PRAISE FOR *UNCONFESSED*

"Christiansë is able to create an envelo[...............ns
of the specific nature of Sila's crime an  e-
ful plotting shows in both the present ....ɔf
Unconfessed are full of powerful images ....ıg
horrendous evil; yet it is one that cann

—UZODINMA IWEALA, *New York Times Book Review*

"Christiansë's novel isn't just a stunningly intimate, heart-wrenching history of slave life in Africa. Her protagonist's furious yearning for freedom ('Wishes are sometimes just stories that have nowhere to go') becomes a haunting meditation on love, loss, and the stories we choose to tell in order to survive. Gorgeous and tragic, *Unconfessed* ultimately reveals a confession almost too terrible to bear and impossible to forget."

—*People*

"[A] beautifully written historical novel."

—*Ms. Magazine*

"Poet Christiansë (*Castaway*), born in apartheid-era South Africa and now living in New York City, channels the torturous history of South African slavery in her debut novel."

—*Publishers Weekly*

"Impossible to put down, this work deserves a place beside such classics as Toni Morrison's *Beloved* and Edward P. Jones's *The Known World*. Highly recommended."

—*Library Journal* (starred review)

"Little has been written about what it was like to be a slave in South Africa under the early white settlers. This debut novel tells it through the first-person, present-tense narrative of Sila, once a slave, now a prisoner on Robben Island off Cape Town in the 1820s...the history is authentic, and Sila's brave, desperate voice reveals the vicious brutality as well as surprising discoveries of love and friendship. Readers of Toni Morrison's classic *Beloved* will recognize the story of a mother driven to save her children at any cost."

—*Booklist*

"[*Unconfessed*] is a compelling story and a remarkable book."

—*Milwaukee Journal Sentinel*

"[An] evocative novel is spun from the protagonist's memory, which reveals the sad and powerful story of the life of a slave woman in the South African outback in the early 1800s."

—*Ebony Magazine*

"From the first ominous sentence to the last, echoing line, Yvette Christiansë has brought into being a compulsively readable novel, the gripping tale of a nineteenth-century slave woman imprisoned on Robben Island in South Africa. Richly layered and uncompromising, this mesmerizing story of a woman's life from her childhood abduction in Mozambique to her travails in the South African outback in the early 1800s is hypnotically and convincingly told. The main character, Sila van den Kaap, is inspired by actual court records, and Christiansë has given her both the strength and a unique voice to tell her own story."

—LALITA TADEMY, author of *Cane River* and *Red River*

"*Unconfessed* is the story of Sila, a slave woman who cannot be owned, who finds and loses her freedom but saves herself through the telling of her fearsome tale. With the shards of Sila's broken life, Yvette Christiansë powerfully evokes a forgotten world unsurpassed in its savagery and stark beauty."

—ANNE LANDSMAN, author of *The Devil's Chimney*

"I am overwhelmed—Sila van den Kaap will forever haunt the southern African landscape (in a powerful countervoice to mythical Adamastor). Yvette Christiansë *made* a new language: a slave woman is no longer the Imagined Other, but simply herself, and through her, from now on, other women."

—ANTJIE KROG, author of *Country of My Skull*

Unconfessed

YVETTE CHRISTIANSË

OTHER PRESS • NEW YORK

Second softcover edition 2023
ISBN 978-1-63542-427-0

Production Editor: Robert D. Hack
Text designed by Rachel Reiss
This book was set in Sabon by Alpha Graphics of Pittsfield, NH.

10 9 8 7 6 5 4 3 2 1

Library of Congress Cataloging-in-Publication Data

Christiansë, Yvette.
Unconfessed / by Yvette Christiansë.
p. cm.
ISBN-13: 978-1-59051-240-1
ISBN-10: 1-59051-240-5
1. Women slaves–South Africa–Fiction.   I. Title.
PS3553.H7286U63 2006
813'.54–dc22
2006005940

For my mother Sally, my sister Lynette, my nephew Jean-Pierre, and for Roz, always

Unconfessed

He stood just in the entrance of the cell, a tall man with his hat in his hands. She could make out the cream of his necktie. She knew why he had come. She waited and could see him struggle with irritation and uncertainty as she remained seated on the bed. The smell had assailed his nostrils when he first entered, but now he could smell the bed. She let it reach him and relished the satisfaction of seeing his small step backward.

She knew about him. The very famous new superintendent about whom everyone talked. Once, when she was out in the yard, he had come clattering to visit the warden. She had been invisible except as one of those people he had been so good at keeping obedient. He looked at her now as if she were a fool. She said nothing.

"What is that stench?" He did not ask this of her.

"Sanitation is a problem, Excellency."

He turned abruptly to face the guard who remained invisible on the other side of the doorframe.

"What the hell does that mean, man?"

He asked for meaning. She felt the laughter bubble up in her throat.

"The warden will explain, Excellency, when he comes back, Excellency."

Sila could hear the guard shifting from foot to foot.

"Has she been here all this time?"

"Excellency? Yes. Warden will explain, Excellency. We have nowhere else . . . this is why we put her and her child here with the other . . ."

"Child? What child?"

She understood his surprise. How on earth could she have been here all this time, under their noses, and not be noticed, she and her child, the one she called Meisie despite the name they wanted her to use? How could they have forgotten about her, *forgotten*? But he could not bring himself to ask these questions, they would have exposed his ignorance, and a great superintendent of order could never admit to such a thing.

For a moment the walls spun. The sour damp straw of her bed reached her nostrils. Her move to grip the wall made him turn.

"What have you to say for yourself?" he demanded, but she could see it was to stave off his alarm. "*Ek se, wat het jy vir jouself te sê?*"

His accent was so stupid. She lay back and laughed, drawing her skirt up. This was how they liked it, filthy and stinking. He should know that, superintendent of cleanliness and order. The *naai maintje* was here. Yes, he should know who and what this place had made of her in all these years she had been forgotten.

"Sit up! Sit up!"

She disobeyed.

"Can you confirm that you are Sila van den Kaap, slave to the burgher Jacobus Stephanus Van der Wat?"

Slave? Who was he calling slave? She sat up and pulled her dress into place.

"Are you the woman who came from Van der Wat?"

"From Van der Wat, yes." Something old and cold, heavy and dull was pushing her heart down.

"What child is with you? Is this one of your children that came with you from Van der Wat's farm?"

"Meisie. She was born here."

The superintendent's mouth opened. He looked around the cell, then turned toward the door.

The guard's silhouette vanished with a jump. "She is a very bad woman, Excellency!"

She had no energy to deny this. She was a prisoner in the country of lies. Truth was a foreign language here. She rested her head back against the wall and inhaled. Soon she would be done with it all. Not even the thought of Meisie, or Pieter who was still on Van der Wat's farm, could keep her in this world. The demons of this world had swallowed up her children as they had swallowed so many before them.

"I am Sila who was taken from Cape Town to Van der Wat."

"You were sold to him?"

Sold? Sold? That old pain made her cough. Her throat was closing up as if a rope had at last been placed around it. She thought of a freedom so close, a freedom stolen.

"Where is your child?"

"They put her outside with the other women when they heard you were coming."

"Excellency? It's so that Excellency can talk with the prisoner."

The superintendent was talking to her again. Something in his voice made her look closely at him. Before he had only been a tall man with black, black hair, black eyebrows, no beard, black clothes. Now she heard something in his voice. He was speaking to her, asking questions that were not orders or commands that had all the answers already. These questions said, "There are things I need to know. Can you help?"

"Help me, Master!"

When he left, so quickly she thought she had dreamed the whole visit, it was hard to stop the room's spinning. This time would be different from all the other times, all the other visitors. She knew the guard was aware of this because he did not come back. There would be no quick counting of coins, or the rough laugh he gave as the visitor ran to wash himself. The shadow of death had come into her life once again and announced that, for the final time, she had run out of all luck.

And what a lucky girl she had been as a girl. All those years ago, in a place these people knew nothing about, she had been the luckiest girl. Now she was locked between walls in a country where real murderers walked free with the right to real buttons, and fancy dresses, and cream neckties, waistcoats on Sundays.

Sometimes she imagined that swine Van der Wat and his family pronking off to prayers at a neighbor's farm with their pious stout faces served up on the platter of their holy words like *vet* little piglets snorting in the Lord's trough. Sometimes she imagined them sitting before a visiting minister and scratching themselves as fleas nibbled and scuttered away under their woolens and muslins.

"There is a valley far, far away," they sang, swaying and swaying away as one with the rest of the congregation, while secretly trying to shift against their clothing for the tiniest bit of relief. The hymn ended and they had to sit, Van der Wat so stiff and righteous in daylight and public, beside his fish-belly wife, and their greedy children.

For a whole day no one came near her. The next day, she was not allowed out of her cell. When the other women left for the yard they jeered and laughed at her, every one of them but Rachel, who came back with one of the younger guards to offer to take Meisie out on her back.

While they were binding Meisie to Rachel's back, Sila spoke quickly.

"I do not know when they will come for me. You must get news to my friend Spaasie. Tell her she must fight to keep them from sending Meisie to Van der Wat."

"Have courage, Sila."

"Courage is one thing, Rachel. The law here is another."

Sila kissed the top of Meisie's head.

"*Kom!*" The young guard was jumping from foot to foot.

After that, no one came. Once, through the dull plug of her damaged ear, she thought she heard Meisie cry. She called out. Nothing.

She sensed the guards. There was a new urgency in their lowered voices. Sometimes someone passed by the bars set high in the door, but she did not bother to look. She kept her face to the wall. Very little time remained now. Although it was not as if she were losing a life she had. A long time ago she would have thought that any life was worth living, that she had to hold on to the tiniest amount of living and find in it the same sweetness that she found in a simple flower growing on a *grens* or even in a crack at the doorstep to the big house into which she had first been taken as a *meid*, just a child who should have been with her own mother. But this could not be called a life. For three years she had been on the path to death. Now she was standing on death's doorstep.

Or was she passing into life? She had yet to be born. If she could pray, she would sing to a god that kind of song babies sing when they begin coming, coming, pushing into the world, a song very few understand for they hear it as the cry of anguish, not the music of prayers from the other world where there is light and joy and freedom.

Very little time remained. She could tell. It was not of any concern how they would come when they did. She had died so many times. The only surprise would be the sense of familiarity: "Ah, this way," she would think as they tied a bag around her head and threw her into the sea, or when they strangled her as they did that other woman, Hester. Let them throw her in. She would rock like her own baby. If only there was a song she could sing.

"Sing along, Sila. You never sing with us."

She looked across the green light to where Spaasie was clapping and stomping her feet. Everyone else was gathering in front of the huts. The big house was all tucked away in their *kerk klere* and already halfway to their encounter with their god in that smelly old church across the valley. To a man and woman, they all hated the master. His mother, Hendrina Jansen, separated wife of Petrus Theron, deceased, and mother of Theron the liar and thief, was a different matter. *Oumiesies* was the one who held everything in those thin little hands of hers. Mean as a *poff-adder* when she wanted to be, and hard in business and money, but afraid of dying and meeting her maker, so she was always looking over both shoulders.

She kept an eye on that son of hers. He knew, she knew, everyone knew that he would be no real master until she was gone. Everyone knew she watched him and felt, each day, his breathing close to the thinnest part of her neck. She also kept an eye out for the first sign of a vengeful angel come to ask the whys and whats of a ledger keeper. *Oumiesies* took precautions in this world to make sure she would be properly received in the next, and so her people, as she called all for whom she had paid *rix dollars*, could be guaranteed a half-day on Sunday, enough food, moments that felt like kindness. Her people did not mind her, though they kept one eye on her and the other on the son, and sometimes they watched his wife who could not keep her eyes from her mother-in-law's china or rings. And sometimes they watched the son's children who clunked about in big shoes and wanted this and that with no concern for the trouble they caused.

"Sing, Sila, sing. *Nooi, nooi die riet kooi nooi, die riet kooi is gemaak.*"

The world would not keep still today. The new superintendent of police had asked if she was the woman who had come from Van der Wat's farm. He knew nothing. That was the way this world worked. The superintendent would learn. The guards said he came to the Cape to fix up prisons because that *kgosi*, the king of the English, was pleased to send him. The guards and the field cornets, the police, the *landdrosts*, the court clerks, the fiscal, the judges, everyone was going to teach him, this man, just how things were done here. She knew this, and she knew that what she had seen when he stood inside her cell was the first sign of a thread working its way loose around a button. Yes. They would try to undo the very secrets of life that held this man together.

Yes, she knew enough of the world to know what would become of this man. And it was useless worrying about him. She had her own worries. What could happen to him? His cuffs would fray. His buttons would fall, roll away, and be lost. His sharp blue eyes—hidden by the darkness of her cell, but clear in her mind from her first sighting of him—would cloud with anger, confusion, disappointment, defeat, and he would sail back to his king's land and disappear.

What did he know? She should have told him of the people he would be dealing with. She would tell him the truth about how she came to be on Van der Wat's farm. She would tell him that Theron was a liar and thief. And Van der Wat was filth. She should have said neither Van der Wat nor Theron was her master. Not that she had not lived the life of a slave, for there had been masters and there had been mistresses. First, when they brought her here as a child, there had been old Minister Neethling and his wife. Then *Oumiesies*, Hendrina Jansen. And then Theron who . . .

She had to get up, move about the cell because those "What if" and "If only" thoughts were coming fast and strong and she needed to swat them away. She marched on the spot—one-two, one-two, arms jerking up-down, bent at the elbows.

When they first brought her out of that dark and rolling world that made her so sick, she was just a child and she had gone to people who were not bad, just stupid. She knew now how much pain and sorrow stupid people brought to others. Minister Neethling and his wife were stupid. And she had been a child stolen from her own mother and pushed into a hole with others only to be pushed out into this world.

"Sing, Sila, sing. *Nooi, nooi* . . ."

She longed for other songs.

But the world was breaking up and all the old places were coming through the holes. First there was Neethling's farm. And she, just a child. Then *Oumiesies'* farm. She could see it rise up and there she was, her own self, standing still while others danced. She knew that younger self.

"You are without joy today, Sila," that gray-haired old Johannes van Bengal said as she twisted away from the dance Anthony was trying to pull her toward. Johannes could talk. They had brought him fresh from Java to *Oumiesies* when she was still married and he was young and puffed up with the chest of a cock, so Spaasie said. Johannes did not like the place they brought him to so he tried to run away with Barend van Bengal and a whole pack of others from that Java place. The punishment was heavy. You could still see where the *sjambok* had tenderized him. He laughed about it now and teased her about the old rhino that had made many paths across his back.

"*Nee, man*, Johannes. They took that hide from old rhino to turn you into an ox. You look there, they use it only to make the ox move faster."

"Sila, *meisie*, then rhino and me has got an understanding. I go at my pace, he goes at his and together we make a dance called *sjambok*-wins-everytime-for-Master."

Johannes made her laugh. Of all the men, he alone had not tried his luck with her. A little squeeze, a little pat, and she was supposed to be grateful and just lie down for them as if she were one of those women who had to, there in the Dutch Company's Lodge. Long before she came to this land she had been meant for other things.

"You must get ready."

Sila looked at the guard when he finally appeared. He was making an iron gate of his heart. Never mind, the smell was there to help him with that. They kept her like this because it helped them sleep at night.

"Do you want a priest?"

She was still a little girl when she came out of the demon's belly and found herself with the Neethlings. Those days Minister Neethling was still preaching and she had to wait outside of the church with all the other slaves while he called upon his god and waved his fist and pointed his finger. Otherwise Missus Neethling kept her at her side as if she were a toy dog. And then the minister offended his parishioners because he refused to pray over the condemned. They called him unholy and said that Christ had ministered to the fallen. The parishioners began to stay away. He lost his church and then, after the drinking began, he lost the farm that had come as part of the Missus's dowry.

"It is repugnant unto the Lord insomuch as any mere mortal could imagine the ways of the Lord's mind. 'Vengeance is mine' sayeth the Lord."

Young as she was and new to another terror brought to life through the minister's drunkeness, Sila listened to the talk in the kitchen as she helped polish silver, or fetched or carried, or sewed. She listened at night when the day's work was done and the older people talked around the communal fire in front of their huts while the big house sank into itself with a full stomach. The question they asked became hers. What was to become of them all? The answer came quickly. The first to be sold away was a woman named Saartje. The next was a man named Klaas. Child though she was, she felt the world tilt again and feared being plunged into yet another dark heat. She heard Missus Neethling speak of her own fears to the woman that all the children had to call Ma.

"I may come to curse my own husband. He has cast us upon the mercy of unkind people. What is to become of us all?"

When Missus Neethling cried a long aw-aw-aw as if she were one of the farm girls, the woman Sila called Ma cried too.

"What of these children? What of my children?"

"I will never let him sell them, or you."

That was the first of the big, big lies.

Ma told everyone around the fire at night that she was afraid for her children. She had been made to lie with men before the Neethlings bought her, and of the seven children she had carried only three were left. They were all the brothers and sisters Sila remembered: Loedewyk, Adam, and Annetjie.

For a long time she did not want to remember the years before arriving at the Neethlings and let herself live only in the stories that Ma had told. It hurt too much to remember her own mother and father, and each time she did there was nothing that would make her move, hear, speak, eat. When she did not remember, things were as good as they could be. Which did not mean that there was no ache. She had to be smacked out of rubbing her nose, especially when Missus Neethling brought her in to serve tea, which Ma said was only to show her off and have visitors admire the way that the Neethlings could teach pretty manners to such a young slave girl, a Mozbieker slave girl no less. Rubbing her nose with the back of her hand spoilt the game and made the visitors smirk or pull their noses up and that made the missus angry. And *that* meant slaps.

She learned to keep her hands away from her face and to concentrate on the sewing lessons, the cooking lessons, the baking, the manners, and the Bible lessons, scratching on slate that spoke when you pointed at it and said what the missus said it said, and which then took on its chalk body, which transfixed her as she tried to understand what else it was saying behind all the blood banging in her ears.

She worked hard, curtsied in a row with Loedewyk, Adam, and Annetjie when visitors came. And when Missus Neethling promised them all their freedom—them and Ma—when they were grown, she joined in the laughter and clapping. So much for that.

When the Neethlings lost their crops and were forced to stave off greater debt, they sold Ma. On that day, Missus Neethling and Ma wept before each other and Missus Neethling made another promise —that not one of the children would be sold.

Standing at the end of the road to the farmhouse, Sila tried to see Ma go, but the sun was in her eyes. She heard Ma calling out of the ball of light that seemed to dance around the cart, but what was called was lost because of Missus Neethling's terrible wailing back in the house and Minister Neethling's loud praying. And then that was that.

There was no more cart and no more Ma. They never told her where Ma went or, the next week, where her two brothers and sister went. She alone, the youngest and the prettiest as Missus Neethling said over and over, remained. And then the farmhouse, which had been so bright with the laughter of her brothers and sister, became an ugly old thing, cold and damp in winter, and full of fleas in the newly broken summer. Left alone to wander around the farm as she pleased, Sila wished she had not been pretty. She might have gone with Ma, or with Loedewyk, who had been fierce in his anger as he was pulled up in the new cart that had come to fetch him. He had looked ahead. As with Ma's going, there had been no time to say goodbye. There had only been the sudden rush of the wheels and then the cart coming into sight. Then the orders, as Minister Neethling had never ordered before. And then Loedewyk came, a question in his eye that vanished as soon as he saw the man counting money into Minister Neethling's hands. Adam told her afterward that the man had come the day before to look at them all, but Missus Neethling had fought her husband and taken Sila away. So Sila watched as Loedewyk went. A day later, another cart and another man—a fat one this time, with no manners—who pushed money into Neethling's hands and then insisted that it was Annetjie and not Adam that he had agreed to sell. So Annetjie went, crying.

"Childbearing age," was what Neethling said as he insisted upon more money.

Another day, Adam went stiff with tears in his eyes. By then Sila was grateful that she had no more family. In a week she had learnt again all there was to learn about family. For weeks it was as if she had been hurt. She examined her body for the bruises. Missus Neethling was more determined than ever that she read without tracing the words with her fingers.

"It will be time to baptize her," Missus Neethling told her husband. "The new young minister, Armstrong, can baptize her."

Freshly drunk again, his head wobbled on his neck. "In time."

"There *is* no time."

"When I say it is time, it will be time."

Sila knew enough by now. She had to be baptized or not even a promise to Ma would be able to keep her if they ran out of money again. Loedewyk was right, Neethling was a stupid master, not like the others who knew how to make money. He sat in his room and where he had only prayed and written long letters to his wealthy relatives back in that faraway place he and Missus Neethling had come from, he now drank and prayed, prayed and drank. His wife was a good woman, but she hated being poor, and her fond memories, as she called her memories of Ma, were fading. Sila tried to think of a way of being baptized. She read the Bible. She tried to leave it open on Neethling's desk: *Suffer the little children* . . . He must never have read it, or she must not have been one of the suffering children. She let him see her pray. She prayed so much a neighbor declared it unnatural and advised that she be stopped. And still Missus Neethling kept the lessons up, reading and writing. But Neethling put an end to that.

"What?" He stood at the door to the kitchen with his empty wine jar in his hand. He pointed to the chalk that Sila held. "*That* must stop. I cannot have that."

So, the writing stopped at a struggling, cramped "My name is Sila van Mozambique."

And just who was Sila all those years ago? Now they called her Sila van den Kaap, slave woman of Jacobus Stephanus Van der Wat of Plettenberg Bay in the District of George. A woman moved from master to master, farm to farm, from the district's prison, to the big town's prison. A woman fit for a hanging. Child murderer.

On good days she could see the sky into which a woman might suddenly jump and disappear. In winter she longed for things for which she could not find words, so she made other things do: a piece of honeycomb fresh from a beehive, a little bunch of grapes stolen from a vine and delivered magically in someone's old rag that had been kept damp to keep the grapes cool. Her older girl and boy, Carolina and Camies spitting grape seeds to see who could spit further. To lie in the *riet kooi* and hear Baro breathing beside her, his tiny baby breathing strangely fierce and rough. Cape Town—all those years before they arrived at Van der Wat's farm.

Baro. No. She did not want to start thinking these things again. His name made her heart twist as if someone had reached in to pull it out. Baro.

"Get that child to fetch the horses now."

"But, Master, he is too young."

That dog Karel said he had sent Baro to fetch the horses, but the boy had disobeyed him and gone playing with another child instead. She listened to them talk about her son as if he were a grown man.

Perhaps her mistake had been that she had not used the knife on herself. But that day, that day . . . Her legs itched. More than anything her legs itched. Too many fleas. They must let her clean this place out before they take her away. She had to meet her end in clean clothes, not like the animal they said she was.

All the other women, including Rachel, were taken to the yard early the next morning. They knew. Most of them could not look at her. Someone said, "Go well." Someone said, "Courage." Rachel wept at Sila's questions. How would Meisie end up in safe hands? Why had Spaasie not come?

The child was crying and squirming in her arms by the time the guard came. She tried asking what was to become of Meisie, but the guard spat and threw what looked like a bundle of cloth at her.

Even before she touched it she knew it was a new dress. She could smell the newness of the fabric.

"What will happen to Meisie?"

But the guard was gone.

She sank down to the stale bed and cradled Meisie against her chest. Not even in her last moments alive could she help a child of hers. How many times had she felt this uselessness? How many times had a child of hers cried and how many times had she not been allowed to be the mother she should have been? And now she was weeping like her own child who would be left in this world of demons.

The dull sound of the door opening made her turn to see and hear properly.

"Rachel!"

"Warden is sending me to Robben Island!" Rachel cried, voice trembling.

Robben Island? Sila gripped Rachel's hand. Who could take care of Meisie now?

"Hey!" The guard appeared again. "Warden said you must not keep him or the superintendent waiting."

"The superintendent?"

"He is with the warden," Rachel said. "And your *advocaat*, the one sent by the Protector of Slaves, is also there."

Sila set Meisie down and shook the new dress out. The guard remained in the doorway. When she did not begin undressing he waved his hands at her, but backed away, closing the door.

Rachel was speaking, helping her change dresses, but nothing made any sense.

She was shivering in the perfume of new fabric when the guard returned.

"Come!"

Sila put her hand out and Rachel caught it. Then the guard was shoving her forward. She lifted Meisie and hurried down the dark corridor between the cells, with the guard pushing and shoving so that she found it hard to walk as she had wanted—tall, strong. She jerked her shoulder away from his hand.

He snorted, but stopped his shoving.

She gathered, or tried to gather, herself. Her heart was not behaving as she had ordered it to. When Meisie was born, she had lived with the hope that Spaasie could come and take her. Then Rachel arrived and there was new hope that she would take care of Meisie until Spaasie could. Now, all hope was gone. And the warden was sending for her. In this face of death, her body was beginning to shake. What was it like to die? She, who had summoned death and drawn a space for it in the world through the living throat of her boy, she had no knowledge of what it would be like to feel her life going out of the body that had been her very own burden in this world. Her stomach trembled.

What had she done?

"Come! Come!"

She walked past the very guard who had been so happy to sell her to any man for three years, the guard who had carried her dead baby away with a look of disgust. Today he did not even look at her face.

The light of full day hit her eyes as she stepped into the courtyard that separated the women's cell from the building in which the warden had his office. Someone had just opened the prison gates and she glimpsed the town outside. If her legs were stronger, she could have run right out and up that Signal Hill with Meisie, into the barrel of the noonday gun and been shot out across the ocean. Instead, she walked toward the warden's office on shaking legs, like an old woman. When she reached the door to his office, the guard pushed her aside and knocked.

The voice that called was not the warden's. She stepped into the square white-washed room and there she saw the warden standing beside his desk, the superintendent seated at it, and her *advocaat*, van Ryneveld, seated in the only other chair in the room. The warden turned his back to look out of the small window.

"Come, come forward," the new superintendent said.

"Master?" She was pleading for her life in that one word. Would he hear it? He alone, she believed, might hear what it cost to utter that word. All those years ago she had learned that van Ryneveld, although not a bad man, loved fighting the farmers of the outlands more than he cared about her.

The superintendent *smiled*. And then he stood up. The warden twisted around like a snake. She was a tall woman, but felt herself small in front of the superintendent. She could feel the world growing around her. She alone shrank. Table Mountain, Lion's Head, Signal Hill were all so high now they pushed the sky out of their way. She alone stood like a tiny mushroom woman under the burden of these last moments of life. Then van Ryneveld was talking to her. What was he saying?

There was nothing new. She had heard that language of the court before. The "whereas a female slave named Sila" was not new. She was thinking fast. For three years she had been asking them to let Spaasie take Meisie but, no, they would not permit this. Perhaps there would be a way, now, with the new superintendent.

Her life was being summed up in that same language that said how she was: "At a Court of Justice holden in and for our Colony of the Cape of Good Hope and its Dependencies on Wednesday the 30th Day of April 1823 tried and Convicted of Murder, and had Sentence of Death passed upon her for the same . . ." That much was old, over three years old, but strange words came from van Ryneveld's mouth now.

"I, Baron Konrad de Laurentz, in consideration of some extenuating circumstances of her having been allowed from some neglect . . ."

The warden started to say something, but the superintendent held a hand up.

Van Ryneveld looked from one to the other over the rims of his spectacles, inhaled and continued reading: ". . . from some neglect or other to linger in prison for three and a half years with a sentence of death hanging over her head, and to demean herself dur-

ing that time in a manner little calculated to prepare her for another world . . ."

What was this? This language was like too much cream on the
top of milk—pretty, tasty, but even with the first taste it was making you sick. Her head was spinning. She wanted to shake her fist at
them and shout, "Just tell me . . . Death, or not death!"

"I humbly petition his Gracious Majesty on her behalf to Extend
Your Grace and Mercy . . . and grant her your pardon . . ."

Van Ryneveld was nodding. The superintendent was smiling at her.

"Is my life spared?" she asked.

When van Ryneveld shook his head and explained the petition,
nausea was all she felt instead of the gratitude and relief he clearly
expected.

The warden stepped forward. "You are to be taken to Robben
Island."

She tried to ask the superintendent about her children.

"They are the children of a free woman . . ." but her voice was
drowned out by the warden shouting for the guard.

"Your daughter goes too," the warden said.

She looked directly at the superintendent.

"My boy Pieter is still with Van der Wat. Do not leave him there,
Master. And Carolina, Camies . . . They are the children of a free
woman, wrongly sold by Van der Wat. Pieter . . . My children . . . !"

The warden was trying to get her away from the one man who
could help her. Why? What was it to him? The guard was pulling at
her. She fought him.

"Excellency! My children! I was wrongly sold to Van der Wat.
You can see, I was first brought here to the Neethlings' farm when I
was a child . . ."

"You will leave my office . . ."

"And then . . ."

"I said . . ."

". . . to *Oumiesies*, Hendrina Jansen . . . then . . ."

"Out!"

The superintendent put his hand up and the warden's mouth shut. The guard let go of her.

It came tumbling out. Neethling to *Oumiesies, Oumiesies'* last will, the freedom that had been stolen by Theron . . .

"Ask my friend Spaasie who works in Rondebosch. She was on the farm and she was in the will and she has her freedom."

The secret sale to Hancke, the secret smuggling . . .

". . . of me and my children, Carolina, Camies, and Baro, to Van der Wat's farm, named Stoffpad, in Plettenberg Bay."

Van Ryneveld, never a man to be rushed, cleared his throat now. The superintendent looked at him and then back to her.

"I have set an investigation into this matter, but you have committed a crime, Sila, and for that you must pay a penalty. The law requires this."

Investigation. Her breath slipped out of her mouth like a small thing finding a hole through which to escape, quickly, easily, gone. Then her body moved her to the door. She knew what these people thought about time when it came to the likes of her.

Rachel was happy. She laughed when she heard the news.

"I will be waiting there for you."

It was a small comfort. Robben Island. Nothing good was ever said about it except by the white people who went over to picnic and catch fish.

Everything moved quickly then. Rachel went the next day, calling back that all would be well. That left Sila with the other women who were hard, loud, rough, not interested in helping her with Meisie, only interested in snatching any food for themselves.

A week later, the warden sent news that he wanted her up early the next day and cleaning her space. By the time dawn arrived she had already risen, folded her straw mattress, folded what little she and Meisie had into an old dress, and tied it into a bundle. Then she strapped Meisie to her back and was waiting at the door before the guard came. Not one of the other women stirred and she had nothing to say to any of them.

The early January air was warm when she stepped out of the prison gates, the only woman in a small group of prisoners being led down to the water and the boat that would take them to the island. To her left lay the shuttered face of the town. Hancke's store was just over there, on the Parade. She would not look at it. It was a place of lost hope. If she looked, all the dreams that she had dreamed when she was sent to him, thinking herself a free woman, would come back to bite at her. She had been silly. What free woman is sent by one white man to another? The small group, herded by tired and irritable guards, began making its way down the northern edge of the Parade, close by the *kasteel*.

Early though the day was, people were already moving about. Two men hurried by with baskets suspended from each end of poles balanced across their shoulders. The heavy sway of the baskets made the poles sag and rise at both ends, so that carrying made the men seem to sag and rise too. One of the guards called out, asking for something from the baskets. Neither man replied, and no sooner had they gone out of earshot than another pair of men came by, this time carrying baskets suspended from a pole that rested, each end on one of the men's shoulders. This time ears of corn were visible. One of the guards called out. One of the men waved him off and the swaying, sagging, barefoot basket dance went its way. As the group neared the *kasteel*, it began to attract attention. Some people stopped to look, some only glanced as they went on with their business. Sila kept her head up, her face closed. But she was used to the way people stared at her.

"What'd she do?" a man called, close enough for her to hear.

"*Kindermoord*," the guard nearest to her answered and spat.

The mild attention that the group had drawn stiffened. Sila felt the change. She kept her head high. She was thankful for her damaged hearing. Things were being said and they were behind a thick wall. Then someone was bumping against her. She had to look. It was a woman. For a second, longing made her think it was Spaasie, even though the face before her was unknown. Unknown? Then why had it stretched into an open mouth, bared teeth and wide eyes?

"Animal!" the woman shouted.

She did not look at her accuser. Her life was taking yet another turn. How many more could she endure? How many had she already endured? That dark and stinking, rolling place had spat her out in this country. One turn. The Neethlings. Another turn. Neethling to *Oumiesies*, Hendrina Jansen, separated wife of Theron, mother of the thief Theron, the son whose backside never filled the seat of his trousers. A man more like a rat than a pig, but whose grunts made him more pig than rat. Another turn. But not even Theron was as bad as that pig Van der Wat who came into her room the very first night she had arrived on his farm with Carolina, Camies, and Baro, and another child on the way. Pieter. She tried to tell Van der Wat, insisted on telling him, that *Oumiesies* had given her and her children freedom, that Theron had been wrong to sell her to Hancke, that Hancke had been wrong to sell her again, that Van der Wat should know this.

The two men who worked Van der Wat's fields and cared for his cattle had drawn their noses up at her, and so had the women who were on loan from Van der Wat's mother-in-law, the very wealthy Maria Martha Cruywagen. Sila had expected understanding from them, help of some kind, even if only because she was carrying a child, but they all sniffed and pulled their mouths up when they heard her insist that she was a free woman with free children. It did not matter to them when Van der Wat beat her so hard, and then beat her children. How they had looked at her the first morning she came out of the barn with bruises on her arms and legs, her face. One of the men,

Jeptha, even laughed and told her to give up thinking she was better than everyone else.

In those days she was fierce. She spat. The two men, Jeptha and Talmag, spat back. But she knew enough on that morning to know that Sara and Boora had nothing to say to her that could not be said back to them. And she knew the men were jealous and ashamed, and that was why their eyes went dull with hatred when they looked at her. She knew there would be no Sunday afternoon dancing or singing with these people.

Van der Wat's was a large farm. It had a river that ran right by the house on its way down to the ocean. She never saw that ocean, though Jeptha and Talmag went there when Van der Wat and his family took themselves to fish. Her work was in the house and then, later, when things were getting very bad, in the fields. Once Sara and Boora returned to Maria Martha Cruywagen, she was the only adult maid— she refused to call herself a slave—and all of her time was taken up in the big house. She cleaned, washed and ironed, sewed and cooked. And she thought about the ocean and heard it rush through the chambers of her ears at night as Van der Wat sweated on her, and Jeptha and Talmag ground their teeth with rage in their hut.

Daytime meant cleaning, washing, ironing, sewing, and cooking. She managed to listen to gossip in the house and in the yard when visitors sent their drivers to the kitchen door for food. Those who came from the same region in which she had been born had the same story of being taken up in the same way, of losing family, of being brought to this world where the farmers answered to no one or spent a great deal of time bamboozling the governor's laws when it caught up with them. Sila listened to the stories and found herself longing for news of her own father and mother. It startled her, but she could not help it. She began to put faces where there had only been ovals of blankness, but the faces changed. And there was no voice she could imagine as her mother's.

She dreamed of her mother and father. They walked without faces, without hands. Yet she heard them calling her, and she, waking, longed for news of them and of her own village, which she barely remembered. The more she realized that she would never find her way back to Cape Town, the more she dreamed of a place far away from Van der Wat's farm. And the more she dreamed of that place, the more she relived its destruction. This time, she was her own mother, running to gather her children and find a place to hide. Sometimes it was in a river, with things eeling around their legs while men with guns ran shouting. Sometimes it was in the ground itself. She would lay her children down and pull the earth over them like a sweet-smelling blanket before she rolled herself into it as well. Sometimes they flew up into the trees, she with her arms folded around her children, her feet kicking and kicking against the air until they were entering the kingdom of a green-leafed silence that put all the noise at a distance. They never looked down, then. They sat, perched on branches like birds and smiled without speaking. She liked this dream best of all but had to learn how to endure waking to a world in which Van der Wat was king.

She also learned that, unlike his neighbors—who included the very wealthy De La Rey, who had thirty slaves and whose man Adonis was blacksmith to all other farmers in the area—Van der Wat was a man who puffed himself up. His land was good, but he was all talk, big talk, and what he had he had because of his father and his wife's family. Sila knew that it was his wife's mother, Maria Martha Cruywagen, who helped him purchase her and her children. When her husband died, the widow Cruywagen gave part of her land to her daughter as a dowry, but her own farm remained strong enough to need fourteen slaves whose ages ranged in a perfect arc from able-bodied men and women to teenagers to children. There were young girls who would grow into women and bear more children, young boys who would grow and take over the heavier work of their elders. Those who gossiped behind Van der Wat's back said Maria Martha

Cruywagen would never be in the predicament in which her son-in-law found himself when two of his slave women died, one in child-birth, the other from an unspecified illness.

On a day when they were willing to make small talk, Sara and Boora said that it was only after much pleading from her daughter that Widow Cruywagen sent them to work in Van der Wat's kitchen and household. Until then, Van der Wat had to make do with Jeptha and Talmag, and the youth Fortuin. It was a difficult shift, and both women were still angry with their mistress for the carelessness with which she had treated them, especially when they found themselves subject to Van der Wat's beatings, and other attentions, and then his wife's jealousy.

"He's a dog!"

"Ja. He likes to open his hand when he hits you over the ear. *Klap*!"

Sila kept her lips pressed together. They could talk. Since she had come neither of them had been beaten. She, on the other hand, had been beaten daily despite the advanced state of her pregnancy. Not one of them had tried to help her when she covered her belly and tried to duck from Missus Van der Wat's blows, either. Yet she discovered that she was glad of their company, irritated and irritating as it was.

A few weeks after she arrived at Van der Wat's, Maria Martha Cruywagen came clattering up the road in her carriage, followed by an open cart. She announced that she had come to visit her daughter, but she came straight into the kitchen. She looked at Sara and Boora, her girls as she called them, and ordered them back to her own farm. While they were away collecting their belongings, she made Sila stand before her.

"You have been here a short time and already I hear things about you."

"She's disobedient, Ma." Van der Wat's wife had come in too.

Sila said nothing. She looked at the two women, one a younger version of the other, and thought them ugly and squat. Under her square bonnet of which she was no doubt very proud, Maria Martha Cruywagen was a set of fat squares. Her body was a square in black, her face was a square pudding, pink and red.

"Are you looking at me!"

Sila looked at the floor that she had only just dried off after a solid scrubbing.

"You are going to have trouble with her if you do not use an iron fist."

"Ja, Ma. Jacobus is training her."

"*Hmph*. Jacobus. And what, I want to know, is he training her for?"

"Ma!"

"An iron fist, Martjie. I know this stock. I have enough from Mozambique to know them. Remember, Mozbiekers are strong, troublesome if not handled properly."

"But Ma! Why did Ma buy her?"

"You keep a strong hand here. And *you*," she was pointing at Sila. "You be careful how you look at your betters. You hear? Your master will teach you how to look at your betters. If you misbehave, you will be sold. Do you hear?"

Sila kept her head down.

"When is your pup due?"

Sila put a hand on her belly.

"Soon."

A small tunnel went burrowing all the way back to Cape Town, to sounds, to smells, a sleeve brushing against her face, a short cough of pleasure, things lost, things broken. The tunnel closed.

"You be careful who you go with from now on."

Why was she not able to be the ox they wanted her to be? Why could she not nod and put her mind where it could just sleep and sleep and sleep until the end of all days?

"Make sure that Jacobus registers it as soon as it's born. I do not want the English sniffing about our business."

"Yes, Ma."

Maria Martha Cruywagen turned and walked out of the kitchen, her namesake daughter in her wake.

"You wanted to marry that man. You wanted a love match. I told you he was trouble, but no, you wanted a love match. If your father was alive, he would have given you 'love match.'"

"Ma!"

"You whine more as a woman than you did as a child. I blame your father for that. He gave you too much."

They were moving into another room, but Sila could still hear the high-pitched voice promising to do her mother's bidding, and then Van der Wat's voice joined them. It was impossible to hear what he was saying. His tone was another matter—anger, like the fumes of long-brewed beer, stank up the air.

Sila picked up a broom and went out into the yard to where Sara and Boora sat in a cart alongside two men, one who held the reigns and another, older, who was dressed in a way that told her he had driven the widow's carriage. The first man smiled and nodded.

"So you are the one," he said and leapt down from the driver's seat.

He was surprised. She could see it in his eyes when he did not have to look down at her. And she herself was amused by his height. He laughed. She liked the sound of his voice. It put her in a mood for play. She held the broom lengthwise behind her back, not worrying about the fact that her baby showed.

"So. You are the free woman?"

"I told them all," she answered and twisted so that the broom handle was pointing toward the house.

Sara and Boora jeered. "Free woman! Free woman! 'Maaaa-ster, I am a free woman.'"

The man turned back and they both clamped their mouths shut.

"They call you Drusilia?"

"They can call me what they like. The widow gave Sila freedom. I am that Sila. What is your name?"

"January."

"January?"

"January."

Something skipped in her chest, a story that could be told, a life that could be lived, but she was already wiser than that skip and so she just nodded and swung the broom back into sweeping position.

"Go well," she said to Sara and Boora. To him she nodded again. He nodded back.

Fancy ideas were not what she needed now, and a tall man who sat in the driver's seat of a cart that was not his own was not what he could have been. She had seen the decrepit state of his trousers, and his smile was broken by missing teeth. She turned away because it was not right that a man who leapt to the ground with such grace, and spoke with such ease that it put her in mind of honey, should stand in such old and dirty clothes and with a mouth that was old before its time. And her, carrying the child of another man whose smile she would never see again.

And then Maria Martha Cruywagen was bustling out of the house, calling, "Cupido! January! January!"

She stopped long enough to remind her son-in-law that she had advanced him the money to purchase a woman of his own, one who had years of childbearing ahead of her. That way he could increase his own stock.

The child in her suddenly seemed to grow three, four times in size. Sila glanced at January who was already in his driver's seat, staring straight ahead. Even Sara and Boora had nothing to say. But there was laughter coming from somewhere, somewhere. Sila closed her heart and ears to the sound of it and still it was there. Yes. It was laughter of the worst kind, the kind she imagined others would laugh if they could.

She gripped the broom to steady herself. A gate was opening somewhere. She turned and looked at the widow, who was being lifted into her carriage by Van der Wat. The gate opened further.

Yes! She *had* heard that voice before. Sila felt her heart beat faster than hooves riding out a storm. It was back there in Cape Town, in Hancke's store. She was in the yard sweeping while Hancke was in his store, talking to a woman dressed in black. What was Hancke saying?

"If I could only find a way to teach Theron a lesson for trying to cheat me."

"Oh, you must!" The woman said. "There is a way. If you are prepared to accept a modest price, my dear Hancke, I might be able to help you."

Same voice! The gate was wide open now, everything made sense —the sudden flow of cash into Hancke's business where there had been talk of bankruptcy before.

Why had she not been alert? She knew Theron had lied to everyone. She knew he wanted her and her children back and that Hancke was fighting him. Spaasie was like a wasp in the fiscal's ear—Spaasie who worked as a maid, not slave, just as *Oumiesies'* will had allowed, Spaasie had not taken her freedom and run on tiptoes as far away from their old life as possible. There was a week when Spaasie came almost every day to find a priest or *advocaat* who could make a strong case to the fiscal. In those days of fighting both Hancke and Theron, Sila had never been more grateful for Spaasie. If there was one person in the world who cared about her, it was Spaasie. Perhaps because of Spaasie, perhaps because of *Oumiesies'* will, perhaps because they were all stupid women who could not see enough to know they had no say in the way the world turned, she had believed in the governor's law, that it would step in and honor *Oumiesies* Hendrina Jansen's dying wishes.

And all the time, as she swept Hancke's yard, she had thought the woman in black was buying something else from him, as so many did who came into his store—cloth, quills, paper, ink, lamps, oil, string, wax, candle holders.

She had never liked Hancke, but preferred being in Cape Town to being on Theron's farm. She missed everyone who had been on

Oumiesies' farm—Spaasie, Alima, Johannes, Roosje, Philipina, everyone—but there were also people she could speak to at Hancke's, and she was in the town.

Yes. It was better to be with Hancke than with Theron, and better to be with Theron than with Van der Wat. But best of all would have been the freedom promised by *Oumiesies*.

Sila watched the carriage bearing Maria Martha Cruywagen turn away from the house, the smaller cart that bore January and the others trailing behind. Suddenly, to her right, Missus Van der Wat was crying out.

"Ma! You forgot your *konfyt*! Jacobus! Jacobus, quick!"

The jar thrust at him, the carriage moving away, Van der Wat stiffened.

"Jacobus!"

Sila knew exactly what Van der Wat saw when he looked at that carriage. All that money rolling away. She watched him run, the jar held out in his hand. The carriage halted briefly. The driver began to climb down but stopped and then jerked as if prodded from behind. He sat down. The quick, sharp whip snapped the air and the horses sprang forward, the weight of the carriage pulling against them for just a second so that it seemed as if they were caught, as if in one of those paintings back there on *Oumiesies'* walls. Then the carriage wheels moved and the horses were away. The cart driven by January picked up its pace as well. Van der Wat stopped and threw the jar into the bushes. His wife squawked and ran into the house.

Sila stood with her hand resting on the broom.

With Sara and Boora gone, he came each night. It mattered nothing to him that she was carrying a child. He came to the hut, called her out in a clipped, hoarse whisper and then he shoved, pushed, and it was over, quickly, without his ever looking into her face. He would turn and walk away even before her skirts had dropped. That was how it was, night after night. Now she thought of that time as endless washing, scrubbing, sweeping, polishing, worrying about her children, and listening to the ocean in the chambers of her ears while Van der Wat did what he had to do. Time stood still during those first weeks after Maria Martha Cruywagen took her women back to her farm.

It was hard in those weeks because there was still hope that someone would come from Cape Town, maybe even Spaasie with one of the governor's black constables. Those men who struck such fear in the *witmens'* hearts. Maybe the constables would fetch her when they learned that Theron and Hancke had broken the law. No one came.

Pieter was born and for a while Van der Wat stayed away. Then it started all over again. He came whispering at the door of the hut, waking the children. Pieter cried until she came back, waking the men in their hut. It was time to give up tears and look at the world in which she and her children had found themselves.

On the night that she decided enough was enough, she was waiting outside, determined to say no, ready to be beaten. But she did not say no. In a heartbeat she knew what had to be done. She walked away from him toward the barn. She could have walked tall and proud, but that was not the time. She kept her heart tall and proud, but lowered her head as she entered the barn. It did not matter how rough he was, she had shifted the line between them and knowing this shifted it even more.

She had understood something about this man and needed to hide what she knew. Filth, was what he was. And filth was what she called him. *Vuilgoed.* She reserved a part of herself for the barn. It made him excited and he could not stay away. She learned to listen to this excitement as he came seeking her. She could feel his mind circling her and trying to cut her away from the rest of her time, reducing her to just those times in the barn. She kept herself from him in the day, cleaning, washing, scrubbing, in the house.

She could see, too, in his wife's glances each morning that they were both prowling around her, bemused, but filled with hate. The eldest daughter, Susanna, took her cue from her mother, but Sila was not concerned with her. That girl was too busy worrying about the fashions in Cape Town or the neighbors' eligible son. The elder boy had no thought in his head but guns and horses. It was the mother and father that she had to watch. They could not help themselves. They wanted something of her. What it was neither she nor they could say but, slowly, she began to understand that this wanting was born of a thing that these two people who claimed that they owned her, like a cow or horse, feared. And so she told her body to bring forth some sign of her power. At first it was the way Van der Wat trembled when he pushed himself away when he had finished. She willed her body to speak to his, not before, not during, but after. And he trembled, always. After. And was confused. And grew angrier by the day.

The missus said nothing, but under her skin there could be seen yet more of that cold ash that the fires of rage had dumped after burning in that big, ugly bed. Nothing suited her then. The floor was not clean enough, the gravy too thick, the milk too sour. If the dog came into the kitchen and dropped at her feet, she kicked it. Jeptha, Talmag, and Fortuin were strangely untouched. They received nothing but complaint and warning. But if Carolina did not carry water quickly enough, it was cause for boxing and slapping. If Camies brought damp wood, even though rain had fallen for days, it was cause for more boxing and slapping. If Baro ran by the kitchen, she rushed out, her skirts whoomphing the air as she caught him and shook him, accused him of stealing sugar, or milk, or honey, of having broken flowers in her garden, of having tramped mud into her house when in fact it had been her own children who had done so. It was her triumph, to summon Van der Wat and have him beat the boy after she had pummeled and clipped him about the head herself. How that mouth of hers pulled up at the corners, pushed out in the middle while the strap found its soft marks. She made Sila her worst enemy.

Then there was that December and the big feast for which neighbors had come. And there was the new horse. Van der Wat was showing it off before the neighbors, picking his youngest son up high into the saddle with him when Baro came running, calling to be lifted up to the horse as well. There was Van der Wat, stunned with embarrassment, the neighbors shocked but laughing and the missus swollen with outrage. That was a day of broken things. The first break was the missus's favorite jug. Sila dropped it, a torrent of curses bursting out of her and splashing their way to Van der Wat as he picked Baro up by the arm and swung him away like a piece of rubbish. There was a silence that could have cracked the world in two. Then they forgot their guests and came at her from two sides, swinging and beating as if they were croppers desperate to beat the frost. When they were finished, Sila could hardly move and the guests had hurried to some other place, hiding their faces but not their disgust and that made the pig and his missus even angrier. Jeptha had to come and carry her to her hut. There was no visit from Van der Wat that night, and there was no fire in the kitchen the next morning, and when the missus came to curse and accuse from the doorway of the hut into which she could not make herself enter, nothing could stir Sila. The others—Jeptha, Talmag, and Fortuin—were quiet around the yard, quiet in the house. Van der Wat and his wife talked between themselves. One came, then the other, to look in. On the second day, they sent for De La Rey's man, the one who worked with animals.

Lying in her hut, she felt a heavy ring tightening around her. She dreamed strange things. At the end of a week, she woke, looked at the hills and spoke to Jeptha of a plan.

Neethling to Hendrina Jansen who preferred to be called *Oumiesies*, *Oumiesies* to her son Theron, Theron to Hancke under a cloud of lies. Hancke to Van der Wat, pig of Plettenberg Bay.

Sila tried to think of a life that might have been if only Missus Neethling had kept her promise and resisted her drunken husband.

They would all have stayed together—Ma, Loedewyk, Adam, Annetjie, herself. There would not have been a Theron. And there would not have been Theron and Hancke fighting over who owned her and her children. And there would not have been a Van der Wat.

Perhaps she would not have had children. Or perhaps they would have come, each one as the child who had to come to her and to her alone. Or, perhaps, if, as was the case, nothing could be done to save Neethling from liquor, *Oumiesies* had bought them all—Ma, Loedewyk, Adam, Annetjie as well. And if *Oumiesies* had not died, what life might have been had then? Even if *Oumiesies* had lived, Theron would have come to the huts for her just as he had come looking for Spaasie and Roosje, or Philipina. But *Oumiesies* could have lived long enough to see him chased by the courts for stealing another widow's name and owing so much money that the superintendent of police wanted to send him away, out of the colony to another place far, far on the other side of the world.

So many lives, and each one of them gone. Once she and her children were delivered to Van der Wat way out there where the law could not see or ask questions, all other lives vanished. For a time even Spaasie was like someone lost to another world.

If *Oumiesies* had lived, *Oumiesies* for whom the world was her god's test, Sila knew they would all have been happier. She would have taken good care of *Oumiesies*.

She thought of *Oumiesies*' last days, of listening to *Oumiesies* moan in her sleep at night, calling for a little *branwyn* to take the pain away but not calling, not once, for her own son who only came riding over from the property that had been his father's when he needed money. In the end, all that fierce widow had was the people she had bought. Every morning it was Roosje or Johannes who inspected her chamber pot closely. They murmured and frowned. *Oumiesies*' health was their health, her longevity theirs.

"Sila, you must keep her chest warm."

"You tell her."

"You tell."

Johannes was the one who decided to speak, but it was too late.

On some winter days, the light at the close of day is yellow on the green of the vines and the hills begin to give up the perfume of their moist insides. On such days, it is not a strange thing to wish to lie down in the side of a hill and be allowed to sleep a sleep that would be a journey into another place, one that could only be reached by sleep and entered by a different waking. And then, then . . .

The sound of water comes into the prison. She can hear it and wishes so much to go down to the water and be washed right down, clean to the bone.

A woman named Hester threw her children, then herself into the water of Table Bay. Dragged out, she found herself and one child saved. And then they tied a leather strap around her neck. One man took one end, another the other end, and they pulled and pulled. That was how she was punished. And then they threw her into the sea.

Out of my way!
What is the good of a door if it does not let you through?
If you don't mind . . .

Baro?

Baro! *Hai,* boy? My boy. Is this you? Can it be you?
My boy!

This is a good day. Stand over here. Let me see you. My boy. My
lovely boy. I *knew* you would not forget your mother. I *knew* you
would come. My clever boy, finding your mother all this way out
on the water. Stand here where I can see you. Ja. Ja. It is exactly as
I thought. All those bruises, gone! My boy, have you any idea how
much your mother has missed you?

I knew this would be a good day and when I came to sit here out
of the wind—*look* at you! I felt—is this you?—that the world was
about to change. I felt you, yesyesyes, even before you stepped between me and the sun. I have longed for you, you have no idea how
much. Or perhaps you do. Is this why you have come? Sweet boy.
Sweet, sweet boy.

I knew today would be a good day. I said to myself, Sila, take
yourself out of the huts and go for a walk, get away from the
compound.

I come here on a Sunday afternoon—my boyboy, come closer!—
when we have some time for rest. I like to find a quiet place out of
the wind, yes, and out of sight of the guards who are also resting—
they do not worry about us running away on this island. There are
no boats for us to jump into, oh, not one, no, not a single boat, and
it is too far, much much too far to swim and even if you try, the sharks
are waiting out there and then . . . *chomp*! A man drowned only a

few weeks ago. The warden was so angry he kicked the man who lay there, dead as a whale dragged up onto the pebbles by the waves.

Is this you? My boy, my own dear boy come back to find your mother like the good son that you are.

There is so much to say.

What can I give you? There is nothing to give you. I have never seen a boy shine so. You look as if you have been drinking that sun in.

How hard it must have been for you to find me. Did you go back along the Stoffpad to Van der Wat's farm to look for me? Who told you to find me here? Did you go to the town of George to find me in the prison where they took me after you were gone? And then did you come all the way to Cape Town to find me in the prison where they kept me for three years. Yes, three years before they brought me here and in all those years the shadow of death was on me. You could have knocked me over with a feather when they sent me here. They said, get your things, and they put me into a boat.

How glad you have made your mother's grateful heart even though this place is not what I had in mind for our reunion. I had hoped for something better.

Heish! Boarding that boat to come here. The sun was in my eyes.

When they sent me here, all I could think was goodbye, goodbye. Born to die one day, stepping into a small boat the next.

I held my baby girl, your sister, held her tight in my dress. Yes. A sister. But that is not all the news. You have no idea what your mother has gone through since you were sent away. I had two more babies since I sent you away from Van der Wat. There was a brother. He was not strong. He did not want to be in this world. And I was sick, too sick of heart with missing you, and Carolina and Camies, Pieter. I was heartsore and not the mother he needed. He left this world. It was hard. And then your sister came just before they brought me here. Of Pieter I have no news. He is there, still, with Van der Wat. Yes.

Ooh. Get me a big stick, get me a gun, a knife, get me an axe and let me go there, all the way to Stoffpad, to the house near the river and I will cut that house in two with one swipe of the axe and your brother will come dancing off that land.

I call your sister Meisie, plain and simple. Girl. They wanted another name. It meant nothing to me and nothing to her. Meisie is what she is. But do not go looking at her. Why? Because she is young, so young, in a hard place and you are her brother who has come back shining, a surprise that has turned the world around. She will see you shining and she will begin to turn away from this world. So. So, Baro, do not look at your sister. Let her be. Stay here and let me tell you what is to be seen. Let me see you.

You have no idea what things have happened to me.

This island . . . *Hmph.* Look at it. Look, look around you. I know your eyes must learn how to look upon this world again, and they can, they will.

Can you see how flat it is? You can see right across to the mountains on the mainland. For the men—there are men here too, prisoners, we are prisoners here—that sight is a promise broken every day, every time they look up. They see where they are.

This is not a good place, Baro. But it is where you found me. It is where I am.

There is much to tell you. So much.

Come, come. Sit. I have never seen a boy shine so. My boy. My boy. Sit low with me. Yes. If they come by, the guards will think Sila has gone mad. What do I care? But I do not want them to step close, not today, hey, not today. Sit. Sit. Ja. I sit here on a Sunday. I look at the world.

Do not be afraid to look at this place. When I first came here I did not want to see or know anything. The tip of my nose was as good a view of the world as I needed, and you know how I hear only half of what the world has to say for itself. So, do not sit on the side of the ear that has been broken inside. Ja. Ja. When I came here . . .

Hmph! I could not look at anything but what was right in front of me. It was my shame, you see. I know. How good it would be to tell you that your mother never had shame. The wind that crosses this island in such haste to reach the mainland—there, look at it, rising over there, and there Bloubergstrand—the wind has blown away all need to lie about such things. I am a tree stripped of loose things and some lies can be loose things, they have no way of holding on. Sooner or later they are shaken loose and they fall to the ground and everyone can see them and you are in trouble. Some lies. Other lies are like roots, they feed you and keep you from drying up and dying.

But why am I talking about such things? Look at you. Baro! What is it like to be as free as you are now, free to come and go? What is it like to belong to a place where there can never be another lie? What can it be like to never have your name stolen?

The trouble is that you never know which lie will save you, which will break you.

I dream? Forgive your mother. *Ha-ha!* It *is* you.

I want to say how much better it would have been if you had not found me like this, on this place, in these clothes. How much better it would be if I could say my rage made me blind when I came here. Or that I kept my head high with dignity and the knowledge that I am worth more than ten of these guards—*have there not been* rix dollars *exchanged for me*! It does not work this way here. Perhaps, one day, I could make up stories that would tell of a Sila who did not get rolled by the surf, who did not come out of the water with the back of her dress over her head, who did not have to pull her dress down and who, though angry with the men standing there, was angrier with a piece of old cloth for its thin stupidity, and was angry even with herself for not having the legs to stomp against a wave's power. Here, when you step out of the boat, they start you off scrambling and stumbling. Now there is talk of a jetty. The warden wants one, but, in the meantime, scrambling is what the water does to you. The water, even crossing that water, softens you so that you come out of it and onto this place with less strength than a baby.

No kindness. No care. The boatmen say nothing to you. They do not look at you with any kindness. There is no warning.

This place is filled with sadness. I thought we—you, your sisters and brothers, and I—had known sad people, but there are sadder people here than you can imagine. And there are worse than you can imagine. The warden, for one, is bad. He does not care about us women. The guards care too much about us. And there are people who have been sent here so that they can wait for ships that will take them to the very end of the world, they say. I thought this was the end of the world, but what do I know, hey!

Let me look at you, boy!

What? That is the wind. And what comes on the wind is nothing but the guards telling jokes to each other. They cannot hurt you.

Rest. You have come a long way. I know because this is not the look of anyone from this island, or from that town over the water. You look like someone from far, far away. Rest. Even though you cannot be hurt by this place, it takes a lot to land here. I can see that in your face. I am still recovering from my landing! You came prancing on such heels, but you should have seen me. You do not need the boat in which flesh comes to this place. If you did, you would feel the first chain that holds us here. The water moves like a thing that lives deep beneath its own skin. The moving is what makes you afraid. All you can think about is the deep down there. They said to us, get into the boat. Your sister was crying, but her crying was nothing in the sound of all that water.

At night I wake up. Hau! Is that? Is it? My little girl's hands holding my dress. My heart is preparing for that loss. I want to take her hands away. I want to hold her. I am useless, useless as a mother. I am not the woman I want to be.

When I came to this place, it took many hours in the boat. We left early and by the time we were near we heard the noonday gun. That is how long it took.

I held your sister. I thought, and now? What now? Not the hands of men, but water will roll the one child I have left away from me. When water moves like that you know it goes deep. Some of the men were sick over the side of the boat. The waves were big, hey. Up, down we went. Meisie was crying hard. Sometimes I cried out with the men when the boat's nose went up, free of a wave and then hit down, hard. Then . . . when the boat pointed down! *Hoo!* All you see is a valley of water and you think now I am going to drown. But up the boat came again. I had one arm tight around Meisie, the other around the nearest man. We were all holding to each other.

I am holding you, girl, holding, holding. Van der Wat will not find you.

What?

There we were, rocking in the boat and your sister went quiet with her eyes big, but still holding my dress in those little fists of hers. I was afraid but I was also laughing.

Better with me in the water than back with Van der Wat.

I will call up bad things and send them there and they will crawl into Van der Wat's ear and scream at him until he runs into a wall, head first, until he breaks his head open the way he broke our lives.

The other prisoners, the guards and boatmen thought I was loose in the head because I was laughing. It was all that openness and the salt on my lips, and the noise of the waves slapping the boat, and my own head bobbing on my neck, my stomach a knot. And your sister was looking at me with eyes so big.

Then the sound of the water changed. The boatmen were shouting to each other, pulling and pulling on the oars to get the boat away from the rocks and closer to the sand. The guards were shouting to us to get ready. I could see land and men standing on the other side of the waves. And there I was, only new to the sky again, new to so much open world, staring at a new place from a boat that was rocking fast with waves splashing salt on my face. Your sister stopped crying. I looked at her. That girl! She liked that rocking.

The guards said, jump! They hit us with the ends of their rifles as if we were pigs or sheep. Jump. That is how a person arrives here if you are not a fancy lady or gentleman. If you are, they get prisoners to carry you on their backs. The rest of us have to jump into this cold water that opens your mouth so your breath can be snatched away.

The water snatches a breath away to make place for itself. I know these things. There have been people who did not come out of the water with their breath in their body.

I jumped, holding your sister up so that she would not go under the water. I held my mouth up. So, like a spout on a teapot. I jumped. And the sea clamped its lock.

When the sea grips like that, it says give me something, give me, give-give. That something is your breath. If you give just one breath, it wants another, and another, because it longs for that sweetness that is squeezed out of only the last breath taken in this world. So, I gave that sea just a little breath—not for me, for your sister—and it rolled me and rolled me to get more because I am a woman who learned back there in the Cape Town prison to take each breath as if it is the last. And that is how I fooled the sea itself. Ja. Rolling around with the water up to my chest. Even on my toes it was hard to find the bottom. But I held on to your sister and held her high.

The men had to get into that water with supplies on their heads. I was laughing and holding on to your sister, but then—fear, fear will always get you—I thought of the sharks. My head went under and I thought your sister would be pulled from my hands by that sea. I started to shout, your sister was crying again. One of the men threw aside the load he was carrying to grab her. He called to me, a white man, he called me woman. Woman, I will save her. He grabbed her and made for land. I saw him climbing through the waves and I saw your sister arrive on the island before me and then the sea pulled my legs down. I thought, now Sila, now you will die in the mouth of this big water or in the mouth of a shark and that will be that.

So that is how it is. You arrive and no one says, let me catch the wave that will push this boat right up. No one leans and says, be careful. But for the man who saved my baby and gave her to me before being kicked back into the water to fetch what he had thrown aside to save her, there was no, let me help you. No, put your hand on my shoulder. No, hold on to me. Nothing.

But I fooled the sea itself with false breaths and with laughter even though I was afraid. So, even though your mother came stumbling and slipping out of that water like a calf that has yet to find its legs, she had already fought and won a great battle.

Those guards, that warden, they stood there. Guns held out, or hands behind a back. Those men and their guns. You know how a man stands when he has a gun in his arms. He holds that gun with the same ease that a woman holds her baby. The guards stood there the way men do when they are watching the world, lazy hips, one up, maybe a leg raised on a nearby something, or a foot placed back, on a bit of wall, or against a tree on which the man is leaning. That look of their bodies. Watching. And those guns.

What kind of people are these?

I came out of that water a woman who lost too many things. They marched us to the warden who goes by the name of Pedder. He was standing where the beach sand and the island's sand run into each other like enemies in a battle—it is like this here, fighting, fighting to live. We had to stand in front of Pedder. He said, no disobedience, no drinking, behave, hard labor, break stones, stack them, be good. His face, you will see, is red, and small veins stitch his cheeks. His eyes are hard. His hair is thin. And his chest is a fat pillow in a tight cover, his legs are skinny from too much drinking.

He said to me, You will go to the hut with the other women. You will work in my house some days and some days you will work with the men in the quarry.

So they brought me here, to these huts, right up from the landing place.

The sound of the ground is the sound of sand and small stones, small shells that have been blown by the wind—I even find the powder of shells on the floor of our hut after the wind has been strong.

So. I did not want to see a thing of this island. But that was then. Now, this place has changed. You have changed it by coming to find your mother who loves you. It is your island now, Baro. I am giving it to you because I have already worked enough to claim it for you. Three years in the town prison and fourteen more to look forward to, but I have already as good as paid them. So. There. Take it. I am stealing this island for you and it is the best stealing I have ever done, hey. Remember the honey from Van der Wat's kitchen? And those juicy pieces of meat? He beat that poor old dog that day. Steal my meat! He said. *Blam! Skop!* I felt bad for that poor old dog, Baro. She never did me any harm. But I was happy that it was the dog and not me. Ja. She never carried another litter. Perhaps it was a good thing after all. But I feel, still, a sharp sickness in here, just under my breasts, when I think of how he beat her.

Hshh. Your mother has done some bad things.

Listen, if you go about this place, there are two things you must keep in mind. First, remember that the island will lead you. Here is how—the edge of the island is its own path. Second, remember too that the sea will always call you to the edge. And the edge becomes everything here. If you come to visit me when I am working in the quarry, you will find that something is pulling you, bothering you. You may try to swat it, but it is no fly. It is the water in your ear. From your first landing on this place, you will have water in your ear and that water longs to go back to its own kind. Those are the two things—the edge, the water.

Oh, there is a third. Look. Those mountains of the mainland. They seem to be everywhere, but that is their trick, like everything on the mainland that wants to take hold of every thought. That mainland is just there, but—and this is the truth—it is not everywhere. And that is why you must use it. When you walk about, until you get to know what goes on this side of the edge, you can use that mainland. Put it on your left cheek, or right cheek, at your back, or stick your face out at it. Those are your directions. I give them to you because, small as this island is, you may be pulled about by the wind or the sound of the sea—oh, and sometimes it is not the sea you hear at all, but the wind sounding like the sea. So, be awake. You will hear the difference when you go near the *fynbos*, you will hear wind and think it is the sea. But, remember, the sound is thinner.

And there is nothing that grows high enough on this place to give you shade unless you are lying flat on your back, or sitting low, like this. Oh, some bushes can be up to a man's shoulders, and when I walk in them my head and shoulders stick through, but most of the *fynbos* in which the birds hide their eggs reaches no higher than my thigh. The waves are higher than the *fynbos*.

So. Now. If you want, you can go this way, first in a straight line to the water. You will walk with your back to the mountains of the mainland, then stay with the edge of the island and walk all around it. This will take you just a short time, not even half a day on those strong legs of yours. You see, this island is small, smaller than Van der Wat's farm. And if you were walking around it, along its edges as if your feet were scissors cutting the shape of a cloth, it would take less than half a morning. You will walk with your face toward the ocean first and the mainland will be on your left cheek until you come around like the wind, pulled back toward the mainland. But stay at the edge of the land. Follow it as if you are following the tracks of an animal that has dragged itself over rocks, over stones, over more rocks and some sand. I want you to see how this place is all edge. That is what keeps us here. Small, but all edge, and wind and flatness in between, with the carpenter's shop, the warden's house, a graveyard, one quarry of white stones and another, there, closer to the water. And a place we call the Black Hole.

Unconfessed

This island is a prison, but the Black Hole is a prison in the prison. Bad things happen there.

And when you walk away from the edge, if you keep the water at your back and walk a straight line from this point where you found me, you will go by the place where I break stones for Cape Town's streets and walls. Yes, even women break stones here.

The warden must count each stone and write the number in a book and in that book he must also tell the superintendent of police how it is with all of us who live here. We are in the same book as the stones. Rounders. Oblongs. Squares. Pounders. And the lime that must be burned. Do you smell that smell? It comes from where they cure lime.

This stone beats you in the eyes.

When we are not breaking stones, we carry them, Lys, Mina, and me. We are told, stack them! When we are not carrying stones, we work in the warden's house with the men who keep his garden and his clothes. When he has guests we work extra hard.

And watch where you walk, adder is king in the *fynbos*. He lets me pass and because you are my son he will know you and let you go by without striking, but, since you are new, take care. Show him respect.

But do not go in search of the quarry or King Adder today. The edge is your business today, lovely boy, where there is sand, where the rocks are black and white—black as they shine where the waves polish, white where the salt has dried.

And remember, when you have come right around, the mainland will be behind your back and you will be at the place where I landed. Turn left and walk to the huts. The mainland will be on your left cheek again. Do you understand this? Repeat it and you will have it right. It is not difficult.

Are you listening to me?

Perhaps, if we had been able to run from Van der Wat's farm . . . perhaps if we had found and followed the land's edge we too might have come back to the place from which I had been taken as a girl. If there had been someone to tell me these things . . .

Listen to me. I am telling you things that will save us all. I am telling you what kind of place your mother has been living in all these years since last you saw her. Do not remember those old and terrible times. I do not want to think of Van der Wat's farm. See where you have found me and what I am giving to you as your own island.

And listen to me, you need to take care here among the sad people. *Tsst!* Now! *Tsst!* If you come when I am working in that quarry and if you get lost—you may not think you can, but the wind and sun can make your head spin some days—listen first for the hammer of my heart. Listen. And remember how to go and come back, sweet boy.

Now let us go and find out how the island leads you around. *Hooooooo!* Boy! Grab my hand, your mother is in a mood to run.

Quick, we are close to the warden's house. See? It has a wooden floor, but there is nothing fancy inside. He brought a big bed from the mainland and the guards laughed. They sleep in hammocks. We women sleep on *riet* beds. But Pedder sleeps on a big, dry bed. When you walk in that house the floor makes an empty sound. It is a lonely house. Even his chairs and tables are lonely. They sit there, waiting like Pedder for visitors. He has many plates and cups and saucers. And knives, forks, teaspoons, a clock. There are rooms. It is not like our dirt floors and *riet koois*. You will see how we sleep.

But, you listen to me, there are places you do not want to enter by mistake. And keep away from the quarry after dark unless you go exactly where I tell you. And do not come to visit me when the door is pushed in and the candles go out.

I said, listen!

If you hear guns, it might be someone shooting rabbits. Visitors come to hunt rabbits. Or they come to catch fish. Some days, you will get used to this, you hear the laughter of visitors resting on the rocks after a good hunt. The men light pipes. The women sit under parasols.

What kind of people are these?

46

Here, always, the wind and sand are at my face. It is not the home I had wished for and it is not where I hoped to see you again. But here we are.

It is not a good place, but I have found a way to cheat it, and now that you have found your way to me I will be stronger and my cheating will be like a pick, pick-picking away until I have left this place where, some days, visitors come to shoot rabbits or catch fish while—even with my bad ear—I can hear a prisoner calling out from the Black Hole for more water, or food, or to have the irons taken off of his ankles before they rub right down to the bone.

Some people wait out their days here and will not leave except to go deeper into this island. You see, there? The graves. See how they turn the feet of the dead away from the mainland. Some try to find someone on the mainland who will remember them. They scribble-scratch-scribble and it is not hard to imagine what they write. It is not hard to see that they are finding a way into the years that line up on the other side of the horizon. Even if it is the single year away that they imagine, moving from December into the return of a January bearing the next number in the years of their lord, it is not for the now that they write.

There is a minister who comes. He is thin, hey, and brittle as twigs. He crosses the water with his wife and when he comes he sits in the warden's house and argues. He says, build me a church. But the warden does not want him to stay. So, he comes in the boat and stays with his wife in one of the huts and then he goes back. When he stays he prays and prays, then he writes what he is going to tell us his god has told him to tell us.

The minister's wife writes letters for the prisoners. And she writes letters to people she longs to see again in that faraway place where she was born. When the storm stops her from going back to the mainland she rubs her hands together and her tongue darts out of her mouth, over her lips. Then she sits in the hut in which she sleeps with the minister and writes more letters.

The guards write too and I say they write with spit. I spit at them. There.

Vuilgoed.

The warden writes about the jetty, and how many stones have been cut. Me, I say he is weighed down by the lists he must fill each month to make a year. Every month he is weighed down like this island by the rounders, the pounders, the half-pounders. The warden thinks he writes about months past and he does not see that the year comes to him from over the horizon and that the stones we must break loose from the island are bits of the future we give to that growing town across the water.

This island is weighed to its place in the waters with all that land in sight. That land is like a heaven. But what if we take too much? What if we sink the roads before they have set themselves down? What if we send the island to the bottom of the waters in which I hear, on clear nights, voices humming?

The island is a ship on which I have been sailing across the years to you. And look how it is that I sail so grandly that the world draws to me and not I to it. And look how it is you who comes out of the sunset, or from behind the sun at any hour, laughing when I feel that my hair will never be clean again.

If I see myself, will I know that it is me? Oh, my boy, come, come, let your mother see her face again in you.

Back again? Be careful. Pedder is cross today. This is not a good place for you today, you who have come in finely spun clothes and with such heels that water makes itself your dancing ground. You will hear why. Listen. There. You think that is the wind going fast and low through the *fynbos*? Listen again. You heard that sound when you were still of this world. Such things have not changed. Here they call the whip the cat of nine tails. And it is true. Not one whip, but nine growing from one handle. They call the sound of that splashing against the skin a stroke. I ask you, what kind of stroke is that? The warden is fond of this whip, but he never lifts it himself. He says, why must I bark when I have dogs to bark for me? He sends one of the prisoners. And sometimes we are made to watch how one man is ordered to beat another. Sometimes the men beat us too.

Pedder. *Tchah*. He likes to keep his hands behind his back when he stands on those skinny legs. I know that way of standing. It is to show you who is master and who is not. You, it says, you are without help. The hands behind the back say, I am the one and you better know it.

But. *Hah*. When the superintendent of police comes, Pedder is not the master. He keeps his hands behind his back but his shoulders are stiff. Ja. Pedder. His shoulders go stiff because they do not want to do as someone tells them to do. But he must because the superintendent is his master. They do not like each other. The superintendent complains about Pedder. And when Pedder beat a man named Jacob for not making him three new shirts, there was a big stink.

You see, Pedder put Jacob in the Black Hole for eight days with only bread and water. It was hot, hot-hot. And when Jacob came out, he was not Pedder's favorite anymore. One day, we all had to go to the Black Hole to watch Pedder's new favorite, a man named Van Graaf, tie Jacob to a post and give him so many lashes that he had to go across the mainland to hospital. When Jacob came back, he was quiet. He spoke to no one. But Pedder was not finished with him. On a Tuesday he sent for Jacob and said, Jacob, make me two new shirts, bring them on Thursday, I have visitors coming.

I was there in the house. I heard. I knew Jacob could not make those shirts. I could have helped him, but he was one of the men who stood with Pedder and cursed us—me, Lys, and Mina. And when I had to work in the house and he was there, he acted as if he was my master. So. I said nothing.

I am not a bad woman.

Thursday came. Pedder sent another man named Frederick to Jacob. But it was not to ask where the shirts were. It was to tell him to go back into the Black Hole.

Now, this is what I think—Jacob must have known that Pedder was going to punish him, so he took a knife from the carpenter's shed.

Knife!

And he cut his finger off. Just like that!

I knew Pedder did not want those shirts! He knew Jacob would not finish in time. Pedder is cruel. And we are all, every one of us, grains of sand under his eyelid.

He is especially cross with us women. He does not like women here on the island. Some days we catch his fish for him but we do not laugh like the visitors who come here to fish. You can hear them laugh. For them catching fish is not work. They come here to play like children and do not see how we live. Pedder sells his fish to the mainland. And he is jealous of the shells we collect. That man! If you take a shell, he calls for the cat of nine tails. He has his own men who collect all shells. These, too, he sells.

So much for Pedder.

You see those big pots? Big, hey? That is where our food is made. I have to help there sometimes. We put meat and rice together in the pots after the quarry. We eat like animals. There are no dishes or spoons unless you can find something yourself. No knives. Pedder says we will have a big boiler soon. *Hmph.*

The evening meal is better than breakfast. Breakfast is bread. Pedder eats eggs from his own chickens and vegetables from his own garden. And fruit from the mainland.

Some of the prisoners find pots or kettles or something to put food in. If you walk along the sea you can find things but you have to know they are from the dead who no longer have use for them. I have two little *bakkies* from the man who saved your sister from the water. They sent him far away to a place called Sidneecove. They

send a lot of prisoners there, and when the men are told that it is time to go there they look as if they are facing their own death. The man who gave me the two *bakkies* gave them to me because the distance to that place is greater than the heart can survive, he said.

You see these huts? That one with two doors is where I live. It is two huts joined by one wall. One is empty. Meisie and I live in this one with Lys and Mina and Mina's girl, Flora. It takes time to see when you come inside, but I see everything I need to see here. We live where they put us.

This bed is for me and Meisie. You know how I like to be near a wall. Lys has that wall. That is Mina's bed near the door. She does not like to be near the door. Mina has been here the longest of us women. When I came, she was already here, and so was Rachel who was in Cape Town prison with me. Then Rachel went and Lys came, wet too, carrying her bundle. I liked her, from that first day I liked her.

Lys is my friend, Baro. Yes, your mother has a friend here. She is from the same master as Rachel who is a good woman. Lys says it will not be long before Rachel is with us again because Rachel also does not like Truter, their master. Truter is the judge who does not like disobedience. All of us have had dealings with Truter. Lys says that if you are in his household and do not jump when he says jump, he punishes you. He tells the court that you are im-pyu-dent and you end up in prison. Lys says he has no patience. She said to him, why am I in your house? She said to him, you are a man of law, you must know it is wrong to keep me here, let me go. So here she is.

Mina is another story. She can sleep near the door.

I am watching you! You be careful how you look at this room. Maybe you have a room made of gold, maybe you are made of gold yourself nowadays, but you remember, I am your mother.

You will see Lys soon. On Sundays she also likes to find a place far away from anyone. But she will come back soon. You will know her by her height. She is the smallest of us women. She is the best of us. Lys is not the name her mother gave her but, like all of us, it is the name she has. She laughs—she can laugh like nobody's business— she laughs and says she keeps the name because the name that her mother gave her does not belong in this world of liars and thieves. I did not hear her called Lys when I first met her. I heard some shouting, but it was on the side of my bad ear. I turned my head and the guard was calling a small woman lazy yellow bitch. I heard laughter and there she was, laughing at the guard. That was the first time I met her. She was fresh out of that rolling in the salt and with nothing dry to wear, sitting on the doorstep of this hut. She looked at me and laughed again but with good laughter. Here, you know, laughter is a way of crying or of adding salt to a beating, but her laughter is not like that. I took my spare dress and gave it to her. What did that make her look like, the smallest one in the tallest one's dress? If we stand side by side she comes under my arm. She laughed about that. Right there and then, she laughed.

Lys is the one who taught me how to live here. Lazy Lys. She works hardest at that name. And some days she answers to impudence. At night, I am Miss Sullen, she is Miss Impudence. We laugh. Listen. That is her laughing out there with Mina. She is friends with Mina. I do not mind. That is the sound of her voice. Learn it. Yes. That clicking is her tongue. The guards have no idea what she is saying.

You will like Lys. Her people have been called the worst of people by those who do the worst things. Do not listen. She had sisters and brothers a long time ago. She was taken to work for a farmer who had no wife. Those were terrible days for her.

What? No. No-no. That is nothing. Come. Stand close to me. You will come to know that noise. It is just the guards telling jokes to each other. They cannot hurt you. They live in those huts that are only just a little bigger than ours. I remind myself of that when I have to find something to keep them in shape. I tell myself, those who guard prisoners are prisoners of the prisoners. Some days it is a lie that works. These men cannot hurt you. It is what moves around them that calls for care. Step wide of them, for this reason.

But let me finish telling you about Lys. If you see a woman whose face is wide and the color of pale and beautiful clay, you will know it is her. There is no one else like her on this island. Her eyes are sad but there is kindness in them.

And me?

I can see how you look and look at me. I understand.

Mina. *Sheesh!* Thin. No meat on that bone. If I did not hate her so I would help her. A woman that thin has trouble carrying what anyone of us can carry. Me, I am thin, but not that thin. She is skin and bone, nothing in between. Lys says, Sila, have pity, sorrow and anger have eaten Mina's flesh away. But Mina hates me. Why should I care about her?

You will know her by the ring around her neck. That is where the collar that dragged her into this country left its mark. That was a long time ago, but the mark is still there. She says I am like her. I say, *get!*

Sometimes they call Mina by another name, Philida. If we were friends, she and I, we could help each other bear the burden of our many names.

Mina. You know what that name means. Wet nurse. She is proud of that name. She talks of the babies she suckled for the *witmens*. When she talks like that, so proud, I want to hit her.

When I first came here she helped me, she and Rachel. Rachel took my dress and dried it. Mina took your sister while I changed clothes. It was sunny, but I was shivering. Your sister was shivering. They wrapped her up tight in a blanket. They wrapped us both up as if we were both babies and I had a day of rest in this very hut.

Mina was sad and happy when Rachel went. That is how it is here, as it is everywhere else in this country for those like us. I tried to be Mina's friend. She was good with me in those first days. And she was good with your sister. That has not changed.

But. One day, after I first started working in the warden's kitchen, I brought two pieces of orange, one for Meisie, one for Mina's girl who is named Flora. You should have seen them sucking on those pieces. It made them laugh. Mina was happy to see her child laughing, but when one of the men came knocking to say the warden wanted me back at the house, she started to shake and cry. She said, you! You stole the warden's orange and now he is going to punish you. If he learns that my child ate the orange, he is going to punish me too. I told her, Mina, I said, if we get punished for this it is nothing. A mother has to do what she has to do for her child. Mina said that I was bringing trouble to her and her child. She said I was a shameful creature who was not to be trusted and she did not want me near her child anymore and I had to keep my child from hers. And then she pulled Flora up and went to the other side of the hut.

Trouble for her child? Did I harm her child? Or did I bring laughter to her child and my own. Flora loved that orange. It made her laugh. A child needs to laugh. I did not bring one piece of orange. No. I brought two. I did not think of keeping the other piece for myself. No. I brought it to give to Flora so that she could have the same as my own child. I made Mina's child happy. And for what? To be cursed out.

That was how things went sour between us. Lys tried to tell me that Mina was scared for Flora and that I must understand. I said, go and tell Mina to do the understanding. I said, back there in the town prison I was the one who watched a child of mine pine away for want of something small. For nearly seven months my child was sick. He was like a cloud that gets thinner and thinner until you think it is still there, but the truth is, your eyes are tricking you with a memory of something no longer there. The prison doctor, Lieschung, came and shook his head. What good was he? How did a shake of the head help my child? He sent a man to hospital, but not my child.

He gave me nothing for my child. If I worked in that prison kitchen, I would have stolen a whole bowl of oranges if oranges were to be had. I would have stolen meat, milk, everything.

Born in a prison, died in a prison.

I do not remember his face. He was too young. He is in a place I cannot see or reach.

Lys said, Mina too is a mother with a child in a place that is bad for children. You are mothers together.

Then tell her she must not think she can be the judge of me. How many children have I lost? Carolina, Camies, gone. Pieter kept from me. A boy who came and went so quickly he had no name, there in the Cape Town prison. Only you have come back to me.

Do not look at your sister. No. Nono.

I hold on to this one so hard. Your sister must live to leave this place with me, Baro. And that is why you must not long for her. She will hear you and turn her head away from here. If you leave her, she will grow strong. She has already come through rolling water to land on this place. And she is perhaps lucky because I have seen how, when I was going under the water, another's hands reached and carried her to land for me.

Let me be all the family you need.

The man who saved your sister was beaten by the guards to show him who was boss. His name was Aaron. I saw him in the quarry and he waved and asked with kindness how I was and how my girl was. I said, thank you, we are both well. Lys said, Master did a good thing. He said there are no masters on this island, only the warden and his guards. Sad eyes. They sent him to the other place far away, another prison that takes months on a ship to reach, they say. He gave me these *bakkies* and some clothes. It is his shirt I wear over my dress in winter. And his socks on my feet. He gave me two pairs when he left. That was after Rachel had gone back to her master, Truter, and Lys had come. I gave a pair of socks to Lys, but she just went and gave them to Mina, and that made me cross but who can be cross with Lys for long. So, Mina has socks and I have socks, which I sometimes let Lys wear, but only if she comes to keep me warm.

We have ways of getting on in this hut, even me and Mina.

I think that man Aaron gave me so much because he would not step off that boat on his own two feet. I might be wrong. Maybe he did. Maybe he is walking around on his two feet in that place right now and here I am imagining him a dead man.

This island can make you think all kinds of strange things and that is why you must listen to me when I say to be careful.

And remember, do not go too near the guards' huts, not because of anything they can do to you, but because of what hangs around them. You will know their huts. You can smell them. They eat meat that has been hanging on hooks for longer than a stomach can bear. But that is how it is with them. Their hungers go beyond all decency and bad things hang around them, sucking things that could get near you and I do not want that.

You should hear the things my bad ear hears. Until you came, I heard demons singing. Now even demons bow before you and they leave me in peace.

Faraway eyes. Can you see me with your faraway eyes?

Not all of the men on this island are animals. Some walk this world but they have left it behind a long time. Perhaps you have seen those four, Matroos, Soldaat, Keizer, and Vigiland? Ah. You wait. They have fallen into madness. It could be because they heard things that do not belong to this world and believed their ears, or it could be that they went with demons. All I know is that they are slowly disappearing from this world. The warden and guards look at them and shake their heads. The other prisoners give them a bit of this, a bit of that. But these four are gone in the head.

I look at them and think, Sila, that is a blanket you can pull over your head. But, no, that peace can never come to me. *Nee.* Peace. You leave behind the carcass, even the heart, give it over to the demons, you go somewhere else until the body is called away. It is like a carriage. You lend it to your neighbors—and we all have demons for neighbors—while you go walking out in a good late afternoon light with nothing in your hands but grapes and honey. Perhaps that is where those four have gone, walking somewhere in a good light, while the demons tramp about this island in their bodies.

The warden no longer punishes them with crowbars and does not force them to wear heavy irons when they wander away from the quarry. They do no harm. They are never far from each other. The demons that ride around in them like to be close. Demons have their own families, their own tribes. Remember their names. Matroos, Soldaat, Keizer, and Vigiland. They are all the color of milk in tea. We know what that means. They are the children of fathers only their mothers know. So, what is different?

Now. Matroos is the one who walks like a boat that leans too far to one side. He holds his head so. Lys says it is as if he has been hung. But he killed no one. He came here for theft. His face has the marks of coming to manhood, lines that move from left to right. These days, they are where demons play games and roll stones. He digs the warden's garden, but I have seen him piss against the house.

Soldaat is younger. He is what his name says, a soldier, and that is strange because he cries like a baby when he sees a rifle. He must have his father's eyes. Sky eyes watching with fever. He is lighter than Lys, but she thinks his mother might be from the same people as her. He speaks nothing of her language. He speaks a language only the demons that live in him can understand. Some days, when the demons are sleeping on their job, you can hear words that you think you should know, but the meanings are all in the wrong place and there is no time to put them back where they fit. All of his teeth are missing and he holds his right arm as if it is a broken wing. Lys speaks to him over and over. She is a better person than I am. Soldaat also works in the warden's garden.

You will smell Keizer before you see him. Some days he cannot hold his bowels. It makes the guards angry. But why beat him? No one wants to be near him, so he is always on the edge of everything, even in the demon family that keeps those four men close. But he is pretty! A more pretty man you cannot find on this island and when his bowels are strong he is much desired. He holds his right cheek so, as if it has been slapped. To look into his eyes is the same as looking at a stone. Look away. I do. Those are eyes I never want to see if I can help it.

Vigiland is the youngest and the saddest. He is thin. His arms and legs are still like a boy's—a young tree, new branches. His is a face that had not yet come into the world, but already it has been dragged out. It is like watching something that cannot come out of the mist and be solid before you. He was sent here because he did nothing but walk around town. He was not a slave, not a servant, although I want to know where he got a name like that. That is the name of a slave, Vigiland. But there he was in that town, belonging to no one. He would not work. They called him vagrant, then they called him thief because he was stealing time for himself. I think he came to the town to find someone, or he just came to see what all the fuss is about, or perhaps he lost his way. Now here he is and the demons have entered. I think his mother must be mourning for him, waiting for him to come back to where he belongs.

Perhaps he got that name from those meddling people, the ministers and their followers. I think he listened to them and got that name and wandered away into lost air, thinking of worlds that do not exist, of creatures called angels and of prophets who would never come. Some days he says words that make me think he has been disappointed by great, great hopes. If he were my son, I would have told him to block his ears to the confusion that comes on the wings of those who live inside that world folded between black covers. He does not do much here even though he is meant to work the quarry. He wanders away and always comes to stand in the warden's garden.

So, now you know something about Matroos, Soldaat, Keizer, and Vigiland. I have nothing against them, but they are men and I keep from them because I am one of the few women on an island of men. In another place, I would do more for them, even give them bits of food, but here I need all the food I can get. Lys always has something to say to them, something to give. She is a better person than I am. Even Mina has something to say to them. I keep to myself around them. But I watch and look, look and watch. I have nothing against them. They are like big warning beacons for all of us, not just me. I do not want to be like them. I want the superintendent of police to hurry up and take me off this place even though the minister's wife tells me that I am a lucky woman who does not deserve mercy for I had not given any.

She wants me to pray. Let her pray. Me, I keep my head right up and she says, do not dash against rocks when god sends you a message of hope. *Tcha*!

Today, when I stood outside of our hut, just as the sun came up, I felt the first cooling of the air that tells me summer is leaving us. Lys said, Sila, you are mistaken, there are still many days of summer. Well, then, I said, you tell me, you tell me why I feel this change?

I thought, perhaps I will receive a message. Perhaps the superintendent of police, Mr. Baron de Laurentz will send me a message because he is making an investigation. But you are my message, *hey*.

I do not want summer to go.

This light hurts my eyes.

Can you see me? What do you see when you see me, my son?

Sometimes I look around and what I see is strangeness. This world is strange, stranger than strange. It is always more than I can imagine and it always surprises me. There are things that are beyond words—and these can be good or bad. You know this as much as I do—that good things can be as strange as the bad. Remember the time Van der Wat's neighbor sent his driver to give me trousers for Camies? Until that day, who knew if he had ever looked at my child? He never so much as looked in my eyes. But there his man was, holding out the bundle, saying this is for you from my master. I thought my bad ear was making me hear wrong, but . . . no. There the driver was, giving me strange things. What can a person make of something like that?

A man by the name of De La Rey. Do you remember him? Van der Wat was jealous of everything about De La Rey. Do you remember? And how he tried to please him, even sending me over to make a dress for De Lay Rey's wife.

Do you remember De La Rey? He was rich. He had many cattle and he had forests. His house was very big and all who worked for him were happy. I wanted to work there. De La Rey would not hear of it. He did not like Van der Wat although they were neighbors. But he sent old trousers to cut down for Camies.

Everything that De La Rey had, Van der Wat wanted. The missus was the same. When De La Rey bought a new horse, Van der Wat had to do the same. When De La Rey's wife grew flowers around her house, the missus told us to dig up the ground around her house. She bought seeds from a traveling merchant. No. Not Mokke. They never let me see that traveling merchant, Mokke, when he came. Do you remember Mokke?

Mokke! I do not want to talk about him now. Tomorrow, maybe. We had to plant seeds. Me, I had to work, digging, like a man.

Van der Wat wanted to be rich as De La Rey. I saw that from the start. You were small then, just this high. A few weeks after we arrived at Van der Wat's farm, when I was big with Pieter, the missus told me to make a big meal because special guests were coming. That was De La Rey and his wife.

Who ever saw such carrying on? And the noise! On the day, the missus ran around. She shouted for me to get the two youngest children dressed. Do you remember them, Dirk and Maria, the girl who was named after her grandmother, Maria Martha Cruywagen? Dirk, that boy, would not stand still. And Maria did not want her hair brushed. The two older children were just as much trouble. *Sheesh!* The oldest boy was out in the field, and late coming home, so the missus was screeching his name from the window, Stephanus! Stephanus! Susanna was running around too, crying about her hair. Her mother told me to help her when I finished with Dirk and Maria. Then Susanna cried that she did not have enough dresses. The missus complained that De La Rey's wife always had a new dress. Susanna said, oh, that was because she went to Cape Town. Susanna always wanted to go to that town. She always wanted to know how the ladies of Cape Town were wearing their hair. Her mother said, *ffff* to the ladies of Cape Town, but I saw how she took her own plaits down and brushed the middle path away to make one knot at the back of her head. She put her wooden comb away and took a shell comb. She took off her plain dress and put on a yellow thing. And what do you think she kept on? Hey? Hey? She kept her old red flannel bloomers on! And what did I see? A big hole?

I was careful. It was no good if she caught you looking at such things.

Van der Wat and Stephanus were riding around, putting cattle in the field near the house. Talmag and Jeptha had to work hard to help bring them in so quickly because, as Talmag told me, Van der Wat's cattle were not half the number of De La Rey's. But there Van der Wat was, trying to impress De La Rey. He made Fortuin and Camies sweep the dirt from the front of the house. The missus sent Carolina to find flowers to put in vases.

My child!

I was chasing after Van der Wat's children that day, and if anyone asked me what my own children were thinking, I would have nothing to say. You were too small, Baro. But what was Carolina thinking? And what was Camies thinking there when he had to work like a boy older than his years? What kind of mother did that make me?

Susanna was shouting for stockings. She worried that De La Rey's wife always wore stockings. Every day.

You were in the kitchen with me when Jeptha shouted that De La Rey's carriage—yes, carriage, not wagon—was coming. The missus screamed that it was too soon. *Yeesh!* Then there was so much running. And Van der Wat still in his work trousers. I remember those things only too well. Leather, like Theron, like all the farmers wear when they ride about everyday, stiff and hard from rain and wet branches, wet grass. Van der Wat's were bad—mud all over, fresh and old. They should have been thrown away a long time ago.

How could I be told to clean things that can never be clean again?

Well. There Van der Wat was. His blue shirt was splattered with mud too. He was trying to undo the flap of his trousers, calling to Stephanus to help him.

When De Lay Rey and his wife stepped out of the carriage I did not see people who ran about shouting for their clothes to impress their neighbors. I saw a man in clothes that knew his body—nice shirt, good shoes. His shirt was a very fine linen—this I know about from those days with Hancke at the store in Cape Town. It did not fight his body. And Mevrou De La Rey did not pull at her dress. She wore her hair in a single bun, pinned with a nice comb of silver and mother-of-pearl, just as the missus had feared. Ja. They were of money, those people.

And when I made a dress for his wife, De La Rey sent his driver with a pair of old trousers to cut down for Camies. I fixed your trousers too with what was left.

Haish! There are things that make me laugh, but everything, funny or not . . . *Hai,* there are days when no name can hold a single thing in place. A bush is more than a bush on such days. It is not where it belongs and it will not stand as it should. The whole world is a place that makes no sense and I am sore with looking for things I know.

Can you see me?

I see how you are looking at me. Is it because I have changed?

This world is strange. It hurts my eyes to look at it. But I do not turn away. Since when have I turned away?

Can you see me?

Here, look, here, here, Baro. I am over here. Yes. Here.

I waited for you all week. I saw you watching when I was in the quarry.

My thoughts are like birds breaking out of the *fynbos* when I think of the years that brought me to this island and, now, you to me.

But look at me now. Lys asked me who I was preparing for. I told her to keep combing my hair and not to ask questions. Mina said it must be a man. I said I will not comb my hair for any man of this world.

If I had cloth I would have made a new dress, but here we make do. So this dress is what you find me in. I have this one and the one for working. Pedder does not like to give us dresses. He counts the cost. With him it is all money. The superintendent of police watches him, even from across the water, so he must do as he is told. But if I had cloth I would have been dressed to meet you. It has been a long time since these fingers touched good thread, good cloth. I do what I can here to get a little extra food for Meisie.

No. No looking. She plays there with Flora and they are not for you to look at.

The guards ask me to help now that Jacob has cut off his fingers. There are no fancy clothes here, and Pedder goes to the mainland for shirts now. I sew a button, mend a tear. The guards let me keep what thread I can save.

When I sew I think of Alima and Roosje, who taught me, all the way back there with *Oumiesies*. Alima taught me how to cut cloth for a dress and how to sew it. Roosje taught me how to make trousers. And *Oumiesies* taught me how to sew fine thread on tablecloth. That is why Hancke did not want Theron to take me back.

When I told Lys how we found ourselves on Van der Wat's farm, she did not laugh when I said I am a free woman and my children are the children of a free woman. When *Oumiesies* put me in her will, she meant for my children to be free too. That is how the law is. I know that. The children of a free woman are free. And when *Oumiesies* died I became free. Eighteen and oh-six. Carolina was born in eighteen and ten. Camies came in eighteen and fourteen. And you, my boy, you came to me in eighteen and thirteen. All of you came long after *Oumiesies* was in the ground. Free! Mina laughs, but Lys does not. I told her how I was taken from my own people when I was a girl, and how it was there with Minister Neethling and his wife—long before you were born, when I was a girl. I told Lys how Neethling drank and when they sold me to *Oumiesies* I was already on my third life. And then *Oumiesies* died and that son of hers lied to me.

It was not right! Not right. No.

And this has been a bad week. The warden is cross with me because my thoughts were on you. He said, be insolent again and your door will be blocked up.

Me, I say, Warden, a door is not made of stones.

But I know. Roads push up from the water's edge and lead across rivers. In the distance, far over there, only the eyes can travel when the body is weary. In that distance the wheels creak and complain and crack sometimes, dragging away from the town that keeps growing. So many wagons. They drag slowly. And men and women, children, stand at the edge of cliffs and shake. They want years that no one can live in. They shake. Can you see them? It is as if they are at the place where not a step more can be taken and—*Hoo!* Watch! Watch! They beg their god for rewards. They make promises that bind.

Blood for blood.

And some days I look hard through the sun that jumps off the water and see how ships keep bringing more of them. And I remember another ship.

This is a task I must do for myself to keep all that is behind from coming up and taking my mind. Those who have passed on know what it is to be kept from life. And here I am so close to them that I must keep myself sharp or they will believe I am theirs already. It is hard, but I try to keep my nails clean because you can see how the dead find rest beneath others' fingernails, and also in the creases of their skin, in their nostrils. I do not want this.

And sometimes I set myself the task of staring at the ships that come for the whales. When they go, they pull their big anchors up. And some days I make my eyes reach far, further still, and I tell you I see the anchors splash into the water off that coast, there, that Cape of Tears, Cape of Death, Cape of Struggles, whose contagion will spread up, into land far from the sea—a dry land. See that, how red the soil is. Let your mother teach you how to see such things.

And how some days the sun turns gold. You can see this, just like me when I stare through all that light to that red soil. And then the earth opens and men go down, down, like creatures hungry for death. They pull the earth like an old dress and there is waste piled upon waste. I can see this. I see the waste. It is yellow and my throat stings, my eyes tear up with the grit that blows and blows.

Women sweep daily, and often, to keep the thin lines of yellow sand from creeping beyond the doorstep or window ledge. One woman sings as she sweeps and there are no stones that pave the roads, but a flat river of black soil that children run across, as do dogs.

I keep myself sharp here, or the dead will make me believe that I am going mad. I hear them call me. Baro, you alone may use my name.

And some days I weep nothing but tears and there are no fancies and the sea is the sea and the island is the island.

Now that you are back, my thoughts are like bees in a bottle. Days long ago are back, fresh and with them a pain that is sharp. When I see you, I see Carolina. Camies. How could they have known what was waiting for them? It was my business as a mother to know what snakes lay ahead on the road. Is that not what a mother does? A mother watches out. A mother teaches her children—do not sit on a cold stone, do not step over a log without looking, do not roll a big stone over without care, keep your head covered in winter, keep your chest covered when the winds blow, rub fat on a bruise, aloe into a burn. I could not see what was waiting for them.

I thought, well, now we are here with the worst of demons, but, still, I can fight. My friend Spaasie or maybe even Philipina will try to find me and they will worry at the hems of the fiscal's coat until me and my children are found and brought away from such a pig of a man and such a pig of a wife. But Van der Wat said no one would find me or my children. I should have known.

Do not ask me to go to that day that he took Carolina and Camies. *What breaks, breaks. What is broken stays broken.*

Something heavy sits in my throat when I look at this place. Stones in my throat. Stones in my stomach. I have been swallowing stones for years. I am sick of stones, but they are not done with me.

There are some things you do not know. I remember my mother— my mother from whom I was born—and her dancing when the day had grown late. And she could sing. *Jirre!* Baro, my mother, your grandmother, could sing. They all said I was like her, but I know she was pretty. And you, my boy, you have her prettiness. *Ag,* when you laugh . . . I hear you laugh. Do not forget that laughter, real laughter, keeps the stones from breaking into tears and drowning the world.

Some days, I thought I heard tears in my mother's voice. It was not always good, back there, but it was where we came from.

Well. So. Here I am. If you want to know how I am, this island is how I am.

Ag, my boy, keep out of the light so I can see you.

Draw back the curtain, Baro. It hangs its shadow and this hut is deep within the valley of secrets. Call my name, hold it. My name is newborn where it sits best on the sides of your tongue. On the sides of my tongue there is a taste of lead. It takes my mind off things.

They say there is a coach that takes passengers as far as Rondebosch these days. Have you seen it?

At dawn, when the cold slows even the rustle of cockroaches, a child cries.

When I was with the Neethlings, we sang to their god. I never knew why. Now we sing to this god because another minister tells us to. And Mina sings hardest of all. She closes her eyes and sometimes she cries as she sings. She keeps asking the minister to baptize her and Flora. She tells me I must do the same for Meisie.

What for? She believes that old law that these people must not transfer for sale any of us who have been baptized. Now, I ask you? If this god is so powerful, and so irritable, will there not be trouble if we pretend to be his people when in our hearts all we want is to defy those who say he is their father?

And do I not know of the thinness of laws and the words that speak them?

When I was a girl, Missus Neethling promised Ma that we would all be baptized, but Neethling himself said no. And later, when *Oumiesies* wanted us all baptized, even she, with all her stubbornness, could not defy her neighbors, her *advocaat* and her own minister, who refused her wishes in this.

Mina says there are good ministers who are collecting the purchase price for children and old men and women, and they set these people free.

Where do they go then?

She says they go to a farm inland, near the winegrowers of Stellenbosch. Am I stupid? Do you think those farmers will let good hands sit idle? I am not so stupid that I cannot tell a thorn in my foot when I feel it. But that is where Mina wants to go with Flora. Well. Good.

Let her go. I will step off this island with Meisie and go find Carolina, Camies, and Pieter. I will knock and knock on the door of that Orphan Chamber and I will find Spaasie, who will help me find a good *advocaat* who will make them see that I am a free woman freed by *Oumiesies*, and my children are the children of a free woman. And Mina can go inland to find her rich ministers.

Sing for me, Baro. Do you remember any songs?

The sun is going again. Can you see the lights over there on the mainland? The ladies of Cape Town are making their evening visits as their mothers did before them. They put on their skirts and go pronking on those silly heels to gossip. Go pinch one of them for me today. Go lift a skirt . . .

These are things a father should teach a son. How to go visiting ladies. I know about visits, but what I know comes from those lessons. Those lessons teach a man how to forget his mother or sister. He must. He must forget that a woman is a mother or a sister. How else can he do what he does.

I should smack you, my son, for all the forgetting that would make a man of you.

Things stink here, but in that town they drink wine from the governor's vines and you can smell them as they go pricking by from visit to visit in the visiting hours. The sound of their heels is little different from the stumble of horses. That is what Pedder hears, all the way out here. Pedder longs to go visiting in the town. And, look, I see the shape of a man walking in black robes, the gleam of his god's collar at his throat. Be careful now, be careful of his shadow.

The minister comes in black, clutching his Bible, and—look there, see?—his wooden heels are worn. His clothes stink of tobacco and too much wine. His face glows. I remember Minister Neethling from long before you were born, when I was just a young, young girl.

Some days, the sun flies up like a hundred buckles.

If I had enough *rix dollars*, I would buy a hundred silver buckles for your dear shoes and you would take up the practice of pricking your way out across the streets like the very best of them and make a gift of your smiles as you grace their sitting rooms. You could take them my greetings. Say, your mother thinks of them, kindly, and will be pleased to receive word of their health.

Do I long to be one of those ladies? I pick up pebbles and throw them into the water when I get a chance. I say to each pebble, *So het god jou gemaak.* Go down. Go down to where you will never forget that you are a stone. Stones are not made for walking on water. Stones must sink when they imagine that they are fish. Go down. Go down.

Today a man and three ladies are visiting the warden. This is why Pedder sent for me and Mina to clean his house, but the guests came tramping mud in. You should have seen those ladies arrive, shaking the water from the hems of their skirts. Now they have gone walking. The man is in there with Pedder. Listen to how they talk about those ladies of Cape Town. Come, listen to what goes on behind the backs of words. Just now the warden told his visitor, ah, but those women do not hold any upeel.

Upeel? Ah-peel. Does he mean they are not his kind of woman? He said, I have no sympathy for their prattle and complaint.

Mina and I were right here, cleaning the floor. Mina spat when the warden and his visitor were not looking. She laughed. Pedder said, you! Get! So we came into the kitchen. Pedder said, *meid*! Where is our tea and cake? Mina said, do you think they are asking us to tea? We laughed, and Mina spat again.

I say we are all the women this island can hold, that is why they make us pay. We are too many and not enough. Mina will agree with me.

What do you think of Pedder's visitor? You tell me, why a bald man needs such a big moustache? I know why he has come. Pedder had us catching fish again. The men were in the water with nets. We women were on the shore rubbing salt into the fish. This man will beat Pedder down to a sorry price. Look how he pretends he is not interested and how Pedder does not see him eye the baskets. See? Now they talk about other things when one wonders how to cheat

72

the other. Before you came the visitor said, aah, Pedder, but for certain necessities, a man would rather a good dog than a woman. They laughed. And Pedder said, in all this beauty, those damned women long for endless balls.

That is not what he said when those ladies of Cape Town were here. He could not prance enough in the wakes of their skirts. He made four prisoners carry them off the boats and when they landed, laughing and bright pink, he promised that the jetty he is building is for them and them alone. *Psh!* Pedder can lie! He needs the jetty so that the town can get its stones quicker, and so his fish can get to town and he can get richer.

Those ladies looked at us. One said, it is a shame that such wretched creatures should be in a place of such beauty.

Are we not here? Hey! I am asking you something, Miss Bring Me My Parasol. Are we made of air that you see through? Ek gaan jou klap!

Pedder said, I fear they do not see the beauty, my dear.

The ladies covered their mouths. Dear Pedder! How dreadful for you. It must be a great sadness to be among such creatures.

Ah. Dear ladies, how kind of you to think of me. I serve the law.

Hold my tongue! Hold me, keep me from growing ten times my height and taking their heads off as if I pluck dead blooms from the bush as Van der Wat's wife taught me.

Pedder puffs and puffs up with pleasure when his visitors talk of him with concern. He likes to be thought of by these people. He wants them to think of him. Do you think they really care about him?

Listen to him and the moustache now. Listen, Baro, and learn to know what goes uncleanly behind the backs of ordinary words.

Is there a more glorious spot on this earth, Pedder?

No slums.

Ah, the mountains. The cloudless sky. No crime to speak of, in spite of this place.

Oh, indeed, indeed, my dear Thomas. Hence the need for the law. It is what such wretches as these before us deserve and it is my duty to keep them at hard labor. There are desperate creatures on this island.

Their actions curse the boundless generosity of God himself.

Hsst. Baro, what is it with you? Watch out! Here the ladies come. Three. One is young. Wake up! Their skirts make the sounds of small waves sighing quickly.

I can tell you what they are saying. I have heard this many times before.

Dear Mr. Bowler, Mr. Pedder, if it were not for the unfortunate use to which this island has been put it would surely be the most glorious fairground for the town.

Oh, yes, Mariah has it exactly. Mr. Pedder, do you not agree that the town is in need of a place where ladies and gentlemen could have the best balls and parties. It is so dull otherwise.

Dull? Ladies, ladies! What of the freedoms we all enjoy? In the midst of the wildflowers? Consider those that give us such brilliance and beauty in brief blooms that last but a day, though full and generous. Consider the nights we enjoy. So calm.

And so cold, Mr. Big Nose.

So clear.

So that some can see the mainland stretch into the length of their longings, Mr. Bald Head Big Nose.

So serene. A serenity that, surely, puts one in mind of god's paradise.

And let us not forget that snakes go about at night, Mr. Flabby Crotch Bald Head Big Nose. And men.

Stars trembling . . .

The men tremble as their toes dig in and push, push.

. . . shivering.

You can say that again!

The mainland floats into the dark like my home as we are loaded into the ship. We are taken out at night in long boats and we are pulled up in a big net and that net puts us in a night darker than the demon's heart. Do not come here talking nonsense, Mister.

Do you think these people tell the truth? Do you think Pedder does not like these women, or that Mr. Moustache would rather have a dog? It is all about the price of those fish. For these ladies of Cape Town, it is about another price altogether.

Hsst! Are you there, boy? Sometimes your mother sees things that make her think she is going mad. Sometimes I look across at that town and see things that would make the minister reach for his black book and throw it at me. Perhaps you know what these are, wonderful boy. Tell your mother what it means when she sees men whose bodies have been swallowed up by great monsters that have no legs. I see inside these bodies. I see those who have been swallowed. And these monsters move fast. Faster than you. What can it mean? Is your mother mad?

Some days I do not want to open my eyes and some days not even that saves me.

The guard shouts. Lazy.

I lift my right shoulder and look to the left, slowly. I make my chin dip and come up again, like a small boat. I *am* a small boat bobbing just there off Cape Town, there at Roggerberg. I have come to pick up Hester and her babies. She walked into the water with her children so that they would escape this country. But cruelty of cruelties, she and one child were pulled free of the water. They punished her, as they wanted to punish me.

For women it is different. Two men get hold of a piece of rope. They call it strangulation. For men it is hanging.

Hester is gone from this world. I am still here.

Kom, Hester. I am your boat. I will take you up. I will talk of what it is to be mothers in this country of people with stomachs full of irritation and eyes that always watch us. And I will take you to wherever you want to go, even to your god even though I have no god of my own and do not want another's. So step inside, Hester. Take hold of the sides, I am your boat, I am your friendly little boat. I will point my nose into that line where the sky takes up the earth like coins placed in the plate by the congregation of fancy white ladies who hide the flea bites under their high tides of skirts. Climb in, climb in. We are bound for the place where sun and sky hide a gate that only we will be let through. Come, Hester. Come, come.

This guard who shouts and calls me lazy whore thinks I do not know him. Tonight I will send him fleas that will swim in the folds of his manliness. I am not a nice woman.

The guards say, open up! We stare at the door. We can hear them. They whisper together. The same three guards have tried to come in on other nights. I know the other guards know what is going on and have turned their faces to the wall or have walked to where the wind will cover their ears.

Open up. They whisper and whisper. The door rattles. There are more voices. They are all joining together to become one command. I know the other voices. They are the contractors who have come to build Pedder's jetty.

Build that thing and go! Go!

Open, open!

Pedder dreams of lifting the skirts of those women who have sucked at his mutton. Pedder does not know that he will be writing a report about this. He will write about this. He will write.

Pedder!!!!!!!!!!!!!!

They think they know me. Death! Death to them and their children.

Peddddderrrrrrrrrrrrrr!

Pedder walks about our hut with such a look on his face. I see him through one eye. He pulls his nose back like a *vark*. He covers his nose with a rag.

Gulls above our hut. Their wings open rusty doors. It is a strange time. Crickets have not yet finished with the air and the sun is impatient to arrive. The gulls pull doors open but today the doors are the doors to the dwellings of demons. Me, I do not care. I have all the demons I need. The gulls bring me twigs when I have had trees fall upon me.

Pedder's clothes struggle against his body. He has dressed in a big hurry because we have screamed and screamed and we have all the marks to show it.

Lys has a broken nose.

Pedder curses the guard, one of those who went to the other side of the island to find wood for his fire because the wood collected in front of his door was not fit for the old meat he wanted to cook last night.

Pedder asks the air, how am I to explain this? I will have to send them to the surgeon. You!

Me, I put my shoulder up. I look away. Mina wants to tell him everything. They this, they that. The door, the latch, the wind that blew in like a bad relative. The pulling. The this, the that. I keep one eye on the world where I can see it, outside where the sun shines.

Pedder talks of punishment for the guards and other prisoners, and those who came to build the jetty. What is punishment? Bread and water for . . . how many days? He punishes the punishers.

Baro. Bring me some of their nails, some of their hair. You will find these things in our hut this morning. I have a meal to prepare.

Listen! Help me, boy. You know how hard it is for me to hear. I see their mouths move at me, but hear nothing. Pedder is writing. Go listen to the scratching of his nib. He must find a way to tell the superintendent of police what has happened. Pedder is god on this island. He is a flea on the mainland. He watches us. The superintendent watches him.

Fleas on his page. The sssswine!

What?

He is taking up his book as if it is the end of the month? Return of . . . what? Convicts? Ah. Yes. That is the name of his book. It is his record that he must send each month, as if he is returning a sum of money that has been lent him. What does it say? Hey? What? Does it speak as it always does, of detained prisoners, as he calls us, and of lunatics. He calls Matroos, Soldaat, Keizer, and Vigiland lunatics. Me, I have seen their eyes. They are not so much lunatic as sick in the heart and home to demons.

What else does it say, that book of his? How many stones have been cut. Tell me what he is writing, that Pedder. Tell me.

I said, what? You know I hear nothing if you stand on this side of my head. Come around here. Now.

From the first of January to the first of February, eighteen and twenty-seven. Yes. That is exactly one month. I am counting years, he is counting months.

Who is in his book? Oh, forget the men. They are all the same to me. Is Lys there? Yes. My dear friend. He says what about her? Lys Hottentot. Well. She and I laugh about that. Who is next on the list? Ah. Yes. Philida. Today he calls Mina Philida. *Tsh*! I wonder what she would have to say about that. Never mind, she hates both names. Philida slave. Well, slave she is. That, at least is true. What? Me? He says what?

Stones cut and sent to the Cape. That much I know. That is all I need to know.

One Lys Hottentot. Two Philida slave. Three Sila.

I have heard enough. That pen of his is scratching, scratching. He must explain February eighteen and twenty-seven.

The contractors. Hottentots Sent. Punished with thirty-eight lashes and nine days' solitary confinement on bread and water for picking the lock of the female prisoners' door on the night of the twenty-fifth instant. Twice attempting to force the women and cruelly using them, being aided by three soldiers of the guard. The jetty sufficiently completed for all purpose of landing and shipment of stones being 3/9 feet long. The sea face seventeen feet in height by twenty—I shall no doubt be able to complete it by the twenty-fourth of this month. G. M. Pedder, Commandant.

I heard him read out their names. Their names were D. Donnahoe, his majesty's forty-ninth regiment. W. Stewart, his majesty's fifty-fifth regiment. C. Logan, his majesty's fifty-fifth regiment. M. Cary, his majesty's fifty-fifth regiment. P. Dogherty, his majesty's forty-ninth regiment and sent to the town prison. Ja. Get him off this island and into prison over there. M. Ellas? Cellins? His majesty's Hottentot corps. J. Katte, his majesty's . . . *what*? Sixtieth regiment.

There were not enough lashes, and bread and water was too good for them.

Wild things. My thoughts break and fly like wild things, but I am a wild thing. The warden, the guards, they say I am a wild thing.

They come at night as if there is gold in this place. I hear them open their doors and close their doors. I hear them, even their shadows make a noise, but one that is not of this world and that is why I can hear them with my ear that is not turned outward to everyday things.

They long for love.

Let them grow long, then.

And if they think I am going to welcome them . . . Well, that is not what they care about. These men are not interested in welcome.

But, if they think I will forget, they can think again.

So, come to your mother, Baro, and bring those things that will make them forget all but things that move under their skin.

And then let them fetch a priest. Let them call for whatever medicine they think can be painted over their skin. I will make a poison of all that they touch.

Let them call out to each other that there is something that moves amongst their huts at night.

Let them bathe themselves where the ocean is strongest and will whip them into a feeling of cleanliness. I will have ash waiting at the ridge and a wind that will blow them back into the water until their skin sails away like a shirt that has not enough buttons.

Let them cry like boys. I will tell them of boys who have been made to cry.

Let them turn around in circles. I will close them in the circle of my curses and their tears will be as a liquid that melts rocks.

Let them point their guns. I will push my lips together and eat those guns and when I laugh in their faces they will fall as if cattle.

And, for a special few, bring your mother the king of adders. The pleasures of striking are many and your mother is teaching you what is what in these matters.

Another month. Another report. Pedder's pen is scratching out lies. He says to himself what he writes. I have heard enough through my good ear.

The whole of the prisoners have conducted themselves extremely well with the exception of the two females—Sila and Mina. The jetty will be completed this day.

So much for April. And eighteen and twenty-seven. I am counting. Perhaps if I count fast, years will move like clouds in a Berg wind.

I see you looking at me. I know something wild moves in my eyes. Can you see it, my once-again boy? I feel it. It changes how the world looks. The world will not be still. It flies about in silver. The wildness in my knees, my fingernails, in the first cave of my ears, in my ankles, between my toes, in my nostrils, in my nipples, in my navel, in my cheeks, in the palms of my hands. Sharp. Shaking. It makes soft things of me.

In the warden's kitchen, I put my hands in so much meat for his table. He likes liver and kidneys.

Plates breaking . . . soft things . . . soft things . . . inside things . . . soft . . . soft . . . inside things that can also make the sound of plates breaking, or bones.

I am hungry enough to bite this island. Yes. I bite it. I bite a chunk out of the quarry. There. And tomorrow I'll shit the stones they want so much.

Mina and me? We will never see eye to eye. I pushed her today.

Lys says, Sila! Mina!

The trouble with Mina is that she wants the warden to see her as if she is a good girl. I tell her, the man calls you girl. You are a woman! A woman! Look at her. Mina, I tell her, Mina, have the courage to squat in front of him and shit and shit and shit. Then he will see just what your goodness is made of.

Me, I drag my hair across his shadow and his skin flakes and leaves him like leaves falling from a tree for which there will be no new season. Ja, that is what I say.

The warden has punished the punishers. He spoke the words and it was done. Me, I can already feel the new baby move within. I talk to her.

Baby, I am your mother. I am the one who should know all things about you because I was there, but I am already less than your mother because I do not know which one is your father.

Turn your face to the wall.

My hands shake. I hold them up to the light but the shaking is inside. It is a deep shaking and now I see that it is my whole body, but especially my right hand. My right hand shaketh and if it shaketh must I not do something to it?

The guards watch me. Pedder complains in his reports. I say to them all, you think this is what you think it is. You know nothing. You are fools. You must go and put your head where a fool should put her head. You go. You go and bury your head. You go and get away from me and you stay away from me and you get away and stay away

and do not think you know what you think is true because you know
nothing and nothing is what you know and that is how a fool is and
you are a fool and you must go and be a fool elsewhere. This is my
place. Get!

It would be nice to have a piece of melon. It would be so nice to sit
in the sun and eat a piece. I like to bite in, right to the rind and suck,
and I like the sound. It is the sound of sweetness and my head fills
with sweetness and light and just for this I am happy, just this alone.
   Where did I put my apron?

It takes time to understand what is being done to you. There is a
space, like a hole in a door and that hole takes a key and that key
goes into a space that has, in it, other things that spring a door open.
I do not claim to understand how a lock works, Baro. I am not a
woman who has been taught such things. Few people have been. But
I do understand why a lock has been made, and what work it must
do. And I understand how some people have been turned into locks
that work against them and others.
   Some days I think I am going mad, but that would make life easy
for them. The them-them I mean. The them who take us as they
please. The them that we must feed. Them. Ja.
   Quick. Come give me a hair or two. I have threads of grass in
need of plaiting. Grass and hair today, hair growing with the grass
tomorrow. I know how to dig a hole.

What I heard today is not for all ears. Lys came out of the shed with bruises on her face. She does not speak to me. She threw her bowl of soup at a guard. I threw mine too. She must know that I am her friend.

The warden says, impertinent, sullen, disobedient, trouble makers. I say, make me a gun and I will bring us all peace. More bread, more water. In the lock up, I say nothing out loud. I give them no excuse to treat me like Matroos, or Soldaat, or Keizer, or Vigiland.

To make a good soup, you must have a generous heart. You cannot ask a carrot to boil and boil for twenty people or more. A carrot has just so much to give and no more.

To make a good soup, you need more than water.

Who blames a cook in this place? Only fools. And the hungry. I give my bowl to Lys. She throws two today. I laugh for two. The warden says, uncivilized.

One bone for how many? I say, let whoever wants the bone have it. This is too little to fight for. I suck the air and my tongue searches for anything sweet. Yes. This warden thinks he is teaching us. I say, it is better to know.

Ai. Boy, your mother cannot move today. The surgeon has come. His lips are closed and pressed. He pulls them down at the corners.

Another baby.

As if I did not know what goes on in my own body.

Missus Minister says, you will call her Catherina if she is a girl.

Pedder is pulling at his hair. How will he explain this? Mina is also growing big. Yes. Soon there will be two more babies on this island.

And how many fathers?

Look at Mina, afraid of everything—the warden, the guards, King Adder, thunder, lightning, the wind. Even now, when the guards say, Come! she goes—right there, behind the hut, against the wall. Then she looks to see if we have heard. She pretends she sees nothing but our deafness. Even if I point to my good ear she pretends it is my bad ear.

Wake up!

Mina says, why do you hate me? I say nothing and sit with Lys. Sometimes it is best to cling tight. Wider circles are easier to break. Mina says, I hear you two laughing at me. Lys says, no, no. We are laughing at the guards. Mina puts her hands over her face and turns to the wall. Well. That is what walls are for.

You must do what you must do, and I do what I can.

I am not the kind of woman who can be good and kind and sweet. If I could I would put Mina out there each night, like a dog with a collar, tied to a pot at the door. Let her swallow up all the *vuilgoed* that come to that door. Let her do her work. Why should I be moved by a face that stops up holes in the wall? I have my own wall and nowadays when I put my face into it I see my life sliding out.

Lys says, enough. Sila. I say, let Mina eat her soup and suck on the bones that come her way. Suck-suck. Ja. See if that will make her fat. See if that will make her happy. Just wait and see. What grows first is the belly. What grows in the belly is a worm that wriggles out of the marrow of that bone. What grows is a worm. A worm grows and makes you the nest it loves. See how that will make her happy. See what she does when that worm wants to sit up, or turn over, or eat what you eat, even the thinnest soup. See what that feels like to have a worm chewing on you.

Sila!

Lys? Lys says, Sila, a child is not a worm.

Those men. They look at us in new ways. Some of the men put wide spaces between us when they walk. Others laugh. They say things. Some nod. Some grab themselves. Some spit. What do they know?

And the way they walk . . .

I . . .

Lys, I say to Lys. What has been stolen? Sila, Sila, there is nothing gone. But, I say to Lys, something is gone. Something inside me has been taken away. They walk as if they are gods, coming and going. They do not even know who Sila is, or where she has come from, who her mother was, who her father was.

Lys says, it is not to you or to me they do these things. It does not matter who Lys is or Sila. You must hold on to that. It is not you.

Ja? Let me tell you, that is the worst thing. They steal me away. It is a thing men do here.

I am thinking!

Let your mother think. Your mother is looking for the smallest crack and you know that will be the moment we fly away. Just the tiniest crack.

There are ways of flying. Some are not what you think. Some keep the fools for what they are, *fools*. But, *when we fly you will know it.*

Look! Hsst! This place is a boat.

This place is a horse with a wagon that just brings itself along.

This place is a grand hall and we are the guests invited to dance.

Take up your mother's hand. I want those ladies of Cape Town to break their necks as they crane to watch us. We will move as swiftly as leaves in an afternoon sun when the winds begin to lift the corners of the tablecloth.

Hai. Then. Let death take a seat in the corner of a cold cave on the other side of the mountain. Today we are making life itself stand up and tap its toes because I am stepping out with my son who dances with a high head and such fine shoulders.

Death, we will sing, *death. You have to go to that place alone.*
Death. No one to go with you but some fine, fine ladies.
Their necks are broken and their clothes are torn,
But their faces are pretty and their breath still warm.
Death, we will sing, *death. You will go to that place alone.*
Yes, by yourself.

With nobody but those who are now your own.

What do you think? Just what we need. Yes? A bit of music and even our own song.

This place is a steppingstone and we are the ones who are not young, not old, not rich or poor, not slave or owner. There is not a name for us, even those we tell each other have fallen away. And you remember that, boy. Your mother is teaching you how to make a crack in the floor of the world itself.

In due time, Baro, we will shed even our names, but until then, let us dance on the tips of our toes to keep warm. We will call this our July dance. I was a girl once who loved to dance. And when I sang all stopped work, and there were no curses for that rest we took.

Dance with me, and I will sing and those ladies in Cape Town will wish they were as lucky as I.

Let me rest. This child is pushing on my bones.

Who is coming? Is this a boy or a girl?

The warden's garden is putting on a new face. Soon more visitors will come, like flies in warmer weather.

Next month the farmers will turn their soil now. I remember the smell of fresh diggings. That is the smell of September. I can feel it coming.

After the rain, the flies leave us alone. If I was a woman given to the minister's language, I would pray for rain, but since I am that thing she sometimes calls evil and without mercy, I am willing to live with a fly or two.

Such whipping. Do you know how happy your mother is to see this morning? I was back there on Van der Wat's farm last night. He was whipping me again. With my good ear I could hear the whipping. It woke me up. My good ear is always awake. Lys, who knows of good whippings herself, said be still, Sila, it is the wind. She said, be happy that it is the corner of the hut that takes the beating this time. Her back is warm. I do not understand how it is that I, who am, yes, the worst of all creatures, have come to be so lucky in this, my friend whose back keeps me warm and brings me happiness. I say, thank you for the happiness even though it whips me.

I am not well today. The smell of meat makes me sick. I hold nothing down. It is not just the baby.

They say there is a blue clay that will make you well. The people who live inland, find this clay in the ground and they grind it and make a paste. They eat this paste and those who are sick get well.

Yes. Good boy! And be quick. Your mother feels the weight of all these stones settling on her heart as if a grave is being made.

I will not go even though a sweet bird called today in a voice I have never heard before. I thought . . . bird, if you have white feathers, go past my door, go beat your wings for another. I have a war to fight.

Do not come too close. This is, yes, yes, a new sister. She came early.

Do not come too close. This is not a place for a child and if your sister sees you she will want to go with you because there is nothing that can hold her to this place, not even me, her own mother.

This place.

I have called her Catherina, not because the minister's wife wanted that name. I have called her Catherina because I am too tired to find a name. Do not ask me what kind of mother this makes me.

And do not come too close. Do not wake her. She will see you and she will let go of me and Meisie who sleeps next to her. My new girl will let go of this place and go laughing with you if she sees you.

Do not long for her. Or Meisie.

Two children in this place. What am I to do?

One of the men brought me a piece of wood. He carved the date into it. Number nine and September and eighteen and twenty-seven. She came too early.

Can this be? Now? Of all times for this. A message came from Spaasie. Yes, yes. Spaasie. She paid someone to write a message that Missus Minister read to me. Spaasie says the superintendent of police has written a letter to the governor, Bathurst, to say that *Oumiesies* gave me, all of us that she called property, our freedom and that, yes, yes, Theron was a thief. Who knows what will come of this? What is important is that Spaasie said, too, that she has had news, by way of a man who works for a traveling merchant, that Stroebel sold Carolina to someone named Sterling, also in the District of George. Spaasie says she will go to the fiscal again and ask what news there is of Carolina.

Perhaps the superintendent will come soon and take me and my girls away from this place. He knows now. He has put it down on paper.

Tchaaa! Paper? Paper burns, paper is blown away, paper can be folded like eyes that close from things they do not want to see.

But the superintendent is a different man. I saw this in his eyes when I told him I am a free woman and my children are the children of a free woman. He will not let me sit here. Perhaps I will work for him in his house and he will pay me and make sure my children go to the governor's school so they can grow into freedom. I will go and fetch Carolina from Sterling. I do not care if it is on the other side of the world.

And no news of Camies? What is my boy doing there, on Stroebel's farm?

And Pieter? I want to see that boy and be a good mother to him.

And why no news of Roosje or Johannes or the others from *Oumiesies'* farm?

The superintendent will come and Pedder will have to say sorry and I will set off from this place. I will say Lys must come too. It is the price I ask for all the years that the Orphan Chamber did nothing for me and mine. And I will go and find Camies and tell him, you see, your mother never forgot you. Perhaps I will get a small house up there in the Bo Kaap, on Signal Hill where the gun goes off each day to tell us it is noon.

Is that the superintendent's boat? Baro, go across the water to that Cape Town and find out why the superintendent does not come.

I asked Pedder, what happens now, because the superintendent of police, de Laurentz himself, wrote to tell the governor that I have been cheated. Pedder did not chase me because he is worried that the superintendent wants him in a prison of his own. He said, this is not for me to think about, it is for the courts of law and the governor.

Not for me!

Lys says, Sila, Sila. Mina scoffs. She says, so, you think you are special. Even the guards are talking.

The superintendent must come soon. The truth has been told.

How long does it take for a governor to read a letter?

How could I do it? The minister's wife asks me the question she has wanted me to answer all these months. She asked the warden if I could help her clean the hut in which she sleeps with her minister husband. I know she wants to see Meisie and Catherina. Well. Meisie is like me. She does not like this woman whose tongue wipes and wipes at her lips and whose hair is flat and thin under her bonnet.

The minister's wife watches Catherina. She wants me to take your sister off my back so that she can hold her. And that is how it is today. I pretend, again, that I do not hear her. Look at her now, rubbing her hands. Her hands want my children. If she comes too close, Baro, take those hands and let her feel you. Hiss in her ear.

She says, Sila, you are my spoken test. She says, god has placed me here on this island for a purpose, Sila. He has granted me a test of my very own and it is you. God has spoken to me and said you will be saved and it is I who will save you. Let us work together. Kneel with me.

I kneel enough. It is also called work. And I can see the results.

The minister's wife says, you are a stubborn woman. She calls me wretched.

My father, all that way back over that water there, called me stubborn and there was laughter in his voice, pride.

The minister's wife says, kneel, Sila, and stop babbling. God has placed me here for a purpose, Sila. May he look down upon you in this world. As he sees me in this world. He is your God too.

My god?

94

My God.
Your god says things I cannot hear.
My God takes the blossoms of a special tree.
My god takes such blossoms and makes this girl, me.
God has spoken to me and said you will be saved.
My god has a tooth the shape of a blade.
And it is I who will save you.
Ah. You and your god.
My God cuts down the proud as if they were reeds.
My god moves, I take up the task.
Let us work together.
Your god says things I cannot hear.
Kneel with me.
Who is speaking now?
May God look down upon you in this world. Kneel . . . stubborn woman.
I was made by a great god. I was made to sing . . .

That woman takes all of my energy. I need my energy even more these days, with the baby, the warden's kitchen, his linens, the stones that must be carried in the quarry. These days I do not break stones, but that is no relief. Carrying stones is heavy work and with a baby on my back I cannot think straight for fear of what is happening to her.

The minister's wife talks of god, of salvation, god and salvation, god's salvation, repentance, shame, salvation from shame, mercy for the repentant, and her eyes gleam at all times. Look at her eyes as she watches your sister at my breast. Her hands are like birds looking for some morsel in a long winter. Her nose is a bird's beak. She will pick at me and pull at me and pick and pick and pull a sinew out of the corner of my eye.

She talks. God, salvation, repentance. And she says something so quickly it comes from under her tongue, a place where she keeps other words that might run away from her to make a noise in the room, or outside, where the neighbors could hear. She says it quickly and those hands fly at last and land. Wings at her mouth. They beat and in her eyes are years of secret things that swim up in the way that secret things swim up and shimmer because they do not have bodies themselves, not even the body of a word.

She says it quickly and I see secrets that seek life and I turn away. H-h-h-how c-c-could you do it?

It bangs against my ears and I hear the rushing of too many winds, the kind that bring trees—and I mean *big* trees—not just down but up, right up out of the earth so that their roots are torn free.

Her hands are at her book and the pages are wings trying to fly from her hands because, flit and fret and fuss as her hands do, the pages will not land where she wishes. She looks at me. She looks at Meisie. Her eyes shine.

No. Do not say anything more.

She sees what my eyes tell her. In her cheeks, white things are pushing up under the scarlet. Things are moving in there. She says . . . I shake my head. She says . . . No, no. Sssila! No. This woman . . . She wants . . . I want . . . this island is a small mark in a big world. There are things . . . I say . . . I say . . . No, no. She wants . . . Ssssilaaa! Her eyes . . .

There are things I will not stand for.

The minister's wife takes her book between two firm hands. She bends her face to the page she has pinned down. Obedient servant, she searches in there for what she must say. She wants that book to speak to me so that I will hear what is buried there. It speaks like winds beating the tops of trees, or the sails of a ship that carries the dead.

There are secrets here that must never be spoken. I, Sila, wretched stubborn creature, will not let her make me the vessel of her secrets.

And. Before you ask me such questions and desire of me such things as you do, Missus Minister, you must know what places I have seen, what people, what creatures. You must know what sounds I have heard and from which direction they came. You must know what birds woke me, and what birds crowded the day out with their chatter. How could they be told apart? You must know this by learning the way they move. Learn who it was who coughed sometimes at night and could be heard across the compound where my father sat with the men, talking. You must know who got up first to go to his hut. And you must know how he got up. On which knee did he rest his hand to push himself up? Who did that dragging footstep belong to? And which children teased him in daylight?

You have to learn these things. And then tell me if I should be emptied out so easily to become the vessel of your bad dreams.

How? I will tell you.

With the smell of lemon juice in the air. With the sound of the rushes as they are cut and gathered to make a bed. With the taste of those lemons. And there is nothing like the taste of lemons, and if you dip the tip of your finger into the fresh new face of a cut lemon and rub the insides of your eyes you will keep your eyes from getting sores, though the sting will make you groan and laugh at the same time.

Yes. With deep roots in my veins. With glass in my belly and glass in my heart. With the dullness of lead in my left ear. And, yes, with care. That is all.

Huh! A dream. Lys says, Sila, it is only the wind and rocks herself so that I, grown woman and mother, one child only new in this world, I who am a wretched creature, the worst creature, fool without hope and condemned to learn this lesson each day, I who answer to this name she calls, I will be rocked like a child.

Catherina looks at the world with wide eyes. She is quiet. Even when I leave her with Lys. Even when Meisie waves her hands in front of her.

Meisie. The warden talks of taking her away from me. Missus Minister has been talking to him and he wants Meisie to go to Van der Wat because there are too many children on the island. Lys says the new Protector of Slaves will not let him do this.

The protector? Where was he when I needed him? He has slaves of his own, I hear. So. Tell me, what does he protect?

One of the guards gave me a blanket for your sisters. I thanked him. He has never come and kicked our door down, but I still keep a wall in my voice. Doors are opened in more than one way.

The warden says Van der Wat has registered Catherina as his property. When I heard that my stomach went tight and there were bright spots before my eyes.

What is it with these people? They count us like buttons their jealous hands do not want to lose.

Who told him?

The wind howls in my throat.

When the minister's wife says again that Meisie must go from this place I say, then let me go too and take Catherina. The minister's wife says I am a selfish woman. She says Meisie will die here, or worse.

Let me be buried and I will grow into a tree that will shade a whole village.

Let me lie in a shallow grave and be found by hyenas. Let me be food to creatures that deserve to live. Only those who must eat and are not plagued by words can forgive me. I will say, hyenas, I surrender to you and you will not care that what you eat had a name, was called by that name before I came to live in the wretched stink of this place called Sila. And you will not care about anything at all but the meal. A meal is only one meal. It interrupts the hunt and you are a slave to the hunt. I will find my peace. And I will not seek to live in you. I will not seek to speak through you. You will laugh your shivering laugh, because you will have tasted surrender.

Lys is angry. She says, get up Sila! Do I want to be beaten? Catherina is crying. I hold her too hard. For this reason I let Lys take her. Meisie plays with Flora. That is good. I will not move from this bed.

Even when Lys tips the cot I will not move from the floor where I have fallen. I smell the dust. I close my eyes. The floor is good against my cheek. The floor speaks to the bones in my body. Hardness to hardness. The floor makes me feel what lies beneath all the flesh. A truth we all carry and fear when life is good. My good ear is turned away and Lys is a muffled voice. My bad ear is the ear that hears what the floor says to the bones in my body. My bad ear was born for this.

The surgeon has come over in a boat. Pedder is angry. The surgeon says do not let me find out that you are malingering.

I am doing what I am doing. Go drown yourself, ugly man, go drown those crooked teeth of yours. Drown your beard and the bits of breakfast that still cling to it. Go put your head in your chamber pot and drown yourself. I am doing what I must do.

I have spent today remembering things I have never wanted to remember. Your visits bring me joy, but they also make what should be still shadows crawl. Now that you are back, my son, everything else comes back—the first day we arrived at Van der Wat's farm and, before that, all the years I thought I was working my freedom price off at Hancke's. I have been counting years. I worked so hard to keep you children with me. Even before any of you were born I saw what happened to women and their children. There was the time back there with the Neethlings when I was, *eh!*, so small.

Loedewyk, Adam, and Annetjie. Gone. The woman I had to call Ma. Gone. Then, I was taken to *Oumiesies* like a present one person buys for another.

I do not want to think of such things. But I must. That is the difference between me and Mina, even between me and Lys, who is closest in my heart.

When I was a girl with *Oumiesies*, Theron kept trying to get us away so that he could sell us. He wanted to sell Spaasie and Roosje's children. You see, they were born on his farm because there was a time when *Oumiesies* sent Spaasie and Roosje there to help him before he was married. Then she brought them back and he was cross. Spaasie told me all about this. She said she had run all the way from his farm to *Oumiesies*' one night because she heard that he wanted to sell her and her children.

Say what you like about *Oumiesies*, a woman who kept us as if we were lap dogs to play with, but she was there and fierce about what she called hers.

Who did I have when she was gone? Who could I run to?

Spaasie's children were Galant, who could run after cattle faster than any of the other young men, Arend, who could find honey, Frederik, who was quiet, and that sweet girl Sariel, who could not sew but cooked *tert* that melted in your mouth.

Roosje's eldest was Galate. When I asked why Galant and Galate were so close in name, Roosje was angry with me. I was young. What did I know? *Oumiesies* kept me from the things that Spaasie and Roosje had to live. Galate was like my big sister. Skin like butter, like her brother Cesar, but also like Galant.

Spaasie and Roosje's children were brothers and sister to me like Loedewyk, Adam, and Annetjie back there with the Neethlings.

When I first went to *Oumiesies* I slept with Sariel and Galate. We were the youngest, me the youngest of all. Then I slept with Philipina, but after she went to Theron I had to sleep in the kitchen because *Oumiesies* did not want to be alone in the big house. Sometimes, when *Oumiesies* was snoring so hard you could hear her all the way to the kitchen, Galate and Sariel would come and sit with me and we would talk nonsense until Spaasie or Roosje came and told us we would be sorry come morning.

Spaasie's boys were good. They would not be men who hit women. I do not know what kind of man Cesar would have become. Galant and Arend were both older than me, but not by many years. They were brothers to me.

Those children came at a high price for Spaasie and Roosje, but they loved them and they worried about them. When I was young, before I reached childbearing age, I listened to Alima and Johannes, Spaasie and Roosje talk about what could happen if *Oumiesies* was not there to stop Theron. Johannes used to talk about things he heard in town—how the English did not want slaves, but did not want to drive the farmers deeper inland. One time he said that, as soon as they could, the English would set us free. Spaasie was sharp with him. She said this was rubbish talk, the English also kept slaves, and they would have to chase the Dutch from government house again. Johannes said they did this once before, they could do it again. He said, remember, when the English took the country from the Dutch they ended all torture, in seventeen and ninety-eight. I remember because Johannes told me. It was the year that I went from the Neethlings to *Oumiesies*, Spaasie said, well, but the talk is that the Dutch will have the country again and no English care enough about us anyway.

She and Roosje worried about their children. Theron was always trying to make *Oumiesies* give them to him or sell them. So, Spaasie said Johannes was wrong, there would be no freedom for her or her children. Roosje agreed and said, Sila, there will be a time when you will bear children and then you will be afraid of the world in ways that are new and terrible.

I was lucky, you know, *Oumiesies* did not push me to have babies. Before she told her husband to get out of her house, he pushed Alima to have many babies. Then he sold them. Only Spaasie and Philipina were left because he sold the others away. *Oumiesies* would not let him get Spaasie or Philipina. When he left, he wanted them and Alima, but *Oumiesies* said no because Alima had come to her as a gift from her own mother. So I was lucky that he was gone when I came to *Oumiesies* but, young as I was, I knew Roosje was right. No matter how much *Oumiesies* did not push me, babies would come. It made me afraid. How many times did I hear her and Spaasie talk with Alima and Johannes about what would happen to us when *Oumiesies* left this world. They worried about Spaasie and Roosje's children. They said Theron would come and sell us all.

When they talked about such things, I remembered the time with Minister Neethling and Missus Neethling and I knew why they sold Ma first. It was because they tried to be good in the tight stockings of their hearts. They did not want her to see them sell us like pieces of furniture or animals. And I knew that, one day, I could be a mother. That was what came to all women, especially those of us who were called slave. I could see it as if it was before me like one of those pictures that *Oumiesies* liked to keep on her walls and that Theron said were a waste of money.

One day, Spaasie said, *Oumiesies*, I am afraid that my children will be sold away from me. *Oumiesies* said, Spaasie, as god is my witness, this will not be. Spaasie said, *Oumiesies* does not know that this life I live with my children is not any of that god's business. She gave Spaasie a hard look and reached for that big book and to read about the suffering children who would be taken in by a father who did not care what they are. Afterward, Spaasie said she had to shut her mouth to stop herself saying that she and her children were not in *Oumiesies'* book and Theron was not afraid of *Oumiesies'* god.

We wanted *Oumiesies* to stay alive, but she was not well. She had those cheeks that spot with heart weakness. We were all worried for ourselves. She was cross with me one day. She said, you people, you care for me because you are afraid of what will happen when I die. Ja, she was right. She asked, who is there in the world who cares about me? She said, it is not my son, that man cares only for himself and that wife of his cares only for the bowls and furniture she will get. And the land, I thought, but my mouth stood just so, not a word spilling out of it. But *Oumiesies* knew and I lied with my face and with the shaking of my head and the care of my hands. I was young.

Then, just after the fields had been ploughed and seeding begun —July?—Theron visited. He told her she had too many people on her farm and he needed more. He said she had cheated his father out of his marriage due and as his father's heir he wanted some of us. He pointed at me. *Oumiesies* told me to get to the kitchen. But I was young, maybe fourteen years old. I said, *Oumiesies*, if we go from your farm, what will happen to us? Theron shouted, keep your place! He shouted at his mother. He said, you have no control, it is dangerous, you must let me take these people, especially this one off your hands.

Right in front of me, *Oumiesies* asked him, what would happen if she sent us to him? She said, you and your debts, you will sell them off, and sell their children, already they are all worrying about that. What was she thinking, to say such a thing? Theron looked at me. He said, you baboons talk about me? You *gam* talk about *me*? He gave me a *klap*. *Oumiesies* shouted, you will not lift your hands in my house, these are my people. He told her, you are a stupid woman and you will die in your bed with your throat cut by one of these heathen savages. How many times have I told you you must have a *mandoor*? He said, I will send my *mandoor* to look over these lazy good-for-nothings who speak back to their betters as if they are on the same footing. It is your fault, he said, you put ideas in their heads. *Oumiesies* said, I have all the *mandoors* I want. Theron said, *mandoor*? You call that old cripple baboon a *mandoor*? *Oumiesies* said nothing but I saw her grip on her scissors. He saw it too. His eyes went big. He said, old woman, you be careful. She said, no, no, it is you who must be careful. Do not think that what is mine will be yours so easily. He kicked a chair over. It made a big crash. I jumped. I thought he was going to hit *Oumiesies* and I called for Johannes to come, come quickly. *Oumiesies* was calling too, Johannes! Johannes! The dogs were barking. Alima ran in, then Roosje and Spaasie, and then Johannes. Theron pointed and said to his mother, you call upon these things? You will be sorry. Johannes looked, but said nothing to him or to *Oumiesies*. He and Alima said to us, come, and made us leave. But you could hear the shouting all the way down in the kitchen and the dogs were like mad things.

Then Theron shouted for Johannes to fetch his horse, and while Johannes was gone, Theron came into the kitchen with his *mandoor*, a man not one of us liked, a man into whose food we spat when we could. Theron looked at me and said, so, you worry about yourself. Well, you will have something to worry about, that I promise you.

That was July of eighteen hundred because it was just before *Oumiesies* made her will. The bad, bad days had not arrived yet, but they were gathering themselves.

My eyes hurt. They burn. All that dust from the quarries, all that noise of hammers and stones. This island is filled with the noise of hammers and men coughing.

It is time those stones flew up like bullets into the warden's house. Faithful messengers. And then they can pick themselves up and fly over the water, low as birds, until they reach the town and further still. I want one stone to break a certain head at the prison. I want another to find Theron's head, and Hancke's and Mokke the trader's, and I want it to smash his cart so hard it turns into kindling. Let his children know what it is to be hungry. Let another stone break his heart. Let him know as he dies that his children will be hungry. And I want a big pounder to hit Theron.

I will say this to the day I die, it was all the fighting with her son that made *Oumiesies* sick. When *Oumiesies* died and Theron came rubbing his hands like a fly over her grave, I told Theron's eldest daughter—the one who was the same age as me, what was her name? —that *Oumiesies* had said we should be free on the day of her death. I said, Theron must let us go, we are free. I told that no-name daughter because she hated her father. You see, their seed turns on them. I know why she hated him.

Family secrets are not so secret. Just ask me.

I told that daughter how *Oumiesies* made the *advocaat* write down her last wishes and I was there with Spaasie, Roosje, Alima, and Johannes, everyone, to hear when she told him to read it. And, more! Isac—you do not know him, Baro, because it was before you were born—Isac was there and he could read more than his own name. *Oumiesies* was worried about her son and she said I must keep the paper. Then, the next year in July eighteen and oh two, when our huts almost burned down because a Berg wind came up and blew candles over, she told me to give it back so she could keep it safe. It was the year the English took the country from the Dutch, and Johannes thought we would all be set free. Poor Johannes. I gave the paper back to *Oumiesies*. She put it in a box and showed me where the key should always be found—behind the headboard of her bed. One day, when she went to town, I promised Isac some *melktert* if he read the paper to me again. His name was not in that paper. He laughed and said *Oumiesies* liked him too much to let him go, even if she was to die. I gave him two pieces of milk tart.

Isac. He laughed and ate the *melktert* even though his name was not in that paper and I gave some of the *tert* to Spaasie and Roosje, and to Alima and Johannes, and Spaasie's children. Then I made a whole new *tert* and *Oumiesies* never knew.

When *Oumiesies* died, I tried to tell Theron and the *advocaat*, even the *mandoor*, where she kept the paper. Even though I could not read the words I remembered who was in it and what it said. I said, Johannes, Spaasie, Roosje, and Isac all knew. And the *advocaat*. But Theron said there was no paper.

When I told his daughter about that paper, I even drew the shape and size in the sand. I said *Oumiesies* said it was god's will. I was stupid to tell that daughter. She went to her father. She gave me up so that he could be pleased with her. Yes. Theron beat me. He said, *meid*, did you murder my mother so that you can tell lies? I said no, no. But the price of my stupidity was already mounting. Theron said, never speak of *Oumiesies* again. Well. That daughter made her bed and she can lie in it. I heard she got married. I want to see the face of her first child and then I will tell her what I know.

Sheeeeagh. All this remembering.

There should be a time for one cool, clear, steady breath. I want to inhale air that does not come through this world where everything has a name, whether that thing deserves that name or not, whether that name *is* a name or just a big bucket that they put over all kinds of different things to be sure there is nothing that has not been given a name. A name, I am learning, all over again, is like a place. When you have a certain name, you can be like Missus Minister. Things can be sent to you. But, as I learnt from the day I was taken onto that boat, even before I went into that great hole where we had to lie down like people not yet dead but dying, I knew that who I was, who my mother was or my father, did not matter. None of that could help me. Everything that was part of the who that made me—my bowl, cracked as it was, the place where our headman sat, the place where the boys went to become men—nothing mattered. And it matters less now. There is no going back. There is only my forehead and where it points me.

And where it points me some days is right in the warden's face. Ja. Lys says, Sila, some people just do not know when to sit down and die.

I am one of those people. Yes, yes. Even though I faced dying for a long time, I have also given up trying. This life keeps me from life itself.

I said to Lys just yesterday, they take us out of life and we are not people anymore, we are not women. And then they come kicking in here to remind themselves that they are men.

There are many hungers. We are not to allow ourselves hunger. Do you hear me? I have begun to understand something. It is the beginning of an understanding. Soon, I will be able to tell you what it is I understand. In the meantime, we must protect ourselves from hunger.

Someone always has to pay.

What?

Time for you to grow up, boy.

My pretty boy with the sun in your eyes. Look, it is me, your mother.
I sing a song for you and it will carry over the years and the light in
your eyes will finally become true as the light of the end of one day,
and the sunrise of another. Keep your heart safe. Son of my heart,
son of my life, I know the meaning of the light in your eyes.

I tell Lys about you. I say, a pretty boy. She likes to hear about
you. She alone understands why I was so sad and so happy when
you were born. And so I say, you could see the flecks of sunset in
his eyes when he laughed and those flecks came from the oranges I
ate when I carried him. I tell her, he was born of me and a man
who danced away with me when the stars were out and the grass
was so wet our feet were cold and shining. And when he was born,
there while I was working for my freedom at merchant Hancke's,
I would put Baro before a looking glass. It took him a long time to
see what was in that looking glass. I should have been warned. I
say, Lys, you know, he looked at everything before him, but it was
as if there was a blank patch right before his eyes. He could not
look at himself, but when he did, ah, a little shock that first time,
a little start, a little light and those flecks came alive. He laughed
to see himself.

What were you thinking when you looked and looked so hard?

I told Lys, how, after Carolina and Camies were already gone and
only you and Pieter were left with Van der Wat, one day, when I
was working in the field where I should not have been working because I am not a field hand, you went into their big upstairs that cost

money borrowed from Maria Martha Cruywagen. You went into their big room and was found.

What did you think? Did you speak to that boy in the mirror? Did you ask him what life he lived?

The first of your beatings behind my back.

I send a message across that water now. I tell that water to take my curse deep into the belly of generations and to find their rooms hundreds and hundreds of sunsets away, and I tell the wind to go into their rooms, make the bedding rustle and crawl. Let them sit up and turn for light, more light. Let them be weary for days and let them be afraid of the face that peers back at them from their mirrors.

I want so much to see Carolina's face today, and Camies's face, and Pieter's.

Did I tell you why I named your sister Carolina even though it was not my mother's name, or anything that came from my family back there in the time before the world tilted into darkness and spat me out in this place of demons?

Did I tell you about old Johannes who liked to see me dance? Johannes was like a father to me. I was a child when he lifted me out of a wagon for *Oumiesies*. And he was father to Spaasie and Philipina, who were my sisters there. A good man. I miss him.

I wish . . . I try not to, but I do, I wish . . . Well. Some things are best left unsaid.

But I remember. When your body begins to talk silly things to your head, all sense goes. One day, after many years on *Oumiesies'* farm, when I was a young woman, maybe fourteen, and the men were beginning to look at me, I came into the hut and there, on our bed, was a bunch of flowers. Those pretty pink ones that look like they have been dipped in candle wax. They made me smile and I put them in a cup of water, right there. Alima pinched me. She said, someone notices you. I laughed like a little girl. But Spaasie said Philipina put those flowers there. I said, she did not. She said, you think they came from Johannes. I said, what if they did?

Sila, you must not get fancy ideas about Johannes.

I made myself cross. My nose was in the air.

He is an old man.

I said, I do not care. She said, he is not for you.

I was cross, cross. I knocked the milk over and she got the blame when *Oumiesies* came into the kitchen and saw it all over the floor. When *Oumiesies* went out of the kitchen Spaasie hit me on the backside with the broom. Now, I can laugh. Then, *heesh*, it was a different story. We did not speak for days.

Then Alima told me to carry water to the vegetable garden where Mars and Petro were weeding. We walked slowly because she was old already. The men were sitting under the trees when we brought their water. We talked with them for a while, then Alima and I turned to go back. But when we had gone a little way she said, Sila, sit with me.

It was pretty, sitting there under a tree with the pea hens nearby. I loved Alima. She was a good, good woman.

She said to me, Sila, you are lucky.

Lucky? What happened?

Alima said, *Oumiesies* has not made you lie with men, *Oumiesies* is good that way, even if she is also stupid when it comes to Theron who is the true son of his father.

I remember. Winter was over because the fields had just been turned and the men were pruning the vines. Spring. Perhaps August. I asked Alima what she meant. She said, Sila, you are coming of age and you must be careful of Theron. My heart jumped. She said, Johannes and I have done what we can to keep him away from you, but he wants *Oumiesies* to send you to his house. No, I said, I will not go. Alima shook her head. She said, that is what Spaasie said and it was what Roosje said.

So that is how I learned the truth about Spaasie and Roosje's children. Alima said Theron wanted to sell their children because everyone knew and his wife screamed at him about his bastards when she got cross.

Alima told me how, before she went to *Oumiesies'* farm she was made to lie with men so that she would make babies who were sold from her even though the law said no child should be sold from a mother.

But, Spaasie and Philipina? I said, they are Johannes's children. She said, only Philipina, but Johannes is a father to Spaasie because she was a baby and Johannes took her up as his own without question. She said, Johannes is a good man, Sila. I said, yes, Alima, when I have a man of my own I want him to be like Johannes. She did not get cross with me like Spaasie. She said, I hope that you find a good man, Sila. But in my heart I was afraid. I asked who Spaasie's father was. She said it did not matter because that is how it is in this country. He was a man on another farm, in another time.

I asked Spaasie about Theron. She said, so, you just found out? She asked me where I thought her children and Roosje's came from. Not from under a bush, I said. She said, a bush but not the kind you mean. We laughed, but Spaasie said, why do you think we hate Theron? When she told me how he grabbed her when she was cleaning his bedroom, I felt spiders crawl over me. I said, why did *Oumiesies* let him do this? She said, *Oumiesies* sees what *Oumiesies* needs to see. What is too hard is not there, that is all. And you, she said, you must watch out for him. Be careful.

Alima. I think how she must have felt when she and Philipina were sent to Theron's farm and, when Philipina was sold away, with no one else to talk to, trying to send a message across the valleys to *Oumiesies*. Those days you had to wait for one of the mail runners or a traveler who came with servants who could pass a message to someone who could pass it on again. Sometimes, who knows, a message for someone in a next valley might go all the way to Franschoek and back before it reached the right person. And I think about Johannes, how it must have been to see Alima taken away, then Philipina.

And Philipina. I think of what she must have had to live with there on Theron's farm. When I put my face in the sun I can see her face. I put my finger on her nose or her cheek. I was young before I could see her and talk to her as a woman. Then she was gone.

Hai, but Alima was all the mother I had after I arrived at *Oumiesies'* farm. Alima was a Mozbieker like me, and so were Isac and Roosje and Mars. Mozbieker, from all the way up the coast in that direction.

If we follow it, will we come there? Why not? What is it that stops us? I ask you, this is a very, very important question.

Alima, Roosje, Mars, they were already grown when they were taken. Not like me. What I remember is very thin. What I had was feelings. A smell of something would make my head spin like nobody's business. I could just be walking, or in the kitchen, making bread and then something would be like a smack. For a long time the smell of summer made me sad even though it was warm and easier for living. It was Alima who saw this and understood how, on a hot day, when the air was wet and covered your skin with drops of sweat, how it made me cry for back there. She said, do not hold your tears. Let them come.

But it was Spaasie—born when Alima was too young to carry children—who asked me about my home. Perhaps it was because she was a mother of four children, one younger than me, that made her so good to me. Perhaps it was just that she is good, like her own mother, and like Johannes who was father to her, and like her sister Philipina who loved me and gave me pink flowers once. Spaasie asked me about my mother and father. I ran away from the kitchen the first time she asked. It meant trouble and there would have been a beating but she told *Oumiesies* that she had sent me to fetch wood. Then *Oumiesies* said, use one of the boys, what is wrong with you, she could get ideas in her head. Spaasie said, sssssssorry *Oumiesies*. I was cross.

Spaasie asked me, did anyone else from your family come with you? I said, you.

Was it not? It was her. It was her body that I lay against and it was her whose arms held me and cried on me and called me little daughter. It was her I called Ma.

Spaasie said, did they bring anyone else from your family? I said the little girl was in that big hole by herself. She said, what girl? I said, that girl. Spaasie wanted to smack me for making a joke, but Johannes came from the corner of the room where he had been tying *riet* for new beds. He said, no, leave her. Then Spaasie nodded. Then she asked me, what about that girl's mother and father? What were their names?

She told me that she had another name, one that her mother Alima had given her, like a small gift from that other place where her mother was born. She told me that name. She said it was Alima's own name from that other place.

Alima gave me bread with honey, just like the *Oumiesies* ate. Alima was all the mother I had then.

But Theron got her and Philipina because *Oumiesies* was trying to be a mother to him even though he was no son to her. That was a big day.

I do not like to think about these things.

You see, Theron came to the farm when *Oumiesies'* sister was visiting. It was a big visit. It always was when her sister came because *Oumiesies* loved her so and missed her when she was far away inland. *Oumiesies* used to say, let me sell all of my land and go live with my sister. But she never did. *Oumiesies* loved her farm as much as she loved her sister and one was always nearer than the other one. But when her sister came, it was a big visit. And it always meant that Theron came with his family and his wife's family, and *Oumiesies* tried to hide her anger from her sister. And that was how he got Alima and Philipina. Right there in front of everyone, just when I was carrying the last dishes to the kitchen, I heard him say, *Moeder, Moeder* you are so lucky to have so many hands to help you. *Oumiesies* said nothing. I knew something bad was coming, Baro. I felt it as if it was a wind bringing the smell of a big storm. Theron said, my own wife has to make do with little help and we are so many more than one person living in such a big house. *Oumiesies* said, we will talk of this later. But her sister, who loved Theron because she knew nothing of his badness, said, oh, Hendrina, sister, you must let him have someone to help out. I did not hear what happened next because Philipina was behind me and gave me a push and out I went and the door was closed.

The next day, Theron and his family were gone. And then the next day it was time for *Oumiesies*' sister to leave. We all had to wave goodbye to her, as if we were also sad to see her going. *Oumiesies* was sad. She was like a lost thing, going from one room to another. She came and stood on the back step and asked what I was doing. I said, hanging the linens, *Oumiesies*. She said, then do a good job. Then she called Alima and Philipina.

I was still hanging the linens when I saw Alima going slowly to the huts with Johannes. He was holding her hand. Spaasie came running out of the house. She was crying. Then there was a big cry from the house and Philipina came out as if demons chased her. She was shouting, why? She ran left to right, right to left in front of the house, shouting at the house that *Oumiesies* was wrong. Alima turned around and from across the yard she called to Philipina. Come, she said, come, there is a long way to go.

Baro, you must know that your mother's whole body went cold. It was like seeing Ma go all over again. This time was as different as it was the same. We were like dogs chasing our tails. Because that was all we were. Dogs and cows, pigs and horses. When Alima put her head high and walked to the wagon that Johannes had made ready, there was no proud woman loved by all. There was only an old horse. When Johannes helped her onto the wagon, there was no kind old man who never put a hand on my body. There was only an old pig snorting. And when Philipina came crying and holding on to Spaasie, there were no sisters weeping. There were only chickens making stupid chicken sounds.

When Johannes came back the next day, he was not alone. They were all in the wagon with him. But there was Theron too, and his *mandoor*. I was stupid. I ran to greet Alima. I said, you are back! She was tired. She just hugged me. I thought Theron had decided not to take them from *Oumiesies*. But it was not so easy. Yes, he was sending them back. But only because he was cross. He shouted when he saw *Oumiesies*. He said, you send me an old woman! And then he pointed to Philipina and said, that one is stupid in the head. Why do you send me an old thing and a stupid thing? Are you trying to insult me? I thought, now *Oumiesies* will tell him to get on his horse and take his *mandoor* with him, and Alima and Philipina would be back with us and we would all go back to pretending that we were not horses and pigs, chickens and cows. But, no. *Oumiesies* said, you take them or no one. Then there was more shouting. Theron pointed at me. He said, give me that one. *Oumiesies* said, you take what you get. So he got on his horse and called to his *mandoor*, who was the real dog, looking to please his master and win a bone.

A few days later, Theron's wife and daughter came to visit *Oumiesies*. The daughter was the same age as me. I remember, she was fourteen because *Oumiesies* sent her a pretty dress for her birthday. Me. I never had a birthday here. Never. So, there was Theron's first born with her mother who said there was a new baby coming and she needed more help. But *Oumiesies* was cross. She said a gift had been made and a gift had been thrown back in the giver's face. Theron's wife said, oh, *Moeder*, you must not get so cross with him, he is proud. Then she asked for me and Galate. *Oumiesies* said no. She said Alima and Philipina could go but only until Theron could buy his own slaves. She said, he must do that by the new year. *Oumiesies* said, this is August. You will send my women back to me by the end of January. I remember. Everything was green.

Theron's wife was not happy. When she was leaving with her daughter, I saw her face. She saw me. She said, you! Get from my sight! Her daughter put her tongue out.

We were sad, hey. For a long time. Then one day we heard that Philipina was gone. *Oumiesies* was not well so she sent her *advocaat* who came back and said, no, Philipina was still at Theron's, but Alima sent news to say that this was not so. We told *Oumiesies*. She sent her *advocaat* back and this time she went to the fiscal. Theron told the fiscal that Philipina was dead. That was a bad day. Spaasie cried. Johannes held his head. Then Spaasie asked *Oumiesies* if she could bury her sister. *Oumiesies* said, you are reaching above your station. But then she said, Johannes, take the wagon. I wanted to go too, but *Oumiesies* was sick and I had to stay. When Johannes and Spaasie returned, they said Theron chased them away because Alima told them that Philipina was not dead but sold away. Johannes did not want to leave Alima there, but Theron and his *mandoor* beat him. So, he and Spaasie came and told *Oumiesies*. She was sick, but she climbed into her carriage. Johannes said there was shouting but Philipina was gone.

Hai, Philipina. Sweet, just older than me. She could cook, hey. And I still do not know why Theron called her stupid. She was quiet, different, not like other women, but not stupid. A woman dead, then alive, then gone.

We had word that Alima died on Theron's farm. Spaasie did not believe that. She still does not. She is still looking. She is strong, that Spaasie.

It was only a short time later when news came that *Oumiesies'* sister was dead. The trip back inland killed her. *Oumiesies* locked herself up in her bedroom for many days and cried. You could hear her if you went upstairs. When she came out, it was to call us all together to pray for her sister. Then she went back into her room. This was how it was until October when weeds kept Mars, Anthony, and Petro busy all day in the cornfield. One morning, *Oumiesies* came out dressed as usual. She sent Isac to town with Johannes to give her *advocaat* a letter. When they came back, she said, Isac, make a list of all of my people. Give it to my *advocaat*. I am making my will.

Unconfessed

Oumiesies trusted that man but he was more friend to Theron than *advocaat* to her. And do not ask me why she did not put Isac in her will.

After making her will, *Oumiesies* felt a bit better, but something had gone out of her, like freshness out of a stem. That was how she was, like one of her own cut flowers. She thought that piece of paper would keep what was hers from going to Theron. But when she died Theron took some of us to his farm and tricked me. That is when I saw just how much *Oumiesies' advocaat* had been a friend to Theron because he helped Theron trick the Orphan Chamber that looks after all estates. He helped Theron sell Johannes. And Mars. And Isac who was not even in *Oumiesies'* will.

Why am I remembering these things?

Spaasie was one of those who got freedom as *Oumiesies* wanted. In eighteen and oh six. She can read, you know. She was too much trouble for Theron. She found work with some English in Rondebosch and took in extra sewing to pay for Sariel.

Galant and Arend sold, also inland. And Frederik. Philipina, gone. And Anthony, Mars, and Petro, sold away. Not even Spaasie could find out what happened to Johannes.

Theron kept me on his farm for two years, and for two years I fought him. He used to come to me at night and then his wife got cross. And his daughter got cross. And then he needed money. That was why he sent me to Hancke. And that is where you, Carolina, and Camies were born. Carolina first. In eighteen and ten.

I wish I found work with Spaasie. She is a good woman. She sent word out, asking where I was and, one day, I was sweeping Hancke's store on Market Square and there she was. She came to see me in Cape Town because the English woman let her ride to the store with her. The English man went to the fiscal to try to help her find Galant, Frederik, and Arend because she said they would all work for him. She said the English did not call them slaves but made them work as hard.

The English let her come sometimes and Hancke never let me travel and then there was all that business with him and Theron and no one would let me out of their sight. But when she could, Spaasie came to see me and told me to keep fighting for my freedom. So, when your sister was born, I gave Spaasie the right to choose a name. Spaasie took the name Carolina.

I chose your name. It is a box that holds something from my father's people.

I have been thinking of the stories that Alima liked to tell us when I was a child. When she was gone, it was Spaasie who told the same stories, as if they were hers. I was older then and I could hear them differently. They were like songs. You do not sing a song once, but many times in your lifetime. So, we liked to listen to Spaasie tell the stories that Alima had told her about back there, in Mozbiek. Galant could not think of what it was like. No matter how she tried to tell him he could not see the place. Arend liked to hear those stories. Frederik and Sariel just listened and they never said anything.

Spaasie was good, but not as good as Alima. She could tell a story, hey. When I was a child and Alima talked about back there, it was as if I had come from her village. One day I told Galant that I was from her village. He asked her if that was true. She said to me, you mind yourself. She said, you want to be silly, girl, go ahead. But she made me say, over and over, my mother's name and my father's name. Who was who in my village. Who was the headman. Do not ask me what name I gave her!

Alima asked, what tree grew in front of your home? What sounds do you remember? Fierce. She was fierce.

And what . . . ? And who . . . ? And what . . . ? Who . . . ?

Sometimes, when we were alone in the house, when *Oumiesies* had gone to visit that son and his wife and their noisy children, Alima made me shout.

Shout, who . . . ? Shout, what . . . ?

I shouted. We laughed. I shouted and perhaps that is where I made a mistake because sometimes I could not remember or wanted to make more, put an extra tree in, make my father important. I shouted lies.

And now I remember *her*, her stories. The rest is gone. All that she said I must remember is like a story I have heard, a story another person told me about her life.

Who is Sila?

Mothers and children, and mothers of children not theirs. That is how we are in this country.

Today I miss everyone from *Oumiesies'* farm. I think of Alima who was all the mother I really had on this side of the world when I arrived at *Oumiesies'* farm. I think of Johannes with his crooked leg. And of Philipina who was quiet and kept to herself but was always ready to help with anything you needed.

Where is she now?

I think of Alima telling Spaasie and Roosje's children about the place that she and I came from. Spaasie held on to her stories. Spaasie. Who got her freedom and is working there in Rondebosch.

Go and see if you can find her for me, Baro. Blow a soft wind across her if the day is hot. Make the sun shine on her if it is cold.

After *Oumiesies* gave this world up over a bowl of soup, we all went in different directions. Except for me and Spaasie's boys. Theron did not want to give them freedom. Spaasie said to me, I know you will take care of them for me while I find work for them. When I fetch them he will have to let them go because he will get much money if we all pay our freedom price. I will make it hard for him to sell them. I will tell everyone that he is the father of these children and I will tell everyone what I know of other things about him. Then she was gone, for a long time. That was in eighteen and oh six because it was two years before Theron let me work for Hancke. I had to look after Spaasie's boys. They would have been your brothers if we were people who could say what our lives must be. I would have taken them with me when I went to Hancke. And you would have had so many big brothers to take care of you and not a single pig would have been able to beat you without fear for his own bones breaking under the wrath of your brothers.

Go and listen carefully and tell me if Spaasie blames me. It has worried me all these years. I have never been able to protect anyone, but you.

I tried with her sons. Frederik was the hardest. He wanted Spaasie's stories. I tried, but things got bigger and bigger. Too many trees in front of my father's hut. Even he asked one day, did you have a forest in front of your father's door? Was your father a king? Why did they bring him so much gold? Why did he not buy you back?

That is why your sisters and brothers know nothing about back there. But you, you can know everything. Do not go back there. They will not know me. How can they know a liar? My father was not a king. In the moonlight, my mother's hands were silver. She sang to me. So . . . *eh-la-la lala lalalala*. The rest I do not know.

It is hard to be a mother in this country. Now, Spaasie, she is made of strong stuff. She is out there, chasing after Theron to make him give her sons back. Go and see how she is doing in this business.

I have told Lys how you, your brothers and sisters came into this world. I told her, Camies came into the world like fresh butter. Pain, yes, there is always pain with children. There is always pain and, if I believed in that god of the *Oumiesies*, I would ask for forgiveness because I was stubborn and deaf in my stubbornness, because I was defiant, because I was stupid, because I believed in things I was not allowed to believe in, because everyone warned me of a pain beyond bearing. I could not hear them. The arrival of my children filled me with joy.

You, Carolina, Camies, Pieter—I brought you . . . my *body* brought you all. I waited on the shore of my miserable days for each arrival like someone starving and I gobbled my children's arrival like food for my heart.

Hunger is a demon with two heads. One head lives in a person's stomach, one head lives in a person's heart.

I was hungry for the arrival of my babies, the first three.

Camies was like butter. He shone like butter when he was given to me. A shining baby boy. And who was Camies in my life that I should be told to call my butter boy by that name? I call my boy Butter. I call my boy Yellow Ball, Shining Yellow Joy Ball. I call my boy Goodness Arrived in the Last Moments of Light. I call my boy Sad Light that Steals Across the Doorstep with the Smoothness of Butter.

Baro, today your mother is a mess of words. My words today are like the hair of Van der Wat's children. Not a strand will stay in place. Not a strand will stay true but goes rather into a tight knot, a tiny tight knot that has made use of a speck of dust, a stray thing caught from the air and tied and held, but only to be stuck thing that causes pain.

Listen to Mina eating there. She chews her food like a cow. The men are worse. Listen to them. You hear the inside of their mouths. *Sluip*, *sluip*, the tea goes. Listen to the warden and his visitors. The sound of their knives and forks is the sound of their bones. It is the sound of death moving them. The sound of the salt cellar hitting the side of that woman's plate. Smell the vinegar. Smell the meat. Smell the fat. They talk and there are remains in their mouths. Listen to the bone crunch between the warden's teeth when the guests have left and he hurries to the kitchen to fetch back the bones so that he can sit with them at his desk and . . . *Haish*, but he sucks at those bones.

Today, the rain. We stop breaking stones because the rain falls as hard as anger that never has to wait for the right word. But I do not hurry back to the huts like everyone else. I stand up . . . Baro, your mother stands up and . . . *ek is hertseer.*

I stand in this place, with the stones and sand, in the wind. I stand on my legs that should break from the heartache, but which hold me up, make me stand like a tree that is pushed about by the wind. Is this your doing? Is it you? Are you doing this to me? Me? Your mother?

If only I had good stories. What a lovely time we would have. But this place is not for stories.

Where have you been all these months?

News came by accident in November. Hancke is in big money trouble. His creditors wanted to send him here to the island. That would have been a day. But he has gone inland with wagons full of goods to try and make money to pay.

Hancke did not beat me, not like Theron and never like Van der Wat. And he never forced me to lie with him. But he cheated me. He knew I was a free woman when I went to work for him. I told him. He knew. But he made his ears deaf because he had paid my money to Theron, not me. That is why he did not want to pay me when I asked where my money was. He said ask Theron. But Theron wanted more money when he heard I had children. He wanted money for them. But even then Hancke had no money. Now he is in trouble, rushing inland to squeeze pebbles out of the farmers' pockets.

What about his wife and children?

So much for November.

But you should have been here for December. The minister and his wife brought puddings for us. They wanted us to make a place with straw and to make a baby out of materials and straw and put in the straw bed and stand there and sing songs to it. The children had to get close and look at the straw baby, but they did not like it. Meisie asked, what is this? The minister's wife said, baby Jesus. Meisie said, that is not a baby. Even Flora said, that is not a baby. Mina said, it is! She wants so hard for Flora to be baptized.

Even the warden's goats had to come and stand with us.

Yaish! These people.

Lys and I were laughing. Mina was cross with us. Even Pedder's favorite, Van Graaf, was cross because he wants to be a minister, so he prays hard and wants us to learn how to read this black book. He said, this is sacred! His face was red from the heat and anger. The men laughed. Van Graaf said he would get the warden to put us on bread and water.

And where was the warden? Sitting on the mainland with his mouth full of English pudding.

We had to sing. Mina sang with all her heart and the minister's wife kept her eye on me.

. . . born but to die.

English songs for the minister and his wife. Dutch for Van Graaf. Straw for the goats who did not know this was a baby. Even Mina had to laugh.

The minister and his wife wanted us to stand with goats. What do they know? We stand with goats while the men sniff around us. Stand with goats, lie with men.

December.

Where have you been?

While you were away a whole new year came. Ja. Eighteen and twenty-eight is with us. And three more women came. Rachel came back for the crime of desertion. She had enough of Judge Truter. Deel is new. She is like Lys, but not of the same village. They have words that are the same. The third woman was Rosalyn, but she came and went quickly. The superintendent of police sent a message to say she should not be on the island. She came in January and went in February.

And what about me? And my Meisie and Catherina? Has the superintendent forgotten about me and his promise to make an inquiry about how I came to be with Van der Wat, how I came to be at Hancke's?

I told Lys, I said to her, when I first saw him I thought this is a man whose coat sleeves will fray at the edge and he will be worn thin himself from all the fighting with these people here.

He has forgotten about me.

Who is Sila anyway?

I am the woman who will spit like a snake if they do not take me off this place with my girls.

I asked that woman, Rosalyn, to take a message to Spaasie. She promised. What is happening with the superintendent? And what news of Carolina, Camies, and Pieter? I sent a message with Rosalyn but I wanted to leave instead of her.

I am a bad woman sometimes. I was, yes, I was jealous.

What kind of woman am I to be like this?

This world makes you like this. In this world, good things are like food set down for two or three when many, many people have come to eat.

Deel is afraid of this place. She is next door, on the other side of this wall, with Rachel. Pedder had to open that side up so there would be space for the new women. Mina wants to move in with them.

Let me be, today. I am not talking to anyone. After all these years, my body still has no say in what happens to it. Another child. How can I be in the warden's kitchen, do his linens, then chop and carry stones with two babies and Meisie to take care of? Lys says the warden will have to keep me out of the quarry and let me stay near the hut with Meisie, Catherina, and the new baby.

I know this one is a girl. You see how she rides? I will call her Debora.

The warden curses me, he curses the guards. He asks me, *who, who*? I ask him for bigger candles to see in the dark.

The guards look nervous. Someone puts meat on our doorstep.

Well, *someone* can go and throw himself into the water and never come out.

The warden orders all guards to stand before him. He says, stay away from the women. They look across the water to the mainland. Some I recognize. The warden says there will be leave. The guards look at him and fight hard not to smile. There are women in town to take care of them, fancy women on Berg Street. Lys says only the officers can go there, and men who wear fine buttons. I send those women my greetings and thanks.

So. Here we sit. There they go and come, come and go. And my body has no say in what happens to it. And Mina has no leg to stand on. She is bigger than a mountain already.

So much for March.

Now let me be. Go find something to do. See if you can find the trail to the future and come back to tell me if this sister of yours will be worth the pain.

Mina asked why I hate her so. Hate her? I said, now why would I hate you when I do not even think of you. *Aisha.* There is poison in me and I do not know where it comes from. I am afraid of it. It comes snaking up out of a pot in my belly and right up my throat and into my mouth and . . . *Pik!* It strikes. I am afraid of it myself. When I talk with Mina, I hear myself trying to run from something I do not know.

I have been fighting all kinds of fears in my sleep. I dreamed that Lys told me my body stinks. She looked at me and said, go wash, Sila. And when I looked at my body I was ashamed. There I was, trying to show everyone here, Lys included, what a good dancer I am. And I tried to sing, to let them hear how I can sing. I wanted my voice to do things that no voice has done before.

Where does this come from?

I wanted to leap over their heads so that their faces would turn up and their mouths would open with aahs.

What for, why, why do I dream such things?

And Mina? In truth, I do not care to hit her. Perhaps this poison that springs out of my belly and *piks* at her comes from knowing how things stand in my life. Ja? In the space between now and maybe, there is a home for poison.

Or perhaps it is not so simple. I just want it to go. I feel it in the mornings. It is as if Lys was telling the truth in my dream. There is something about me that stinks. What to do about it? This thing even swallows me. I feel it going down my throat, back to its pot where it will wait and wait for someone like Mina.

And what has Mina ever done to me?

Lys asks what Mina has done to me? I remember the orange. Lys says enough, we must be strong together, Sila. We share this life and we must be as a wall against it.

Lys is right. Mina has it hard, just like me. Her baby is pushing already. Boy, girl. It is hard to tell. This will be hard for her too. She will have two children on this place. I will try to be better to her. I have put her on the outside of my friendship and made it hard for her. I will help her with her baby when she is tired, and when she must crack stones I will take the baby to the warden's kitchen with me and Catherina and let Meisie and Flora be in the yard when I can look out and see them. I will give Mina's baby bread dipped in milk to suck on until she comes back. You wait and see. I can be better to her. And when my girl is born, we will all be together here.

I think there can be nothing as cruel as a life lived in the halfway of things. If you live all alone, or with the knowledge that this life is all there is, or this loneliness is all there is, then you just live. But if you live such a life and have dreams, or you know that there is something else and—*look across the water!*—if you know there are others in this world and that they are together as friends, or man and wife, or as man to man, or woman to woman, then you begin to feel the dust of loneliness settle on your face and hands. That dust becomes so thick that you walk with your cheeks dragged down, and your hands clumsy. Everyone can see. They see the dust of loneliness and failure all over you and it is like a disease to them, and to you, and they keep away. They see you as someone who forgot to do something, who neglected to wash, who has a crack or mark inside, and they pity you and that pity accuses you and punishes you. And you begin to feel them seeing you in these ways. And you begin to apologize for all of your faults and then at last you think that everyone is better than you are.

Today your mother found a bird. The guards set traps for pigeons. They like to eat pigeons. This one escaped. One broken wing. One broken leg.

You may say, what good was that escape?

Everything depends on how you stand.

Me, I hopped after that bird. It was afraid and why not. I also like to eat, but today my hands were like those hands the minister tells us are the hands of Jesus in prayer. Come, bird.

Hop-hop. Hop-hop. Lys was laughing, but her laugh is not healthy these days. She holds her right side even when she has not been lifting stones.

Come, bird.

He looked at me. My heart was water early in the morning in winter.

Now, why are you here listening to this when you have all this island to play on? Go. And do not come back until you have found which is the prettiest of the birds' eggs.

Such things to tell you! Such news came while you were away! Lys ran to say Pedder was cursing because the superintendent of police and Van Ryneveld arrived. Then one of Pedder's men came for me. I thought, now what? And what do you know? The king of the English sent a message across the water and Van Ryneveld and the superintendent of police brought it. Van Ryneveld's mouth belonged to the paper. He said, in the case of the female slave Sila, I now transmit to you a pardon, which his Majesty . . .

A pardon! I asked, when do I leave this place? But the warden told me to shut my mouth. The superintendent told me to listen. And Van Ryneveld kept reading about the we who this and the we who that.

When I asked who all these people are who say they give me their grace and mercy and grant me their pardon, Van Ryneveld looked at me as if I was an ox. He said, they are one man. The king, the king is they and them and I must give thanks to god.

For what? Fourteen years.

I asked, what is to become of Meisie and my new baby? I do not want Van der Wat to take them. The superintendent said they would stay with me. Van Ryneveld said I must make the best of what I have been given. Pedder said nothing. Van Ryneveld folded his papers and wanted to be gone. The superintendent of police said I could keep this paper with the king's message.

I asked the guard who does not come to us at night to read it to me again. I must learn it all because, already, I am forgetting some of what that king said.

Whereas—they always begin with that word—a female slave named Sila was at a court of justice holden in and . . . something about the Cape of Good Hope and its dependings on Wednesday the thirtieth day of April eighteen and twenty three and . . . something I do not like to hear again, yes, had death passed upon her . . . And, listen, we consider some circumstances humbly presented to us and, graciously pleased, we give our mercy to her, and pardon her, on condition . . . But this knocked the wind out of me again . . . they give and they take like that god of theirs. The king said I must stay in prison to labor as the governor thinks fit for the *fourteen years.*

Help me count. Eighteen and twenty-seven. They said, fourteen years, yes, but to take off the time I stayed in the Cape Town *tronk.* So, eighteen and twenty-three, twenty-four, -five, -six, and some of twenty-seven. How many is that? Five. And I have been here for . . .What? *Yeesh.* And I thought I knew years that dragged their heels. This one is too long.

And the they and them of that king said it was their will and pleasure at Saintjames on the ninth day of November eighteen and twenty-seven, eight years of our rain.

The king, it seems, is a house in which many live in pleasure and good hope and their grace and mercy is upon me, as is their pardon but my condition of years goes on.

Pff! Giving me this ninth-day address! Nine days of lying is what I say. Those who speak as a king live in a place of fish stinking after nine days.

I should send a message of my own, tell them, *you bags of piss and wind who blew the stench of your nine days into fourteen years, you know nothing.*

And what makes that English king think, *whereas,* I, Sila, *so holden,* am standing still enough for him to send that message, *in the condition of my imprisonment?* What makes him think, *pleased as he is,* I can be found so easily? As if I am at home like one of those ladies!

This rain will soak into my bones one day, but nothing stops the warden's book. It is a big hole. It must be filled. Every month he makes a big fuss, counting, counting. Lys says he is like a woman at her time of month.

He does not like visitors on the final days of the month. They come to fish and get in his way. His face is all smiles as they come ashore, but his curses under his breath are swarms of anger that go *fftt, fftt* through the air.

Smile, Pedder, smile! Say, welcome! Welcome! Ask, will you take some tea when you want to take that scrawny neck in your big thick fingers and squeeze it until she drops her parasol. Ja. Pedder, smile.

I still do not know why Pedder smiles so, Baro. When was the last time anyone invited him to leave the island and visit their dining room? A person must have someone who cares about them.

Hey! Fancy parasol? Fancy moustache! Ja! Are the fish here different from the fish that swim around that mainland? Jirre! Julle vokking mense maak my vokking siek!

I have heard that the places these people have left to come here are cold.

It is a strange thing to live among such people. They make me ache in a place you would not expect, even in the roots of my fingernails. It came to me one day when the sky had sagged and rain was pouring down the sides of our roof, as it does now—on such a day, when there is no color left in the world and the mainland is just a shadow, and you do not see a single light, and you hear nothing but the ocean in the wind's mouth, and when your toes ache and your back is chilled against the wall—on such a day I was sitting just as we are now, glad to be in the huts and glad that not even the warden's book could make the guards drive us out to cut stones. On such a day I was sitting here and I felt irritation where my fingernails enter my skin. The cold does that. It makes you feel as if your fingernails are shrinking out of your flesh.

These people suck the life out of the world. But I can smell things fighting back. You do not believe me? Hah! Smell the air. What do you smell? What is *in* the air? Wake up! Cold air has a smell that is different from hot air. You know this. Summer has one smell, winter another. Now you can smell the *fynbos*. Right? You can smell the *fynbos* as if it is the inside of a stem, and the wetness and cold are the bark. What you smell is the *inside* of things. That is the surprise of cold air. When it rains or when the ocean puts mist up over the mainland, you can understand the inside of things if you take the trouble.

And I love to see, then, a bird fly low and black against that sky.

Listen, it is like this—cold air smells one way, hot air smells another. You see, hot days bring something that these people cannot leave. I think that, perhaps, no, I know, deep in my bones, I know that their air must smell of their trees and that these days of cold and wet stirs something in their hearts.

I know our hot days do something to them for which they can never forgive us. Hot days make these people bolder than bold in the face of moving among other beings. You see, it is like this . . . I have seen them stand crisp, only to sag and wrinkle and grow sleepy all at the same time as the heat opened all windows in the air and all smells overcame them so that they grouped and pushed rather than stumble.

At night, in the shadows, behind doors, behind walls, under bushes, against trees . . . ! My, my! How they grope and reach out, how they stumble and come undone, slipping and grunting. My. My. My. The things I know.

These people begin by holding together and pushing at us. Distrust is what follows, but they will tell you it is not themselves they distrust behind all those buttons and belts, all the leather and buckles.

There is so much more, but I will try to draw the net in before my greed to catch all explanation makes me lose the bounty of a good few. Some things are delicate in the weaving. Pull too tight and things break, pull and bind too hard and things have no beauty and the eye turns away.

And I know that I talk of knowing these people as if I am on a high chair, looking down upon them. Do not think that I have forgotten what the truth of the world is.

But there is something that tells me I do see them.

Tomorrow there will be fog. That is how it is when it rains so and I will not have to see the mainland where the superintendent goes pricking his way around the canals that stink so.

What is happening with his investigation? Has he forgotten me?

Go quietly, quietly, Baro. Lys is sleeping over there. Remember, Sunday is our half day of rest. On Van der Wat's farm there was no rest day for me. It was the same cleaning and cooking. And you, fetching wood, carrying things for Jeptha. So, when Lys sleeps on our half day I do not even let your sister play near her.

The sunlight is getting thin. That is how it is when March draws to an end. And so Lys is like me, we try to find a place out of the wind but in the sun so that we can try and help our bodies remember warmth when winter comes.

You see where she sleeps? Do you see what is happening? She goes far away in her sleep. She tells me that this comes from her father's mother who was named !Kweitan. It was she who gave to Lys's father this way of seeing. Her father could bring rain. In her language he was called !giten.

I say, find him and let him send so much rain that Van der Wat must turn into a fish or drown.

Lys tells me to watch her when she sleeps so that the guards will not find her body and move it. She will not come back to it if they do. When she sleeps she goes far away, and sees things. Then she comes and tells me where she went, what she saw.

That is the secret of her laughter. Here is not where she belongs and here is not what keeps her in place. There is no prison for Lys. But when she comes back from this kind of sleeping, on days like this, she does not answer to Lys and I alone whisper her name to her, the name that her mother called her, the name that her father called her.

Kammean.

Kam-meh-aaaan. Your tongue must kick itself free of its root and send the first sound back into your throat, like a key that opens a lock, and then the rest will come out.

Kammean.

She told me that *boere* took her mother a long time ago, and when she was a young woman herself, her father was away and *boere* came with horses and guns and took her. They gave her to a man who was the color of the dead. Red hair. Red beard. Spots on his face like fly shit, she said.

Kamme-aan.

I asked if there were children.

Kammean. What have you seen this time? Why do you never see my father or mother? Why do you not come back and tell me of my children?

What do you think, Baro? She never answers when I ask, what of my people, my children?

Sometimes, she sees only the shadows of people who are now and will be no more. Then, there is no laughter. She says, Sila, I will not speak for two days, or three. She counts the days and I know why. If she speaks, she will vomit up grass and pebbles, sand and perhaps even a whole riverbed that has not seen water for a long, long time.

Other times, she tells me, Sila, I have seen who is left. She tells me there is one hut and her father's brother lives in it with his wife. Over there are more huts with the married children of her father's brother. She says, Sila, my sister has two children now.

I tell you, Baro, at such times it is as if I too have gone with her, visiting as if we were kin from a neighboring village.

Kammean.

This is her little name, she says.

Sometimes, when she wakes, she shows me what she has seen. She takes a stick, like so. She draws in the sand. She says, Sila, this is what I saw running, or crawling, or hiding from a hunter.

Whai gwai the hunter looks for his favorite meat.

Whai gwai! The hunter's feet were itching and look, look, you were standing on ants.

Kahori-kahori.

Kuken-te walks over dead leaves.

Kuken-te, anteater find the fat little rice.

Kusan-te, xe has laid rice.

When *Kammean* speaks to me I am a child listening to words I must learn.

Xe. Ant. Or the head of the ant who lays her eggs and these eggs look like the rice that the white settlers eat. *Xe.*

Xe lays *kwari-kwari.*

Or *ssuen-ssuen.* Lys, *Kammean,* says this is what her mother's people called the ants' eggs. *Ssuen-ssuen.*

Dju. That is the beetle.

Baro, your mother teaches you another mother's language.

Tcshau! Hau-au. Perhaps if I put my head next to Lys when she sleeps so I would ride with her and perhaps I will go back to where my father's hut stood and there will be all the names I have forgotten, kept in a nice basket on the roof, dry, out of the way of all things that would eat them, or chew at their edges.

Kammean.

Sometimes she wakes and shows me how to dance as her people do.

Koa! She says, *koa!* And then I must fetch Mina, and Soldaat, Galant and Matroos. The men stand there in a line. Us women stand here in a line.

Koa!

Soldaat, Keizer, Matroos. Hey! What do they know? Mina and I laugh at them, we laugh at ourselves. Lys pushes us. She says, do this, so, with your feet. Do so.

Koa!

On other days, this word does not mean dancing. It means water. Perhaps dancing is like water for Lys. On such days, Mina and I try hard, but we always end laughing and I swear our laughter is like spoor that Lys follows, but before you know it she is back with us. She is Lys again and there is no *Kammean* until the next Sunday when the sun has gone from the tops of our heads and she says, Sila, watch me, do not let the guards near me, do not let them take my body, keep my body where I can find it again.

Baro, some days I am afraid that she will not come back. Then what will I do?

Xo opua.

Porcupine!

This rain will stay for days. Everything will be wet and cold and we will all smell of smoke. Our hut will smell of smoke and ash. Our feet will be wet. The floor of our hut will have mud inside and around the door and the mud will make paths from the door to our beds. It is bad for the children because they have to sit inside the hut all day. Catherina does not like this. She cries. Meisie and Flora are good with her. They make faces, they wave their hands. I try to take her out on my back, but the wind has daggers and the rain gets on her. So, she must stay inside with Meisie and Flora, who has begun to cough in a way that makes Mina's hands fly about and knock things over.

Hai. Mina. I know what it is to have my hands fly like birds caught in a trap.

I wanted to hold Mina's hands today, but she would just spit at me and I would spit back. She is afraid. She wants Flora off this island. I do not blame her. This is no place for children. And now we are both bringing two more into this world.

Suurlemoene. Yes, yes. This is how this place makes me feel. It is like lemon juice in my chest.

Hsst! A woman named Sila is running like a mad thing from one end of the island to the other. She moans like a cat, whines like a dog, and shits like a cow.

Help me! Help me!

Some days I fear I will walk the path of Matroos, Soldaat, Vigiland, and Keizer.

No, no. Where are you going? Stay.

It is just the cold that makes me shake my hands so. Just the cold. It makes my breath tremble. Nothing else. It makes it feel as if my insides are falling out. The cold. But I am strong. Right? Strong. This not trembling. The cold makes me shake. Everyone shakes in the cold. See? Go and see how the men shiver. Yes. Big, strong men who can lift the warden's biggest stones. They shake too. See?

Now, come and sit close by but do not look at your sisters or they will want to come tripping after you. And stay clear of Flora.

Sit, sit. I am feeling better now.

It is hard, you see, but I do not give up. I have tried to keep the mud from making its way in by laying small mats of *fynbos* and grass. It is something. When I can, I will make more mats. Mina and I brought driftwood from the beach to put in front of the door, but some of the guards have taken it piece by piece, all of it, as it suited their needs.

We do not mind if Matroos, or Soldaat, or Keizer, or Vigiland take our wood. What do they know? They are like birds. You do not get angry with a bird.

This rain will keep the days gray. The mountains will keep dissolving until the sun breaks through and dries up all of this wetness. Only then will the mountains grow firm again, be rock again. Blouberg. Hottentot's Holland. Tafelberg. Lion's Head. Signal Hill. For now they are all just soft and cloud. And all the time the rain is running down the edges of the roof and through the roof. It is a sound that means neglect. I cannot think about that too much. I must just listen to the sound and like it and it alone.

Some fruit you pick, others you do not touch for fear of poison!

Heesh! You wonder why I tell you all of these things? You have been asleep, but it has been a sleep that has saved you. Let me tell you . . . Those first years of being in this world of the *vuilgoed*, those years after they came and stole me from my own home, I was asleep. I know that now. And that it is sleep that saves a person from madness, or from running into a wall, head down, or from being mauled and eaten by the beasts that live in the pit of one's own stomach. I moved from day to day, stumbling through all the things they wanted me to learn, all the new words I had to listen to. I had to keep to myself those I was never to say. And all the new laws that lived in the new words! *Meid*—a rule lives in that. *Come here*—another law that grows from *Meid*. *Clean this*—still another law that grows out of *Meid* and *Come here*. *Open up*—perhaps the worst law.

I was like a baby again. I fell. I got up. I spoke and they did not understand me. They spoke to me, said words slowly. I said the words back, slowly. It was hard. And it hurt to look. I did not know what I was looking at. They had the forms of people, but they behaved like demons. I understood.

Do you understand what I am telling you?

I had to wake up. There is a time for sleeping—I put myself to sleep in those first days. There was no one who could do that for me, and so I woke up in the same place. But you . . . Baro. You have been asleep and now you have woken, but you must open your eyes and your ears. It is time to wake up, boy, and look at the world. Eyes that are open but are still as water upon which no breeze blows do not see the world.

Look at me when I am speaking to you!

Have you heard the news? Is that where you have been? All the people from the old Dutch Slave Lodge have been set free by the English governor. If Johannes was here he would say, you see, I was right. Lys is also happy because those who are closest to her people have also been set loose from that place.

I am happy for the women there. They lived bad lives.

The news is that there is now a big worry in the town because all of these people are walking about free.

I think they must go and find some land and build a place and make fields and plant all the things the town needs.

What about us?

Lys says, this means that freedom for all of us is coming soon. She is like Johannes. The two of them would be patting each other on the back if he was here.

I think she is right. But when?

Lys talks of trees. *Oumiesies'* farm had many big trees. Everyone said it was like the governor's mansion where the trees grew tall around the carriage road.

It was late in the day when I arrived at *Oumiesies'* farm. The sun was no longer stomping on my head. The oxen were dragging us forward, but the wagon moved slowly because they had pulled a long way.

They came to fetch me in a big wagon—big and flat with only one seat up front for the driver. There was another wagon, covered with seats that faced each other inside. A woman rode in there. She was *Oumiesies'* sister who saw me when she was visiting Missus Neethling. She came with the wagons and dogs, two men and a woman. It was that sister who bought me for *Oumiesies* as if I was a cup or a shawl.

I thought they had come to fetch someone else. Then, early the next morning Missus Neethling came crying all the way from her house to the huts. I sat up.

Why so early? What is happening?

Missus Neethling said, *kind, opstaan.* Then I knew. I tried to hide under the blanket. They pulled me out but I fought them. The women who traveled with the visitor said, *kind,* my mother is Mozbieker like you. My name is Spaasie. You can come with us. It is nice where we live with *Oumiesies,* who is very rich and good to us.

I was like a person at the end of a long path. The rest of the world was on the other end. I was not in the world, only walking near it.

So many kings and queens in this country.

We rode for a long time, days. Sometimes we stopped and the driver gave me water from a sack tied to the back of the wagon. Once we stopped at a watering place and Spaasie went to take care of the woman in the carriage. When she came back, she brought me a piece of cold tongue. The old man gave me bread with quince jam. He smiled and nodded. I ate the bread, not the tongue. I have never liked tongue. I do not eat anything that can taste me back.

I remember that we stopped on a farm for one night. The kitchen woman asked where my mother was. I slept with five children. They all called her mother. In the morning I cried because I wanted to stay with her, but *Oumiesies'* sister was already in her soft seats and wanted to go on.

After more traveling, not even the whip could make the oxen move faster. I sat flat on the planks with my hand on the side of the wagon, my chin was so, on my hand. I remember, because I was looking at the grass and listening to it against the wagon's wheels. The sound made me dizzy because it was like the washing of water against the big ship that carried us Mozbiekers to this land. I thought, so this is how it would have been if I was not down in that hole. I would not have been so sick, and there would not have been that stink of all the others who were sick with the rolling and the smell and with the sound of their voices calling names that never answered or, if they answered, Baro, it was as if a spirit had taken the one you loved and was speaking with her name. That was how it was when I cried for my mother.

Well. Enough of that.

I smelled the farmhouse before I saw it and I saw it just after I smelled it. A wood fire. Even the oxen must have smelled it because the yokes creaked as they changed their pace. And then I saw smoke rising out of the valley. And there was the house, big and orange, glowing with many trees around it, trees covered in white flowers.

The dogs began to bark and I saw people—a man stood upright there, another over there, a woman, another one. And I saw how the land had changed. There were fields. The land bent away into rows and rows of green and more green. The driver cracked the whip and the whole world cracked.

And you know how it is in the evening, when the ground is already cold and that cold ground has a smell that is sweet and the sweetness opens a door in you, a door you do not even know, but one you feel.

My heart was beating hard. I was scared. But the beauty of that place. *Seeshh.* After all this time I can still smell that farm and when I smell it it is wood fire and green, long shadows growing longer and longer as we went down into the valley and the big house came closer and the trees grew bigger until the house disappeared behind them.

And then we were on a road from which all rocks had been pulled and even while I was trying to see where the house had gone, what the road was like, where the few people I had seen had gone, we came to two big white walls that curled and curled over at the top, like waves, or like a very important man's moustache. We turned into the road that went between the walls. The trees grew high on each side of the road. I did not know where to look first. There was the house, not orange, but white, waiting like a queen on a wide throne, looking down through a robe of white that curled over itself like the walls through which we had passed. I would not take my eyes off the house, but the white flowers *moved*. Yes, they moved. It gave me a fright. Then I saw, it was not flowers flapping their big petals. They were not flowers, but birds. Big, white birds.

Look, the house said, look here. I looked and could not raise my eyes. That is how a person knows the presence of a great being. Yes?

The king came through our village when I was a girl, there where I was born.

This is not one of my stories that I made up to please Galant or to feel closer to Alima. This is what happened.

For days there were preparations. Messages flew back and forth through the drums. Each day for many days the news of his approach grew in size and it was as if our village was in the way of a storm that would soon burst out of the trees. My father had a new robe. My mother worked with the other women to prepare the feast. And when they were not pounding grain for bread and beer, or sweeping the compound before the chief's hut, the women were taking care of each other's hair. And when he came, the whole world rushed toward him so that it was the world I saw, craning its neck, clearing itself, praising, pushing, and bowing with a sound that was a sigh and a moan. And that was how I saw the king, in all the world, as he entered our village and disappeared into the chief's hut that swelled and groaned all night under the glow of fires and drumming, the dancing. When I woke in the morning, the king was gone and we were an exhausted people. My father was angry. My mother was angry. The village smelled of ash and food scraps and something else that was still swirling in the direction of the king—a sweetness, perhaps, whose flower you cannot see in the thickness of the forest.

So. That was how *Oumiesies*' house arrived before me. I saw nothing but the way it bent its walls and made square eyes that looked out and told the trees where to stand, and pushed a long road out from itself. And opened its big brown door.

The creaking stopped, but the dogs ran on and barked. The whip cracked and the dogs stopped on their heels.

Oumiesies came out, but I did not know her as *Oumiesies* then. I saw a woman in black skirts and a white widow's cap. The shadows were long already and she was a small shadow with a big white hat. She did not come down the steps. She stood.

I was afraid, but child enough to be excited. The look of that big house in that valley and the perfume of the soil that was already giving itself up to the night air comforted me. Someone put a blanket and I had it over my shoulders.

The dogs were barking hard but one wave of her hand made them duck and fall away. She said, Johannes, you made good time. And the driver limped over to her. He said, ja, ja, *Oumiesies, Oumiesies* knows Johannes does not like to be out there when leopard is looking for food. She laughed. He laughed. Then she said, let me see her.

The driver called to me gently. I tried to hold on to Spaasie who told me not to be afraid. The driver said, *kom kleintjie, kom*, we must not keep *Oumiesies* waiting. He came to the side of the wagon where I was sitting and he reached right up into the wagon, that man with the bent legs, and lifted me out. I went up the stairs and all the time I could not see anything because the light was falling out of the house, into my eyes. So, that was how I arrived at *Oumiesies'* farm, blind and wrapped in a blanket, holding a broken man's hand when the air was getting cold and the ground was putting out a perfume of dampness.

Ja. Johannes. The first hands to touch me in that place were the hands of a kind man who walked with a bent leg.

Ag, and now the sun steps back and takes itself to the other side of the sky. I see it lower itself, as if it is visiting a king. It is a sad moment. But one bit of light still reaches into the bush, this one here, by my left shoulder. Winter is on the next horizon. You can feel your breath change. Soon the ships will have to drop their anchors deep or break loose and come smashing against our rocks.

More firewood for us.

The sun goes down. The air gets thin, like me. I am a thin woman now. I saw my dress hang on the string that Deel and I tied from the back of our hut to a pole that Soldaat fished from the ocean and carried like a gun until he tired of it. I saw my dress and thought, *hm*, Sila, is that you swinging so high, like a spirit trying to get to its own world? A blue dress. The material is heavy, but our string is strong. I looked at that dress and it was long. Its hem folded and folded away from the earth, its neck was the door for a ghost. I saw my dress. I saw myself, floating up there.

I have come close to leaving this world.

Those days after I sent you away were hard. They beat me. They said, evil woman, bad woman, cruel woman, animal. Van der Wat was so upset when he learned how I had tricked him. He could say nothing for a long time. He hit me, but Van Huysteen stopped him, and said, why does a woman do such a thing? Is she mad? Van der Wat said nothing, but the next day after their *kersfees*, he came to where the field cornet had locked me up. The field cornet was still visiting with De La Rey and there was a man who had to guard me. Van der Wat came in his fancy new Sunday clothes.

Perhaps you remember those clothes that he wanted for Christmas. All that money he spent on the silk for that coat so that he could look like a wealthy man.

I could hear him argue with the guard, loud, then soft and fast. And then there was the sound of money. I know that sound. The guard went outside to smoke his pipe and Van der Wat came in. He said nothing. He folded his jacket and put it on a chair, and then he took off his belt. He said nothing to me. I stood up straight. I was not afraid of him.

Pipe smoke from outside.

You see this, here, over my right eye? Did you see it when you came again? Van der Wat put it on me that day, for tricking him and sending you to where he could not get you. I said, I told him, send me the one child I have left, send my Pieter to me and you will see, I will also make sure he gets far away from you. I called him *vuilgoed*. So, he hit me again. He hit my head against the wall many times. Many times. The bones of my head were a wall that day. I said to him, you hit my head, what good does it do for you, you have lost. I said, you get, *get*! He put his fist into my eye, like so and I felt the inside of my head, as if it was a room I was falling into, a room where the walls were breaking like egg shells. Then the field cornet came in and shouted, Van der Wat! Jacobus! *Genoeg*. Van der Wat was breathing so hard he had to lean on the wall.

When he went, the field cornet fixed my eye himself. But it was still closed when the *landdrost* came. He asked no questions. I told him why I sent you away, just as I told the field cornet. They did not understand a word I said. I was a creature that made sounds to them. *Keek-keek-keek-kiew-kiew-keek-kroo-kiek-croo-croo-crooo.*

They took me to George. It was small. Not big like Cape Town. But Van der Wat wanted me back. The field cornet said, this is not your matter now. I listened, but said nothing anymore. They put me in the *tronk*. Then the justice came. They talked around me. They said, death by strangulation. I kept myself quiet, I was not afraid.

What? Asleep? Baro! Wake up! I am telling you of the days after I sent you away. They kept me in the George Town *tronk*. I was there for some weeks.

. . . Out of the dark . . . the prison door opens.

Pipe smoke.

Hy sê, meid! meid, is jy wakker?

Am I awake? My ears are awake. They hear things and I think, *aha*, a big rat crawling. A big dog snuffling to get under my skirts as if I am a bed and my skirt is a blanket and the prison is a dark winter a dog needs to escape. My ears hear breathing.

And my teeth grow long, my nails get sharp. My teeth are like a small animal's. My teeth are ringed with his blood. And my eyes swell the next morning so that there is no seeing out of them. With my good ear I hear how the other guard holds his breath and then the argument.

My heart grows strong when I want it to behave like any other heart and just break. My heart gets so strong, as if it is a fist that is getting ready to knock these walls into the faraway of things I cannot see.

Wait, I tell myself. And I send him fleas. A flea will get under his foot and bite and bite and his foot will squirm in his big, dirty shoe, press against the buckle and the buckle will hold his foot in the shoe and his shoe will be a prison of itching and more itching. And I send him something for his lungs so that he will lie in his own bed with his wife and they will hear his breathing and know that it is because he breathes that he dies. A little something for his lungs.

Eighteen and twenty three. They brought me all the way to Cape Town and put me in the *tronk* near Hancke's shop. Do you remember where it was, on The Market? The prison was on the other side.

They were getting ready to strangle me when they got a big shock. I said I am going to have a baby. They did not believe me. Then they sent for the doctor. He asked me how, when? I pretended I could not hear. I pointed to my ears and shook my head. They were cross. They wanted to put out my lights but I was cheating them again.

Your brother saved my life. He came to me like a gift. But he was sick. A prison is bad for a child. He was sick for many months. I was sick too, sick in the heart, and I thought, well, now, you have lost children before, this will not be so hard. It was hard.

In this world there are roads. Some roads are where people live. Some are where people pass through. My boy was born to a road of passings.

When the superintendent of police asked me what happened to your brother, I said this is not a place for a child. Then the superintendent asked the warden, what was done? The warden said all effort was made. I said, the food is bad, ask anyone. The warden would have liked to hit me. The superintendent told me not to speak unless he asked me to, but I could see that he was not angry with me. He was protecting me.

Perhaps we can get off this island and I can work for him.

I watched over your brother, but with a sickness of heart that made me useless. I did ask for a surgeon. I told the superintendent that. The superintendent asked the warden did the prison surgeon, Lieschung, not see that my child was ill and send us to hospital. The warden said, ask Lieschung. I would not be quiet. I said, the surgeon saw my child in January and my child was sick until November.

The warden said, her child pined.

Yes, my child pined in eighteen and twenty-three. I was marked for death but it was he that died. Now, how is that?

Your brother is like a button on my long, thin, blue dress that hangs out there, trying to dry itself in the thin leftover sunlight.

If you sit here you may hear how the winter sun passes through the water in the surgeon's bottle—the one he left for me—and makes a sound like a *viol* made to play a mournful tune. My heart makes this sound in my ears all day. It is a lovely tune, too. So lovely, and so sad from one heartbeat to another. There are nights when my singing heart wakes me. I listen and listen, not knowing what the melody will do with itself next.

Heee, Hiiiiiiii, Heeeeeee, Humm-hummm, hee-heee.

Some things just cannot be told. Hey?

At night, water in our basin gets thick with cold. Come morning, we have to break the ice cover. Your sisters cry when they drink water. It is good when I have to work in the warden's kitchen. Then they can come, and Flora too. I have nothing against Flora.

The men stand together, shoulders hunched, blowing on their hands before they are marched off to the quarries.

Catherina blows her breath out in small puffs, laughing.

Oh for a heart to praise my Lord . . .

The minister's wife *pomps en pomps* the air to make us sing the words exactly as she wants us to. We must all sing. That is how it is here on Sunday mornings. Then the minister pats his thin hair and stands up and the wind stands up with him and his hair lifts up again so that the baldness he tries to hide is revealed to us like the will of his.

Nou, ja. That is how it is here on Sundays.

. . . take your burdens to the Lord.

The minister's wife lifts her eyes but I have seen where she looks and it is not to heaven. She looks out of the square that we make with our bodies in front of her husband. She looks out across the water to the town. She can see herself walking there.

There are mornings when my eyes just will not see anything but the rocks that have waited all night for our hammers. The warden says, we have orders to fill. He even sends me and Mina to the quarries these days. I pointed to my belly and hers and asked him how we could lift stones. He gave us small hammers and said, work at the quarry wall over there or stir the lime. We took the hammers. I said to Mina, do not work hard. What can he do? Nothing. For once she has listened to me. When the guards are not watching we wave to Lys and Deel and do a dance. They laugh. Deel is not strong enough for this work. Lys has to watch her. And Mina and I have to hit small stones loose and watch out for our girls at the same time.

But what does the warden care? He just gives orders like nobody's business.

Then the guards open their mouths and their orders are farts and when they walk their backsides waddle as if filled with wind that squeezes and rasps against their cheeks.

Lys and I save our laughter for when the night is curled around itself. Then we start. First one, then the other. We just start a little laugh, then it is big but we keep our blankets against our mouths. We come together in one bed so that our laughter does not have even the space of the small room to cross. When Lys laughs against me I feel something of peace. Our bodies are warm and laughing. I lie against her back or I feel her against my back and we laugh as if we are two little girls put to bed early by our mother just so that we can learn how it is to have a world that is our own.

In the morning, we are women again and our eyes are slits and our mouths closed tight as we take up our hammers. I hit the stone. I believe I would thank the minister's god for the stone to hit. I would thank the minister's god for the hammer that is allowed to come down so hard on the stone that is Van der Wat's head, that is his stupid wife's head, that is Theron's head. I break open head after head and sometimes it is very hard to make myself remember that what covers my hands and is all over my dress and even on my face and in my hair is just dust.

Dust, I say.

And dust will be all that becomes of their offspring and their offspring's offspring. I say it so that it will go down as if it is writing on paper.

When I walk back to our hut, my dress is heavy. The gulls make a sound that is like the Saturday afternoon scratching on the chalkboard that the minister has brought to try and teach us how to read our Bibles by ourselves. The gulls confuse me because, sometimes, the sound is also like old doors opening.

I look up, put my hand to my eyes. The light flutters and shakes and the sound is not from the gulls at all. It is the sound of the stones moving against each other as the waves shift the island. The island is dragging against the water. The mainland is dragging against the stones that lie beneath it.

The whole world is moving away!

But what does it move away from? Where does it move to?

If I stand still, the mainland will arrive from behind my back and I will walk off this island in a dress that is yellow as the lemons my darling boy went to pick for me. I will walk off the island and the whole world will lay itself down to greet me.

Get out of my way!

I like being sent to clean the kitchen. I make myself walk slowly and when I can I let my shadow make a small step, a dance that we do. All the way to the kitchen. Then I take a pot and give it a smack. I take another, give it a smack. I hit the rim of a glass from the warden's table against another of its kind. *Ching!*

Pank

Pank

Ching

I make the dishes chuckle in the soapy water.

Ping-kle!

And the sun's thin yellow song is the song that my heart knows best and my heart sings along, so sad and so lovely. My blood makes a deep sound.

My heart is a voice that has been soaked in lemon.

Let us talk about the things these guards do.

Let us not.

Is there a message from the superintendent yet?

I miss those who were family to me on *Oumiesies*' farm. I have been thinking about them. I wish you had been with me then, all of you children. They would have looked after you. If I counted everyone I call family, we would fill a village of our own.

Now. Let me see if I can still remember. The number of lives that *Oumiesies* said she could do with as she wanted was fifteen before she sent some to Theron in the hope of peace between them.

There was Philip from Malabar. His name was Philip but he was not brother to Philipina who was, is, Alima's daughter and Spaasie's sister. You know how it is. They just give us names that lie around and sometimes the names make us brothers and sisters. Philip spoke a language that none of us understood. He had a mark over his left eyebrow, like this, and he was gentle with the animals. His job was the garden around the house and the fields. He was the only one from that place, Malabar.

Amerant came from Batavia. She worked in the house. Perhaps it was because they had no one else from their lands that she and Philip kept close together. Some days I would hear them talking, each in his or her own tongue, laughing. Amerant. She had two children who were sold away from her before she came to *Oumiesies*. It was Philip who brought some life back to her. She pleased *Oumiesies* greatly. But who knows what goes on in the hearts of *witmens*? *Oumiesies* was so pleased that, one day, when she had us all sewing, she said, Amerant, tomorrow you will go to Master Theron's farm. Amerant said, *Oumiesies*? What does *Oumiesies* want me to do there? *Oumiesies* said, you will be housemaid there. Amerant asked, and when must I come back? *Oumiesies* did not even look up from the stitching. She said, give me the green thread, you will stay there. Amerant began crying. *Oumiesies* was cross. She said, you will not cry. If you cry I will send for Master Theron's *mandoor* and he will give you something to cry about.

Philip's eyes went dull the day he asked if he could go with Amerant. *Oumiesies* said she needed him, but that he could drive the wagon when she went to see Theron. So, he saw Amerant sometimes, but not enough. He worked *Oumiesies*' fields in sadness. Then, after a long time, when *Oumiesies* saw how sad he was, she said she would read that big black book and find out what her god had to tell her. Her god must have liked Philip and Amerant because *Oumiesies* said to go to Master Theron. But that god does not see what goes on on Theron's farm because Theron sold them. *Oumiesies* was cross. She sent her *advocaat* to tell him that Amerant and Philip must be sent back or he must pay her. The *advocaat* came and said there was no money. So *Oumiesies* said Theron had to find Amerant and Philip and send them back to her. But we did not see them again. Maybe they are still together. I do not know. *Oumiesies* was angry. She said, never again. But it was too late for Amerant and Philip. And it was not true anyway.

Now. Who else? Oh. Yes. It would have been better if *Oumiesies* had sent Petro away. He also worked in the field. His anger made him unpleasant. Philip kept him in line. Petro was afraid that Philip might curse him in that language, you see.

And then there were those of us who are called Mozbiekers. We all came in ships and we never got that rolling world out of our ears because, on some days, one of us would stumble and the others knew the ocean was sending us a message.

Spaasie you know about. And Roosje, who was Mozbieker like me and Alima, but did not want to talk about it. She said it made a person mad with anger that had nowhere to go but across a room, or a table. Spaasie said no, anger came from not knowing there was something else.

Spaasie taught me many things—how to cook, how to make quince wine. Spaasie and Philipina, daughters of Alima, who was with *Oumiesies* for many years until she was old and then *Oumiesies*, who, good as she could be to us, could not be trusted and sent her and Philipina to Theron.

There were others who made that long journey in the ships. There were Mars, Anthony, and Isac. Mars and Anthony worked in the fields too, but Mars also kept the cattle. Isac was *Oumiesies*' favorite, after Alima and Johannes. Isac was clever. Sometimes we laughed and said he walked like a woman. Mars was sad and quiet, but Anthony was angry all the time, like Petro. Mars said that Anthony saw no difference between himself and the cattle. We all learned to find happiness, however it came. We tried with him, but happiness walked on the other side of his valley. He wanted to fight his way out of the place into which he had been brought. Who could blame him? But what could he do? So, he was always angry and he and Petro were always fighting. *Oumiesies* told Isac he must whip them if they fought. Isac swore at them for this. One morning Mars had a broken nose. Petro had a broken finger. *Oumiesies* took a *sjambok* and hit them both herself. I want to say more about Anthony, but there is nothing more to say. He longed for an army to lead against the *witmens*. I did not dislike him. We were close in years. I kept myself away from him. A woman's heart would break over such an unhappy man. I heard he was taken up by a man named Van der Riet, but that may not be so.

Mars was older than me. Once, he asked me to lie with him. I said no. He asked Amerant. Philip wanted to hit him. He apologized. Then he wanted Philipina, but she said she would never go with a man. I do not know what happened to Mars.

Isac was gentle. He alone could reach Anthony. He put his arm around Anthony's shoulders and the anger would settle. Some nights, I know this, he lay with Anthony. Then, Anthony would be quieter but not happier. Ja, Isac. A good man. He understood things and even *Oumiesies* asked him what should be done with this, or that, when to plant this, when to take care of that. When she called him valuable, he said he liked Isac better and she just laughed. I heard he went to Cape Town and is now one of those men who prays five times a day. I heard he went to Stellenbosch and is working for two winemakers. I heard he died when a horse kicked him in the head. Someone said he got his freedom and started walking back to where he was born. I do not know. You tell me which is true. Maybe one, maybe none.

Spaasie and Roosje's children you know of. Galate, Roosje's eldest, liked to chew on a stem of grass. Galate is the smell of grass and hay. Her brother Cesar needed caring. Spaasie cared for him and Galate because Roosje's care was filled with sadness and anger. She was too busy keeping anger on the horizon and her children reminded her of things she wanted to forget.

How much is too much?

I have told you about Spaasie's children. Galant her eldest, the same age as Roosje's girl, Galate. Roosje was angry when I asked why their names were so close. Spaasie said, Theron named them. Her face told me not to ask any more questions when Johannes walked out of the kitchen. If Galant was on this island, he would be in the same hut as Matroos, Soldaat, Keizer, and Vigiland. But you could trust his brother Arend, to find honey when no one else could. On a Sunday afternoon, while we rested, he searched for honey. He would sit near water and wait for the bees, then follow them. Quick on his feet, sharp eyes, charming to bees. Frederik was the next for Spaasie. He kept to her like a shadow, like Sariel, his sister, who was the baby of Spaasie's babies.

You would have liked them. We were all together on *Oumiesies'* farm and that was the year eighteen and six.

All this talk of *Oumiesies'* farm. Last night I dreamed of it again.

The big change began on day when Theron visited with his wife and children. Spaasie said, you watch, he brings the children when he wants money. Roosje said, then he is a fool who never learns.

I carried the tray with tea and *koek* for the children, and Spaasie brought the cups and plates. So, we were in the room when *Oumiesies* was saying no. She did not stop when we came in, even though Theron and his wife tried to tell her to be quiet. In my house, *Oumiesies* said, you tell me what to do in my own house? Theron's wife told me and Spaasie to get out. *Oumiesies* said, I am mistress of this house until the day I die. You do not come into my house and tell my people what to do. Then she told us to leave everything on the table and go.

Well, you know we did not go far. We leaned at the door. Theron argued again for money. When his mother said no again, his wife said they needed extra hands to work on their land, young hands. *Oumiesies* said no. She asked them where Amerant and Philip were. She wanted to know where Philipina was. Theron said it was not his fault that he had debts. And his wife said, *Moeder*, you have so much and you are one person, we are two with four children. We could not hear what *Oumiesies* said to that, but we heard Theron shout that what she said was not true. And his wife cried, Jesus in heaven protect me from hearing such things. She said, my husband is a good husband. Then we did hear *Oumiesies*. She said, he knows, the Lord knows, I know it, everyone who has eyes in their head can see your husband's bastards.

Spaasie pulled me away and said, go, take the children to the far field and stay there until I send for you. My heart was shaking when I took all the children. Sariel was on my back. We went into the far field and waited. I watched the path. The shadows grew long, longer, and then it was dark. Then the children were not happy. I had to make up a game and then I had to tell them to just sit still. It was late when the lamp swayed at the edge of the field. Johannes came with Spaasie. They said nothing until we were all back in our hut and Sariel was asleep.

Johannes said, Spaasie, you and Roosje must get *Oumiesies* to baptize you and your children. He said many people like us had been baptized and there was one woman in Cape Town who had children from her master, but made sure that she and they were baptized. When the master died and his family tried to sell them, she went to the fiscal, who told the master's family that they could not sell those who had been baptized. Spaasie said, I know, I know. Johannes said, Sila, you must help them. You must speak to *Oumiesies* and make sure that all the children are baptized. I said yes.

The next day I tried to speak to *Oumiesies*, but she was too cross. She looked at me and then at Frederik, who was next to me. She would not talk to me all that day and told Spaasie to keep the children out of her rooms. But that night, when Isac brought the Bible to her for *boekevat*, she called all of us, even Anthony and Petro. She read about a man with many sores. She read until her voice trembled.

When she stopped, she looked at Spaasie and Roosje. She said, I want to know, once and for all. Johannes turned his face away, but Spaasie touched his shoulder. She said, *Oumiesies* knows I have done nothing wrong. *Oumiesies* said, spit it out! Spaasie said, ja. Roosje nodded too. *Oumiesies* went red in the face, then pale, then red again.

She looked at me. And you? Her eyes were hard. You tell the truth, here in front of everyone. In front of this book!

Me? I did not have any children.

Oumiesies lifted the big book in the air. She said, you will tell me in the presence of god, have you lain with my son?

Spaasie said, *Oumiesies*, we have all kept him away from her.

Oumiesies threw the book down on the table and shouted at me. Me! Why did she not go and shout at that son of hers? She said, what kind of women are you to let such things happen? I said, *hai*! *Oumiesies* must know I never did this. I was cross. I said, *Oumiesies* must go ask her son.

She turned her face away. But I remembered what Johannes asked me to do. So I said outright, just like that, can *Oumiesies* help us and the children? She looked at me. She said what are you talking about? I said, can the children be baptized? For a long time she said nothing. Then she took cake and gave some to Sariel and the other children. She said, I will see about Spaasie and Roosje and their children. And then she sent us away.

Spaasie and Roosje were happy with me. Johannes said, you are not afraid. But my mouth was sour. What kind of heart did *Oumiesies* have? I thought of Amerant and Philip, and of Alima and Philipina. That old woman could do what she liked with us. I told Spaasie and Roosje. They said, do not worry, we will make sure that *Oumiesies* takes care of you too. But I had seen something in *Oumiesies*' eyes, something for which I did not have words. It made me cold inside. And that night I dreamed of so many tiny white snakes crawling all over the world.

A week later, Theron came back to shout at *Oumiesies*. Isac was in the room with *Oumiesies*, helping her with her accounts. He told us everything, how Theron shouted that the priest had been to him and some of *Oumiesies*' neighbors too, and the priest had asked him to come and speak to his mother to ask her what she was thinking. Why did she ask a priest to baptize slave children? He said he would tell anyone that she was a madwoman and would lose everything. Isac told us how *Oumiesies* told her son that she had promised her god that she would set things right. Theron said he would wash his hands of her. Isac said that when Theron rode off *Oumiesies* was shaking and went into her room. There was no *boekevat* that night. Or the next. And never again.

A few days after Theron stamped out of the house, Johannes came back from the town with many things on the wagon and news that made him come quickly to the kitchen where I was sewing with Roosje. I remember. Spaasie was making bread. We laughed when we saw Johannes hop-hopping and asked if he had been drinking *arak*. He said, Spaasie, give me a cup of *Oumiesies*' fresh *melk*, today is a day for celebration. He said, good things will begin for us, the English have become rulers again. There is a governor who does not like the settlers, and there is talk that they will end all slavery. He said there is someone who will watch out for us.

Spaasie said, speak up, old man. Who is this who is going to care for us?

Many people, Johannes said.

Where are these people? we asked.

Far away, in the English country. We laughed even more. Johannes would not listen. He said there was talk of people who did not like slavery and they were pushing the English *kgosi* to make a law that would protect us. Johannes said that the governor was already very cross with the settlers and wanted them to answer when they mistreated slaves. If Theron beats any of us again, we can go to the governor.

You should have heard us laugh. Roosje said, ja? And how do we get to the governor? I said, we can ride in *Oumiesies*' carriage like ladies.

We were all still laughing when the kitchen door was kicked in. It was Theron. He pointed at us and said he was going to punish us all. He called *Oumiesies* and when she came he said to her, the British are taking away our land and now they are trying to take our right to be our own masters. It was as Johannes said. *Oumiesies* and Theron and all their people had to make a list of who we were. That is what made Theron very angry.

You see, this is what it was, the governor sent a message to all masters and mistresses and said all of those that they called slaves had to be registered. The governor said in that message that the king of England and those who help him now desired that we be written into a book. Spaasie said this was good. Roosje asked for what. Spaasie said it meant someone wanted to know where we were and that could only be good. Roosje asked if she thought the world would one day wake up and fix itself up.

We all laughed, except for *Oumiesies'* son. I heard him fight with his mother when he told her not to put all of us down on paper and she told him he had too much of his weak father in him. She said he lied on paper about who was and was not on his farm. We should have listened to that, more than we listened to our own laughter.

But, too late for that. And that is why I tell you, *listen*, Baro. Listen. This is my family in this world of demons. This is your family too. Together we hold the demons from swallowing us up completely. Do you understand me? This is our family. Johannes, he who said I danced like a slender branch in a gentle breeze.

Poor Johannes with that broken body of his.

You see. Johannes looked at the world and wanted it to be different, but also knew what was what. When Spaasie wanted us to remember where we came from, he said, you Mozbiekers make it hard for yourselves. You do not know when to stop. You hit your heads on the wall because you do not like the wall where it is, but wall has no thought. Wall is wall. And these people who call themselves masters and madams have walls inside them. Teach this girl how to live here, now, not like a bird born with two heads, one to look behind, one to look forward. There is no behind. This is behind. And there is no forward. This is forward. Teach her this and you will take the pain away.

Roosje agreed with him, but liked to tease him. When he said there is no behind, she hit herself and said, hey, Johannes, here's behind, here's a good *gat*, that's all the behind I have. He did not like this, but he laughed. And Spaasie was cross, but she said nothing. She let them laugh at her. Sometimes, if Johannes was really cross about the words she wanted me to remember, if he shouted, give this up, she would tell him quietly, Johannes that is your leg speaking to you. Then he would go away, limping that limp and she would be upset with herself.

Alima once said, Sila, be careful of pain. It is a chain they fix to you. It is a chain they want you to pull around your own heart. Be careful. *Heesh.* That woman knew things.

I wanted Johannes to like me. I liked to dance for him, even when I knew about him and Alima. I learned that I could just like a man. This is important for us. In the business of men and women we are on the top of a long slope and we get kicked down. No time to say, hey, wait. So I learned to have a special place in my heart for Johannes, and it made me happy when he smiled and clapped to keep time as I danced.

These are all family. And you must know that we all share the same parent. We have that parent's eyes. Look. Next time you go past Lys or Mina or Rachel—yes, even Mina because she too is family—look into their eyes and you will see your own and your mother's. We are the offspring of that Cape of Good Hope, and that Cape of Good Hope is the place that fathers one branch of what the minister's wife calls a family tree, while another is mothered. And, let me tell you, that place makes us who we are but it will deny us. I know this as sure as I stand here and look upon that town today. It is those wives of those fathers that you must watch with the most careful eye. They are jealous and they tell themselves lies. They stare over our heads and clutch their pretty, well-pressed children to their sides, staring and waiting for the man of the house to come home.

But then, there are mothers. And then there are mothers.

Sewing. That is how it began with Theron, just before *Oumiesies* sent Alima and Philipina to him.

He came riding to *Oumiesies'* farm one day when I was walking from the river where Philipina and I had been washing linens. We heard a horse and Philipina said, quick, hide, someone is coming. She ran into the bush with the basket on her head. I was proud. I wanted to stand firm. Why did we have to hide?

Then there he was. He rode by and then stopped his horse and turned it around. I wanted to run. Something was buzzing at me. I should have listened to Philipina.

He asked what I was doing so far from the house. I said I was washing linens for *Oumiesies*. He pointed and said I was lying because I did not have a basket. Was I out meeting a man? I said the basket was with Philipina. Then she came out of the bushes. So, he said, you walk about by yourselves? I said, no, we walk together. He said, you watch yourself and get to the house. Then he clicked his tongue at us and gave me a kick. So, that was how we walked to the house, with him on the horse next to us as if we were cows.

After that, he came riding to the house nearly every week. Sometimes he stayed overnight. It made *Oumiesies* happy because, in those days, she was still trying to mend the broken fences between them. And she longed for the company of her grandchildren even if she did not long for the company of their mother. But she did not trust him.

It happened that Theron went to Cape Town for business and stopped in at *Oumiesies'* farm on his way home. He was angry. He

166

said he was the man of the family and did not have the wealth that a man should have because his mother held it all in her hands. He said, look at my trousers, I must have new trousers.

In the kitchen I told Spaasie that it was true, Theron's trousers were up to his ankle and he had wooden buttons for the flap, and his *dopper* was so short his shirt pushed out between it and the top of his trousers. Spaasie said, you pay no attention to Theron's trousers.

There was shouting. *Oumiesies* came into the kitchen and took the key that she hid under the big table. She went to her room. Then we heard her say to Theron that there was all the money he needed for one long jacket, two pairs of good working trousers, two new *doppers*, and some shirts. She told him to get the clothes. Before he left, she asked him when he would come with her grandchildren.

He came back the next week, without his wife, without his children. He asked for more money. When his mother looked at the trousers and jacket that he wore, she asked why he was wearing the same old clothes when she had given him money for two trousers, a new jacket, and *doppers* and shirts. He shouted at her. He called her an old woman who knew nothing about the world. He said he bought one pair of trousers, one jacket. That was all. *Oumiesies* shouted back that he was like his father. She had driven his father out of her house because he wasted money.

Theron shouted, I am the man of the family, I want my money. She said, this is my farm, it was my mother's farm from her mother and you will not succeed where your father did not. *Hoo!* It was ugly. When he was gone, *Oumiesies* was small. She sat at her table for a long time and there were no prayers that night. In the days that followed, she sat alone at her table, drinking tea, calling out only when the pot was empty. After many days Theron came back.

I was sewing the wings of a blue bird on a new tablecloth that *Oumiesies* was to give to her priest's wife. Theron looked at me. He said, fetch Johannes and tell him to bring the big roll from my saddle. I did this and helped Johannes carry the roll in to where Theron was standing over his mother. Theron said, there is enough cloth for two trousers and Sila will make them. *Oumiesies* did not like this. She asked him where the money came from. He said he had sold an old gun. She looked at him. Even I could see it was a lie. It sat in the open between them, but she said nothing. Then she nodded.

And that was how Theron called me to the room upstairs the next day. I was in the kitchen. Spaasie said, you will not go alone. She told Roosje, you go because you can sew too. But when Theron saw Roosje he told her to get out. She said, Master, Sila does not know how to make trousers. He said, she will learn.

I knew, then. I said, no, Master, Roosje is telling the truth.

He said, do not tell me what I know.

I said, Master.

Where was Oumiesies?

Roosje said, Master, if you want good trousers, let Roosje make them. He shouted. I ran to the kitchen. Spaasie, Roosje, and Alima put themselves between me and him when he came in. He said to them, you wait, the day will come when you will be sorry. He tried to push Roosje, but she said, as if she was talking to a child, no, no, Master, Sila is not good at making trousers. I will make them for you. He pulled her and hit her on the backside, hard. She kept saying, no, Master, no, I will make your trousers.

He walked out of the kitchen and rode off. That night, in our huts, Johannes, Alima, Spaasie, Roosje, and Philipina said we must all watch out now. They said Philipina and I were not to go anywhere without one of them and we were to stay together, close, day and night.

So, for many days we went everywhere together. Spaasie said, that old crocodile will come on wash day. So, she went with us, and told Mars and Petro to come too. And, there was Theron, waiting on the path when we were carrying the washing back. He said nothing but rode his horse away.

Haish. I was scared. Spaasie said if he was still living here, we could crush glass and put it in his food. She said she wanted to do that when she and Roosje were on his farm, before he was married, but they were scared. Demons look after their own.

Then, some weeks later, I was carrying wet sheets back to the house with Philipina. We were slow and Spaasie and Roosje were already at the house. We came around the corner of the path and there was Theron. He said, you come here. I said, no. I held on to Philipina and we spun about as he tried to grab me. Then he clapped Philipina and she went flying. Her nose was bleeding. I was shouting. But he grabbed me and pulled me into the bushes. I shouted, fetch Spaasie! Fetch Spaasie! And I heard Philipina running and shouting.

He said to me, you must learn a lesson. And I felt that thing of his pushing out of his trousers. His face was close and his eyes were hard as stone. But I fought him. And I was quick. I was young, you know. And soon I could hear Spaasie and Roosje shouting. Then Anthony. Theron got a fright. He gave me one big fist in the eye and I had to hold on to a tree so that I did not fall to the ground. But then he was gone and I was safe with Spaasie and Roosje. Philipina saved me. Her nose was broken and her finger was cut where a piece of wood had gone into it. A few days later Alima had to make a poultice with linseed to keep it from going bad.

Johannes told Isac that something must be said to *Oumiesies*. When he tried, she told him to get from her room. She went deep into her black book, praying and praying.

Alima said she would not let him get to another one of hers. Ja, she called me hers. And Spaasie and Roosje saved me from what had happened to them.

Sewing.

Tsh! Tsh! In that bush.

Oumiesies. That dress of hers hisses and all the *fynbos* is alive. *Oumiesies*.

She smiles when I say goodnight.

'n Sagte hand vir 'n harde stok. Glimlagent.

She sees nothing but the lips of her god, there in that great house she tells me she is going to. Then she writes a letter and that letter fetches the *advocaat*.

She says, I want the names of my people in my will.

Put it down, *Oumiesies*! Freedom for Sila, Spaasie, Johannes, Roosje everyone. And the children of Spaasie and Roosje. Do not forget Alima who was mother to us all, and do not forget Philipina with her crooked nose. And Mars, and Anthony, and Petro, and Isac who is your favorite.

Sila, she says to me when I am sitting next to her sewing more birds with more blue thread. Sila, it is good to have you here. Then she pats me and says, I do not understand these things, but sometimes I feel as if my sister is in my house.

Oumiesies can lie when she thinks God's ears are not listening.

Ooh, *Oumiesies*? Does *Oumiesies* mean me? Thank you. *Hai*? Thank you.

Ja, Sila can lie too because god's ears hear nothing she says.

Sisters. Sssssssissters. She gives me a hug. Then another. Then one more. She kisses my cheek and looks to the hills *from whence cometh* the *advocaat* on a slow horse.

That *advocaat* wants to know if she has told her son what she is planning. Her son is the master of the house, is he not? *Oumiesies* is cross. *Hoo!* That face of hers that can smile so is gone. Gone! Tomorrow it may come back, but today is another story. Clouds and lightning. Cross! She holds that table under her fist.

I, she says, and there is a long silence that is the washing of all words that she does not want dirtying her room. I am the head of this family. I. I, Hendrina Jansen Theron. This is *my* house. These people are *mine* to do with as I will, and God has told me what *His* will is. *His* will be done. And *you* are *my advocaat* and you will have no traffic with that son of mine.

Oumiesies. Poor stupid *Oumiesies.* Ja. *Ons is sisters en jou seun is onse pa, onse man, onse advocaat, onse judge, onse god.* Say what you want. Even I, yours to do with as you will, I know how you know nothing about the world. And you can sign that paper over and over, across the table, across the years. That paper will swallow up your name as if your name is a bit of dry bread.

Why do you think that son of yours came to kick my door in? And why did he hit Mars so hard?

And who said Mars did die? I saw that cart come, like the cart that took that first woman who was kind to me, all the way back there when first I came into this place of demons. Her name was Ma. I saw that cart take her and then another cart, and another, took the boys and girl who were like a brother and sisters to me. Loedewyk, and Annetjie, and Adam. I saw carts come and take them all. And that is what I saw with Mars. I saw a living man put in that cart and I saw his face as he saw mine. I saw him ask about that paper and your wishes. I saw a living man get into that cart and come out dead by another paper. Mars, who once asked me to lie with him.

Stupid *Oumiesies!* Let your god hear that! Your god must love stupid people.

She said, Sila, as the lord is my witness, it feels some days as if my sister is in my house. I remember as if it was, not yesterday, but today, right now. And if she were alive she would have come to hold my babies and pretend you were hers too.

A pinch, a pat, another little pinch and a tickle. They laugh and hold their arms up over their chests. Laughing, laughing. She puts honey in their mouths.

When demons come with honey, be careful.

Now she is moving those skirts through the *fynbos* and I know who she looks for. But you are mine, Baro, and you are good to keep out of her way. She thinks she will see in you a son who will never disobey a mother because she is lonely now. There is not one person who says her name on this earth and she can feel what it is to be a dress that goes grayer and thinner with each year, and she can already feel the light shining through—one place today, another one a week later. Soon there will be only one patch left and that patch will not even remember it was once a woman who owned so much land and had people she could call hers to do with as she would.

And to call her *Oumiesies* is not name enough to help her, for her other names were forbidden and my mouth cannot begin to speak the forbidden, even when it is a forgiveness needed.

And that is why *Oumiesies* comes with those skirts in the *fynbos*, looking for you, Baro, and me, looking to see if we can at last be disobedient and forget that she is *Oumiesies* and not that name on the paper that her son disobeyed. Empty paper. Empty name. And . . .

Look! There! There!

Ag, you must be quicker than that.

She runs so when the birds pick at her and the snake king comes to see who is calling him with a voice that is forgetting its own name.

Shhh. Shhh.

Softly now. Soft.

Keep still.

Tchoep.

Do not look.

Shh.

There.
Still.
She is passing.
Let her pass.
Do not look.

Ja. She goes so quickly but one sound from us and she would have been here with those torn skirts and wild hair. She would want you for a tooth. She would, my Baro-boy-boy-Baro. No teeth in that head, no cheeks. No cheeks, no smile. No smile, no friends. No friends, no one to remember your name. And you would make a sweet tooth.

Let her go. She will not come again for a long time now. She wants what little hair she has and the birds want it too. Maybe she will forget and come no more.

Come no more *Oumiesies*. Sleep *Oumiesies*, there where the forgotten ones lie. Sleep and keep that little bit of hair. Forget Sila. Forget her boy. Sleeping is forgetting and forgetting is peace. Remember only this.

Peace. *Rustig hart*. When the farm went still after the long day, the hot day. We were like birds that had been busy all day. Then we went down the path with each other to our huts. Spaasie, Roosje, Johannes, Isac. Our feet made dust. Behind us the house stood still as day passed. The house stood still and those trees stood green and still, waiting while day passed and night came up the path, a slow carriage that made a big, quiet dust. And that dust came slowly and sweetly from under the stones, from under the grass, from inside the leaves and the trees themselves, even from under the chairs and tables, from inside the water jugs, the wine bottle, even from inside the bird's throats. Ja, and you could hear that.

Then. *Tchss*. Quiet.

The house stood open. The doors open and the windows putting on their widow's weeds.

The day she left was a quiet one and we, Johannes, Spaasie, Roosje, Isac, and me, went to our huts with our bundles that were our hearts and we got ready. We took the children and we got them ready. Mars, he wanted to dance and shout, but kept as still and quiet as the house when Spaasie gave him one look. Petro and Anthony went to take things from the house. Johannes and Mars blocked their way. Isac went to sit by himself.

I looked at those hills where the sky was making its fire quietly and without big claims. The birds were making their last flights, quiet too in this. Only a wood pigeon called out to that house and its call was only the echo of what lay in there and what was gone for good from this world of days and nights, nights and days.

Johannes was sad when he came to sit with Spaasie and me. Spaasie had her boys close. They said nothing. Johannes held her hand and we all sat like a family with our backs straight against the wall, waiting. I wanted to ask Johannes why the world was leaning too far on one side like that day they put me on the boat and I saw a boy's head go down into that big hole before I too went, when my throat was my enemy, choking me and my heart kicked me and kicked me as if I, I was the demon and the thief. Why, Johannes, I wanted to ask him, why was I seeing that time all over again when this was the day that *Oumiesies'* paper would speak and make the governor himself listen?

We waited. And then Johannes wept and I knew why the world was leaning so and why I had to hold on to his hand.

Three days. Johannes said at last that someone must go over to that son's farm to tell him. Spaasie had a wild look. She said no. Johannes said, woman, do you think we can go on like this without them coming? Spaasie said that son came only when money was low and

Oumiesies had given him so much just two days before she dropped her soup spoon and said aah-aah with soup going down her chin and her eyes so big and her hands grabbing-grabbing the table. A lot of money. He would not come for a long time.

For three days we waited and then Johannes spoke. Anthony said the road was a long one in one direction but longer in another and that was the way to go, far away, over there. I said yes, let us go. Johannes looked at his feet and I felt that old bone bend again in his leg and its crack come again as if I was there that day his first master taught him the price of running. Spaasie said nothing.

It was night again. The house sat still and what was in there was stiller than still.

Then Spaasie spoke and it was the sound of a bird and the trees hung above our heads as a light passed from window to window. And we knew *Oumiesies* was looking for us from a place we could not see.

Why did we not take the wagon? Or the carriage and the horses and ride, ride?

It went like this, *klap*! That was for Spaasie. She fell and when she got up again her face hung on one side like old meat. *Klap*! For Roosje who went *owffff* and danced a slow dance of sagging knees before she sat down on her heels like a drunk woman.

Johannes.

Someone out there is beating the carpet as if spring has come again, but I see only darkness.

Mars?

Someone is killing a pig.

Children are crying while I am dancing out of *sjambok's* way.

And in those trees that *Oumiesies* loved so, there are white birds flying and trying to stitch night back together again.

A soft rain. Easter Friday. Or, no. No. Now *what* day *was* it?

Your mother has such trouble these days. There is a noise in this useless ear and in my eyes there are birds that fly with such a sound that echoes in the hills.

Can you hear the wood pigeons? When they talk like that it means rain.

I am cold. Winter is coming. But the smell of that farm stays the same. How did we not grow tired of it?

Someone is killing a pig.

Someone is beating a carpet. Children cry like baby birds.

I am dancing and dancing.

It is raining. Winter will come like a soft rain at first, then we will all think it is Good Friday and the world is ending and a new one beginning in the cracks that open in the ground beneath our feet.

Block your ears! The sound riding to shore with every wave is the sound of the dead clearing their throats to speak to you this morning. Close your ears. Quick. Listen to this melody of pot against pot in the soapy water. Listen to the guards' tin cups bumping in the soap over there near their kitchen. Listen. Think of the hens clucking in the farmyard where you ran on your shiny little legs. Think of the broom, its stiff bristles that brush the yard clean of hens' droppings. When I pick that broom up those bristles sing their sh-shing song to the ground and the ground sings back. Listen to this.

Do not make me fight so.

I am tired of pecking and scrounging to find things to keep your head from turning away. I am no mother bird and you are no chick. What is wrong with you? You go off and stay away without a word. The world is full of demons and this island has more than its share. They would chew down on your bones and suck them dry. You will become like *Oumiesies*. She wants you for her family. Is that what you want?

Be careful. Naughty boy. You will be joking on the other side of your face if *Oumiesies* hears you. Do not be fooled by her cooing and calling. She is no dove. She only uses the language of wood pigeons to fool us. Listen. For the difference. Which is the wood pigeon, which is *Oumiesies* squeezing herself into a wood pigeon's throat? Be careful. And think of me. I do not want to see that old woman looking at me with your eyes. I had enough of her when she was covered with flesh.

Cheeky boy. You will know the difference when *she* pinches your cheek. She will pinch to test for what she can get. The demon dead get hungry for company and such is their hunger that they devour what they long for. Be careful! Do you want to become just so much demon shit? There is enough of it piling up and making a road into the future. Look at Soldaat. Why do you think he holds his arm like a broken wing? It is because a demon has grabbed hold. Look how he fights to shake it off. You are not so strong. The demons will make a meal of you in no time. Is that what you want?

And do not think those voices that come in on the waves are any better. They will suck you into the prison of their loneliness. You think those are the voices of Flora, or of Hester's children. I made that mistake. Be careful. Hester's children do not belong to the demon dead. But, who knows what goes on there in the waters of Roggerberg.

Who knows anything anymore? I am tired. Wake up, boy, and give me some rest.

I am going to teach you the difference between all of these voices that you can hear, and how to tell the difference between all those people you see. The first lot to be careful of are like *Oumiesies*. I have warned you enough about her and I am not going over that again. You better have listened or there will be holes in what you know and those holes can become the holes through which demons like her can sniff you.

There are the usual demon dead whose purpose is simply to distress us. You have little to fear from them. You are beyond them. They only reach the likes of Matroos, Keizer, or Vigiland. Those demons left this life, but the poison that kept them alive now eats them. They are the ones who could never be satisfied. They ate land just as they ate meat. They made places of hunger and they taught us hungers that devour us. Now they are hungrier than ever.

You must also be careful of those who will break your heart. They are the voices of Hester's children. They cry because there is no one who will sing for them, and they are also down there in the waters of Roggerberg. I once tried calling them, to be a mother to them, but they trust no one. Who can blame them?

There are some who sound like children. They want to swallow that whole town, thinking it is their mother. That is why the town fights so to keep its shore from being swallowed. So, be careful of the voices of the doomed who were not wicked in their fleshy lives but have been cast aside. Their voices plead and make you cry, but you must not even so much as reach out. Leave something for them instead, something small. It will make them happy for a while. But stay clear.

Then there are those who have suffered at the hands of those who were dearest to them. Well. We have all heard them. They make me cry.

There are things I do not know. Here is one of them—I do not know how it is that we are all living, and what holds some of us together, while others seem to drift by without seeing anything or anyone. Some days I think I know how it is. Some days I think I have seen how we all move in the world – there are threads that lead to one ball of light. Other days I see only a mess of dry straw cast about in the air and on the ground.

They are everywhere.

I woke up. *What?* It was the gulls.

Gulls can cry like newborn babies. And newborn babies can sound like little creatures sent to us so that we may teach them how to become like us.

Why do such a thing?

I have called her Debora, as I promised. August baby. She came quietly, quickly.

No, no. Remember, if she sees you, she will want to come with you.

Lys and Rachel helped me. They bound me tight afterward, and Mina kept Meisie and Catherina with her.

Debora. I do not think she is breathing properly. Mina says do not worry, she is strong. But I saw how she and Lys looked at each other.

I want to be happy for this child, but I am without happiness.

Lys and I keep her in bed with us. Catherina and Meisie sleep in Mina's old bed.

Meisie is happy. She thinks this is very good to have a new sister.

Catherina puts her face close to her new sister's, but Debora sees nothing. She has eyes like yours.

The hinges on these doors sound like a baby. I tell myself I am a fool. I tell myself, *You are going mad, girl.* And my hair wants to run off my head and smash against the walls, but I keep my hair to myself.

My hair has been growing and growing all by itself. It throws its own shadow when I sit near the wall and now I let my hair's shadow

fall across the warden's door. I like this. It falls like a door knock.
The warden comes to the door.

Who?

I make my eyes wide, as if I do not speak the language of the living anymore. I stand like a ghost. He believes I am a ghost because he slips back into his office, quickly, like a crab afraid of the shadow that my hair throws. My hair is wings, my hair is the wings of a gull with a hunger. The warden slips back into his office, crab arse first, and when my hair knocks at his door again he does not come to see. My hair makes me laugh so. It springs up when the guards try to come near me. They clear their throats, each one, to a man. My hair gets bigger and bigger.

One day my hair will cover the whole island like a big bushy forest filled with things that laugh and sing inside. People will come in their boats. The ladies of Cape Town will give up visiting each other and come out in boats that trail ribbons. They will do this just to float a little ways off, bringing their picnic hampers and they will be happy and sometimes their throats will hiccup and it will be as if they do not know what makes them say my name. And yours, Baro.

They will say it is the wine and they will cover their mouths with their hands and apologize while they giggle. And my hair will send a bird or two out. They will cover their heads quickly and duck under their parasols because the birds that fly out of my hair will be known for the size and accuracy of their shit.

Dit is what ek sê!

Now. Where did your sister Carolina come from? The fathers do not matter to me. Except one. Perhaps I will tell you about him one day. Perhaps you remember him. A big face, big eyes, big heart. But a wife he did not tell me about. How was that?

My girl is my girl.

Things have happened to me, yes, but I was not like one of those women from the Company's Lodge. They talk about those women who, like the men, were called holdings. Men, women, and children. Holdings. What is that? Holdings? Me, I have always had a place in my heart for those Lodge women. Masters let their wives go visiting every afternoon and while their wives were visiting, carried in their sedans by the Lodge men, the husbands went to the Lodge to relieve themselves of all that cargo they carry with such pride. I heard that the Lodge women had to take whoever came to them.

I do not want to talk of that town prison, or the district prison near Plettenberg Bay. There is nothing to say. Those days and nights are not mine and the woman who lived them in my name was not me.

Your brother was born in Cape Town *tronk*. But from my body. I am all the parent my children needed. As I am now with Debora, whose eyes are wide as if she is looking through the world. This is not a good look for a baby.

Ag, and what good did I ever do for my children? I do not want to talk anymore. Let me rest. My head aches and there is a worm in my heart.

Do you think there could be something inside us that makes us slaves and them our masters and misses?

That day they came—all the way back there where I was born—it was as if we were just useless things that did not even have legs to run. Our mouths made noises that made no sense. The village was not a village. We were not people. I am telling you, there was no one I recognized. I did not even know who I was. There were strangers, crazed creatures banging against themselves like shadows trying to get back the shape of their bodies. My mother was a shadow bumping into the trees, my father was fighting a snake as it wrapped itself around his neck and ankles, using the necks and ankles of others to give it strength.

And then I saw the whipping. Men walked in a wide row that soon circled us. They were whipping the air and the ground and we were like deer whipped into the smaller and smaller circle of our fear until we were standing, backs to the center, faces to what drove us and what was coming for us. I thought, there will be more. My father and uncles would break such small men. Then, in all that noise, all sound was sucked out of the air. Oh, the air was still being whipped, mouths were still open, and arms and legs were moving, moving on the spot. We were holding on to each other, trying to get behind each other. But there was no sound. And that was when I knew, young as I was, something not of this life was there in the trees. I thought, it will come out of the trees where it stands and watches.

It never showed its face. Those demons in the forms of men were its signs, the circle the shape it made, and those chains that snaked around us were all that was needed to let us know that we were like animals drawn into a valley that is the death of our lives with these people. On that day the world changed itself and it leaned so hard that we poured into a place from which all our generations will have to struggle to leave.

Well. That is how it feels today and I must sleep now so that one more of those tomorrows can come quickly.

Close the door. Walk quietly, your mother needs to sleep. Your sister needs to sleep. And keep an eye out for anyone who might come to take her away from us. Be our guard, Baro. It is time for you to do something for your sister.

Go carefully today. Mina has lost her baby.

I have taken food from the warden's kitchen for her and she has not been afraid to eat it. She cries. Flora cries.

Lys sits with Mina. And Deel. I just bring food and say, sorry, sorry Mina, sorry for your loss.

One of the men brought a small box made from driftwood. We put the baby in the box and stood over the grave while the prisoner Van Graaf said words in Dutch. Lys and Rachel had to hold Mina up.

Sorry, Mina, sorry for your loss.

Help that baby, Baro. Do not let him wander near the *fynbos*.

Such a storm came last night. I thought—an army of redcoats crossing the roof. Such lightning. I thought—someone sharpening very big knives. And the wind! That wind blew the *fynbos* out of the ground and I heard the warden's roof come to pieces, the guards crying out as they ran. I heard the warden coughing as he grabbed his trousers.

Look at all of this. The sea threw itself this far last night and left these things for us. This wood. What could it have come from? Maybe a ship has died somewhere between this place and that one over there. Look there. Yes. More wood. Well. One ship goes down. Fires get fat tonight on this place.

Can you see how tired your mother is today? I have not the heart to lift a finger. The Minister and Missus Minister are back. She looks at me and says I am sick from woman's business. As if I do not know what she is talking about. A woman's business. I tell Lys, that woman has no business being here and talking to us. That woman and her husband have no business here.

Lys says, Sila, we are their business, just as we are the warden's business. I say, let the warden mind his business and mind it well.

The storm leaves so much work. Pick this up. Sweep here. Carry that. Put that back. This body wants nothing of it. This body wants to lie down in the mess and be carried away by ants. This body wants to sleep and wake up in a place where the sun shines like a boy's laughter and where children are all well fed. This body does not want a torn dress. This body does not want food that rats will not eat. This body does not want this ground, these huts. This body does not want to hear anything but welcome in a voice.

The sky gets that look again. Well! Let all ships sink!

Is this good or bad to say such things? Is it good or bad that there is a town over there that grows so fast in the hands of men who can do no good but for themselves?

I ask myself, what kind of woman are you, Sila van den Kaap? I ask myself because there is no one who can tell me. Except, perhaps, Lys.

The storm makes nothing but noise. My head aches today. My body aches. Your sister is not well. Do not come close. She will turn her eyes and see you and then Meisie will be sad.

My skin itches. The minister's wife is here, like a fly after all these months away. She comes and sniffs around Debora. She asks me, what are you giving her? How are you holding her? She says, give the child to me to hold. She tries, but your sister is like me. We do not like this woman.

[✦] [✦]

Have you been looking for me and Debora? We have been very sick.
We had to go to the hospital on the mainland. They call it Somerset
after the governor. Lys had to keep Catherina and Meisie.

Were you lost? Were you counting the days we were there?

The warden was cross when the surgeon said we must go. The surgeon said there are too many fleas here, and the warden must do something about the rats. He says the fleas from these rats make us sick.

They put us in a big room with other women and children. It was
good, even though Debora was coughing so hard and crying, and I
longed for Meisie and Catherina. And Lys. We had food there. And
the sick do not get up to break stones or clean house. But your sister
was too sick. The surgeon came and said the island is no good for
your child. And the minister's wife came to wipe her hands and stare
at Debora.

What am I to do?

Spaasie came to see me. But no news of Carolina or Camies. Pieter
is still with Van der Wat. No news of Johannes. Sariel is well and
reads and writes, and cooks better than any of us. And Philipina is
found. Yes! Living in town now. She sent a message that she will
care for me and my children as a husband would. I told Spaasie,
Philipina does what she wants. Spaasie says, Philipina will have no
one to look after her when she gets old. I said, I will. And my children. Spaasie shook her head. For the first time she looked old. She
says she is sick of cleaning for *witmens*. But what can we do, hey?

She wants a small piece of land and when Sariel marries she can give this to her and then live with her until she dies. I do not like to hear Spaasie talk of death.

The minister's wife has thorns in her words. And very few smiles. She looks at your sisters and says this is not the place for children. I say, then send us to a better place. She calls me insolent and selfish because a good mother would sacrifice her own pleasure for the sake of sending her child to a better place. She says there is a priest, a good man, who is working with others to buy children and old people and set them free.

Now I know Mina has been talking with the minister's wife. Mina wants Flora to go to this place. I know what she plans. She thinks that they will take her too, but she forgets what the warden calls her in his book, and what the law says she is. Mina prisoner, Mina convict. If they take my child I will be left here, chained to the rock of Sila prisoner, Sila convict. So will Mina.

Perhaps Missus Minister told Mina they will help her leave this place if she helps them take my children away.

What?

It is one thing to say this is no place for a child, another to have your child stolen.

What can I do?

The minister's wife says there is good food. And a school. She says there are other children, and women who will take care of them. Her words are thorns.

What else can I do?

Baro? Your mother is a leaf blowing in the wind.

And Lys is ill today. The surgeon says she is lying. But I can see. She says she feels nothing in her fingers. And her eyes hurt. And now even she says, this is no place for children.

I say Meisie and Catherina are not sick on this place. Lys shakes
her head.

Deel is no help. She says, look at Debora. And Rachel shakes her
head.

Who are they to say? What do they know?

Go and listen to the wind. Bring me an answer. The minister's
wife is breathing on my neck and her eyes are on your sister's heart.
She says, look at your baby, look at how sick this place makes her.
How long before the healthy ones get sick too.

Hurry! The ground is breaking under my feet.

That woman has run to fetch her husband. He will come in here
again with that book in his hand and say that this thing my soul must
go into that book. It is a word, that book, he says. One word. But he
keeps that word to himself and puts up many, many words between
me and that word.

Where were you? They came, Mina said, they came when I was in
the quarry. Missus Minister and the warden came.

I ran to the jetty, but there was no boat to be seen.

Meisie!

I would have jumped in the water to fetch her back. Yes, even to
this place. She is my child. A child's place is with her mother.

My child!

I asked Mina, why did you not fetch me? She had to run from
me. Lys had to hold me back. The warden sent the guards but they
did nothing. Even they know this is wrong. But the warden came,
cross, shouting that he would put me in the lockup for a whole day.

Lock me up? When I did nothing? Let him lock himself up. I will
spit in his food, you wait. I will put goat shit in his stew.

Pedder sent Van Graaf to say that he would put me on bread
and water if I do not stop shouting. Hah! Bread and water. He can

give me stones and sand and that will not stop me. What does he think?

I must get a message to the superintendent of police, or the protector of slaves, or to Van Ryneveld, or to the Orphan Chamber. Lys says that Meisie, Catherina and Debora, and Pieter are still the concern of the Orphan Chamber. The Orphan Chamber will make them bring Meisie back.

Does she think I do not know what is what? All those years before reaching Van der Wat's farm? I know who was *supposed* to take care of me and my children. Knowing is one thing. Knowing is useless if no one will do anything for you.

Only last week when Missus Minister asked if Meisie could go and live with her on the mainland, I said no. A child must be with her mother. Then Missus Minister asked Mina, who said yes. And Missus Minister said she would be back for Flora. Not Meisie too!

And where were you?

Wake up!

The superintendent must know, but Pedder refuses to see me.

I *knew*. I *knew*. I *knew-knew-knew* as soon as I came into the yard in front of the huts. No. Even before. When I left the hut for the warden's kitchen. When I went from the kitchen to the quarry. No. When I woke up. No. I dreamed of a demon coming into the hut. I should have taken Meisie with me, even if she was coughing.

They took her in a boat in this weather and with that cough. I will kill them all. Get me a gun. Get me an axe. I will chop this world up into tiny pieces.

Lys says, be strong Sila. Think of Catherina and Debora. I do. I listen to Debora cough. Her body is too small for such coughing. But what can I do? They will not let me take my children off this place. They take my healthy child, leave me to listen to my sick child!

Even the guards look away. They leave me alone.

I still ask, why did Mina not run, *run*, to fetch me?

Ag. Farewell. Farewell.
What else can I do?
So many tears. Mina in her corner, me in mine. And Lys blowing on hot soup for Catherina and Debora.

The minister's wife is all smiles.

Bring me news if they do not give your sister the good food they promised. Let nothing happen to Meisie. And look out for Flora too.

The warden's face is a stone set on our graves. It bears our names. We have one name. His face writes our name.

My heart is not a stone. If it were, I would be, yes, comfortable.

Heart, I am speaking to you, you who live in me like another. Listen. Go away.

I turn my face to the wall. I would make the wall the place where I live. A wall waits, but I do not know what it waits for. I am trying to learn what is worth such silence.

A wall is silent. My heart is not.

Heart, I am speaking to you. Listen. Be still, be silent.

My heart speaks back.

I have longed for walls that are my own. I have longed for walls that shift and crane, like guests at a celebration, for the moment my beloved arrives. I long for this. Do not punish me for such things. I am a heart. It is my job to love and to long for love.

We are at war, my heart and I.

My heart speaks, again.

I long for forgiveness. Do not believe me unforgiven.

There are short years left and shorter days. Small things move between us with great weight. Nothing is so bad between us. Forgive me. Do not punish me for such requests. I am a heart. It is my job to seek forgiveness and to forgive in return.

Well, then. What will become of us, me and my heart?

It is hard. I have winter in my fingers and my heart longs for summer.

Listen to me, heart, summer is over. This is the winter and it will be long. Prepare yourself. It is a lesson I have learnt. Accept this now. There are less breaks. You know this as much as I, you break like a bone.

My heart speaks, in spite of me.

I . . . I . . . Do not go . . . Do not.

I cannot. Do not punish me for staying.

I am a heart. It is my job to stay where I have been placed.

Well. So, I am to be made into a demon. I, the cruel one. As if I am the liar. As if I am the one who has lost all joy and blamed my heart. So I am to be made the angry one, the joyless one. *I am not without joy. You, heart! L-i-s-t-e-n!* Go away. There will be no more talk between us. I forget you. I forget you. I forget you. What need do I have for joy? I am the wretched one, the unforgiven one, the stealer of joy, the creature of despair. Go. *Go!* I dismiss thee. I dismiss thee. I dismiss thee. *Enemy!*

The wind. The cold is like salt on my fingers and things do not open easily. I leave Catherina and Debora with Mina, who is also coughing, but what else can I do?

Lys? I know things that are bringing me to my knees. Mina says pray to the minister's god.

Well! Then! Bring me that book and its words.

Who is it that brings me down? What shakes me?

I am like a rose in a valley of death and the shadows fear no evil.

I am like unto a rock that strikes a hill that breaks like a potter's vessel.

I look unto the hills from whence cometh the wrath of a thousand plagues and in the mornings there are vines to bind me to the crusher's wheel. Yea, though I wash and wash at the water's edge, there is no balm and the angel of the Lord breaks bread elsewhere and I must not laugh too loudly.

Pssshh! That book is full of things for miserable people. Missus Minister says it is the word of god and it is therefore powerful. Big word, if you ask me. She says, it speaks to all of us, no matter what color, no matter what station in life, or where we were born. That woman knows nothing about the power of these words and who bears them. She has no color, she has that station and she can say where we were born.

Bring me to the place where I may gaze upon the valley of my youth. I am captive in a captive land where rulers push their mouths out, sucking at barrels in the vineyards, there in the valley of death and their cattle are many and their slaves are many and their sins are like unto a plague of locusts that eat not fields but bodies and hearts. Deliver me, I am weary and know things that bring me to my knees.

There is something in me that has nothing to do with this place or the people who say we are theirs to do with as they will. It has nothing to do with the warden or the minister or Missus Minister, or these guards.

What? Lys, am I going mad at last? What else is there but the world of these people? They send us to make their wine, we make it a red that comes from another world or a green so thin they call it white. They send us to break stones, we break their rocks for their streets. They put us in a kitchen, we cook their food. They tell us who will make babies on us, we make those babies. They tell us where the road stops and we do not set foot beyond it except for some craziness that will not be obedient. They beat us and we cry out, or lose our hearing or the feeling down one side, but we do not strike back, except when we go mad and lose all care for life. And I am saying that there is something in me that twists and twists over itself and it has nothing to do with them.

Look at Matroos, Soldaat, Keizer, and Vigiland. They are telling us something.

Ships that sail by at night leave only the sound of their creaking—wood that longs for forests. If you listen, when there is no storm, you can hear that creaking as if that ship is in the saddle of a horse that swims underneath the water, there in the down there, a horse that rides like the horses in the minister's book. Because surely that is one of the few things on which it tells the truth.

Meisie! I cannot remember where she went. I left her in the hut and when I came back she was gone.

Was I bad?

Ag, Lys, I had a dream that will not let me be. We were all getting onto a ship, me, my children. We had a big chest filled with plates and dresses for me and my girls, satin *broeke* for my sons. Then the ship was moving and my insides were empty with fear. My children. Some were on land, some on the ship, and those on the ship had disappeared. I could feel them moving about, close to me, but could not see them. It was as if one of those big fogs had arrived and settled around my eyes. Near, I could not see. Far, I could. Nothing in between. My children were in between. Then the ship had wheels like a wagon, and my children were still half on the ground and half up with me. Then the ship was a small-small *bakkie* with a small-small horse and I had to ride the horse with my feet on the ground to help it move. My children were behind me. I tried turning to make sure they were on the *bakkie* but my feet were pushing, walking that horse and that *bakkie*. And my heart was beating and aching, my feet pushing and pushing.

The shadow of this dream is heavy, Lys. What do you think it means?

I think that ship was taking us home.

It is hard to think about my children, but there is not a time in the day that I do not. Did these people think I would forget my children as if I am a cow or a pig?

I think of Carolina. I want to know how she is. I dreamed that she had a child. If she has a child, who is the father of that child, and is he good to her? I want to know if she is afraid, sad. Do they beat her? How does she look? Who does her child look like? Does she think of me?

I am a woman surrounded by spirits. These spirits are questions. These tormenting spirits are the questions we cannot answer. The dead hear these questions and send them back to us in anger, for . . . Why? Why would the dead be angry with us?

I am tired. What do I know?

Of Camies, there is nothing. What has happened to that boy? I heard he was with Carolina for a time, but there is only silence about him now. I fear for him, Lys. He was not very strong. Not like Pieter. Now *that* boy was strong. He came out of me with a kick. He did not cry. I thought he was dead—can you imagine how it feels to give thanks, even for the space of one breath, maybe two, when you think that what you have carried in your body is not life, but death? But he was alive. Just quiet. Not weak. Strong. He looked at the world with old, strong eyes.

Pieter! I do not even remember that boy's face.

I am only slenderly on this side of making sense, even to myself.

How do you keep your days so neat and still? You are my good, quiet day, Lys. You make a place for my back to rest and all aching stops, and when my face relaxes I know that it was pulled up, strained. You are my good day, and my quiet, Lys. You make a place for my stomach to relax, and when it does I know that it was twisted and turned like a dirty old sheet taken away by a stream before I could catch it and wash it and lay it out. And my heart is what I thank you for most, Lys, even though it is like a sore where a stick has broken skin. There is no safe place for a heart, but my good days are in you.

Another dream, Lys. These nights there is no rest. I was walking in the town with my children. A big fog was creeping up from the Roggerberg. My children were holding onto my skirts and we were coming out of a big house. Behind us the house was filled with animals. There were monkeys in a cage that covered a whole tree. That cage was a net. There were she-elephants and their young. And deer of every kind and their young. All were caught in cages. I saw men with sticks, poking into the cages. They were laughing and on their belts they wore bags swollen with coins. I took my children and they held my skirts, but when I looked down there were two girls whose faces I had never seen, and then I saw myself and I was a woman I had never seen. I took those girls by their hands and walked away from the fog as if we were going to Buitengracht. And then my eyes were closed and the fog was in my ears and my children were gone.

What do these things mean? I think that Allah Hoo Akbaa man can help me. They say he reads dreams better than anyone. If you see him before I do, tell him I need to ask him about my dreams. Tell him my sleep is filled with things that speak to me in a language I never learned. Tell him it is not for trying. Tell him I can pay him with things from the warden's kitchen, but do not say that I take these without the warden knowing. I hear that he is particular about such business. Tell him they are things left over and the warden does not think twice about them. It is true. Tell him only that I have dreams whose messages are like ships that will sail away without me if I am not quick to catch what is in their sails.

I need to sleep, but not to dream.

Hai! Your mother's lips are burning today. Your mother has a big sore on her lip. It burns. Lys says I am to put salt on it. Deel says it is a disease women get from men. I say, life is a disease women get from men. But who listens to me these days?

What to do? All day in the quarry, the pounding, the dust, the thirst, it all means nothing against this sore. It burns and I think that my lip must be ten times its size but Lys says I imagine things and there is hardly anything to see and what does Deel know, Deel is one of those women who does too much and knows nothing.

Your mother is a tired woman and may just lie down and never get up again. If it was not for Debora and Catherina, who has still not learned how to look at the world, and if it was not for Meisie, who waits for me to fetch her there where they have taken her to give her good food, I would say, get ready to welcome me, there where you really live.

In the quarry, my arms shake . . . so. You see? Look. And at night I feel a shaking that goes on inside my bones. The hammer goes on in my bones. What to do?

Bring me a cloth to cover my face. Bring me a cloth the size of the world and let it cover my face and let my face be as still as the earth when no one walks across it.

Bring me a bed that will sink itself deep into the earth and pull the earth over me like a blanket someone has made for a friend. Bring me the earth, my blanket, and find me a friend who will sing for me while I sleep and sleep and sleep.

Bring me water. I will wash myself and I will make myself clean and the earth will cover not a dirty face but a clean one and smell sweet in all the groves that surround me. Bring me this water, now, I long for clean skin.

Back there, far back there, there I heard them tell about a girl with a hole where her mouth had been. They said her white lover had eaten her mouth. And others said, no, it was her breast, he had eaten her breast. They said that lover did not love like anyone else. That lover took the girl and he had a gold tooth and that tooth needed to be polished with blood and he sucked and sucked and sucked and her blood left her mouth and went into him and her blood left her breast and went into him. They said she was the middle daughter of a headman and her father has covered his head with ash.

My lip burns and swells. There is nothing in the world that is larger than my lip.

I take my broom. I sweep the floor. Near my bed I put water in a bowl. I put salt in the water. I put sugar bush at the door and the ants will stop there and munch on that sugar bush and leave me in peace. There are demon ants biting my lip. Deel says it is the sore from a disease. Lys says she knows nothing and if someone knows nothing it is best that that someone shuts up or nothing will hit her hard in the mouth. Deel says beast and beast is what pulls her hair and makes her run out of the room to Rachel and Mina. Me and Lys put our beast heads together and laugh.

My lip hurts.

I gave myself one small apple from the warden's kitchen. I ate it. I gave the core to the mice. They can leave me be now. It was delicious, that apple.

Is there no special medicine you can bring for your mother? Bring me a boat filled with medicine. Bring a boat with a hundred men to lift me onto that deck. Make their hands soft as a lamb's chin, make their words soft too, and kind. Make their faces good. Keep all beer off their breath. Bring me that boat.

And bring me fresh water to wash my lip. I know the water from that place is better than anything here and it alone will clean me.

Bring me something!

My head.

Perhaps it was the bite of a viper. Perhaps that viper thought I was an apple. Bring me an axe and I will teach that viper how to tell the difference between an apple and a woman with an axe. *Xxxttttt!*

My lip hurtsssssssssssssss.

Lys says pick out a man, kiss him, give it back to him. Me, I say I give nothing anymore, not even a viper's kiss. Let the men kiss themselves.

Quick! The sky is what I was telling you about! Keep it clear and I will see if I can lift my heart above the big fat lip on my face.

I am helping myself. I am using my heart. We are talking to each other, now.

The viper showed me the way. But my lip still hurts.

Things are not so easy.

The island is thick with vipers. You can hear them playing with the stones.

My lip is the size of a stone big enough for a man to stand on and see into a window over there in that Cape of Towns.

My lip is all dressed up. My lip wears a stone as if it is a gold ring. My lip is a jewel and the vipers must keep away or I will bite their heads off. That is what I say.

What is that on the ground?

Perhaps a cockroach.

Perhaps a snake.

Perhaps a pocket that has fallen off a guard's trousers. I will put a stone in it and send it back. Let him sit on that.

What?

Someone hits the side of a wall with his fist and his piss stings the ground. Let him groan. That is not my worry. A centipede crawls inside him. He shakes but it has many claws. Let him groan. That is not my worry. I am helping myself. I am using my heart. We are talking to each other, now.

My lip hurts. I am tired.

Bring me a real bed to lie on. Bring me a cloth for my face and I will be calm and let the sky cover me. The sky is what I was telling you about. And I am tired.

I am helping myself to a big piece of the sky.

Do not look at my face.

[X] [X]

The minister is in there, drawing lines and writing names that Missus Minister points to and reads as the names of his family, the children of children. She points and says, that is her. Ink on paper. She says she has entered her husband's family and when he comes around to drawing her family tree, it will show how he has entered her family. She says this as if she knows she has left her mother's name far behind.

This woman thinks I have nothing, nothing else to do but listen to her. Who does she think I am? Her sister?

She tells me a family is like a tree with branches growing out, big branches, small. Well. If you look around this island you will see. There are no trees worth mentioning.

And where is my girl, Meisie?

Now what?

More visitors. They want tea in that warden's parlor? Tea?

There. Let them taste *that.*

Look at this. *Plop.* She puts sugar into her tea and does not even know that someone holds this tray in front of her. Look at the hair. Needs a wash, *nè.*

Shh. Look at this one. Who does *she* think she is? And this one. Count the chins, is what I say. If I was this ugly I would not be bothering people.

More tea? *Hmph.* Listen to the way Pedder asks, as if he is going to pour it.

Look at her. Lady, *you* do not mind if you do, but someone else does.

The weather these days *slurp* is a matter *slurp* of great *slurp* con-*clink*-cern to the farmers *slurp* and I do believe *slurp* that we shall *slurp* see months of *plop* before we see *slurp* relief *mmm*, god willing.

Animals. When he holds his cup out so, he looks at her but sees a bull mounting the rump of a fat cow. So I say, slurp away in those pretty skirts that want to fill the room. The froth of waves is at our feet and I am the only one who knows which way the tide turns when winds blow into each other and they can *slurpslurp* and *plop* and talk of the *slurp* which *plops* at great cost to the farmers.

I knew a farmer or two once myself. And look where it got me.

Quick, I must try to remember. Today I stood with the sun in my eyes and I could not remember a day before this one. Listen.

Here is how I have been moved about in this country. Neethling to *Oumiesies*, who was named Hendrina Jansen, separated wife of Theron. They called her, also, Widow Theron. From *Oumiesies* to her son Theron, then from Theron to Stroebel. No. That was Carolina and Camies who went to Stroebel. It might as well have been me too. A part of my heart has gone with them, but that part of my heart is lost now. Me, I went from Theron to Hancke, from Hancke back to Theron, from Theron back to Hancke, and then for a time in the prison. Then Hancke sent Mokke to hide me and my children—you, Carolina, Camies—in his wagon. Mokke, it was Mokke who took me all the way over land to Van der Wat there in Plettenberg Bay, on the Stoffpad.

No. I was never on Stroebel's farm. My mind tricks me because my heart went after my girl and my boy.

Carolina! Camies! Your mother thinks about you every day.

Give me the language to curse curses that will make even the stones tremble.

But first there was the boat and before that all that noise. But, before that . . . a place I dare not call home. That word makes the skin between my toes crack and weep.

Before that boat then, is nothing I can bear to live with. Some days.

But your mother is defiant, Baro, even if there is a price to pay.

And prices have been paid. *Hai!* Perhaps it is knowing what we know that makes us laugh here. Lys says to me, look at that guard, he stinks like the meat he has hanging in his room. Now, why that should make us laugh I do not know, but laugh we do. Even when Mina says the guards keep us hanging in our huts at night as if we too are meat, we laugh.

Ja, we laugh together. Sometimes one of us will start—me, or Lys, or Mina, or Rachel. Or Deel, who is not strong enough to break or lift stones and will die if the warden does not take her out of the quarry. Even Deel can find some laughter.

Mina is good with Deel. She watches out for her. That is good. Mina fights the guards away from Deel. I can see that.

There are things that hurt when you remember them, but we can still laugh. I think that, yesterday, Lys stumbled over an old rock in her heart. There were tears, then we were laughing and crying together. I ask myself, sometimes, is there a way to remember without stumbling? Perhaps that writing that Missus Minister does, or that the minister does, or even the warden, is a way. Baro? I want to remember. And I am afraid of that. I look over there at Matroos, or Soldaat, or Keizer, or Vigiland.

So. Yes. Neethling to *Oumiesies.*

Was there another old lady? By name of Cruywagen? No. No. *What is happening?*

My head aches today.

I woke up out of the darkness and the rolling world and the endlessness of weeping—my own and not my own but that too seemed like mine down there—and a woman was there, one of us. She gave me water and then food and she held me while she too cried. I asked her if I had been sick. There was land now, I could feel how the world was not rolling anymore. And I was in a hut made of wood. It was not the kind of hut that my people made. I asked if I was dead. Then a ghost came, an old lady ghost. She said something to me. I was afraid. The old lady was the color of death. I asked, am I dead? The old lady spoke to me in the language of death. And yet I was not among those.

A woman came. She said in the language of the living that I belonged to a new world and that my name was Sila. You see, my mother is the one who gave me my name.

Was she my mother?

I was a girl.

Was that my sister? Was that my brother?

I was a child among children who had eyes like mine. And she too had those eyes, that woman. Was she my mother? She said, you must call me Ma.

That old woman spoke in the language of the demon dead and she answered.

For a time I too spoke two languages. Now I have one.

And that old woman was the first *Miesies*. Missus Neethling. And her husband was the minister who lost everything. That is where I was with Loedewyk. And Adam and Annetjie. And they were brothers and sister to me.

They were your first brothers and sister. No. No. I make a mistake. They were *my* brothers and sister and it was through them and the first woman I called Ma on this side of the darkness, that I learned how to obey these people and speak their language. And the first thing I learned about that language is that you do not speak first. Now that language is everywhere, but there was a time when other languages could be heard.

So. To survive, Ma said, we had to lock some things away so that the demon dead would not leak into all things. That was her first mistake, but it has taken me a long time to know this. And I forgive her.

One must learn to forgive one's mother—as she had to learn to forgive hers. It is the business of children to forgive mothers.

The forgiveness of fathers is another matter.

Was she my mother? It was she who taught me, as a mother should, how to live in the world into which I was born. It was she who taught me the language of the world into which she too had been born.

Neethling drinking himself to death. The missus wailing and forgetting all her promises to Ma. Then *Oumiesies*, Hendrina Jansen, who had one son who took his father's name and was, this everyone said, like his father, but weaker.

I remember these things because, in this world of lies, the peace of forgetting is a lie too. It is better to remember, even though my longing to forget is as strong as my longing to remember.

Shheeeeagh! Your mother confuses even herself!

Come, sit a little to one side and share some of this day's late sun. Let us see what there is to see. Let us see ... that ... there ... And let us not call it sunset, or late light, or thinning light or shadow, or darkness.

Hoo! And bring me some laughter. Your mother has a need to bite into something and taste real laughter, for a change.

The Minister's wife has come with her skirts on the boil, a letter pressed between the pages of her black book. Look at how her tongue moves from side to side in her mouth as that ox Pedder speaks to her about the weather.

She has come to teach me that book of hers. She wants me to put my anger in my pocket. This stupid woman!

Where is my child!

She takes her letter out and reads it to me as if she is my friend. What is she thinking? Look at where her finger rests, on the page she calls Jobninethirteenfourteen. She says, this letter is from her mother who is old and good. Upright. Who let her go because their god's work called her.

> O remember that my life is wind and the wind fills the page
> and the messages that shall return no more no more no
>   more
> and there shall be no peace for generations to come
> and there shall be no peace and the good days shall be
>   cast down
> as it were and it will take generations
> generations I tell you
> before the graves open up and send their pardons
> to the hired hands and their children
> to the women who break rocks, and their children
> and their children will be as the stones

and they will shoot up before the sun
and green branches will fall
and the mouth that shakes itself free
will bite down and find how the years have dwindled,
how the days are swift, as if blown by a wind
that covers the earth, given now like wheat
into the hands of the wicked who do no good and eat
    without end.
I wash myself clean of you
I make my hands clean
I keep my hems down.
My skin is my libation poured over me and still these days
    fence me in
with the ocean, bones and sinews.
Break! Break!
All whose hope is cut off. The stones will cry out
and branches will fall writhing in wickedness and
    confusion.

This language is foul.

Missus Minister's lips move as she reads that letter and there are tears in her eyes. There is more in that paper than meets the eyes. Me, I have had enough of that speech that travels on paper.

Look. She weeps in the face of paper. Her lips move as if demons have taken hold of her. All that confusion on paper. The leaps and bounds, curls and curves, the dots and crosses. It is like a punishment. Let them have all that. I fill this mouth with another cargo and keep watch for a light that will come across the water and throw no shadow. And let this minister's wife fight her tears of longing, for her days are as long as mine.

So. Baro. Listen to me. I have a mind to treat this woman to a day of greater kindness. Give up that tugging at her clothes today.

There is the smell of thin air in her breath. So, keep away, boy. I am keeping my own distance. Let her be. There is a shadow at the corners of her mouth where the words of her yesterdays are seeping through, and in her eyes there are shadows for things that are no longer of this world.

Tsht! I am your mother and you will listen to me. Tomorrow is another day.

She is back. She said, god will strike you. I said, then let it be done. She said, devil! I said, devil? Bring my daughter back! The devil is not the one you are afraid of. She ran off. I said, good, keep running.

Come in here and speak to me like that.

Now her shadow is growing those horns she tells me her devil wears.

Devil like a bull.

I call her cow. Tonight her devil will ride her and she will give birth to creatures that will be taken up and raised for meat. And here I stand in this kitchen at this block.

Hand? Why do you shake so?

Let them come. Look at her pointing at me, complaining. Always, there is complaining. Sila this, Sila that. Since my shadow offends them even when I stand still, I will stand still. Look at the guard, running and cross.

Let them come! They think I am afraid. I will give them afraid. What can they do? Let them give me bread and water. I will give them bread and water. Clumsy *vuilgoed*. Think I do not know what goes on in their underwear? Think I do not know how they stick their snouts in their food? Think I do not know what goes on? Think I do not?

Just come and give me bread and water today.

Then keep me out of that kitchen. I said *keep me out of that kitchen* because I will give you bread and water!

Julle vokking mense maak my vokking siek!

That woman asks too many questions. She asks, Sila, do you forni-cate with the men on this island? I ask, why do you ask me such questions? I say, you must go and ask the men here. She says, you are a heathen. But her tongue moves fast over her lips?

While her husband prays with the men, she brings me here into the warden's house to read to me from her book. But she stands at the window and looks out. She says she loves her husband, it is a union joined by her god. She smiles and says how she loves him. I say nothing. What do I want to know this for? She looks at me. I can see it coming before she herself knows it. She puts her face close. Sila, do you have a special man here?

She stares at me. What would I do with those feelings? You have those feelings and you lose your body to them. What does this stu-pid woman think? Who does she think is on this island? These men did not even see my face, or Lys's, or Mina's. So why would I want to think of a special man when my body is being made strange to me? Lys will agree with me. This woman is a fool because she knows nothing. Do I want my body to become my enemy? Because that is all that can happen. What does she think? That these men even want us to feel something for them?

Missus Minister, you can think again. You take your fool self into whatever fool place you keep your fool thoughts and you can think again. So, get! You take your book of prayers and you get to your husband. Go and find out what it means to kneel before a man and then tell me what this praying of *yours* can mean to me.

Get! Get, I said!

Xh!

Seagulls pick today at the water's face, and the water's face dips away and will not be still and the fish leap and dive behind the seagulls' backs. You can hear their scales chink and clink they chink and clink like charms. And they are charms on a woman's bracelet. I am the woman and I have a mind to go where the fish go in that deep down there where seagulls are not welcome.

Baro, what do you think of your mother's song? Today I am pleased to put my own words to long use and my lips are pleased to push out and hold the door open for things that come from deep in the cave of my heart.

Hai! But is that you laughing so? What a boy you are, what a boy! Come, listen to another one and let us see if it too will bring such light to your eyes.

What if it is not that the seagulls pick at the water, but that they pick today to undo the world? And why would they pick-pick, pick-pick today?

Mina has a man. He is a prisoner called America. I see how it happened. Mina was very sick. The surgeon sent her to the hospital on the mainland. She was there a long time. I think twenty days. And America was sick too.

Give us food that does not make us sick!

Mina came back in the same boat as America. He walked her to huts. Since that day he comes and they sit outside on a bench he made from stone and driftwood. They talk to Lys, but not to me.

Mina says, you see, I have a man. What do you have?

And this is what Lys wants me to make a friend!

I ask Mina, what does America say about the guards who come knocking on our door for you?

Lys says, be happy for her.

What is wrong with me?

There was a man who came riding with one of *Oumiesies'* neighbors one day. When I saw his face I started to smile. He smiled too. And then we were laughing while he wiped the horses down and I hung the washing on the line.

It was in the afternoon and *Oumiesies* and her neighbors were inside. Spaasie and Roosje were in the kitchen. Everyone was busy doing something. Galant was running around, in and out of the kitchen with Sariel chasing him. I could hear Spaasie tell them to stop before *Oumiesies* came to see what the noise was. Arend was helping Petro tie a fence. I could see Anthony helping Isac with wood for the fireplace. Frederik was somewhere in the other shed and Mars was looking after the pigs.

I asked this man what his name was. He said they called him Camies in this country, but in his own country his name was Chirikuloma.

His face. Yes. Yes. I knew those marks. They made my heart beat.

There is a line that reaches down the middle of his forehead, down to the middle of his nose, under his nose, between the soft furrow that runs to the top of his lip, there, where a line of sweat is shining like moonlight. I know this line that goes down to a man's chin from the top of his forehead. And I know, too, the line that goes from ear to ear. And when he smiles I can see that his teeth are filed.

They brought you here as a man, I said. He said, yes. He said, my people are Makua, from Ruvuma. He asked me, do you know these?

I was like a child. I wanted to say yes.

We went to the barn. We went there. He sat down on the hay. I waited. I remember. He did not tell me to sit. He talked. He said things in a tongue that made me shiver and want to cry, but I did not. I was young, proud. And who was this man who thought I would go into a barn with him as soon as we met?

I asked him why he was talking this language to me. He looked at me and his eyes were old, too old for such a young face. He kept speaking in that language that made the backs of my knees feel a different breeze. My eyes were filled with pictures I did not want to see.

Speak to me in a language I know, I said. But he did not stop and so I sat with him, next to him on the hay, and he talked and talked.

I heard Spaasie call my name, but that name was from a time far away, on the other side of a river that was rushing through my ears and carrying me with it.

These are not things a mother tells a son.

He said . . . something in that language.

I was laughter and light.

He said something. I said. He said. I said. He said.

And then that was how it was. A river was rushing and we were two young people holding on to each other because we knew this river, we knew its sound and when it broke out of our bones where it had been lying for so long, we were happy and I was saying yes, yesyes, yesyesyesyes.

I know, this is not what a mother tells a son.

And when we came out of that barn we were washed clean and laughing.

And then *Oumiesies'* neighbor came and the man whose face I knew took up the reigns of the cart and clicked his tongue and was gone.

I thought about him for days. I dropped things and my work was slow. I polished and polished one spot on the big kettle for too long for Roosje, who took it away and told me to sweep the floor instead. Johannes knew. I know he knew.

About one week after Chirikuloma had come, *Oumiesies* decided to visit her neighbor. Johannes told her it would be good for her to take me with her for company.

This was a big day. It was in September of eighteen and oh one. It was a good day. You must know that I had not gone off *Oumiesies'* farm since I arrived there as a child. Can you imagine what that was like? For so long I had seen the sky of the world that was beyond *Oumiesies'* land. I saw her come and go, I saw Theron come and go, and all the people who came to visit *Oumiesies*. I saw *Oumiesies* set off for the town with Isac in one carriage, and Johannes leading the wagon. Sometimes Spaasie went with them. She told me things, about the big market on the Parade. I saw them go and return with the wagon groaning with things bought new in the town. Now it was my turn to set off. It did not matter that it was only to the next farm. I was going off like a lady. I washed my dress. *Oumiesies* said I had to wear a new *doek* and a new apron. So, Roosje and I sat up all night before and when I waved goodbye the next day I was newly pressed and my skin shone from a good rubbing.

And, ja, there he was when we arrived at the neighbor's farm.

How young I was. Until I saw him again I had not thought of anything but meeting him again. I had not thought of what he might think or want. When I saw him and his eyes widened and his face opened as if he had received a gift, *then*, then, I was afraid. Now, what do you think of that? Was your mother silly?

Oumiesies sent me to the kitchen. Johannes and Chirikuloma took me there. There was only one woman there. Johannes was kind and talked to this woman while Chirikuloma and I sat near each other, too scared to touch but laughing and smiling. Then a young woman came in. I looked at her and felt a stone fall in my stomach. She was carrying a child. She was pretty. I thought, is this Chirikuloma's child?

This is what I do not like about the business of women and men. After only one day in the company of this man, I was jealous and afraid. And why? It is to do with the way the world sets itself around men. Are men like the moon, and women like the stars? That is not good enough for me. But I was young then, and thirsty for that river. And jealous. My jealousy was a bigger thirst.

I asked the young woman how soon before her baby would arrive. She said it was not long. The other woman asked me if I had children. I said, no. She said nothing. I could see what she was thinking. I wanted to tell her to mind her own business, but she was not bad. She looked at the young woman who turned away. It was only small, what I saw, but enough. The child was not Chirikuloma's.

There was a sad story here. And I remembered that this farm had a *mandoor* who once tried to grab Amerant, who hit him with the lid of the big pot. I was so ready for that other thirst, the thirst of jealousy, that I had forgotten about the *mandoor*. That was a lesson for me. I knew that, even then. And I was ashamed. This business between men and women is not something I understand. What makes that jealousy is the same thing that makes up stories that are not true. But, back then, in that kitchen, all I knew was that I was happy to know that a man I had seen once was not the father of another pretty woman's child.

So. That was how our second visit was. Just talk in the kitchen, and smiling. Then home again with *Oumiesies* and all I could think was how I would see that man again.

Then, one night as I was closing the door of *Oumiesies'* kitchen, Johannes came and said, Sila, there is someone waiting for you in the shed, behind the wagon.

And there he was. And so that was how we saw each other for a long time, by the stars. He kept talking and talking and for a long time I was happy to hear him. There is much to be said for not understanding a word a man says. I did not have to listen except from outside of the words and so, inside, my breathing was like butter. So, I listened to him talk and talk in that language, and my body went into that river and floated across to a bank it knew. But, after many nights, I began to feel the weight of his head and, one night, the sharpness of his teeth was too sharp. The next night the hay pricked against my back and the river was splashing away from me. Each time after that I tried to make him speak in a language I understood.

Then, one night, I sat on the wagon and would not get down. He climbed up, talking, talking. I said, you talk in a language I understand or I go back to the hut. He stopped talking. I said, I am not a sack you can sleep on, so that you can dream about another place. He said nothing and then he climbed down and left.

So, I said to myself, so much for a face I knew.

But he came back after a while. And he sat down and we spoke together at last. It was not easy for him, but he told me how he came to this country. He was a young man sent from his village with two friends to Inhambe to find a trader who owed their chief a lot of grain. You see, all the villages around his had been raided. It was only because his chief had built a big wall and had trained men to be good guards that his village had been spared. This was why the chief wanted the grain. It would help the village close its gates and keep slavers out. No one would starve inside the high stone walls.

Well, Chirikuloma and his friends found the trader, a *prazero*, who had moved to the big city for a new business. This man made Chirikuloma and his friends guests in his house and brought others to meet them. These people asked many questions about their village. The *prazero* said he remembered it as a fine village. Chirikuloma and his friends were quick to say yes, it was fine. They wanted to impress these people. The *prazero* was bragging with them. He said he had been a good friend of the chief's, but there had been a misunderstanding and these young men, Chirikuloma and his friends, had come to remind him of the friendship he had almost lost. He talked about places near Chirikuloma's village, the land, the people, but always asking the young men to correct him if he was mistaken. He said he had helped the chief build up the walls to protect the village, but that was many years before Chirikuloma would have been old enough to know him. Chirikuloma did not want to offend his host, so he pretended that he did remember this man. The *prazero* said he had told the chief what the best places were to put guards and, as he named places, the young men corrected him. He said, oh, that is much better, much better, I can see that your chief is wiser than me. He asked, is there still a guard here, there. The young men answered, eager to correct his memory further still. He thanked them and they all drank beer and fell asleep.

In the morning, the *prazero* promised to pay the grain, and to take it back himself if they would travel with him. Chirikuloma and his friends were happy and proud. They set off with the *prazero*, who brought horses and a big covered wagon that he said had all the grain he owed, with some extra as an apology. There were other men. Chirikuloma was happy. After only a few days in the big city, he and his friends had done as their chief asked and they were now traveling back with even more than expected.

But, after a little while on the journey back home, Chirikuloma's friends said they did not like the men that the *prazero* was bringing with him. Chirikuloma laughed and told them they did not have to like these people. All he could think of was his father's pride when he returned with this impressive wagon train.

Just before his village, the *prazero* told everyone to make camp. Chirikuloma asked why. The *prazero* said one of his men had learned that there were slave raiders nearby and he had sent scouts to make sure all were safe. Chirikuloma's heart went cold.

The *prazero* asked how to tell the difference between their own guards and any raiders. That way, he said, he could tell if their village was safe or if it had fallen. One of Chirikuloma's friends said the raiders burn villages, that is how you will know if our village has been raided or not. The *prazero* laughed and apologized. He said he did not know about such things and it was therefore good to have three such loyal and brave young men to help him.

Chirikuloma's friends were not happy. They did not trust the *prazero* anymore. They wanted to slip away at night, but Chirikuloma would not listen. He pointed to the wagon with all the grain. Why would the *prazero* bring all of this if he was as evil as they said? They shook their heads. It was a trick. One of the young men said he had tried to look under the cover to see the sacks of grain, but one of the *prazero*'s friends had pushed him away. It was a trick, there was no grain in the sacks. Chirikuloma took a knife and walked to the wagon. He lifted the cover and made a small cut in a sack. Look, he showed them the grain that spilled into his hand.

That night, they slept in the *prazero*'s camp. When they woke up, the *prazero* was gone but one of his men, the ugliest and the rudest, was standing over them. Chirikuloma tried to sit up. The man hit him with the butt of his rifle and he fell back. All the world disappeared. When he woke, he and his friends were in chains. The chains were at their necks and at their waists. They were under a tree. His friends were groaning and crying.

He did not want to believe what was happening. He said, the *prazero* will be back soon. It will all be put right. But he heard a terrible sound in the distance. It was the sound of guns. And soon he could see black smoke coming from where his village lay. His friends had been telling the truth and he had been too proud to listen. Now many were paying the price of his pride.

It was a terrible story, Baro. It made him cry to tell it. And then he did not talk again and I sat there with him until the rooster called. I told him, Chirikuloma, it is time to go. But he would not move. He would not speak. He was like a stone. I thought, this man is dead. But he was breathing.

Then I heard Isac and Anthony. I called them. They could not move him. They went for Johannes. Then Spaasie. Soon it was time to work, and still Chirikuloma sat. We closed the shed door. During the morning we went, one by one, to take him water, bread, soup. He touched nothing. At midday, Johannes called us together. He said something must be done before the search went out. He said this would bring trouble and Theron would be able to shout at *Oumiesies* again. Johannes said we must make a plan. He had to go to the town to deliver pigs to the merchant in time for market. But that was days away. What we had to do was find a way to let *Oumiesies* send him the very next day. Isac said he would find a way to tell *Oumiesies* it was time to send the pigs. Spaasie said, yes, Theron and his family were coming for *Oumiesies*' birthday. She would say they need more things if they are to feed everyone, but she would ask carefully. So, the plan was made. Isac would ask *Oumiesies* about the pigs when she was counting in her book. He would wait until Spaasie brought the afternoon tea for *Oumiesies* and then he would ask her, in front of *Oumiesies*, if Johannes had left for the town already. If *Oumiesies* asked what he was talking about, he would say Johannes had to take the pigs to town first thing in the morning. If she said he was mistaken, he would say, no, no, *Oumiesies*, the pigs must be there by the next day. If she asked why he did not tell her sooner, Isac would say he had. And Spaasie would say she heard him. And if Roosje was nearby she would say, yes, she also heard Isac say when the pigs had to go. Then, before *Oumiesies* could get cross or make her way back to the truth, Spaasie would say, excuse me, *Oumiesies*, but if *Oumiesies* is sending Johannes, perhaps *Oumiesies* would save a later trip for supplies if we could make a list now, there are things to be bought for *Oumiesies'* birthday.

We waited. We were afraid that the neighbor's *mandoor* would come with news of Chirikuloma's absence. I was so nervous that Spaasie kept me out of *Oumiesies'* way. So, I went to see Chirikuloma many times and each time I tried to make him speak or move.

Late that afternoon, Spaasie came running with Isac. Fetch Johannes, she said. *Oumiesies* had decided that the pigs would go first thing in the morning and that she would ride to visit the merchant herself. And she wanted me and Isac to ride with her.

It made me sick. Spaasie told me, stand up, walk straight, get your things ready.

We went the next morning when the sun was only thin on the land. Me and Isac in the carriage with *Oumiesies*. Johannes drove the carriage and Philip took the supply cart that had the pigs in it.

Now, the driver's seat on the wagon was also a big box. Johannes had made it a long time ago to keep *Oumiesies'* goods dry. Chirikuloma did not even make a sound when we picked him up and laid him in that box. I felt for him, that man who made a river flow out of his mouth. I told him, listen, if you can hear me, listen to what I am saying. We are taking you to a place where you can run away.

We rode for a long time without stopping because *Oumiesies* wanted to make good time. That old woman liked the money she got for pigs. It was hard sitting in that carriage with her when Chirikuloma was wrapped up like a piece of bread in the box seat under Johannes. *Oumiesies* wanted to talk. She talked about her sister and how she missed her, how there was no one but us now. She talked about her son, that Theron.

And, then, we were coming up from the back of Table Mountain. Johannes said, *Oumiesies*, the horses are tired. We must stop for a time, let them rest, and we will make a fire and Sila will make tea, *lekker soet tee.*

Haish! Oumiesies liked her tea. I made it strong and sweet, and she drank it with a piece of bread and quince *konfyt* that Spaasie had put in a basket. Then, even though the day was getting late, Isac put a pillow behind *Oumiesies'* head and said, *Oumiesies*, just a little sleep, so that you can be fresh when we arrive in town.

And that is how we took Chirikuloma out of the box, stood him up, and pointed him toward the water. I gave him a bundle of food. There was a shirt from Anthony and a knife from Petro, who had made it from a piece of iron and wood shaped into a handle.

I said his name, but he did not say mine. Johannes said, you must be quick, you go or stay. That way, that way, Johannes pointed. It was north, by the water's edge. We all knew what that was. Nothing.

What could we do?

I want to say he looked at me and said something nice for me to hold on to in my old age. He said nothing. He stood there for too long, and then he sighed like a wagon creaking just before it moves. And he began walking.

Johannes said to me, be strong, girl. You must not cry or *Oumiesies* will ask too many questions. But I put my apron over my head and I cried for a man I would never see again, but whose head was already too heavy on my shoulder.

The world! *Hai!* The world is bigger than anyone can imagine. Listen, I just heard Van Graaf, one of Pedder's favorite men, tell another prisoner about his home. He is from a place where the mountains are higher than even Hottentots Holland.

Soldaat stood with his head to one side, but I saw his eyes grow bright. Another man asked, are you sure the mountains are higher than Hottentots Holland? Yes, said Van Graaf, the mountains on the other side of the world are taller.

Van Graaf has been given the task of teaching us how to read the minister's book. He does not come near us women the way the others do. He is a holy man. It upsets him when the others come through our door. It was he who told Pedder how the men broke our door. But, he told late. And he may be holy, but he did not tell Pedder that he had put his fists in his ears for many nights.

Still, he is one. They are many. And when Pedder is asleep in his own bed Van Graaf must still find a way to be amongst them. So. He had to wait. And now he has a hut to himself and he is to be our teacher, to help the minister until someone else can come.

He says he was born where the mountains are so high there is always snow. And he says that even the English travel to these mountains to wonder at them. Imagine that! Even the English do not have mountains like this.

Baro, the world is a place filled with things that are wonders.

He says the mountains are high and sharp.

How high, the other prisoner asks?

High, higher that those. You can almost touch the stars at night.

You lie.

But I do not think he does.

I want to ask him what people are like in those mountains.

He says there are countries on the other side of his mountain. Here, there is only more of the same on the other side of the Blouberge. And on the other side of Table Mountain, and Devil's Peak, and Signal Hill. When the gun goes off on Signal Hill, I know it is to tell us it is noon, even right out here on the water, but I also think the gun is to say, *hey! This is where things stop.* If I did not know better, I would say the sound of that gun must reach far inland, like an eye that can see.

A running woman could think the noonday gun has a big eye that can see her deep inland. But, can a running woman see what is deep in the mainland without going there first, so that she may plan which way she must travel?

Mina has already tried. She ran with some other women, but they could not see where they were going. Now, everything is no for her. She is like Jeptha.

Haish. All this talk of running makes me think of that man who could not jump high enough to please Van der Wat. Do you remember Jeptha, from back there in Plettenberg Bay, on Stoffpad farm? Jeptha. On Van der Wat's farm.

Tchaa! That man. The one time he tried to see more than the world he was told to see, all he could do was curl up somewhere to wait for them to catch him. If he could see where to go, he could have run until there was no more land to run on. But, no, that man saw nothing but the tip of his nose and what they told him to see. That is why he could tell lies without worrying about anyone else but himself. Jeptha. That man lied, Baro. He lied about me. It was after I got you away from Van der Wat. Jeptha came back and when they told him to say I was a drunken woman who told lies about a good master and mistress, he opened his parrot mouth and out came a big squawking pack of lies.

If I could have taken you and your brother Pieter, I would have run with you both. Imagine, running to a place where the mountains are higher than that flat old thing over there. What it must be! To go to those mountains where the sky's floor is so close.

I have been staring at the air above the Blouberge to see if there are any feet moving about as they say the minister's good people walk around in heaven. Some days, like now, I want it to be true. Otherwise I know a story when I hear one.

But Van Graaf, our teacher, I know he is telling the truth. His words throw clean shadows. Those mountains *are* high and they *are* always covered in snow right at the top as he says. And in the spring there are beautiful flowers. Think of it.

December again. How did that happen? How did this year become a mouse that slips under a door before you can catch it?

Spaasie sent another message and this time it came with gifts of gooseberries, a jar of quince *konfyt*, and some bread. The guards wanted to take it, but one of the men would not let them, so I gave him a piece, but we women and Catherina and Debora ate the rest.

Van Graaf read Spaasie's message to me. He said, you are lucky to have someone who cares for you.

Yes, she is a good friend. Spaasie sent word to say that Meisie is with a priest going deep inland. Spaasie went to the priest to visit with Meisie. She told Meisie that I will come to find her and that she must not forget me.

How is that now? My daughter ends up with a priest going inland. This news makes my heart twist as if it has been caught up in one of the guard's fishing lines. But, Lys says, at least I know where my girl is and this is true.

And here is what Spaasie also says. Van der Wat knows nothing of Meisie. How is this? He saw, all the way from that farm at Stoffpad in Plettenberg Bay, that Catherina and Debora were born. But Spaasie says he never registered Meisie, unless she is under some other name.

Am I cheating them at their own game?

Hooo! Give me some space because I need to dance today.

Lys said if I was a man I would be *Kaggen*. That is the one who plays all tricks on everyone and if he gets into trouble he grows stiff wings and a long green body, and a head the shape of a sheep's heart, but green too and big. Ja. That is me. *Kaggen.*

Deel said, no, not *Kaggen* because I cannot be a man. She said I am anteater woman because I make the rules. But I am not so sure about this. Anteater? Not me.

But Meisie is not with Van der Wat.

A priest. *Yaish!* My head spins even though Lys says, be still Sila, it is good.

But I am a bad woman, Baro, because I have a small snake in my heart when I think that Mina is happy because Flora is close by with Missus Minister and so can come and visit her. Well. That is good for Flora, but Missus Minister wanted Meisie to stay with her and I said no, and now Meisie is far away and Flora is near. Was I wrong? Is my girl paying for my pride? Did Missus Minister send Meisie with that priest because she is paying me back for all the rudeness and for not telling her all the things she wants to hear?

Spaasie said that Meisie wore a nice new dress and will learn how to read. How about that now?

What will she read? My daughter will fall into that black book and when she looks back at me she will have the look of black leather and thin, white paper words in her eyes. And when she speaks to me it will be the sound of fingers turning thin white paper.

Lys said, be still Sila, Meisie is your daughter. She knows how to keep her eye on tomorrow.

Well. I am not sure about that. It is one thing for me to look over today and watch the horizon for the tomorrow of freedom. It is another thing for Meisie to do this.

She will be baptized and have that water on her.

Lys says, water is water.

I want Lys to sleep one of her sleeps and go see where Meisie is being taken.

Spaasie will watch out for her. And if I want to send a message I just send it to Spaasie at a new place. The English have left Rondebosch and gone back to their land and so she and Sariel are now with a man named Kruger. The English gave her a present of money. That is how she sent us presents of gooseberries, quince *konfyt*, and bread.

I asked Van Graaf to write for me.

I said, *Geliefde Spaasie*, how good a friend you are to me. Your news reaches my heart in this place where things are so bad that Meisie was taken from me. I am not a bad mother, you know this because you know the things I will do to save a child of mine from pain. Perhaps I must give Catherina up too, or see her get the look in her eyes that my new baby Debora has.

Van Graaf said, stop, stop, you go too fast. Speak slowly. He said, you must sound nice when you put your words on paper. I said I speak just as I always do with her. He said, well, then, it will just be nonsense. I said, but what happens on paper to make nonsense? If I speak, I speak. He shook his head but said, tell me what to write.

I said it again. And I said, yes, Spaasie, a new baby. I have had two children on this place. If anything happens to me, fetch Catherina and Debora. Never in all those years at *Oumiesies*' did I think this is where I would be, and with children. How is it there with Kruger? Does he treat you well? Have you worked your price off for your freedom as *Oumiesies* wanted for all of us. Theron lied to me and now my child is going deep into the mainland, but you have brought me news of her and you are a good friend because I can think of her now where she is going. What news of your boys and what news of anyone else we knew there on *Oumiesies*' farm?

Van Graaf said, you must say something nice now, to finish the letter.

Your friend, Sila.

Dit bid u voor altoos u geliefde vriendijn, Sila

I did not say as Van Graaf wanted me to say, things about his god.

Ik vaart wel dat god in zyn dogely zoon ons geseegende verlosser en de hylige geest u alle geliefde bewaarden bescherme en seigenen in myne ziel ontfange in syne hemelsche genade, nog eense vaart wel vaar euwig wel, myn geliefde vriendijn.

That is not how I speak. Spaasie would know. It would be like sending her lies.

Spaasie was always fierce about lies, except when it was better than telling the truth. That was a different business, telling *Oumiesies* or Theron what needed to be told. Otherwise, Spaasie did not like lies. We have been put in a prison of lies, she said.

You know this, boy.

When they brought me to Cape Town to be punished for sending you away from Van der Wat, the justice read out all the things that the *landdrost* of the district had taken down, even the lies that Jeptha told. When Spaasie heard what he had said about me she was cross. She said, no, Sila never touched drink.

Jeptha.

You see, Baro, when I sent you away and they took me to the *landdrost*, Van der Riet, I asked Jeptha for help. I asked him, Jeptha, have we not been punished here, beaten? I said, you have seen how badly Van der Wat beat my boy. Tell the court of justice what it is like at Van der Wat's. He told lies instead.

And then I knew. I told myself, say nothing because nothing you say will mean anything. If only I could tell you how well I made a closed gate of my speech.

It was . . . Well. This is not easy. But. It was like this. They asked me to speak for myself, me who was so offensive to them. They wanted to come inside my heart. It was not an entry I could permit. I searched for words, but what came was a new knowledge. For one moment I thought, I, Sila van den Kaap, slave, as they called me, I could keep them from coming inside my heart if I could find words that would make them stop. I thought, oh, that it could be in wonder that they would listen to me if I had words that they understood. But, no, Baro, your mother is not a fool. There is no language to make them ashamed. Nothing I have to say could be beautiful. Not after things done. Not for me. Not for them. I and they were offended by my presence, though I—more than they—know how to love.

This thing we learn, this love, has a mouth that asks and asks for the impossible.

Is it true that . . . ?

The first thing I was told when we got to Van der Wat's farm was to keep my mouth shut. But what could I do? The next time Mokke came through, I talked with his driver and asked him to send word to Spaasie. But he told Mokke and Mokke told Van der Wat.

The next week Carolina and Camies were gone.

Did the *landdrost* want to hear any of this? Truly, I wanted to tell him about Theron, the deal that Hancke made with Maria Martha Cruywagen. But I could not make one sound he or the others would understand.

They told me to speak. Their waiting was a silence filled with noise.

Van der Wat knew how to break silence but he could not do his usual beating. Van der Wat was on his best behavior for the *landdrost*. What a sight. I smelt the sweat of his armpits. You should have seen him. He kept his arms pressed tight against his sides and the sweat was flowing down his cheeks, down his neck, and into his collar. He was so busy being a *meneer*. His shoulders were stiff, his arms were pressed tighter to his sides.

The *landdrost* said, is it true that on the twenty-fourth of December last . . .

Hai. What could I say that would be answer enough for us all? Baro, that day your mother was a stupid slave, too stupid to make two words together.

What could I say that my eyes were not already saying.

I told myself, no tears. My eyes spoke another language.

I told myself, no shaking. My hands did not understand.

I told myself, stand straight. My stomach folded in and my back was an old woman's.

I told myself, Sila you must let them know what it means to be Sila registered to Van der Wat. But my throat was too tight to fit words.

They looked away and would not try and hear the words that would have made them listen. Van der Wat's lips were like a fat worm curling and curling around itself.

Jeptha could have helped me.

Jeptha! Wherever you are, you will wish you are dead. You made their ears deaf.

I asked you to tell the truth. You told lies when my heart was breaking like that honey jar Pieter broke one day. Jeptha, I tell you, and this you will never understand because you have never understood much more than day and night, I tell you and you must listen, I tell you it was a relief and I would do it again, take each stripe on my own back, make it my accident.

It was alright, then, to answer for something I had not done. A mother knows when a lie is necessary to protect the truth. Spaasie understands this. But, them? *Yaish.* It is not as if these people do not lie themselves. But, no, it is one law for them, another for us. For them lies are truth, truth lies. And therefore I could not say as they wanted me to say.

That I had taken my boy.

Cruelly?

Or even that I had loved him and held him in my lap when he at last cried himself to sleep. I could not say that the hand that stole the knife shook, or that I had lifted my dear boy into my lap and held him, and stroked him and known that he was already beyond all of them, even me. And that there was no hope, already, long before I stroked my boy's throat, that he would not sleep in the ground for three days and rise again to tell me that I had made him greater than all of them. No. I could say nothing of the way that love had required that I crush all horror even as I faced it.

I looked at them. They looked at me and looked away. *Speak,* they said.

To say what? What is it you have in your minds when you ask me to make the picture?

Speak, Sila van den Kaap. You have committed a heinous crime.

Yes. Yes. That is its name in this room.

Before God, you must speak.

I looked at them. I prepared my body. I looked at them and I was out of the room where I had put my mind.

Do you refuse?

Jeptha, there was a veil over the days after I picked Baro up onto my lap. I did not tell them how I thought, Baro, you are such a long boy. I did not tell them how I thought, Baro you are too big to be cradled. I held him and I could see how his legs and arms were hanging and I thought, Sila, is it over already. I had hoped for something else. There was such a light, such a light falling into the hut even though I had barred the door.

They wanted me to go behind there. They were sending me as if I was slave to them all. They were sending me to bring for them what they had not seen. Even their shadows leaned forward.

They press me. I keep my mouth tight. I have pressed where a mother should not have pressed. I have pressed as a mother should not. And what flows cannot be stopped.

And still my hand pressing on. Thinking. Not being able to think. Cutting my own mind and heart in two, quickly. Quickly!

They wanted to know about that last moment my boy was of this earth. But not if he suffered.

They said, let it be noted that, in her insolence, the accused refused to answer a further question.

See what is happening now? I cannot stop. For days it has been like this.

Looking, looking. Those men want to know what makes a woman like me.

Bring me a woman who has children! Bring me a girl who is afraid of what is between her legs and I will show you a girl who has been taught to be afraid of being a girl, a woman who is afraid of being a woman, a woman who is afraid of bringing girls into this world and who sees how boys grow up.

The field cornet, the field hand Karel, the surgeon all stand at the bush next to the river. They look and look. Even when they speak there is looking and sometimes, especially with Van der Wat, in those stones for eyes, speaking is a way of making a fence with words because looking is one thing, seeing what you fear to see is another, and seeing what you know is even another thing still.

They look.

The field cornet looks there, he looks at me. He says with words that are like a bad breath, *Meid, wat . . .wat het jy gedoen?*

He covers his mouth, his eyes. He rubs his hair. He turns, spins, stops.

The sun jumps off the river like silver frogs.

Is that my body trembling?

The field cornet is standing against a tree. The truth is there, but it is not what he believes. No. No. What has been done is not what he sees. What he sees is what he puts into words for the *landdrost*, like feet into shoes because the ground has thorns. But he can say it all in polite words—is it true?

I told him, *hertseer*. It is like wind blowing against a closed door. *Pffmph*. I told him on that day. I tell them what must be told and the truth is like a leaf in a big wind.

Is it true, that on the twenty-fourth day of December eighteen and twenty three, you took your son, Baro . . .

Leaves fall.

Ask me how it was to run all the way from the river, then all along the Stoffpad to Wittedrift while the sun was high and the trees stood still in a day without wind. Ask me about the smell of leaves thick on the ground and rotting.

And why do such things have the scent of a lady's perfume?

Ask me why I ran to the field cornet. Do travelers not speak of Van Huisteen as a kind man? So, ask me why that field cornet was angry when I came to his door. Ask me why Karel was scared and sad and why he was gentle when my knees sagged and my skirt was a truth that took us all there to that place.

Better still, ask me why I did not give myself freedom from them all, from going back into the world where demons walk the ground on heels and buckles. That is an answer I need, because it escapes me and I need to know why I did not leave this world of demons and their heels and buckles and their trousers that collect at their ankles.

Shh. My knees sag and my skirt, my red, red skirt, spills and Karel saw what my skirt was showing him and he was more than just that man who was from one day to the next a servant to a life he could not understand.

And I was soft and broken, hard and broken. And my skirt was like the page from the minister's book.

Baro? Baro?

. . . . . . ?

Lys, my friend, leave the quarry and come. The minister's wife is after me again. She sent for me to go to the hut where she and the minister have to lie in their dry bed because the crossing back to the mainland has been too rough these past days.

She asks me, boldly, about Baro. She asks me, have I no guilt?

She asks why Catherina was crying today. She says I must give her to another minister who wants to go to take his god's message inland. She says he will build a town of people he and other ministers have saved and then I can go there when I leave this island. When I say nothing, she says, you are proud and pride goeth before a fall.

Does she think she is the first?

I fall right back into that court of justice, when they were asking questions about Baro. I am there with those men looking at me, wanting to know what makes a woman like me. They want to know, but fill their mouths and ears with roughness.

They gave me very own *advocaat*. Why? Because the English do not like the farmers. Johannes was right about that. That is why Van Ryneveld had to be my *advocaat*. Fancy that, the fiscal had to be the *advocaat* of a slave woman. He is not a bad man. He looks into those books of his and measures the world by what he finds in there. The law said I was bad, but Van Ryneveld was cross with Van der Wat. He said Van der Wat was wrong to make the English think the Dutch are bad.

I heard him say this to the warden at the Cape Town *tronk* when they brought me there from Plettenberg Bay. Van Ryneveld said, we are a country with laws and we are a lawful people and Van der Wat is one of those people who want their own laws.

You see, even a good man could not hear me for all the wind blowing in his own trees.

Whereas it has evidently appeared to the court of Justice . . .

I hear them. They say my name. My name is *prisoner.*

What?

I was heartsore.

What?

I was heartsore.

Jeptha!

He would not tell the truth. He alone could have saved me. He alone.

Van Ryneveld, wake up! Or I will send you aches and pains in your joints and you will have to write in the corner of a page in your almanac, from the third to the seventh I was laid up with rheumatism. Wake up! Listen to what they are saying! They are saying I am a drunk! They are saying I . . .

Van Ryneveld! That man was always writing in his almanac. Even when he was trying to help me, he could not keep his mind off the weather. Perhaps his bones hurt in bad weather. Perhaps he was looking for signs of his god or just wanted to plant good crops.

Verschrikkelynke storm wind uit het N.W.

That is no wind! It is Jeptha blowing lies from his nostrils.

Storm wind geduurende de nacht, wind en regen's morgents. Zur koud.

The cold is the cold that lies in the heart of a man's lies. Someone pays the price of lies. The storm blows in the night but it is a darkness in the making. Van Ryneveld, your joints will not cease aching until you look into Jeptha's eyes and see that shadow of Van der Wat's whip swinging from left to right in them.

And if I had spoken differently . . . ? No. Not a word would have made sense to them. I thought Van Ryneveld would help. But there he is with his almanac and here I am.

Bring me lemons.

They asked me questions. The prosecutor asked, why did you send my boy out?

For lemons.

For citrons, the prosecutor said to the man scribbling away so fast it sounded like that scratch, scratch, scratch of nails against dry, white skin.

Toe seg ek ook, ja, citrons.

But he does not ask me why, or what I wanted them for. I sent my boy on an errand.

Nou, Ja, goed. Ag, Baro, bring vir jou ma suur lemoene.

The prosecutor looks at the wall behind me. And is it true that when you sent him for lemons he came back, complaining of pain caused by a beating from Van der Wat?

They move their lips so fast! Their lips are like the mouths of fish high and dry in the air. They move their mouths and I am the one dying.

Ag, Baro, fetch some lemons for your mother, some lovely sour lemoene.

They point their lips at me.

Laugh now, my boy. I make you a nice lemon drink with water and sugar I have put into my hems. Sweet and sour, like our laughter when they point their lips at me.

I can feel the world that goes on out there. This feeling is like smelling something late on a summer evening, just before you fall asleep, or just as you turn your head to hear what someone has said. You do not hear what is said because that scent speaks like a voice.

Some days, that feeling of what is out there in all directions is a taste. There are things that fill my mouth with yesterdays and even tomorrows and then nothing can keep my mind on the today of what must be done. Then, *bomp*! There goes the bucket of water. *Bomp!* I have spilled ink and have to hurry to wipe it up before the warden sees. And there goes the warden's decanter, and while I am grabbing to save his favorite wine, my tongue is telling me tales of tastes that make my head spin like a drunk's.

But I have no taste for wine or *arak* or beer. Jeptha said I was a drunk. I will find him and make him choke on his words. I am not a drinking woman. I have seen drunks. I have been visited by drunks. The lesson I learned a long time ago was to stay awake. Being drunk is like trying to slip away from the world. It never works. The world is still there when all the drinking finishes. So, no drinking. I keep my eye on the world.

It is about looking. That is what matters. The small things that make up the way a day is remembered are not only to be found in what a person says or does. A piece of bread. A bit of red dust blowing in through the door. The sound of a pot being put on a stove. I remember that sound. When I was first taken into *Oumiesies'* kitchen,

Alima was there and she heated soup for me after my long journey
from the Neethlings' farm.

I want you to listen to me. There was a time when you were not
of this world or any other. I put you there so that, at the right time,
you would take a breath that would change the air for you. You see?
You remember?

No. Do not be afraid. Be still, still. Listen. In that place, you heard
nothing, you smelled nothing and there was no taste but the sharp,
high, thin taste of a life I had no choice but to give you. You remember why? Do not be afraid. Hold my wicked hand, it loves you. It
has always loved you. I knew there would be a time when you would
breathe that breath. And it was that taste calling you back. And I
have wanted nothing but that you look at a world that is unlike the
world I threw away for you. You remember?

Come. Be still. For now, be still. There will always be the wind to
play with. For now . . . Well. Then. Go. Going and coming is a kind
of freedom. So. Go. Sweet bad boy.

Why are your sisters so quiet?

What? March is over?

Catherina found a blue shell on the beach. I told her to hide it
before one of Pedder's men see it. Pedder would even take a shell
from a child if he could get money for it.

[✖] [✖]

There is a man who puts the world onto paper. He asks his family for paper and paint. They send him a pencil sometimes. And sometimes paper. Then he asks me for eggshells from the warden's kitchen and grinds them with water, a bit of grease, sand. Sometimes I steal some ink for him. He is not one of the men who pushes the door in.

I tell myself it is only pencil or sand mixed with eggshell and ink and water and grease. But what I see is a world I know. There are the trees, the penguins, the cat that comes into our hut after a rat, the guards' huts, our huts, the warden's house. Even without colors. These things could cut me loose from myself. My head is like one of *Oumiesies'* vases. I am back there, putting flowers in it as she likes me to and it is as if I have only just learned how, but not well enough because . . . there it goes! Over!

Take my hand, I am walking us into things that you perhaps know better than me.

Baro! Your mother is happy today.

Is this happy? I am not sure.

Is that honey in the air? Can you taste it? I have been leaning all day toward clean water and honey.

I dreamed of a thin blue line in a world that was the color of sand that was the color of oranges left too long in a dry place. And I ate the oranges. They were hard and then they were softer and softer . . .

[X] [X]

Baro, Baro-Baro, beautiful boy. Tell me what you have been doing today? Tell me if you found the hole in the rocks where the sea has made a gate? The spirits of those who die here pass through it. And did you see those ancestors standing, like a welcoming party?

I have a longing to see my own mother today. I have things to tell her and things to ask. I need advice.

Rain so soft, you could forget that April means winter is around the corner. Now, in Cape Town, all the red dust has washed off of everything. And that is also how it is in Plettenberg Bay. From now on, mornings will become tighter and tighter.

I hope the warden remembered jackets for Catherina and a new blanket for Debora.

Mina is happy. She is baptized at last. The minister came in a boat in spite of the big winds. Perhaps he was drunk, perhaps it was all that salt water in his face, but he decided today was a day to baptize. So, there was Mina, first in line. Deel was next because she wants to be like Mina. Lys and Rachel did it too, just to drive Truter mad.

The minister wanted to put water on my forehead. He said, bless you, my child. I am nobody's child. I said, ask your god where is my freedom. He said, your freedom is in god. *Nou, Ja. Wat maak jy van dit?*

Missus Minister stayed away.

Out there, you see the sharks. They stitch the sea together. Baro, the sharks are the tailors of the world. They stitch the sea together to make a place for the land.

Nooi, nooi, die riet kooi nooi,
Die riet kooi is gemaak,
Die riet kooi is vir jou gemaak
Om daar op te slaap

I sang so nicely those days, long before *Oumiesies* died. She liked me. She said to me, Sila, you have a gift from God and you must use it. I said to her . . .

No, the truth, because we always speak the truth to each other, *liefde seun.* I wanted to say to her, your god gives second-hand gifts, then. Tell him to give me my freedom.

I wanted to be my own mistress. Perhaps she saw this in my eyes because she looked away and that was when I saw the sickness in her. It had her by the throat and it had her in the backs of the eyes. Later you could smell it and then she did not like anyone to come near her even though she longed for a hand to touch her. One day I touched her, she pretended to be *so vies!* She smacked me in the face, *klap!* But she gave me one of those hard sweets that she liked to suck. She said, Sila, you are getting too forward. You know that and you are going to pay if someone does not look out for you. I did not mind the *klap.* You must understand, Baro, she had promised us our freedom. I sucked hard on that sweet.

Move over, sweet child, you are sitting in my sun.

What is this weather doing? I am beginning to sound like Van Ryneveld worrying about the weather. The cold is like punishment. Look there. See how the sky begins to suck the mountains into the dark. The mountains go pale and then you know, ja, the day is dying again. Everyone complains about the wind. It whips like a demon.

But no demon whipped as hard as Van der Wat. And when the whip was not enough, he used his fists. *Boff, boff!* I remember. I think about it. He put those fists all over my head, especially in my ears and then my eyes.

What, I asked myself, could make a man so angry? I was not bad. Oh, yes, I fought them, but . . . bad? No one can say that of me.

They try here. They put me and Lys on bread and water and call us insolent and sullen. I do not give a fleck of dust for what they say. I can smell them, long before they come picking our lock. Their stink is something else. It has legs and thoughts. It cooks itself and has a hunger. It is the stink of a hunger big enough to eat the whole world. *Julle stink!*

I can smell things that lie waiting for them in the years to come. Some of them do not even have years to come. That I can smell too.

The cold makes me remember the whip.

Hai! But old Van der Wat had a devil in his *poephal*. He was like a dog with worms, crazy with the crawling. But these worms were in his head. You could see him scratching. Do you remember how crazy he was?

Five long years. My heart gets tired just thinking of it. How did we last that long?

My poor boy. Forgive your mother talking of such things. Some days I think how would it have been if I had turned that knife on Van der Wat and the missus? I should have gone into that house that I kept clean. I should have cut him in that room where he scratched at himself and his books, adding up this and adding up that.

I knew those books. He put us in there with his horses and cows, the carriage and horseshoes. Ja. The day after Carolina and Camies were sent away and my heartache was still fresh, that stupid daughter Susanna called to me. She said to me, you say you are a free woman? I was careful, but I would not hide the truth. I said, *Oumiesies* gave me freedom if I worked the price off and that is what I did for more than eight years with Hancke.

She said, come with me and we went to her father's work room. When we were there, she asked, Sila, do you understand about writing? I made my eyes dull. What did she think? I am not a stupid woman. I knew. But I was not prepared for what she told me. She made my name come out of that book like a crazy thing lost in a big wind when everything is thrown up in the air and spins around. There we all were, the cows and you and me and Carolina and Camies and Pieter. But I was quick. I asked her where her name was. She laughed and smacked that book shut. The skin on my face was tight.

I am cold.

I do not know why he saved his fiercest anger for you and me.

I have a thirst for a nice lemon drink with sugar I have brought from the kitchen. Lemon, hot water, and sugar, maybe a bit of *suikerbos* for extra taste.

I have been remembering the last days of October in eighteen and twenty-three. Van der Wat and his oldest, Stephanus, went hunting with the English who had come with a big party. Do you remember? The English wanted to stay with Van der Wat but he said no and they went to Van Huisteen at Wittedrift.

One of the Englishmen rode over and said he was making a report to send far away and had to write about the things that the farmers do. He asked, what do you do in October? Van der Wat knocked his pipe on his shoe and said, we work as we always work. He said, we are a godly people and we work hard as the Lord wants us to.

Then the Englishman asked me what work I did. I said I work in the kitchen, but I also have to work in the fields even though it is a man's work. Van der Wat was cross. When the Englishman went, he hit me. He said, *meid*, you think you can tell the English things about me? He said, you have been telling them rubbish about being a free woman!

I said no! But Van der Wat hit me until my eyes closed up. When Jeptha saw my face, he said, *Jirre*, Sila look at what he did to your face again. I was cross with him too. I said, why would I want to look when I know already.

Then Van der Wat had even more to be angry about because Van Huisteen came and said that De La Rey had sent his own men to help the English hunt. When the missus heard this she said, you are embarrassing us. She was anxious to please De La Rey because Susanna and De La Rey's oldest were making eyes at each other. This is what Susanna wanted. It was what the missus and Van der Wat wanted, but I know it was not what De La Rey or his wife wanted. So, the Missus told Van der Wat to go hunting with the English. And he went with Stephanus to Wittedrift early one morning.

You could hear the guns cracking through the trees like wet whips that day.

Krak. Goodbye eland.

Krak. Goodbye bontebok.

Klak. Anything that moved.

They even went in search of leopard.

Before he took his guns, Van der Wat told Jeptha to move the cattle closer to the farm and to watch them because he was worried that the Xhosa would come out of the north again and try to take the younger, stronger cattle.

Now, I do not know if you remember how afraid Jeptha was. Talmag would have been the one to do this job, but Van der Wat was rushing off to please Van Huisteen and make good with De La Rey. So it was that Jeptha was the first he saw when he wanted the cattle brought. That is how Jeptha was sent to the other side of the river to fetch the cattle.

Van der Wat and Stephanus were gone for three days. But Jeptha did not come back on the first day. Do you remember? We had to keep it quiet from the missus. Talmag wanted to send you to find him. You thought it was a game. I said no, what if leopard sniffed you out? What if night came and hyena ran laughing after you?

The second day, Talmag came running. He had seen Jeptha who told him that he had lost two of the young cattle because he had fallen asleep and he was afraid to come back because Van der Wat would beat him.

I went with Talmag to the men's hut where Jeptha was tying what he had into a bundle. He said the Xhosa had taken the cattle, but we knew he was lying. I also knew what Jeptha was hoping. If we believed him our numbers could make the lie true. That is how it is with lies. If you can have enough people believe your lies, before you know it, even the one you have lied against will be confused. The lie will make itself at home and the truth will be knocking outside its own door.

Even if we believed Jeptha, it would have been of no use. Van der Wat would do what he did last time Jeptha lost cattle. He would take a stick and beat him on the backs of the legs until he could not walk. Then Talmag, Fortuin, and you would have carried all the work. And I would have to find things to rub into Jeptha's legs and take food to him. And Van der Wat would be angry and say we were all stealing from him.

Stupid man! Where would we put things? What could we steal? Perhaps his guns. He kept those close.

I would only take what was mine—my freedom and yours, and Pieter's and Carolina's and Camies's. But how? Where would I go? How would I feed you and Pieter?

I used to lay at night, thinking about the food we would need, how to take it from the kitchen, how much I could carry, how much you could. Where could we go? In Cape Town, I could change my name and yours and your brothers', and find work with the people in the Bo Kaap, but it was too close to town and Hancke. I could have gone to Rondebosch, near Spaasie and Sariel. But I could also have ended up in that cave in the side of Signal Hill where people like us die, like rats in a hole. Then what would become of you, Pieter? And how would Carolina and Camies find me?

And how would I reach the town anyway? It took many days, weeks to get from Cape Town to Plettenberg Bay when Mokke took us. And then we were riding in his wagon. I could not carry food for so long a journey. And what did I know about hunting? Or you? We would have been eaten by lion or leopard long before we died of hunger.

The other way? It would have been into the forests until I found the Xhosa who made Van der Wat so afraid. I was scared of those people too. What if they did not want me and my children? Some nights I thought, no, these people will not turn us away. I thought, these people are like me. They want the *witmens* to leave us alone. Then I would hear Susanna or the missus telling each other stories that made them shiver, stories about, how, before we arrived at Stoffpad, Van der Wat and his father and the missus's father had to ride out with many men to save women taken and used by the Xhosa.

I told myself, no, the Xhosa have their own women. Why would they want to steal the *witmens'* women? But Susanna and the missus told stories of cattle raids, and of fierce men who threw spears and shouted, death, death!

Even Jeptha was scared. And so were you when you heard those stories.

I thought, Sila, something of this could be true, but something else is happening, even to these people because more and more *witmens* are coming. And, when that Englishman came and asked me what work I did, I also heard him telling Van der Wat that there were many more people coming because his king was sending many new settlers to go further inland, to Grahamstown.

I thought, *hai*, the *witmens* would be so many they would push everyone else off the edge of the world.

Then when Jeptha lost Van der Wat's cattle and was afraid, I saw him look at the trees too. And for the first time I thought we could run together and that would be different. But, *slang* that he is, he would not let me take you or Pieter.

And to think that I tried to help him the day he came with his lies about the Xhosa taking Van der Wat's two cows. I said, Jeptha, take Talmag and go looking for the cattle.

He was not listening to me. He was looking beyond Van der Wat's trees. I saw it in his eyes, Baro, even before he knew what he was thinking. It was a longing I had hidden so well—those days, you had to keep all feelings under the lids of your eyes.

So, *nou waar was ek?* Oh, yes—I am having trouble today. My head is all over the place, like the warden's washing blowing in the wind where I pegged it there on the line.

Jeptha. I said to him, what are you thinking, what are you thinking, but my heart was beating fast. My blood was running away, as if something inside me was getting ready to die. Do not ask me what that means, Baro. I do not have all the answers, even though I have all the time in the world to make answers to questions I must still find.

I said, Jeptha, what are you thinking. He pushed me. So. I pushed him back. He said, woman you will get a smack if you are not careful. I kept quiet. I never liked him. And this I should have remembered when I saw that look in his eyes.

We can do it. I told him. My blood was coming back. My blood was running away.

My children . . . But he said, that is not possible. They will slow us down.

I never liked him. He was easy to see. He could not see beyond the daylight on his nose. Me, I was already thinking how to get all of you out with us.

We can do it, I can tie Pieter to my back, and Baro will . . .

He grips my arm so hard. No, he says.

I said, I will not come. You must go on your own.

You should have seen his eyes then. Big man, big enough to want to give me a *klap* as if he was a master, suddenly afraid. He said, if you stay they will kill you. I was like a snake hissing at him. *They are killing Baro.*

You would think that a person would care when a mother said that. Even him. There were times he tried to be good to you and Pieter. I knew why, but I was hopeful that someone would care about a child of mine.

Then he wanted us to pray. I looked at him kneeling. I looked down at his trousers and how they were torn and I looked at his feet that were hard as stones, so hard sometimes I would have to say to him, Jeptha you have a splinter in your heel. I looked at him and thought, you are a nothing. It was not a good thought. I should have said to him, there, Jeptha, let us be strong together. It would have been kind, the kindness this minister here talks about. But he would not let me take you and Pieter if we ran.

I told him, you go, but we will all pay if you do. He ran and left us behind.

Then Van der Wat came home with a *bok* tied over the back of his horse, and blood and mud all over his clothes. Stephanus had a big wound on his arm where a broken branch had cut it when he fell from his horse. The missus and Susanna had to make a poultice to draw the sickness that was beginning to gather.

Van der Wat shouted for Talmag and Jeptha, and only Talmag came. Van der Wat took his whip and gun and rode off. But he came back at sunset, without Jeptha and without the two cows. Then he made us all stand in a row. He kicked Talmag. He said we knew Jeptha was planning to run away. I said, no. *Klap!*

Sometimes I have to laugh at myself. When will I learn to keep my mouth shut?

Then Van der Wat's horse fell over. He had ridden it too hard. He was wild. He shouted. He kicked the horse. He kicked us all. He wanted to send Talmag in the dark to fetch De La Rey's man, the one who could heal sick animals. Talmag's eyes grew big. I said, if leopard gets Talmag then two men will be gone from the farm. Van der Wat wanted to hit me again, but I was telling the truth.

Haish. Bad times were getting stronger.

Jeptha. I tried to help that man and all he did was tell lies to save himself.

I thought . . . The light plays tricks, Baro. I thought I saw Jeptha step off the boat with the new prisoners. Or do I tell myself this because I want to see him so I can tell him what his lies have done, not just to me, but to my children?

A man afraid. As we had all been taught to be.

Jeptha! Please!

He turned his face away. His eyes were little black stones. His feet were locked into the dance of a good boy. I hated him. He brought the worst days to us.

This man lies.

He says to that magistrate, I have never seen her beaten.

He lies.

She drinks! Your Honor must know how she drinks.

They tell him, just answer. They ask him if I drink. He says I drink.

Jeptha! I have a rope for you and you will dance in the wind, with the branches.

And if a man runs away on his own, if a man who runs away on his own does not know where to run once he has covered ground? If a man who runs runs with very little in the pantry and comes to a river at the end of the day and falls down, there, on the spot because the river is big? If a man is shivering in the cold and feels how hunger is what makes him a slave? If a man thinks, if Sila had come she would have known how to make this water narrow enough to cross? If he thinks, it is Sila's fault that this river is wider than the price of freedom?

And how stupid was the *landdrost*, or the field cornet, when it came to the lies about my drinking? Where do they think I got the drink from?

Oh, Mokke, I will take one of those bottles of fine brandy you have carried all the way from Cape Town. Take this gold. And be sure to give my greetings to Hancke. Xhlll!

I am sure it *is*. It is not just the light. There. Go to the men's huts. *Look!* If it is, come and tell your mother she is not mad. If it is him, I will cut his feet off and cook them and give them to him to eat. I will cut his feet off and send them to Van der Wat.

Your mother has a nest of bees in her ears today. Find me some sugar bush for a nice tea.

Close your ears now. Things must be said. I tell them to the wind, to the stones here, to the sand and the bushes, but not to my son. Close your ears.

Jeptha. He thought, yes, I would just let him come into my bed. As soon as we arrived at Van der Wat's, he thought he could be master of me. Well, he soon learned. I had to put up with Van der Wat, but no slave was going to make a slave of me.

I remembered how I was back then with *Oumiesies*, before that son of hers stretched his legs at me like a spider. I put my mind to being that girl again. I said, no. You find yourself a language for please before you come pushing in through my door. I was not always in this place and I was not always to be treated by the likes of you as you please. I told him, those days there by *Oumiesies*, I could sing and Johannes and everyone else said I was the best singer. Mars would try and squeeze against me. Johannes watched out for me. Those days I still had a picture in my mind of what my mother looked like.

If she had seen what they had in store for me, she *would* have taken a knife.

Jeptha, what kind of woman was *your* mother?

They took my breath away with their lies. Rather that I had been true to my plan to follow you. Rather that I had not been seized by that foolish idea whose first language was lost as I ran over the *veld* to tell them.

I wanted to tell them, *this is . . . this thisthis . . .*

The hills were in a hot sun. There was . . . Who? His trousers were always tied with a piece of chord. What is his name? If you tried to take that chord or give him something you had plaited out of a bit of leather from here and cloth from there, he swore and behaved like a madman.

I asked him for help the day the field cornet asked me what I had done.

What can I say? I was like a madwoman, but I was not mad. My body was making a noise in the world. A waterfall filled my broken ear. I was drowning in that waterfall.

My hands. My feet. My skirt. The dirt on my hands where I fell. They said I was drunk. Drunk?

I cross the fields. Someone has wrung a chicken's neck and feathers are flying up into my nostrils, feathers are stuck to my hair.

Bring me a bucket!

My shadow crouches at my heels, goes springing out when my heels want to rest.

What lies ahead, lies behind.

They look up as I come in bringing the noise of the fields in— a cluttering of stones, a crack, a crunch, the sound that those hills make standing still, the sound of the wagon, the whip, the oxen, the kettle banging onto the stove, the sound of waking and of bees.

They look up and say what? What?

Speak, hands. My mouth is the color of a grape, my tongue swollen.

They look at me and words scatter away from us all.

They are smacking my face.

I was a woman sagging at the knees. I told her, stand up! Say what must be said. They said, are you drunk? Drunk? I said, drunk? And when they were done unraveling their tempers, they covered their eyes with a veil of disgust.

I said to her, stand up. All that has been done is done. Now say so . . .

Some things should not be heard.

The minister's wife looks at me and says, alas.

When my grandmother, my mother's mother, was old, so old her bones were already obeying the call of the earth, my mother carried her like a baby. My mother carried her own mother and . . .

I do not know. Maybe it was so. Perhaps it was my father's mother who was carried. Or perhaps it was my own mother. Then perhaps I was my mother. Perhaps they were my bones breaking out of my thin body.

Alas. What a word.

There are days when this life is like an old dress. Let it fall where it will.

Lys never asks the question.

What did I say? I told my mouth, find words that will make the ground speak, the stones shout. I wanted the stones to curse their mothers' wombs and their wives' and their daughters'.

Baro, you *know* your mother would grab the edge of a blade for you? You *know* your mother would cut off her right hand to save you? And you *know* you are dearer to me than my own right hand?

And you *know* I was never drunk.

Remembering is like being haunted by demons. You open the door to one and the rest come rushing in. *Ssshhhhttt!*

What? What now?

I have been seeing those last days at Van der Wat's again. Why? I do not want to see them. But here they are.

All the excitement about Susanna and De La Rey's son. The missus screamed with happiness and kissed Susanna. Even Van der Wat was happy when De La Rey rode over with his son to ask for Susanna's hand in marriage. Maria Martha Cruywagen sent gifts. And then a big party had to be held. They wanted a dress sewed, but Susanna wanted a special dress all the way from Cape Town. So, off they went, for a whole month.

When they returned it was with many things. Maria Martha Cruywagen asked, where did the money come from? The missus said, Ma, it is Susanna's betrothal and we cannot look bad in front of her new family. Maria Martha Cruywagen said, you and your husband must find the money from elsewhere.

Then she looked at me. She asked, how old is your boy? I said nothing. I left the room and she shouted after me. It was November but my blood was cold, my face felt like ice.

I am a free woman and my children are not slaves but the children of a free woman.

Van der Wat said nothing to me and I thought, perhaps he will not do this thing.

Then it was December and Van der Wat had a new horse. It came in time for the big feast to celebrate their god and Susanna's betrothal. All the neighbors were invited.

That day. Oh. No, nono. I do not want to go to that day. I should have . . .

Pappa! That boy, the youngest, was running after his father on fat little legs. They lifted him up and watched and waved as his father rode with him to the hill and back.

Do you remember this? I can see Van der Wat showing his new horse off. Pieter De La Rey and his son. Petrus Marais and his wife and children from the neighboring farm. Some English who were traveling with a governor's man. Maria Martha Cruywagen and Van der Wat's sister, also named Maria but the Widow of Wasserman. She had come all the way from the other side of Knysna. Her children were with Van der Wat's children and Morgan's, all in front of the house.

And you. I see you run after Van der Wat and before you call out I know what is going to come out of your mouth, in front of all those people.

What were you thinking?

Even that ugly Maria Martha Cruywagen had to say that he hit you too hard. Even Marais who beat his man Geduld until there was no skin on his back, looked away.

What did they think I would *feel*? What did I care about their jug of lemonade? Did they not see? My boy!

I curse them. Once, twice. The third time closes all escape.

If Johannes was alive he would have known how to fix a bone. I asked Jeptha, Jeptha, my boy's bone moves in a terrible way inside his arm.

Demons!

Not one came to help. And that sow squealing about her broken jug.

Ag. Bring your mother something that will make her head quiet. My *liefde* boy.

No more fear of broken bones for you. That is all that matters, *nè*.

It gets dark. The sky gets low over the coals on which the dead are warming themselves before setting out to torment us, here, on this island.

Lys, my friend, sometimes I understand things, but ask me to talk about what I see and the words behave like fish swimming in rock pools after the tide has been in. Catch them in your hands or a big bowl you took from the warden's kitchen to see what they are like, and . . . You know what happens. There is panic and those little wings that move at their sides stop. What is left is the shape of the thing you liked, but there is no life.

Are you listening? Sometimes I think you only listen when you want to. I cannot be quiet. I fear that there is something in us, something that welcomes this wicked world.

Wake up. I have at last owned up to knowing terrible things and these things are about our lives and the lives that will overtake our children and their children's children.

I have wanted disaster to fall upon the generations of the *vuilgoed* and now I know they have wished the same for us. It has been staring me in the face, but I have not wanted to know it. No mother wants to know that her generations are condemned to the life she despises. I have been despised and I have opened my mouth and spoken the language that this has taught me. I have wanted to send fleas into their sores and the soft folds of their bodies. I have wanted to send locusts and flies that would carry their cattle away with diseased blood. And now, it is we who have been condemned for generations. Perhaps it is we who have an agony of plagues that will take generations to cure.

But. There are other things still and I have yet to learn what they are saying to me.

Listen, Lys. I have been dreaming of being back there in those days before I did what I did—the doing of which brought me here to be your friend. When I wake up, it is not now and not here. I am still there.

Are you weary?

Six days before I sent Baro away, they beat me. It was a day the neighbors came together for the first feast of their holy time and to celebrate Susanna's betrothal to De La Rey's son. For weeks, Van der Wat was planning. Every year for Christmas they went to his mother-in-law. This year would be different, he said. He was inviting everyone.

Big talk. His wife had to ask to her mother for help. We were short of hands because Jeptha was still missing. Widow Cruywagen said no. Van der Wat asked his sister. She had no one to spare. He asked his brother who did not reply. Then Hendrik Barnard, another neighbor, said he could spare his man Madagaskar and a woman, Juliana. The missus went crying back to her mother who sent Valentyn.

So, it would be me and Juliana in the kitchen. With Jeptha missing, Talmag, Fortuin, Baro, Valentyn, and Madagaskar, were to do all the other work. I had to make five pairs of trousers and five shirts, and two dresses, one for myself and one for Juliana.

Valentyn, Madagaskar, and Juliana came early on the day before the big feast. Talmag and Madagaskar killed and cleaned a pig. Baro and Fortuin collected wood. Then I had to go into the garden with Fortuin and Baro to clean it up and make it pretty. Juliana helped me clean the house, get the children's clothes ready, and iron the many folds in the missus and Susanna's dresses, and Van der Wat's fancy trousers and jacket. Then, Juliana helped me with the last stitches of the clothes that the rest of us were to wear so that all the neighbors and Maria Martha Cruywagen would think how grand Van der Wat was.

I told Juliana, stick with me or you will know what I have to put up with. Do not let him find you alone in a room. She was a good woman, as nice as Madagaskar was a good man. If this world was different, we would have been friends and we would have visited each other, just as the *vuilgoed* did.

Because they were a day early, Juliana and Madagaskar were our guests in our huts. Juliana was to sleep in the hut with me, Pieter, and Baro. Madagaskar was to sleep with the men and Valentyn. Because we had guests, we decided to have a feast of our own. Talmag trapped pigeons and brought some pig he had kept. Madagaskar brought honey bush for tea. I cooked the pigeons. And we all sat and talked—me, Juliana, Talmag, Fortuin, Valentyn, and Madagaskar, who was good to Baro. Pieter was on my lap. We talked about all things, but not about the people on whose farms we lived. There was too much to talk about. For once, I was a grown woman with visitors. We all laughed and talked.

Juliana was older than me and had been a woman when they took her. She asked me questions and I heard myself speak of things I thought forgotten. She said, Sila, your people must be Nyanja! She said her people were Yao. I said, Juliana! My mother's people were Nyanja. She said, Sila! We have been neighbors all this time, just as we would have been if the *prazo* had not taken us. I said, we called them *prazero*.

Nyanja. I think so. And my father's people were Barroe.

She said her own people worked with the *prazo* who sold gold and took people from Tete, from Zumbo, and Manica. I said, these are names I remember.

I think.

It was like going down into that boat again, only this time there was someone to talk to, Lys. Talmag was fine with this. Jeptha would have been jealous. But he was somewhere else, miserable, alone, afraid, while Madagaskar made us all laugh.

But it was the talk of trees that made us sad. It was because the missus wanted the feast to be outside, in front of the house under one of the big trees. The English call it sneeze wood. I said to Juliana that tree reminds me of the place I was born. She said musicians use it to make music, on that side of the world where we were born. On this side, they use it to burn. Nothing burns as bright as the wood of the *umThati*.

Madagaskar said the trees made him sad. When he landed on this side, he saw a tree that was like one that grew on the big island where he was born. He is named after this island. He said this tree has gray leaves and brown leaves, and the bark of its trunk is gray and rough. He said the flowers of this tree are like red tubes that grow together, tight, in bunches at the ends of each branch. We teased him. We asked him, Madagaskar, how long did you look at that tree? He said, a long time. He said his father was a medicine man and used the bark of this tree for medicine. Talmag said he was talking about a *breekhout* tree. Valentyn said *isiQalaba*, it has a sweet scent.

I remember another scent. And I have inhaled it in this country. The Dutch call it *wildekamferbos*. You know it. The English call it wild camphor bush. I have heard many other names for it. *Moologa. Mofahlana*, but the closest to what I remember is *Mofthalu*. I do not know where I learned that name.

And so, that night was good with Juliana and Madagaskar, our own guests.

Before dawn, the missus was banging on our door. Juliana and I worked in the kitchen, baking. Then I carried furniture with Madagaskar and Talmag. Valentyn made sure that the pig was roasting. Baro carried linens and cutlery. Van der Wat stomped around, making a lot of noise, shouting orders. Crates of wine came from Paarl.

When the carriages started to arrive, the work got harder. Fortuin and Baro never stopped running. They had to lead the carriages to where the missus wanted them.

Hendrik Barnard came first with his family and children. Then Van der Wat's sister and her family, his brother and his. Then the very rich De La Rey, but his wife sent a message to say that she was ill. The missus smiled and made caring sounds, but as soon as De La Rey walked away she pulled her mouth up and said De La Rey's wife thought she was better than everyone else. Maria Martha Cruywagen came last with a very special sour face for the day. She found my *breidi* too thin, my meat too tough.

I never cooked tough meat, Lys. You know what I can do with the little we have here. I know a thing or two about cooking.

I never cooked meat that was tough. And I was never drunk.

De Lay Rey complimented me on my *melktert*.

We worked hard that day. I went from the kitchen to the yard, the yard to the kitchen, the kitchen to the table, the table to the kitchen. Valentyn and Talmag had to carry wine on trays and then they had to carry the food to the table. Baro and Fortuin were in their new trousers and shirts and they had to help carry food, take away the dirty plates, bring clean ones. Madagaskar kept chopping wood for the cooking fires.

The eating went on for a long time while we ran and ran. Then Van der Wat told Talmag to fetch his new horse. He said this horse was what he had been planning for many years. He said it was a gift to himself. When his back was turned, Maria Martha Cruywagen hissed at her daughter. And where will the money for that horse be coming from? She said there would not be a single *rix dollar* coming from her for another horse that will go lame like the other one. And then I saw her look at Baro.

I began counting. I remembered how Minister Neethling sent Ma, Loedewyk, Adam, and Annetjie away when money was tight. And I remembered how Carolina and Camies went to Stroebel.

The missus sent me for more lemonade. She said, bring the best jug. I went. I came back. There was Van der Wat riding high in the saddle of a pretty horse. He was riding it in small circles and the guests, even the children, were smiling. He got off and his youngest boy, younger than Baro, ran and was lifted to ride with him. And then, Baro was running. He called out a terrible word that stopped the whole world.

What made him do that?

Now. Everyone, all the neighbors knew that I had come to the farm with three children at my side and one inside me, and Baro was one of the three who came on their own legs. But that day they forgot. I could see and what I saw stopped my heart. They all thought, so, Van der Wat goes to her at night. Why else would their faces have turned the hot summer day to ice? And even when De La Rey tried to laugh it off, the shock remained. And why else would the missus's eyes have gone from her husband to Baro to me to her husband to her guests and back to me? And when she looked at me again, she hated me even more. And when she looked at Baro I saw bad things in her heart.

And tell me why Van der Wat climbed off that horse even as I was trying to get to Baro who stood there, frozen in the face of all of that frozen day? Tell me why Van der Wat caught him by the arm like that?

I threw that jug of lemonade away.

I took my boy to our hut. One of De La Rey's men, a man named September, helped me bind Baro's arm. I remember him and I remember De La Rey for sending him to help me. September worked De La Rey's fields and sometimes drove his wagon. He was careful with Baro. Then De La Rey came to the door of my hut, there where I slept with my two boys. He did not come in. He said, September, finish up, we must leave.

I knew that it would go badly when he was gone. I asked him, master, maa-ster, if master could take me and my children, if maa-ster could take my boy, Baro. I said, master must know Baro is not a bad boy. De La Rey said, *meid*, you must teach that boy to know his place. And then he said, come. And September followed him like a dog.

Then Talmag came. He said all the other guests were going and Van der Wat wanted me in the kitchen. He said, master is angry and the missus is shouting that he must get rid of you. I told Talmag, things will go badly with me in that kitchen. He said, be strong Sila, be strong for your children.

Then Juliana came and said, Sila, I will sit with Baro and Pieter. And Talmag said, come, before you make it bad for all of us and he pulled me out of my hut and Baro and Pieter were left with Juliana. Talmag said, have strength, Sila.

Strength? I did not see him going to be beaten. What did he know about strength? He worked the fields, he came back, he ate the food I had to cook, he laid down and slept.

They were waiting. Van der Wat caught me when I came in. *Klap!*

The next day Juliana and Madagaskar were gone with Valentyn, but De La Rey came to visit. He sent September to the kitchen where I was moving slowly. September said, *Jirre!* Sila! What have they done? I said, September, go back to your master like the dog that you are. Then I was on the floor. Talmag said afterward that September carried me to my hut. He said September told De La Rey that I was dying. Talmag said September was clever because De La Rey believed him and told Van der Wat there would be an inquiry now that the governor poked his nose into farmers' business. He said, September will fetch the district surgeon. And that is how the surgeon came. He counted and measured my bruises and then he wrote it all down. Van der Wat was angry, but what could he do?

But. *These people.* When I was in the court of justice, the district surgeon read from his report but he said nothing of *when.* He did not say that he came and saw me four days before I did what I did. He said nothing of how Van der Wat would not let him look at Baro's arm. Ja. He read from that piece of paper and I could see how they all thought Van der Wat had beaten me *because* I had taken Baro away from him.

They said I had to come to Cape Town for the end of my life. There was a whole party of people. Van der Wat and the missus went ahead in their carriage. Then there was the field cornet and Karel.

Then the district surgeon who said he must come because he needed supplies. I came behind in a cart with two guards and a driver.

I knew that driver. He was one of Maria Martha Cruywagen's men. The man named January. He was kind to me. I saw him through a cloud. I think he understood. He was gentle. We had many stops along the way. The first night was at a farm. The farmer put the Van der Wats and everyone from the first two carriages in his house. I slept in the cart. The guards were to sleep under it, with January. When one of the guards grabbed me, he took that man up in his hands as if he was lifting a small dog. Van der Wat and the field cornet came running to see what the fuss was. January said nothing. The guard said nothing. I kept my face covered. The next day, the guard kept away from me.

On the second night, they put me in a barn with the animals. January came to me. He said, Sila, you have done a difficult thing.

He said nothing else for a time. Then he said, Sila, do you know the law? I said, January, do not speak to me of the law. It was by the law that *Oumiesies* Hendrina Jansen, separated wife of Theron, gave me and my children freedom. It was by the law that Theron sold Philip and Amerant, all those years back. And then it was by law that he sold Johannes and Spaasie's boys. It was by the law that Theron and Hancke cheated me and my children. The law does not even know how to count years or ask questions.

He was a good man, January. He said, Sila, there is a long way between Plettenberg Bay and Cape Town, we must make a plan to save you. And then I heard my own voice. I said, the law does not take the life of a woman who is carrying life.

Tshhh. That night grew big around us. It was big and quiet. January said, Sila, Sila. He laughed, gently as he took my body in his arms. He said, this place is confusing but there are ways to move around this, even in the little space these people leave for movement. And so we did some moving around of our own, in that barn, in that night, with the guards sleeping outside.

For a long time I kept my head on January's shoulder. He asked what I found most confusing. I said, the language. And the laws. He said, yes, and, just as Madagaskar had said that night before the big feast, the trees had broken his heart.

How many times did I hear that said, Lys? How many times did Alima talk of trees that made her think of her homeland? Even Sara and Boora, who lived on the same farm as January, talked to me of trees when they were at Van der Wat's farm.

Trees. The tree they call yellow wood in this country has another name where I come from. I do not remember it. I asked January if he remembered. He did not. But we remembered the white birds that sat in that tree and January told me that, if a hunter killed one of those birds, death would visit the hunter's family. I said, perhaps my father had killed one of those birds.

There is another tree. The *boere* call it *wildepiesang*, the English call it wild banana. January said it is also called *ikhamanga*. He asked, do I know which tree. I asked him, is it the tree whose leaves are shiny and gray, and do they tear in the wind and look like giant feathers? He said, yes. Its flowers look like a bird's head. I asked, January, do these flowers come out in March? And are they still there in July? He said, yes. I said my father took the stalks of those leaves and dried them to make rope. He said his father used them to trap fish. I said, then your family came from the sea? He said, yes. I said, my family was inland, near Tete. He said, then you had a long walk.

Sunbirds. Monkeys—two kinds. These eat the flowers and we, me and January, we knew this.

I remember that tree you told me about, Lys, the one that the Dutch call *Boesmansgif*, the English bushman's poison. I remember, your people use it to heal and to kill. Hunters dip their arrows in its sap to make their prey weak and slow, easy to kill. The sap is like milk, *nè*? And you can use parts of the tree to treat a person for snake bite, or a bite from a spider, or an ache, or pain.

If I had that bush, I would use it to help you. And I would have used it to help Baro, that day they beat him so badly, the day I sent him out for suur lemoene. *And Van der Wat would have fallen and lain like a* duiker.

I remember another tree. *Umdlandlovu.* I think that is right. The Dutch call it *Beesklau.* What is that? Cattle foot? *Hmph.* What do they know. It is a tree that has flowers like butterflies. The leaves grow like two green ears sown together. And the flowers come out in summer. At night, you can smell them.

That man January gave me a gift and I have never had a chance to thank him.

I will say this. That day. Yes. Wake up. Listen. That day before they welcomed the birth of their lord. The house was hot with cooking and I was tired of it all. Baro came to our hut with bruises. And I, a grown woman, knew what it was to have bruises and how they hurt. He, being a boy, had bruises the same size as mine. I asked, what will the next day bring? What will the years bring? I thought about Jeptha running circles in the forest. I thought of Van der Wat and his children. I was heartsore.

That is what I told them in the *landdrost's* court. I was heartsore. The rest they must tell themselves. They are good at telling the world what it must think of itself.

I saw my boy crying again. Van der Wat beat him because he was picking the lemons that I had asked for.

My boy lay down on the *riet kooi* and I saw things that made my knees fold.

What I did? It was not just to bring him peace. Or freedom. Or just to spite them.

Lys, does that make sense to you? Or is it just stiff dead fish that should have stayed swimming where they belong? I fear there are things I have tried to say without success, because I have a sense of more than can be said, much more.

I do not know. I am walking in the shadow of the valley of bones that cluck against me as I pass. If I am not careful all I will do is cluck in their voice, like the words in that book of the minister and Missus Minister. If I *am* careful, who knows what tiny wings will grow behind my ears? Yes, even my deaf ear.

Tsssht! Listen.

I am afraid for Debora. How can I keep her warm? She coughs and so does Catherina. The wind bangs and bangs at the door of our hut. Even between me and Lys, your sisters cannot get warm. When Debora coughs, my chest cracks. Even Mina brings something for her. I am afraid for your sister. How can I keep my own child warm?

The wind, the cold. The cold is like salt on my fingers. I cannot think straight. And now I have to leave your sisters in the hut with Lys, or with Rachel when I go to the quarry. The warden will not let me stay with my own children.

In the bottom of my stomach, Baro, I feel that something is coming on the wind.

Look out for me. Tell me what you hear. I will tell you what I see.

Fourteen years. Fourteen winters. How many years left?

My girl. My girl.

Did you take her carefully? Is she still coughing? I knew as soon as she stopped that you would take her to a place where there is no coughing.

Why is that not be enough for me to know?

Debora.

Catherina does not understand. She looks for her sister. What can I say?

Lys collected shells yesterday. I did not. She put those shells in a row on the floor near our bed. She put a small twig of *fynbos* there too. She said, we will take these to your baby's grave. I said, yes. She saw my empty hands when the minister was singing his song. My mouth was shut tight. The guards looked at me and said, *ssssss, she has no heart.* Missus Minister was watching me with those sharp eyes. Her tongue rubbed and rubbed at her top lip.

My girl. My girl.

This is not my heart cracking. There is nothing left to crack.

Even Mina comes, quiet and gentle, to say, sorry, Sila, sorry-sorry. And Rachel. Deel just cries. Even Soldaat stands before our huts and nods, but it is a nod that says, sorry for you, Sila, sorry. Matroos, who kept the flies from my girl's head, shakes his head but does not know why.

Sorry, Sila. Sorry. Sorrysorry.

Lys says, this was not a place for a baby. Mina is happy that Flora lives with Missus Minister. She says, your girl came for as long as she needed to be here, no longer.

Is that so? If my girl was so clear that she could choose how long to stay, why did she cough so, and cry? I want to shout at Mina. Is that so? But, today is no day for shouting and Mina has real sadness in her eyes.

I nursed your sister when she was already nursing a taste for rain dancing. And why not? I tried to teach her a language that would not be only a language of stone breaking under hammers? Tell her I have seen the first sign of that language where it made itself visible on her still face.

I see now how the rain rushes into the streets of that town and up the steps. I see how my girl smacks the palms of her hands at their windows there, how she pats a hundred tiny pats at their hair and when they jump to keep dry she laughs into their eyes.

My girl is washing her hands clean of the dust that would keep her, mark her, hold her as a dweller of this place. My girl is cleaning this place out of her skin, she is washing us all away, stone by stone, step by step, brick by brick, house after house goes. When she is done that town will have disappeared like sugar in water. Blind women will say they can see and the towers that hold those Sunday bells will fold themselves away like old parasols torn in all the wrong places.

Baro, tell your sister they call this sea the Atlantic, but we call it the gate. That is what birds have been calling it since before we were all born.

Heart of the wind! Heart of light! Things are cracking here like trees when the axe has delivered its last blows. Give me a language for this. Give me the sound for squatting and spinning on my heels in the dirt. Give me a language that will clean my throat of the noise that death makes when it has crossed a threshold. I need a language that will make hammers shatter, and all the stones in those streets shiver, those houses creak and come apart, crumble and blow away, yes, even before another dawn has passed. In that language, I will give them blisters on their ears and they will wish they had one deaf ear to turn to me. I am in a mood to be a fist of curses at their doors, my son, while you and your sisters and brother go dancing where stars spin and sing.

If Jeptha had been honorable, we would none of us have been in this state.

And still the rain! Taller than any man, the rain dances all over this island on quick, silver heels. The rain is a promise made by thunder to lightning. The rain is the promise of the sea to the sky and the sky promises right back.

Promise your mother you will take your sister into a good house and fill it with fresh food so that she will never have to suck at thin soup. Promise that you will give her a bed of feathers lighter than clouds and a blanket free of fleas.

Your sister has delivered her body to me as if it is a promise I failed to keep.

Tell her, no, this is not so. Tell her there is a washing that tears must do and *that* is the promise that always breaks. Tell her, I long for tears as tall as rain and I would stride over the earth to where those great ships lay at anchor and I would dance all over them until their sails are silver, until their planks are silver, until all the darkness has turned to gold in the down there and when the darkness has turned to gold, the planks and sails to silver, I will make these ships turn from the wasted land and point to the distance of my girl's journey. I will say, ships be strong, ships let us leave this place, let us leave the carriages that rock over the cobbles of Buitengracht, let us leave the doors that close on Green Market Square. Let us leave the noonday gun of Signal Hill, and the fish scales that blow on the ground at Roggerberg, leave the clucking of the Malays sandals. Let us leave the red dust that clings to the hems of those ladies of Cape Town. Let us leave the hems, the dresses, the bring me thisses and the bring me thats. Let us leave the kitchens where pots demand a scrubbing. Let us leave the china, the glass, the knives and forks with their fat, the tableclothes with their rings of wine, and the flowers whose stems are steeped in water that stinks like a dying man's breath. Let us leave the stink of ash, mornings of cold fires and cold cinders shot out of last night's logs. Let us leave the orders and the complaints. Let us leave the inkwells and logbooks, the regulations, the bonds, the promissory notes, the deeds and wills, the bundles of memorials that lie in the Protector's office while he tries to sleep. Let us leave the sleepers, the lovers, and the young to their dreams. Let us leave the old, the stupid, the lonely, the wicked, the fearful, the ignorant, and their victims to their dreams.

Heart of wind! Heart of rain! I will say, fill our sails. Let us follow that disappearing path and be done with this place, let us make a wake that will be wide and full with fleets of farewell and let that be all we leave behind. Let us drown sorrow, now. Let us put happiness into our mouths where there were curses. Let us wash our hair clean to the roots with one song whose one word is our great farewell!

Do not tell your sister that those of us who have veins of blood can only dream like this. You know these things. You have seen how the gods shut their eyes and keep their mouths empty of promises when there are things to be done. You have seen how deep is their silence when there are those who need things to be done. You know how it is to be stranded so in the blood of the living.

Go now, be quick, go to your sister and call her by her name. And sing to her.

Tell your sister she is my girl. Tell her I am her mother and I will come as soon as I am tired of defying this lot. Tell her my life is the defiance of a mother who survives her children.

Tell her, the minister's father's house has many mansions and she is to stay away from each one of them. Woe to those who enter and are good, for there are more that are bad who have worn the robes of goodness.

Tell her, your mother stood at her grave and kept a deaf ear to the preacher who makes walls between the living and the dead with his words. Tell her, I stood at her grave and saw it was small, too small, and that smallness was a wound in the earth. Tell her I kept my good ear to the wind for any sound of her. Tell her I stood at that place and though my eyes looked down my heart went lower and I have left something of that beneath all that earth. Tell her I know one thing and fight another. Tell her I know life learns how to live with the dead. Tell her your mother is resisting this invitation to give up all singing to a belief that death is all there is to death.

Heart of wind! Heart of light! Things are breaking here!

I have lived too long. I know too many things and the space in which I live is too small for half of it.

Get me a bed with a down mattress. Get me a pillow from a cloud passing by.

Tell the geese of my need for the night. Tell a cloud the weight of my thoughts.

Let them eat all the food they can.

What a dream. A table with all the food you can imagine reached from our door here, right down to the jetty, out onto the water and over, over to there, that town. I saw silver plates and gold cups, roast meats, cakes and puddings, pies, even a bowl of fruit covered with cream so fresh you could still hear the cows singing. I sat at the head of that table. A voice said eat all the food you can.

Lys was there. And Mina. There were so many people. My ears, from the sound! Spaasie sat at my left. She had a glass rimmed with gold. It was water. But water you cannot taste on this island. It was sweet and I drank and drank. And when I stopped there was Johannes, dancing that broken leg dance of his to sit on my right. He took a golden knife and cut a piece of melon. The taste! My heart, from the sweetness!

My eyes, from the light!

And there was my boy who died in the town's prison before I could give him a name or study his face. He came to me, laughing. I said, your name is Laughter. I held him to me and that was between us, what we felt. And then Spaasie handed me a basket made of ribbons and, in that basket I saw Debora, my baby girl, strong, and shining. And there was Carolina, and Pieter, and Carolina's children. And Camies grown tall and strong.

And there came Alima, Roosje and Isac, Philip and Amerant, and Petro, and Mars and Anthony. And Philipina came carrying oranges for me.

And up, there, to the right of that mainland's coast, more people were coming. You could hear their feet on the water. It made the water drum.

Over the water they came, a ribbon of gladness coming straight at my heart.

I saw two people. I thought, oh! Is it? It was. It was so!

Come, come! My mother, my father, come and be your daughter's guests. Sit and I will kiss your hands and wash them with new tears. I have been waiting all the years of my bones for you. I am your daughter and I have learnt so many things, good and bad. If I open my mouth now you can look in and see all the bad there is to see. It is what I have been swallowing since the day we were taken from each other.

Now listen my mother, my father, listen to what is worth listening to, to what is the ointment with which I have been anointed by some good spirits whose names I do not even know, but who have kept me alive. I thank them, yes. Now.

Listen, and I will tell you how to make the roots of your hair sing so that the world that stinks and is rife with sores falls away like the scab that it is. Listen to the birds that come from my throat now, and see how clouds stream from my hair, clouds that bring only sweet rain for which the earth will be glad enough to give up its fertile perfume. The earth holds no dead bodies now. Smell, you smell nothing of death, my mother, my father. And I have known how the earth smells when a wounded body has been laid in it. I have lain, with cruel men. Enough. This too gives way to the air that carries with it the messages sent here by an earth that gives up perfumes. And the flowers are the messengers. Breathe in. Is that not the scent of life? Is it not a scent that comes to embrace us?

And they said my nearest name, and I remembered my nearest name and said, this is Baro . . .

What is there if we who live like this do not cling to each other? What is there if we cannot trust each other? What makes us betray each other?

Today, Baro, I heard Mina speaking with Lys.

Well, I have said as much to Lys about Mina. That is one thing. And I have known that Mina never had my heart's ease as her concern. But, Lys!

I am sick of gossip. That is all there really is in our lives, you see, but I have not seen it so clearly, even though it has been before my eyes from the moment we came out of that ship and landed in the hell that stretches from all those farms to here.

All we have is each other. You would have thought this would make us take greater care with each other. I made the mistake myself. I did not see the trap. I made Mina the excuse for my anger. It has been good to give it to her to her face, but only because I have been a coward. Why Mina? She has been in the slop pail with all of us.

All we have is each other and that too is our downfall. What is it we are so jealous of with each other? How can we be jealous even of a moment of laughter someone has with another? Jealousy is the poison that we are collecting as our great gift to generations.

Take care, boy. If there is a place where generations gather, warn them! Tell them, your mother is mad with a worm that has been eating too long at her heart. Tell them, I am sending you to say we are a trapped people, we are a wounded people, we long for freedom, we long for things we have been taught to admire and desire, we long for the courage to desire such things, and we are a jealous people. Tell them, that is the worst thing. We have been taught hunger. And I mean *all* of us. No one is safe.

For this, too, I am heartsore. And I am sick of it.

Lys, Lys, bring me a basin filled with water.

I have been swallowing poison for too long.

Well. Let me tell you it has not only been the sickness of the *vuilgoed* that has been like a snakebite in my heels. It is even our own people. Yes.

I have been playing with you all this time, I admit it. I have wanted to make you smile and even cry because I have wanted someone to cry for me. And sometimes I have wanted someone to cry with me because that would be company. But, after all this time, I have learned that this is false and I am sorry for that.

It has been lonely, you see. I mean we are a lonely people. We keep what is most precious from each other because we fear each other.

What?

Do not make me tell you in less than a plain way.

What?

I had a dream last night and in that dream there were two snakes, brightly colored and small, orange with black bands across their bodies. They were crawling after me. One snake hid in my shoe. I could see its tail. I hit it with a stick. It wanted to bite me. My father's father came and caught the other one just as it tried to bite me. He held it on a stick to keep it away, but it stretched itself to try and reach me. I turned away but could feel it behind my left ear. When I woke, I knew it was a message.

I had those dreams when I was a little girl and my mother took me to a woman who knew how to listen to dreams. That woman said I was being warned of an enemy. She said, next time you have that dream, watch and see what color the snake is and try to feel what its nature is. She said, you will know why and then come back and tell me. That night, I had another snake dream. This time, even as I was afraid and trying to escape it, I noted its color. When I woke up, I had a picture of a girl who was one of a group of children all of my own age. We played together and did our work together, especially fetching water. We both liked to see how much we could carry. My father, who was related to the headman, gave me my own clay pot to carry water in. Everyone admired it. It was not like other pots. This one had a picture of the flower that was my name. Well, when I thought of that girl—and I do not remember her name—I felt the nature of the snake in my dream. My mother took me back to the woman and she asked me what I thought. I said without a second of doubt that this girl was the snake of my dream.

My mother was cross because this girl was the child of her sister's husband from his first wife who had died and so she was almost a sister to me. My mother said the woman was wrong and so was I. But two days later when I was carrying water back from the river with this girl, I felt something on the back of my heel and then I was falling. I heard the pot hit a rock and the crack made me sick on the stomach. There was a look in that girl's eyes that told me she had put her foot out so that I would fall. Her eyes had a pleasure that was cold and it made me afraid. And I knew that the woman was right.

My mother wanted the world to be good. Even my father said that. He said that was also why he loved her, because she was such a good person, but it was also why he got angry with her, because she could not see when a bad person was taking food from her mouth. My knee was bleeding, my pot was broken, and the water had spilled. The girl ran with her water spilling all over. So I thought I had made a mistake and that she was going for help. But, no. She only ran to tell my father that I had tried to show off for other girls by balancing on a rock and that was how I fell and broke the pot.

So. You see. I had been like my mother. Even though I had seen something with my own eyes I did not want to believe that someone I knew was the snake in my dreams. My father shook me and his anger and disappointment made me angry. I told him that she had lied. It was a very big business. She said I was lying. I told him to find the girls she said I was dancing for. He asked her to do this. She said they were strangers. My father asked what strangers, what did they look like, who else had seen them? She was caught. But my father never made me another pot and he never praised my water carrying again. And she hated me even more. Perhaps she still hates me, wherever she is.

The nights before our world ended, I dreamed of snakes. There were many of them and they were all of a color I had never seen. They were pale, like a paste. They had no nature that I could tell of. My stomach was sick and my mother thought I had eaten something bad. She took me back to the woman who said nothing. She put her hand over my eyes and said nothing. Then the world leaned too far to one side and we all spilled into the darkness that stank and would not be still. It has never been still.

Am I bad? You are better than I am, Lys. Let us not fight. Yes. Yes. I will put my head on your shoulder. Yes. We will be as we have been from the start. Yes? You are my good day.

They are reading numbers in the guards' compound. They want to know what the future holds. Fools. Let them look around. This island is full of the future.

I am not in a mood for talking with anyone today, Baro. Let your mother alone. My thoughts are like stones gathered in one side of my head.

This winter light is not good for me. I hear singing in a language from far away. I cannot remember what the words mean. They make my blood move quickly but with ice.

My mother used to sing.

Let them read numbers. No matter what the numbers tell them, they will come away with a pain deeper than the one that took them to the new prisoner who comes from some other place far away and reads numbers.

How many places are there in the world?

My mother was a sweet woman, you know. She loved . . . she loves . . .

Do not stand in my sun, boy. Stand where I can see you.

My mother. I do not know how to think of her. You can say this is silly, but today I want to hold on to a time that no longer exists. So, my mother *is* a sweet woman who loves to sing. My father laughs when he is with us. He says I am like my mother. My mother is singing but I do not understand a word of it.

I am so tired, my dear boy. I could tell those fools something about the future. The future is just more of the past.

Did you hear? The guards are complaining about Pedder again. I thought I heard that tall one, they call him Lieutenant Wall, Englishman, I thought I heard him say he would go straight to the mainland to complain.

Things happened here yesterday while you were away, my boy. A new woman, Louisa, came. Pedder sent her to the quarry even though she was carrying a child. Lys told Pedder this was wrong. He was cross. All he does is count stones—so many flats, so many rounders—so that the mainland will be pleased with him. He is in trouble with the mainland. Lys heard the guards say so. Deel says he thinks that if he sends big loads they will forget why they are angry with him.

We were all helping Louisa—Mina, Lys, Rachel, Deel, me. When Pedder saw this, his face went red and he called her lazy. Stupid is what he called us. Even the guards were quiet. The lieutenant named Wall told Pedder it is not right to make a pregnant woman carry stones. Pedder said, woman? That is no woman? These are animals. Wall said nothing, but I could see in his eyes he was not done.

These are not animals! These are . . . Us. Us.

In the afternoon, Louisa gave a loud cry and fell to the ground. We told Lieutenant Wall and he shouted that Pedder must send her to Somerset Hospital. Pedder closed the door of his office and will not come out. Wall shouted that Pedder must go.

Louisa cries. She is young. She still thinks it is good to have had a baby. What can I say to her?

I am sick of this place.

Mina brings water and *suikerbos* tea with milk that I have taken from Pedder's kitchen. Lys rubs Louisa's stomach. Rachel and Deel come from their hut to bring soup.

Have we not, each one of us, walked on rough or even rougher ground?

The men complain about the fishing. Pedder says, bring me fish. The men complain. Me, I complain. Today Pedder sends me and Lys to catch his fish. I have to shout at Catherina to stay far back from the water. The sea is dark. Lys rolls in the surf and I grab her. The men grab us and bring us to the beach.

No fish for Pedder today. No food for us.

Baro, go down to the fish. Sing to their pretty scales. Sing behind their eyes, in their gills. Tell them, your mother wants some peace and quiet. Tell them to go far away. Tell them to go to that mainland and tell the big policeman that Pedder is a thief. Tell them to say Pedder steals fish and shells to sell to his friends on the mainland.

It is time for Pedder to go.

On all this island, I find no . . . What is it?

My son? Your mother wants to sing as she did when Johannes van Bengal would listen. But there is not a tune that will live in this throat.

Ag, Jesus. There, I say it. If this Jesus is real I want him to come right here, right now and put that lamb's wool over my eyes so that I can have peace.

Longing knocks at my heart like the wind at the door. You are young, put yourself between me and the wind for just a little time so that sleep will be possible.

Your mother has a longing. I ask myself, Sila, is it something sweet? Just a sweet taste of a small something? But big longings make people go mad on this island. I have seen it. I see it in Lys. Lys is sick with longing for the mainland.

My friend. Stay with me.

I ask myself, Sila, do you long for things that must not be spoken? And I know the answer already. And so I must learn to long for something sweet, a little something to suck on. Or is it sour I need to clean my mouth out with? Something sharp and quick?

On all this island, there is not a lemon tree in sight. I long for lemon, just a little piece dipped in salt. The way you liked it, Baro. If you find one . . . Or a green apple. Your mother loves to eat green apple dipped in salt. Then, your mother says, Sila you are eating the ocean and when you eat the ocean you learn how to live in it. You learn how to be a fish and grow scales and fins and dive into that tide and swim far, far away.

Your mother is beginning to feel a little better. Just a little. Let us see what tomorrow brings. And do not block the last sun as it falls across your mother's face.

Well. Goodbye Pedder!

And who cares? He has gone with his face red with anger and his stomach grumbling with all the things he has had to swallow back.

They said, Pedder, pack your bags and be gone from here.

For once we were all happy, men and women here.

Goodbye, Pedder. Stepping off that jetty you had built, and for which we women paid the higher price.

Swallow your spit, Pedder. And go.

That sound woke us last night too. Lys heard it first. She shook me. I had to turn my good ear to the door. I got a fright. Mina came and knocked on our door to say it sounded like someone dying. I told her she did not know what she was talking about. She began crying.

She cries all the time now that Missus Minister wants to move inland with Flora. *Yaish.* Mina was so happy to send her child off, now she cries herself to sleep, cries when she wakes up, cries when I look at her, cries when I do not. I know how it is. In her heart she is holding Flora close. Now she knows.

Sila, Lys said, Sila it is time to give up your hatred of each other.

And she is right, Baro. But what can I say that will not hurt Mina more? So, I keep my mouth shut. Sometimes your mother is not a good woman. But there are things Mina and I know of each other and these things are not pretty.

Now this is not what I am trying to tell you. Listen. While you were somewhere with the sun, we were sleeping, me and Lys, like two shells that fit each other, Catherina lying at my back. That sound woke us. It comes from a box that has folds, like the folds of a skirt washed and pressed clean for one of those dances the ladies of Cape Town like to visit.

But it is not of those ladies I wish to speak. It is of that box out of which the saddest sounds come. The guards were busy with each other last night and Lys went out to see what that sound was. I stayed in the hut with Mina and Catherina. Next door, Rachel, Deel, and Louisa were fast asleep. Mina was crying.

Lys came back and said, Sila come and see. It is the new Warden Wolfe's wife. I went with Lys and, yes, in that warden's house, in the warden's sitting room where Pedder sat only a short while ago, that poor woman was pulling and pushing at a small box that folded and stretched out with sad sounds.

These people even have a thing to do their mourning for them!

I said, this woman must have many reasons to grieve and this place is one of them.

Well. Sometimes life brings strange things to make you laugh.

That poor woman. Listen. There she goes again. She sits alone when others are asleep and therefore I cannot sleep. Such sounds come on the wind and the wind sags, at times, under the weight of so weeping music.

She is not like the minister's wife. This woman has no interest in us. But, like the minister's wife, she keeps her eyes fixed on that town.

Yaish. Is this all there is to this world? Sad women? I have seen laughter, of course I have seen laughter. Even days of laughter and love and happiness, but nothing that lasts. I think some women collect their sadness in pockets that they store around their bodies.

And, I have the luck of being able to put my unhappiness into all kinds of other places that they have provided for me. I can smash unhappiness into the rocks that pave their town. I can spit it into their food. I can send it in those fat little fleas that go seeking their folds and creases. Your mother is one of the lucky ones. But those others? Like this new one? *Tsh!*

Hey! There are bells ringing all over that Cape Town. I said, Lys, Lys, there are bells ringing all over town. She said, Sila you are truly going mad. But I heard them. I say, I know bells when I hear bells. She says, you do not know anything. I push her out of bed and we laugh like children.

They were bells. Go and tell me what the bells mean, Baro. I fear their meaning. I fear that I have been an impatient woman and now the bells are mocking me.

I *know* what those bells are saying. I know.

Johannes? Johannes? *Hai*, Johannes. I have missed you so, old man. I have missed you, but after all these years . . . *years!* . . . there is still a warmth that rises from the soles of my feet when you are near, as if I am standing on ground that has been warmed by the sun all day.

What to say? Where to begin? Sit, sit.

Where did they send you? Do you remember that day of the white birds in *Oumiesies'* trees? What a day. Spaasie has been trying to find you in all this country. But, my boy, yes, that is my boy, he has brought you to me. Baro has brought you to me. Yes. I have had many children since you saw me.

Did you know that Theron cheated me, as he cheated you?

Johannes, I had three children when Theron tried to take me . . .

After *Oumiesies* died in eighteen-oh-six, Theron took me to his farm. What you and Alima, Spaasie and Philipina tried to keep from happening, happened. But I fought him, hey. Everyday, I fought him until he had me fighting on one side, his wife and daughter fighting him on the other side. So, he sent me to a merchant named Hancke. That is where I had my children. Carolina, Camies, and Baro.

So much has happened, Johannes.

Then Pieter, then another boy who came and went too quietly for a name. Then Meisie. She is with a priest, going deep inland. Then Catherina. She is here with me. You will see her. She looks like me. And there was Debora, but this place was not to her liking and she left. She is somewhere out there, dancing wherever the rain makes its celebrations.

Do you remember how you liked the way I sang and danced?
My children never saw me dance.

I heard you went to a farm in the wine lands. I heard you went there with your crooked leg and that your head was crooked too when you arrived.

Well, I was there on Theron's farm for two years. Spaasie's boys were there too. Arend remembered how to tie knots, just as you showed him. And how to catch those grasshoppers. And Frederik, remember how he held on to your finger? Gone. All gone. Only Sariel is left and she is with Spaasie.

You see. I can tell you things.

My boy? Baro. B-aaa-rrrr-oh.

I sent him away from this world, but he is here with me. He went away and came back. My life had a hole. That hole's name was Baro. And then he came back to me. I raised him as well as I could, you know.

What?

You listen to stories you do not understand, old man!

Theron said . . . He told me . . . work for your freedom and your children's there at Master Hancke's store. I thought, it was as *Oumiesies* promised us. She said, work and pay your price back to the farm and then you are free. Five hundred *rix dollars* for me. But when I had children, Theron found out. He wanted one hundred *rix dollars* for each child, because that was what *Oumiesies* asked from Spaasie. I said he was cheating me because my children were not even born on *Oumiesies'* farm. Theron told Hancke to pay him. Hancke said, you go and suck on the devil's tit but you will not get more money. Theron said to me, you give me the money for yourself and for your children and then you can leave Hancke and go your own way. Five hundred *rix dollars* for me, one hundred for each of my children. I asked, how many years will this take? He said, in two years you and your children can do what you like.

I went to Hancke with a glad heart. I worked. I worked like someone who knows their hands are theirs. I worked and my hands were like ribbons blowing in the wind. My skirts, they loved the rooms I moved through. My feet took me to days that were to come and the day that we—me, Carolina, Baro, Camies—would say goodbye to doorsteps that were not our own. I had in mind a place in the Bo Kaap, on Signal Hill, where those Malayas live. I had in mind asking them for that charity that they must promise the world. I would return their charity with the gift of my sewing, and cleaning, and my singing, and my children's happiness. And my children would learn how to make things. But all along, the pages of books were rubbing against each other and whispering things I did not know. I should have been awake.

Why did I believe Theron? I asked Hancke, how will I know when the five hundred *rix dollars*, plus one hundred three times, are paid? What does a day of my working cost? If Carolina helps me, does that help? He said I should not worry. I said, but *Master!* I must worry about these things. Then I knew. I *knew*.

Then. First Theron, then Hancke tried to say me and my children were their slaves.

I tell you, my feet were rags soaked and gray with their dirt. The hem of my dress was mucked. My hands were broken and dirty, the hands of a crude woman whose business is the muck of others. I was no longer Sila van Mozbiek, the place before places. I was who they said I was, Sila van den Kaap, at last. I saw this in my hands. And the stench of grief should have shaken their walls and burned their roof, but it stifled only me.

Is this too much for you?

It is not my plan to smother you with so much of the past. I am trying to tell you how it was. This is how it was from the moment *Oumiesies* died.

In eighteen and oh-eight, when I was still with Theron, he wanted me to lay with him, or with his *mandoor* so that I would make more people for him. But I watched my body and would not let it bring a child to his farm.

Then, when I was working for Hancke, my children came to me. What?

That is my business. No goodness will come of going there. I have enough to take care of right now.

It was us—Baro, Carolina, and Camies. Baro was so small. He liked to sit with Camies. Sometimes Camies pinched him and he cried.

One day, when Hancke was away in Hottentot's Holland and the missus ran the shop alone, Theron came with his *mandoor* and three men. He said, come with me, Hancke is cheating you. He said, come to my farm and you will be free there. But I knew him. He is a bad man, that man. He said, get in the cart or my men will take your children and sell them now.

I remember, Baro fell asleep in the wagon.

Then Hancke came with the police. I knew one of them, the one who did not like them to call him Caffer. I knew him well. But he did not show this. He did not let them see that he knew me. He pointed at me and said, take your children and get into the wagon. Theron was scared of him. All the *witmens* are scared of the Caffer police, hey. How about that?

Then we were back with Hancke. He sent his wife to talk to me. She said, work for us for three more years and you will all go free. And that is how I stayed quiet. All I wanted was to make sure I counted the right days and the right money. Five hundred *rix dollars* plus one hundred three times! My freedom.

I carried myself as a free woman. I was a maid, not a slave. My children were not slaves. I even fixed it so that they learned some letters from a man and woman, Absolon and Clara, who had been government slaves. They took care of a brothel on Dorp Street. They were rough, but they were good. I baked sour milk bread for them. I am not sure how much my children learned. It was not easy. Carolina could write her name. I had some letters, you remember, and when I went to Hancke's I learned many more, and numbers.

Spaasie visited when she could and even brought Sariel when she stayed overnight. A free woman even if she had to get back to Rondebosch and work.

And there was a man who forgot to tell me that he had a wife. Yes, that same policeman who came to fetch me from Theron, the one who did not tell me he had a sad, pretty, wife and four children from her. He always came at night when he was charged with watching the streets. Perhaps that is why it lasted for all those years. I was stupid. He said he lived with other men. But it was not true. His wife and children were out, near Wynberg. Then, three babies of my own later, his wife came to see me, crying. And that was the last day I let him in when he knocked even though Baro was a baby so happy to see him. He looked surprised. Perhaps that is why he never asked Hancke what became of me.

That is all I have to say about him. Except this, he was never in my dream of walking to the Bo Kaap for a little bit of charity.

Those days. Every year I asked Hancke how much I had worked off from the five hundred *rix dollars*. He opened one of those books and said, not enough, back to work. In eighteen and sixteen I said, here are my numbers. He said, what do you know of money? I said, count!

And *that* was when Hancke went to put our names on the slave list. And what do you know? He found that Theron had been there before him. That was in eighteen and sixteen. I said no, *no*. I said, I will go to the Orphan Chamber and the governor. Hancke got a fright. He said, *meid*! He said, do you dare to question me? He said ignorant people imagine things that are not true.

I looked at my children. I could not see straight. A cloud of wasps was rising out of the horizon and coming straight for us. I sent for Spaasie. We went to the slave list and saw what Hancke had done. He was wiping my life, everything away. Where the list asks for the place of my birth, he put *den Kaap*!

Why? Spaasie said, because they must have brought me after the English said they had to stop taking us from Mozbiek! But how could we show this?

And then, who do you think came? I saw Theron walk into Hancke's house. I heard them talk about me. They called me *meid*, not slave. And they shouted at each other. You see, Theron had come for us. He did not want to see us set our feet in the direction of where the Bo Kaapers practice their charity and make dresses, wagon wheels and *riempie* for carriages. No, that man whose trousers sink where his backside should be, that man told Hancke, we belonged to *him*. He grabbed my arm and said, get those children.

All we had went into one cloth. Carolina held it on her lap.

I did not want her on Theron's farm.

What?

We were back with Theron for a year. He was not a well man, then. So he could not chase me the way he used to. And his *mandoor* now had a woman who kept her eye on him. When she saw I had no interest in him, she let me be too. But, Theron! Everytime he tried to catch Carolina, I shouted and screamed so hard that his wife came running. I told her, he is trying to touch my daughter. She was cross with me, she did not like me, but she was not a hitting woman. So, she said to Theron, sell her and keep the children. I shouted at them. Then the *mandoor* waited for me one day. But I hit him, hey. I bit him and hit him. Then his wife went to Theron's wife and said this woman Sila is too much trouble. Theron's wife said, yes. She sent for me. She said, you are trouble.

And that is why, when Hancke came for us again, it was she who said, take this woman and her children.

I said, but we are free. I said I will make trouble. Hancke was afraid. He said, come quietly and you can work your freedom off. I said give me what is mine! So he said, come, come, we will work something out.

But Theron would not let go and . . . Hey. Johannes. There was trouble, but for me. The next thing I knew was that four men came with Hancke and the justice to seize us. I thought, they are selling us! I screamed for my Carolina, for Camies and Baro, on those legs still new to walking. They screamed for me. My children, Johannes, I thought they were sending me one way, and my children another. Carolina was no more than a child. In so few years she had seen all I had seen in my life to that date. And Camies? What could I do? We were dragged to Hancke's wagon. Theron was shouting and cursing.

We were dragged and carried to the *prison*. I shouted my freedom. I shouted, bring me before the governor himself to lay my case before him. But I sat in prison for two weeks with my children. My children saw me treated like a rat!

I am not the young woman you knew. And neither am I the woman she might have become. Well, I have been minding my own business and it has taken me to places you were spared, you with your crooked old bone.

When a man has to open his legs like a woman, he can come and look at me with disbelief! Until then, be very, very careful with your face. I know things.

What?

Two weeks in that prison. Carolina and Camies saw things they should not have seen. Their mouths changed into thick lines. They kept their eyes low. They spoke to me in single words. They were ashamed of me. And we were not people. We were things bought and sold.

Theron came and wanted me to say my name was Drucella. He said it would go easy with me and my children if I said that I was Drucella. I asked who is this Drucella? He said that was the name of his slave, and it was so in the register and that it was me. He said he wrote me down as Drucella. I said, but I am Sila, a free woman.

He said, Sila is already gone with her children. Only Drucella is left.

On another day, he came and said he had spoken to a widow who had asked for me and for my children. He said she knew me by another name still. He told me that there were so many papers with me in different names that the governor would never find me. I said, no Master, Master no, I am Sila, a free woman. My children are the free children of a free woman and I have worked off more than the five hundred *rix dollars* and one hundred three more times, and there is money coming to me and my children from Hancke. We worked longer than five and one three times.

Drucella? Drusilia? As if I did not know why? I knew why. Sila was a free woman. Drucella was the property of Theron. I could not be Drucella because that Drucella could not be the mother of my children. I knew that. It gave me no rest. Children of a slave, slave children.

The court told Theron, give that woman and her children up to Hancke. I told Spaasie, please go to the governor. Take the will of *Oumiesies*. She went, but Hancke sent a man, a traveling merchant named Mokke, to fetch us from the prison—me, Baro, Carolina, and Camies.

I was glad even if only for one thing—Carolina. She was a girl, just years in this world.

Carolina. Camies.

Where were the ministers then? Where were the prayers and the promises? You tell me that, Johannes.

We left that prison just in time for Carolina.

For me it was too late. I was already carrying Pieter in my body. But I am not sure when he came into me. In that prison, or back at Theron's farm.

What? No tears, old man.

Mokke took us in the wagon, hiding us.

And tell me why I did not cry out? Why did I stay in that wagon?

He said, we are taking you away from Theron. He said, Master
Hancke is sending you away from Theron, high up into the country,
but near the sea. I thought, yes, that is the direction from which I
came. I climbed into that wagon with my children and let Mokke
cover us and I told my children to be quiet. I told them we were going
to a place far away from Hancke and Theron.

Mokke left at us the home of Van der Wat. That was how we
came to the end of the world. And whatever remained of the young
girl you knew was gone.

We got there in eighteen and seventeen. But Van der Wat waited
until eighteen and eighteen to register us. He waited for the trouble
between Theron and the slave register to go quiet. So, when he could,
he put us on the slave list, what they call *registration*. He said that if
I tried to get a message to anyone, he would sell me in one direction
and my children in another.

I said *Maa-aaa-aaaster Maa-aaa-aaster.*

He said, you must say Baro is older. How could I pretend that?

Van der Wat said, your name is Drusilia. If anyone asked me I
had to say that I came from the farm of Maria Martha Cruywagen,
widow in the District of George. He said Drusilia is now Pieter's
mother and she, I, was born of this colony. He said Drusilia was also
the mother of Talmag. Talmag? I could not keep my mouth shut. I
did not care how he beat me. So, I asked him, I asked, Master, how
can I be the mother of a man older than I am?

Klap.

Van der Wat told me he knew what kind of woman I was. He
said he knew how I had been with many, many men. I said, no
Massssssssster.

These men have been with me, but I have never been with them.

He said . . . *Ag,* but what does it matter what he said? Let what
he had to say sink like a stone beneath the waves.

I heard that Hancke's children went begging to a minister's wife
who opened her house to them. I heard Hancke's son stood in the

winter rain with his feet in mud and begged for food at a minister's door. I heard that the Orphan Chamber helped Hancke's children.

Or was it Mokke who died and left his family without money?

Mokke took me to Van der Wat. He said, here we are, get down. I asked, where do we live? How do we live? Van der Wat came out with dogs and a whip. He said, put them in there. I said, *Master?* I am *Seeeeeellaaaaaaaaa.*

But that first *klap* in the face told me what a liar Mokke had been. I asked him, I shouted at him. I said, no. No. We are free. I am a free woman. My children are free. Ask the governor.

Take us back!

Where was back? Where was there any place for us?

That she-pig came out. She was thin in the face and thin in the eyes. She said, you will learn to mind yourself here.

You remember how pretty I was, Johannes. You said it. Alima said it. Philipina put pink flowers on my bed. You liked to say, *mooi, mooi meisje.*

I knew I was pretty. Way, way back in my childhood, before the world tilted and delivered me into this world of demons, my own mother took me to an old woman for a charm that would protect me from my own prettiness. My mother said, this is to save you from the envy of others and from wrongful stares. What did I care about envy and looking that could hurt? I was young. My father was strong, my mother was a beautiful woman. I was young and happy.

I saw Van der Wat looking at me on that first day.

Three months after we arrived, Pieter was born. Four months after we arrived Carolina and Camies were gone, sold to Stroebel. I only know his name because another of Van der Wat's people heard his name.

I was beaten that day too. I fought them for my children. I was beaten. I am too tired to tell you how I fought and you are not a bad old man, I have no quarrel with you beyond the wish that you could have stood tall and turned into a god to save us all way back there when *Oumiesies* dropped her soup spoon. Or when she called you up to the house at night. Perhaps you should have taken her throat in your hands and wrung it like a chicken's, and then come to fetch us so that we could all run. Those days, who knew when that son of hers would come again. We could have gone far. We could have gone to the Xhosa. We could have taken the wagon, tied the oxen to the wagon, and loaded it with food and children and gone before anyone knew, we could have disappeared like clouds.

The day Stroebel came for Carolina and Camies I learned of the pleasure Van der Wat took from his strength and, how that wife of his was glad to see him taking up that strength on another woman. For four months there had been beatings. But not like that day. He liked to hit the head and the ears.

Baro!

Baro was a beautiful boy, like his brother and sister. He cried for them. He took the same beating. Yes, he received the blows of a grown man. I have never been able to hear as I did before arriving at Van der Wat's farm, but Baro lost something else.

They would not let me say any of this in that court of justice.

When he was born he had a light in his eyes. It was the light I wanted to strike up for all of my children, to show them a way out of the darkness. It was strong in him. In Carolina, it was strong, but different. That girl! *Hai*, Johannes. You should have seen her as she grew. I saw my mother, *my mother*, in her face, in her eyes. My daughter looked at me with my mother's eyes.

Gone, to Stroebel. And so too my Camies. That boy could wear old trousers as if they were made for him. And he could run, *nè*! Both of them, gone to Stroebel.

Once when we were taken back by Theron and Baro was very small, when he was not looking, those two got hold of an old *riempie* and rubbed it with water and other things until it looked like a snake.

They waited until dark and, just when Baro was coming back in from peeing, they laid the *riempie* across the threshold and dragged it across his feet. You should have seen them laugh! And him! He jumped and cried and then chased and chased them around our room. I was catching them in my skirt. First one, then another. We were laughing.

Being with Van der Wat made being back with Theron look easier.

I dreamed last night that Carolina had a baby. I dreamed that Spaasie sent me a message to say that this daughter's name is Rosie. Not Sila. Rosie.

Van der Wat should not have sent my children from me. I knew the law. They think we are stupid, Johannes. I knew that the law said the separation of mother from child should not be. That is why Hancke sold me and my children to Van der Wat. He was afraid, even though he was cheating me, he was afraid.

I should have taken up a knife the day I arrived at Van der Wat's. *There and then!* I should have taken up the candlestick and driven it into, first, Hancke's throat, then into Mokke's.

What do they think we are made of?

Something in me died when Pieter was born. I did not want that child. I can say it now. Not because of him, but because there would be no Bo Kaap for us. There were no five hundred *rix dollars*. There would be no school for him or any of my children. I saw them and their generations chained to each other in a line that went right up into that land, over mountains, through rivers. I felt my body as if it was giving birth to generations already dead. I wanted Pieter to die.

Pieter used to hold on to Baro's finger and laugh.

Baro was a good boy, Johannes. They said he was a bad child. They sent him—Van der Wat and his wife—to do the work of a man. They beat him as they beat me. And I was a grown woman and he a child. And what had once been a light in him went dull. And it was as if he could not understand me when I spoke to him sometimes. And, then, that day . . .

There was a big feast. And a big beating for me and for my boy. His arm had to be pushed back together where the bone had broken.

And the next day, while I was washing stains out of the linens, I did not want them to say that Baro was lazy even though his arm was not good for work. So, I said, bring me some lemons. I wanted to make him some lemon water and honey. Sometimes I took sugar. I put it in my dress. That day, I took honey from the kitchen.

Later they said I sent my boy to fetch the lemons for stains that needed washing out of the linens. Perhaps it was so. But I wanted the lemons for him. And there were stains that could never be washed out of the linens. There are not enough lemons in the world for the stains that need to come out in that house.

Well. I told Baro, fetch me some lemons. He was gone a long time. I asked the missus, please let me go and see where my boy is. I was washing clothes and she was standing there with a stick.

What kept me from taking that stick and pushing it through her heart?

When Baro came back all the washing was finished, even though the stains hung there for all to see. His eyes were heavy. I saw right away that his arm was worse. It was swollen, so thick, thicker than his leg. When I spoke to him he did not hear me. His eyes were flat. I took him to our hut. I carried him because he could not walk. We had bread with fat for supper but he would not eat and he did nothing when Pieter called his name.

Pieter! I do not know where he is. I cannot ask myself if he asks after me, or how he is growing, or if his face is my face.

What?

I put Pieter to sleep and them I took some fat from our bread and rubbed it on Baro's legs where the hide had left its marks. And then I saw the big bruises on his stomach. I rubbed fat on them too. He moved like an old man, Johannes. I rubbed the fat in and he did not even cry. He went to sleep. I put him in my lap and he went into a sleep that has saved him.

Johannes?

So. Hard to keep away from this place, *nè!*

All these years of missing you.

How is that leg? Does it still pain in damp weather? I remember how you could tell a storm was coming, by the way your leg ached. We used to laugh at you, Spaasie and me. She used to say, look there he goes, watch. We watched you shake that leg and rub it, and ran to get the washing inside.

Those days, when *Oumiesies* was alive. How could we know what was to come? Were we all too stupid? Did easiness make us stupid? Every one of us knew the truth about these people before we arrived at *Oumiesies'* home. Perhaps we thought we had died and gone to that heaven of theirs.

Me, I never use that language of their heaven.

What?

Peace? Peace! Johannes, after all these years, after all these things I have told you . . . ?

Did I tell you how they beat me? They sent for the district surgeon, an Englishman. He read his letter out in the court of justice. I heard him read of this woman and it was me. He said of this woman that there was a livid color on her left eyelid. Red, I know. And black. And blue. Green. Brown. But livid? What is that color? Livid. It makes me think of liver sitting on the kitchen block. But I am not a cow who gives up her liver for a table.

I still have the mark. You see? Here. The surgeon said how long the bruises were and how wide. That was inside my right leg, and on my left shoulder. He said nothing about how deep, or how the flesh came together again. That happened on its own, without him and his letter to the court of justice. He said, these things had the appearance of things I claimed were done to me by my mistress. He said there was no sign that the beating was a bad one.

They said there was no sign of a beating on my boy. They said there was only a small mark on his right leg and that it had been put there by Gerrit, who was in the service of Abraham Van Huisteen. I said, no. Ask Gerrit. Gerrit said in the court of justice that it was indeed him who had beaten my boy. And perhaps he had, since there was no one, not even me, who could protect my boy. But I saw how Gerrit was sweating when he told that lie to the court.

And why did they think anyone could beat my boy as they liked?

Gerrit. Strutting as if he could be a master too. Master of a boy! *Hmph.* Not master enough. And he could not look me in the eye when he told his lies. I looked at him. No matter how he tried not to look at me, he must have felt me looking at him. I know, I *know* he felt my eyes on him. Perhaps my eyes haunt him at night. I hope he sees my boy Pieter and when he sees Pieter he sees me.

Then, the court of justice sent for Karel who worked for a neighbor. That dog said Baro was a bad child. He said Baro never listened when his elders spoke. Perhaps that is so. He was his mother's son. But he was not a bad boy. He was a *boy*! They sent him to do a man's work.

So much for Gerrit and Karel. I did not know Gerrit more than to greet him, even though he tried to grab me into the bushes. Karel was a fool, scared of Van der Wat, scared of his own shadow, drunk from sunset to sunrise. I kept myself away from Karel.

But Jeptha, I knew Jeptha. You would never have liked him. His shadow was not that of a man. His shadow was like oil that had spilled out of the jug. It went like an eel behind him.

I asked him to tell them in the court how Van der Wat flogged us. I saw Van der Wat take the ox thongs to Jeptha. I was the one who put fat on his wounds. I was the one who helped him. He cried on my hands. I helped him. Me. I asked Jeptha, please, tell them.

He said I was a drunk.

You knew me all those years ago, Johannes. And I was *never* drunk.

I could see what was happening. Being woman, I was not man enough to be heard. I needed a man who would speak man to man in that language that would save me. But that language would have had to come before I was born. We have been touched by a language, Johannes. And that is why I cannot listen to the language of that book which calls you on Sundays. I cannot listen to what has already touched me.

Drunk.

Remember how I loved to dance? You are a good man. Warm, like ground that has been under the sun for a whole day. I kept the soles of my feet pressed to the ground when I could. That was how I touched you. And something good was born of that touching. My dancing was a moving away and coming back to you. There was a pleasure in such departures and returns. Secret pleasures. I learned them from looking at you. Alima knew, and forgave me. I was young, Johannes. I miss that girl.

Drunk!

They condemned me. They put their names at the end of a paper that had my life in it. I know some of their names. Truter, father and son. *Ag.* What does it matter what their names are? May their names vanish like spit in the sun.

They put me in a wagon, and brought me all the way back from the district, all the way back to Cape Town so that I could hear the justices of the big court say *strangulation.*

Johannes!

They brought me all that way in a wagon to hang me.

I was truly a slave. Ja. I was not even a mother. My children were gone.

A man named January was kind to me when we stopped at night. He gave me something to keep my neck out of their rope.

What?

I told him they would not strangle a woman who is carrying a child.

January. The beginning of a year.

Johannes, I look up there from the ground, under all those stars in the sky that is black and slowly the beating goes away, it goes away, and there is only beauty. Beauty. The stars are in the backs of my eyes and in my heart and my heart is sealed for the night. And in the morning the backs of my eyelids have a new heat. It has kept me from the ice of their evil.

I dreamed I found a spear. I pointed it at Plettenberg Bay where Van der Wat has my Pieter. If I could find such a spear, I would heave, hard, and that spear would lift and fly all that way and when Van der Wat looked up to see what strange bird was bearing down on him, my spear would find its landing place.

And let the surgeon go measure *that* pain.

I had another baby. A boy. He kept my neck from that rope. He came to save me and then he left. Have you seen him? They wanted to take him from me. I fought them. I fed him from my breasts. Ja! Even in that place, I had milk. I gave him milk and for a time those guards stayed away from me.

Is this too much for you?

Johannes. Listen. I have learned so many things. I have learned . . .

This is so much to bear.

I have not said this before.

Is this too much for you?

Ag, Johannes, it is good to see you even if I am not in a mood for visitors.

Is Baro with you?

What?

My son. Baro, who led you to me. I have not seen him for many days now.

I am tired.

Mina was screaming foul things at me today. I hit her. Lys came to take us apart. I said, why? Why? Mina spat at me. She said, your children were born out of your *gat* because your *poes* was too busy.

Am I not my mother's daughter? Am I not something better than this thing the *vuilgoed* have turned me into? Is Mina just dirt? Is that how she sees herself? I hit her because I am more than what she thinks.

Who is she to speak to me like this?

I hit her.

Catherina was crying and was holding on to my legs. Mina screamed, you think you are better than all of us put together. You! You stink like the rest of us. Worse. You have done worse than all of us put together.

I hit her.

Lys came to pull us apart and took Catherina. Then Mina was shouting, what kind of mother lets her child go with someone who carries sickness? Lys said to her, you leave me out of this. Mina shut her mouth because Lys has always been good to her.

This is Sunday, Lys said. You know that the guards will put you both in the Black Hole. It will be bread and water for both of you. Is that what you want? Hey? You two are making this child cry. Then Lys said she was sick of us and she took herself and Catherina down to sleep under the *fynbos*, there, near the water.

My children came into my body whether I liked it or not, but I love them. I am not dirt. Who does Mina think she is to speak to me like that? Come and call me dirt? I hit her. She must have seen something in my eyes because she ran to the other side of the yard and stayed there all morning until the sun came and banged on her head and she had to edge back to the huts like a crab. But I was waiting. She thought I was sleeping. I made my hand flop onto the ground. I pretended to sleep like the dog she thinks I am. And then I sprang. I hit her again. That will teach her to call me dirt and say my children are shit.

I am not a stupid woman, Johannes. I know that the *vuilgoed* hate us because they are afraid. I know that. You know that. Alima knew that way, way back before I was even born. They only want to be with their own kind and then they are alone, there, in their sameness and the whole world is dark around them. And that is where we come in. They see us and we are the darkness. Ja. I am not stupid. But I do not understand how it is that we fight among ourselves.

What do you think? Did we fight between ourselves back there on *Oumiesies*' farm? You will have to remind me. That *Oumiesies* tried to trick us, like a witch. She tried to make us think we were happy with her, but we knew. When she was eating that big fat leg of mutton and we were stealing bits of fat for ourselves, we knew. When she was sending for new material for her curtains—never mind a dress!—and we walked around in old rags that had to do, we knew. And we knew when that son of hers came and tried to catch me near the river. Do you remember that day? How Philipina ran to fetch Spaasie and Alima? We all knew. Roosje. Alima. We knew, man. But did we fight with each other?

Or am I telling myself lies? Did we hate each other as much as Mina hates me and I her?

I know about the *vuilgoed* hating us. But I must be stupid after all in some things because I do not understand how we can hate each other, we who are supposed to be of the same kind. And here Mina and I are of a kind. We are women. It does not matter that they took her when she was old enough to cry for a life that already had full memories, and that she had to work, like Lys, on a farm for a man who had no wife, and it does not matter that she knows what it is like to be ridden like a horse or milked like a cow. That is another kind that we are. We are women who are horses. We are *poese* up to our chins.

You can wrinkle your nose all you like, old man. I am telling you the truth. And it is the truth even though it is a lie.

I do not want to just sit here on this island and wait to die, Johannes. I do not want to be like a small animal bitten by a snake, going stiff with that poison. I want to bite back. I want to sink my teeth into the snake's head and hold and hold until it dies of thirst or exhaustion from all that wringing and twisting of its body to be free. And I want to be free of even this.

I have spent a long time thinking about freedom. I know what it is, now. It is not what I used to think—getting away from here and being in some place, like the Bo Kaap among the Mullah's people with my children, or even getting back to my mother and father with my children. Yes. These are good pictures and I have not thrown them away yet, but they are not all there is. I think freedom is not being frozen in the Black Hole with no one to talk to, no one to see. And it is not that I am afraid to be with myself, but that I have seen how much damage the *vuilgoed* do by being by themselves. Mina is wrong, I do not think of myself as someone apart from her or Lys— and she knows I do not think of myself as a better person than Lys. Lys is the best of us, the best. I think freedom is not having fear. And in this world, the way we are made to live, it is nothing but fear. On this island, you can think you are free if you do not have to fear that your time in the Black Hole will never end. Freedom is looking and looking. The *vuilgoed* look and see only bad things in the spaces where they are not. Like daylight jealous of anything but itself, they make us darkness. I think this, Johannes. Well, let them wonder what it is like when darkness speaks. That is why Mina makes me angry. She hides in the darkness there, where they want us to be. She is afraid to come out. She thinks I have done evil things. Me! I did what they have been doing to us all along, but I did it for . . .

My children came out of where? I should have taken a knife and marked her face so deep she would be carrying the memory of me each time she touched her cheek.

But I am not like this, Johannes. I am not a bad person. I am not this Sila who cuts people, or who hits people. This is not me. I want to be . . . I feel I am . . . A person who is me hides nearby. She is my companion, Johannes. I wonder how many times she almost leaves me. I do not want to lose that me, the one I want to be, the one I know I can be, that I am. And there is another Sila. I do not want to be her. It is her whose name has changed so many times. There are so many of her. She is the woman who looked up at hills and saw them as the horizon rushing away and she is the woman who was made to live like a dog. She is a woman who kills and who has been made to lie in the dirt with men. She is the woman who looked at the hills and forgot everything but being heartsore. That Sila scares me, Johannes. You did not know her, she is also here. I am not her. I am not a bad person. There is another Sila, the one you knew.

What does Mina know? I ask you, who can she think she is to insult me so? She is not good for me. I hate her and I am not that kind of woman who wants to hate. The *vuilgoed* are one thing, but even I know what little use it is to hate them. I can say that I hate them, but that is just emptying a bucket that has filled up. I splash the whole island by emptying that bucket, but I know it is useless to hate them. It is more useful and better to just despise them. I think there is a difference. Anyone, anything can hate. You have to think about what you despise.

There is another Sila that moves around and around me. I try to find my way back to her. I think it is back but of that I am not sure. I am not sure if I ever arrived at her, or if I even had a chance, but I know she is there and her other name is Chance. Ja. She is the chance I have not had. Maybe. Maybe. She is there. And I am here.

Am I a bad woman, Johannes? You have known me longer than anyone on this island, even longer than my own son. Tell me. Do you recognize me?

I want no lies, hear!

I have found other warmths in these years that we have now closed between us. My children. Ja. Baro. That boy. And Carolina. Camies. And Pieter, even Pieter whose body I did not want. How could I not hold him to me and feel him, and find in myself the answer to his hands as they sought me?

What?

Lys. Lys is the one who brings me warmth. We reach out and we are there. Being woman is enough here. Ja. That is the relief of how it is. A relief, Johannes. That is how it is. And Lys finds everything good in me.

Ag, kind man, let me sit still with my thoughts. Let me rest, old man. Tomorrow is another day.

Nou, ja. What was I saying? Ah. Ja. When I was in the town prison, the superintendent of police came. He was new then. He covered his nose with his handkerchief.

De Laurentz. He asked me questions. A man with black, black hair. I think. He stood in the door of my cell with his handkerchief over his nose, his hat in his hand. He promised me justice and moved the prison walls for me. But the court was not moved enough. And that is how I came to this place. Still, he wrote across the water to that king and said to him, let her be free. That king sent van Ryneveld to tell me his answer. Van Ryneveld was my *advocaat*. A man who worried about the weather so much that he carried his almanacs with him.

Storms all night.

Superintendent de Laurentz was unafraid. I think he carried a shadow of his own. I saw it. I think he had seen things that had made him sick to his stomach. He dragged a shadow of sadness about him.

He listened.

He went away. He wrote letters. I know. I waited. He sent me more clothes for myself and for Meisie, who was with me there in that town *tronk*.

All those days of hope.

And this is when I know, I know how much my tongue has been cut. My tongue is working hard to land upon the language for . . . This!

Johannes. There are days when I have no strength and yet another hand lifts mine, another head rests against mine, another back leans into mine. It is not Lys. It is not Baro who visits me, dutiful son that he is. It is not even the thought of you, or the thought of meeting Spaasie again, or of walking into a boat that will take me from this island I have come to love in a strange way because it is what I know, because I also fear what is new and different. No, this hand, this head, this back that keeps me from breaking like a wave against a rock in a storm, this head, this back, this hand is, I think, Sila herself.

If you want me to hear you, Johannes, you must stand where I can see you. I have to see your lips. My ears are not what they used to be. Remember how I could hear a caterpillar on a leaf? Or how I could tell when *Oumiesies* was ringing that bell for you when no one else could? It saved us all from a lot of trouble, my hearing. Well,

Van der Wat took the hearing from this ear with his open hand. He liked to hit over the ears with his open hand. It made your ear stab inside.

It was the day I shouted at him, you cannot sell Carolina and Camies, they are the free children of a free woman, I am a free woman. He took care of this ear for good. He hit me all around my head with open hands and with a *knobkerrie*. He hit and hit and shouted and my hearing was bursting and spraying away. The pain! Even now I can feel it. It is like a ghost that haunts me, pretending to be real with such skill that I forget there is only the dullness of something that has been without feeling all these years. I could not think straight for many days or bring feeling and language together because there were no words for what was going on inside my head. That was a pain that even took sight from my eyes because, in truth, when my eyes cleared, all I had left was Baro and Pieter.

I have said that I saw Carolina and Camies go with Stroebel. I do not know why I lied. I saw nothing after Stroebel's arrival and the cart being brought around to the hut. I was standing near the big wash tub. Pieter was tied on my back. But when I heard that cart coming in that wrong direction, its wheels breaking stones, my heart stopped. Pieter woke up. He began to make little squeals. And there was Van der Wat, walking around the house just ahead of the horse and then the cart came into view. I knew as soon as I saw them all. Van der Wat's face was set like a rock and when I looked from him to where he was looking, I ran to Carolina and grabbed her and then to Camies. He came straight for me and that *sjambok* went swinging in the air. *Klok!* It got me on the forehead. My knees went down. I got up quickly because Pieter was on my back and if he hit again he could hit Pieter. I got up to keep my back from that demon. I could not see properly, but I could hear Carolina and Camies crying out and they were holding me, holding and holding. I heard the cart's wheels. Van der Wat was cursing. *Klok! Klok!* My legs went away again. They would not get up. Pieter was screaming. All of my children were screaming. Then I stood up and my children were running around the yard like chickens and Van der Wat was running after them, with Stroebel behind him. And another man, one of Stroebel's men. Van der Wat was calling Talmag to come and help. I shouted at Van der Wat. I said, you, you stop this is not right! He stopped and turned and then he looked at me. *Meid?* But I had to speak. I said, *Master! Master!*

You cannot sell Carolina and Camies, they are the free children of a free woman, I am a free woman and Master knows this!

That is when he took care of my hearing with those open hands and a *knobkerrie.* All around my head. With no one lifting their hands to help me.

And then I saw nothing and in that blindness my Carolina and Camies disappeared for good. I did not even hear the direction that cart went with them for behind the blindness and pain something else was waiting for me.

My eyes cleared, but not the pain and I saw that Baro and Pieter were all that I had left. I saw Baro's mouth open wide. I looked at him holding on to my skirts and I could not hear him. I could feel Pieter struggling on my back, but I could not hear a thing.

I thought, what now? What world has he hit me into this time? Where am I now? Have I at last become the ghost that I thought I was when first I went into that ship? But then I thought, things are the wrong way. It is the ghost that cries and clings to the skirts of the living. I thought, my children! I thought he had killed them and now they were ghosts I could see.

I was, yes, perhaps, I was, mad for a short time. That is what pain will do to you.

After a few days, the bleeding from my ears stopped.

I want my boy, Johannes.

Somebody move this island, drink up the water between the land and this island so that I can run up it. I want this land to fold itself like a tablecloth so that I can get to that farm in one step. I want to step onto that farm and pick Pieter up. I want them to see me arrive and I want them to see my right hand as I hold it high. It will be all that they need to see. Ja.

Dear right hand, wicked right hand. Let them see you. Knock three times on their walls and let their walls fall down. Knock three times on the table and let the table turn into dust that falls to their floor.

Let them see me. I have come, my right hand will say, I have come to fetch what is mine and you, you vuilgoed, *can look on and nothing can save you. I have come for my boy Pieter. And where are Carolina and Camies? Hey? Where?*

And when I go in the direction of Stroebel who took my girl and my boy as if they were chickens bought at a market, that pig Van der Wat and his Missus Pig will be left with big eyes. They must live with what they have seen. And all they will be left with is a wounded house, cattle that give nothing but maggots in their meat if killed, hens that lay putrid yolks if broken, cows that give blood and urine if milked. And their hands will have been stripped of all skin and flesh, right to the bone for having beaten us. Their hands will be the sign of all they have done. Yes. And of what will come for them.

That is what the sight of me and my right hand, come for my children, will do to them.

No, no. I am not mad, though there are days when it might seem that way. There were four men here, Matroos, Soldaat, Keizer, and Vigiland. They were the four corners of every direction my mind might take. Matroos alone remains. Keizer went to sleep some years ago and did not wake up. Soldaat was taken back to the mainland and Vigiland too. I keep them in mind. If I get too close to one, I turn and come back.

I am not going to be a lunatic, Johannes. That is a refuge I am not allowed. They would like to think I am mad here. But they know that I am not. That is what used to drive the wife of one of the minister's to her big black book. She was afraid of me. And that warden, Pedder, he wanted to think I was mad, but then he saw I was just angry. For that there were punishments that made him feel safe from me. The guards too. They forgot my right hand for a while. And then they remembered. They leave me alone now. For a time they used to come. And there was even a baby but that baby did not want to live in this place and who could blame her? Not me. Though what was left of my heart made its appearance when she was born. I was happy with her for that short time.

I told you, old man, I do not hear if you stand on this side and speak to me. Stand here, where I can hear with my good ear.

I had to learn how to hear the world all over again. It is a way of tricks and guesses, really. Lys says that is the way it is with her sight.

She has very bad sight and it is growing worse. Lys says of her sight that the world is no longer solid. She says it is all smoke and clouds but for small breaks. That is why she puts her face right up to mine. She likes to see my face. She says that will be the saddest thing if her eyes cloud over completely. I do not tell her that I can see the milk gray of a veil drawing across her eyes. I say to her, Lys, for someone who does not see you have beautiful eyes, the most beautiful eyes, there is not another person who has eyes as beautiful as yours. She does not call me a liar. And I am not a liar about this. Under that veil are beautiful eyes and the veil protects them. And the veil has a terrible beauty of its own. I say to her, Lys, what must that world look like. Hammers are like thick fog? A mountain goes soft? A fist would even, surely, disappear. She laughs. I like to hear her laugh. And, yes, the world does go soft at such times. This is how Lys has taught me to have my own peace.

After the bleeding stopped from that big beating, it felt as if there was a ball of grease in my ears. It still feels this way, even today. But after a few days, the pain grew less and I learned just how big silence could be. Then, behind that, some sound came back and in that coming back the silence that remained was like a great hole in the world. Those days and right up until I met Lys and her eyes started going bad, I felt that what sound there is between both ears only let me know that there is a big hole into which I could fall.

Now, I can say how happy I am not to hear certain things. Waves breaking can make me sick to the stomach when I hear them. A gull crying makes me think of babies.

I remember sounds. And, you may think this strange, perhaps not, I can hear sounds that others do not. I used to hear *Oumiesies* come looking through the *fynbos* for me and my children. I can still hear the way the world shifts when King *Poff-Adder* comes into the compound. I used to hear the way the guards scratched themselves. These other sounds do not bother me because they are a trick that I have named sound. You see, Johannes, the world is full of shifting and other kinds of movement. Look here, you see the way the ground is where you are standing? You see? Now look over here at where my shadow lies. What do you see? *Exactly*. Now. Look here, watch, watch the sand. And . . . There. You see. I knew that guard was coming by. *Tshhh*. Wait. It is not that he always goes running down there at this time of day—he visits one of the men prisoners behind that hut. I have come to know how things move here and I have put this together with my memories of sounds, but also together with things that I see. And I do hear what he gets up to with that prisoner. For that, there are ways that the world moves. You see? Can you see how the light is already tightening with a sweetness in that direction? It is a tightening of light and air, of the thin layer I have learned how to see, the one between light and air. It is like the thin membrane that holds a yolk together. That is how I hear the world. The world drums, like little feathers against that membrane. And that is what I learned here, Johannes. And that is how we can talk, you and I, dear old friend.

I see you have lost another tooth.

Where have you been, Baro? I called for you until the new warden thought I was mad. Why did you not come? Where have you been? You should have been here. Lys was taken away. They have put her over there, a hut by herself. They say a terrible word, *leprosy*.

Me, I say she has never been more beautiful.

Mina drinks every night. The guards give her drink. They like her better now because she does not fight and they are not afraid of the look in her eyes. She is still in the other hut with Rachel, Deel, and Louisa. They say I am unclean because of Lys. Even Mina says this. You see, I was right about her. All these years that Lys has been speaking for her, caring for her. Look what Mina gives in return. Well. Let them keep away. I have a whole hut to myself. A palace.

I go to whisper to Lys at the end of every day when the hammers have all been laid down and a quiet comes over the island that puts my mind with things for which I have never learned words.

Hai, Lys. How are you today?

Sila, look at my face. Is it worse today?

A beautiful face.

You lie. If you lie so I will not speak to you.

You leave me to see what I see.

How is Mina?

She drinks.

Drink is a gift.

From the guards, yes. They give a gift for themselves.

And you, Sila? What news is there of the minister who took Meisie?

321

No news.

What news from Spaasie?

No news.

Spaasie will find Meisie.

But I know better now, Baro. Your sister is gone deep into the mainland. The guards say I have to let her go. I ask them, what? What?

Lys says, Sila, soon you will leave this place.

I say to her, Lys, do not say I have forgotten time. I know I will leave here. I say, I will go and find Meisie and take her. I have not forgotten that king's pardon for things done. I forget nothing. I have already thought, Lys. If I get off this island, my girl will be waiting there on the mainland for me, there at Roggerberg where the boat will put me down. Like all my children.

But I do not tell her of the way this world is pulling in two directions. My heart pulls at one end. It tells me this dream of my children waiting for me at Roggerberg. But my heart has a backdoor and there I see Carolina, Camies, Pieter, and now Debora, all disappearing from me.

And what of my grandchildren? Where is Carolina's baby, Rose? How will my children know about me? Do they even know that I am going to step into that boat and be delivered to Roggerberg?

Lys! More bells. They were ringing because of the news. A guard brought stories of slaves making a procession in The Parade and down The Market because there is no more slavery. If we could have seen it! Hey?

Yes, Lys, we are free women.

My friend, you look at me with that *kappie* they make you wear now so that your face does not show. We have traveled the years together, our faces have been our small boats. I look at you and my heart is a block of ice that falls onto the stone floor in the warden's kitchen.

Free women, Lys.

And, yes, we should laugh and laugh and the other sick people should laugh too because anything to laugh at is good.

Lys, when I go back to our hut it is night and my stomach is tight and filled with butterflies that fly with bright, sharp wings.

Get well. I miss you next to me at night.

What is a heart, then, Johannes? I have spent a long time trying to run away from my own heart. I have pretended.

In this life, I understand that a heart plays a certain game with other hearts. My heart has belonged to my children and, only of late, to Lys who has taught me that a heart is not something to ignore. A heart, I am learning this late in my life, Johannes, is the very curse that I said it was but more, too.

Beyond this, I have no idea what a heart is. Lys tells me things about it. She was born up there, you see, in that place where the sun passes before it goes over the edge of the world. These demons found her and brought her here. She says her people are clever. They went into places where there is not much water, and the demons had a fear of thirst and that was why she and her people could go for a longer time than me and mine before the world tilted and we were scooped up like so many coins from the edge of a table.

Ag, Johannes, I do not have the language to say the kinds of things I know one person can say to another when hearts are involved. I know that people choose each other in spite of the *witmens*. You. Alima. Me and, for a time, a man who did not tell me he had a wife. Me. Lys. I remember that my mother made my father laugh with happiness. I remember my mother leaning her hip into him when he was sitting, talking to his brother. His arm came up and closed around her hip. I remember that and it hurts to remember it. For so long, Johannes, I have not trusted my heart to be free. Birds get shot down, put in cages, eaten.

Lys coughs these days and I go about in fear. She goes out at night to take some fresh air and I am afraid of shadows in ways I have never been afraid. What is this? There is not a thing, not a *thing* that exists in this world that can do anything more to me than has already been done and here I am, afraid of shadows. And, once again, the guards.

There are things I will spare you, Johannes, but not this happiness that Lys has brought me and that has made a coward of me, at last.

This world is a lot of trouble.

Some things you just let slide. You back away and swallow, and think about anything else but that thing from which you must back away. I have learnt that lesson. So. Today I am thinking about the whales that came and the ships that came for them, the men in their boats, chasing blood. I am thinking of the water growing darker and darker and the sharks that came like bread knives through the water.

On Sundays they want us to sing to the law-hawd, the law-hawd. Well.

I smell that darkness come swimming right up under the ground.

And now? Lys, what is going on? Why are you just lying there? Do you want a guard to come in?

What eats your heart these days?

Heart. A thing we must all live with.

My heart is telling me things I never wanted to hear again. My heart has no walls.

Lys? They say the surgeon came again while I was in the quarry. Louisa says you would not speak with the surgeon. She says the surgeon wants someone to help you. She says, Sila? I say, yes, me, I will know what to do.

Look at me. Eat. Or flies and ants will eat your food as if it is a banquet set out for them.

No, no. I was not gone for a long time. You are mistaken. I made a quick visit to the warden's kitchen. This is not meat. Look. Smell it. Does that smell like meat? It is an apple the warden's wife has sent you, but she says tell no one because the warden does not want any of us to think he keeps you special.

Just a little smile.

Put your head in my lap. It is a dear weight that sometimes is as heavy as the whole world but I am happy to hold this too.

What goes on in a body? What can be seen? I want to ask the surgeon, what is it you see and how does it show itself? I think it must be like a storm coming up on the horizon. What are its colors? What is the color of life? What sound does that storm make? What does go on in a body?

I know that the storm of death brings the smell of death and this is why I scream at the guards to cut their meat down and burn it.

Heart! Be quiet!

Heart! Leave this woman alone! Go live elsewhere.

Lys? Lys. Lyslyslyslyslys. Hai, Lys. We are getting closer.

I dreamed of a big ship that came and on it were such people as you have never seen. And they flew a flag of colors that would not be still. Do you think, Lys, that you could be at home with such people? If I tell you about them, do you think you could be at home with them?

Some things must be done quickly. Like dying.

This is what the heart knows and wants. Quick-quick!

This heart that has been like a big mouth eating me all these years and years is a coward's heart. It breaks and does not want to break. It wants things that break to go away, quickly. It is not a kind heart. My head wants kindness. My head wants that ship to come up, real, now, now and those people will get off and come up here with those jars and in those jars there are ointments that they lay on your face and your face stops bubbling quietly, and your fingers come back and when we sleep against each other and our laughter has ceased you will tickle me under the arm and all laughter will begin again even though there is a tomorrow and that tomorrow will need a body to have rested.

So, let them also take away that tomorrow. Let them bring us big pillows to sleep on and in these pillows will be the secret directions for how to get out of tomorrow.

Lys. *Tshh-shhh-shh*. In this pillow there is no tomorrow, only forever and forever.

You say, Amen? As if you believe all that those ministers have been telling us these years, as if you have been keeping a secret from me all these years.

Lys? What secret have you been keeping?

Lys?

Come quickly, boy. Come from wherever you have gone.

They make us stand there and sing about a kind light that will lead Lys. My mouth is still. They tell us god taketh and god waits for what he taketh.

I am sending her to you and you are the one who must snatch her away and so quickly that this god of theirs will be amazed and will call for a loud shout of your name to say that you are indeed a young lion that any mother could be proud of.

Tell her, Sila, my mother, has given you this message, Go well. Visit when you can. Keep to the left of the sun so that she may see you. Do not eat any grain of rice. Rice, like all food, is the language of flesh. Eat only what they tell you there. Do not come searching for that apple you left behind. Keep to the left side of the sun.

And bring me, Sila, sometimes a little bit of a cool breeze in summer and a nice blast of a berg wind in winter. And laugh, sometimes, so that I can hear too. And laugh. But leave the memories of old times for me. That is my work in this place called living.

Baro? Tell her this, tell my friend this.

Wait. This is not how it goes. This—is this?—the only thing I am to have of hers? Take it back. A space in a bed is nothing but a weight that could drown a person who might try to swim from this island.

And if you want to watch me swim you can stop eating that bread and lift those necks of yours to see the great waves I will make and when they come, those great waves of mine, you will have one last thought. So, take care. Measure out your wishes, the ground will be ready for them and they will be as tears washed away and made invisible in the great weight of all that will fall upon your heads, your stupid stupid dull heads. For I am Sila, friend and lover to Lys, mother to children who carry the weight of the world on their faces. I am Sila, prisoner—yes, I can say it, I can speak that language of yours that goes across to the town and from the town to that George whose name is repeated so many times they just say, third. And what is a third son anyway? I am prisoner of George who does not come to this island to see how powerful his word is and how it sends ships in all directions, how it makes waves turn around and go back to him when they want to slide away and take this island out of his kingdom.

And I will take this island of George the fourth son away into the valley of death where my children must go and where they will be safe from the preacher's book and songs.

Lys. Lys. I have been given this small space that was yours and I do not have the strength to carry it. So, let me lay it down on a smooth sheet and let me take the shape of your head out of the pillow and give it to the wind, for the wind alone can carry such great gifts. And

I am only Sila, of this earth and this island and my dreams that knock on doors and windows. I have no relation to the wind, like you, now. Lys, newly welcomed to the family of the wind, remember Sila, remember. Remember.

And if you see Baro, tell him it has been so long. Send him to me. I am his mother. Tell him, Baro. Baaaa-rrroooooo! Tell him his mother has no friend here and the sides of her head need conversation if they are to stay together.

If you see my Debora, tell her I sometimes feel a movement that might be her. In such a short time, such a grip. Tell her I feel her grip on my fingers but, as yet, I have not learned the language of that place into which she has gone rolling, rolling in the laughter of a clear chest.

Ag.

Lys. Maybe I will learn how to give up this hunger that keeps me here. I have to get the taste for soil myself. And who knows, I may swallow the whole world, nè?

Winter again. Baro, your mother can feel how this March is becoming a winter. They call it something else. Autumn. That is just a word to make it easier to deal with. For me it is already winter and this place is cold.

They are leaving me alone with Catherina and that should be so. I have this empty hut and her to care for. She must eat. And there is cleaning to do.

But you are my boy and it is like honey in a glass to have you visit.

Did I tell you that a guard died last night. An adder was waiting in his bed. *Pik!* In the toe. He made a noise. *Pik!* In the left leg. It fell out of bed with him.

An old girlfriend waiting for the likes of him to come back to her.

Harh! This world is a place of strange and timely things. That guard will not be knocking any doors open these nights to come. I do not know what they are singing over his grave. Maybe he is the one who needs that kindly light for that path on which he must go now.

And listen to that bell, how they are ringing it! Hard, hard. When a guard dies they ring the bell hard.

Ja! Open up the gates.

Many years ago, when I first came to this island, a man named Aaron gave me some *bakkies* before they sent him far away. Did I tell you this? He told me that there is a place in these people's afterlife where their spirits go—when they are not wandering places like this island, like *Oumiesies* did. In that place there are hooks and they hang the spirits of those who cannot answer certain questions on those hooks. Well, those demons of that afterlife have hooked one skinny little spirit after last night. Hardly worth the fuss. If the afterlife was an ocean and he a fish, they would toss him back. Hardly worth the fuss. What use is a place like that if it can only boast a pratt?

I have a mind to visit that old adder king and ask him some more favors. Yes. And soon there will be not a guard left on this island, and if that new warden himself displeases me I will send him a message.

Come slither, come slide. Come flow, come glide. Fat little message planted in his side. Come slither, come slide, death is the bride who waits for you, though your wife lies by your side.

Now. Tell your mother what you have been doing all this time, and where you have been, and tell how you did things and what it was that made you laugh the most. There is a need for laughter here, with that bell ringing and the king of adders shining with pride.

One thing weighs on me these days. I feel it at all times even when I do not see it. It is the water that surrounds this island. I feel this water and where it used to make my heart lighter on days—those days when it was all milk spilled onto a smooth table—it just makes me ill now. I have had enough of this island life. I have had enough of water that washes me away from all those years of a childhood to which there is no return. Not that it is the childhood I desire, but the years before this place.

When I leave this island—and I will leave this place—I will take up what little I may have, gather my children—and I will find all of you, even if I am an old, old woman—and I will walk into that land and not stop until there is not a scent of salt water. There will be no edge of the world. There will be no more waves, no more ships, no more surf on the rocks. There will be land on which you can set your feet and walk to what you see and what your eye fancies seeing from close up.

I have made many journeys. Even those days of going down to the river to fetch water and bring it back seem now like the preparation of journeys to come. Now, they are journeys taken and I am tired, especially of the water. So, one more journey is what I am thinking of and it will be deep into that land that lies there as if it is only a thin thing, ending in those mountains. I know better.

All this time has not been for nothing. I have been trying to understand what it means for someone like me around people like these—and I mean the guards, the warden, the ministers and their wives, the judges, the field cornets, governors who come and go, the wives, the doctors, the king. I mean this great weight of masters and madams is like a wave that comes and comes. When such a wave breaks it is on backs like mine. I am tired of them and fear that wherever I go they will follow and make me believe they have always been there. I fear that no matter how far I travel into that land, my children, will end up like me.

Still, when I leave this island, I will take up what little hope I have and gather my children even if I am an old woman, and even if I have to fight a minister to get a grandchild back, I will go into that land and not stop until there is no salt water.

And if I arrive in such a place to find a kingdom of masters I will sit down and break a rock with my teeth and my children and their children will eat rocks. And when the time is right they will give birth to rocks. And I will be in my grave weeping and the seasons will misbehave because I will have cursed my own generations out of all that is good and into a state of vengeance, the likes of which the ministers have found in their book.

The daughters and sons of my generations will say, we are not people, we are things. The sons of my generations will say, we are men made of rock and it is our natures to throw ourselves against all enemies until their skin breaks. I fear for the daughters of my generations for, with such fathers, there will be no home. I fear for the sons of their generations for, with such fathers, there will be no goodness. And I will be weeping in my grave, or running after *Oumiesies*, who will be nothing but a wisp of gray hair snagging from one branch to another, one blade of long grass to another. And I will be wisps of grief myself, forgotten, hungering after other people's children, for my children will be running behind me, forgotten too as their children's children, those rocks who were once people, smash and smash some terrible future into shape.

Well, that is how I feel today.

I am tired of this place. And even more tired of today's dreams. Today, even the guards stay away.

And now? Keep quiet? Well, Sila van den Kaap, it is time we faced each other. Yes.

Yes?

Well. Well. Not so hot today.

And not so cold either.

June has always been a month in which I hold my breath. It has the longest nights, but not the coldest. I know the worst cold is yet to come and then it is a matter of waiting.

There is always the choice of lying down and never getting up.

Some days, I think we have all been tricking ourselves. I mean running from one end of the day to the other to keep from dying, if we believe that dying means the end of us. That must be the hardest thing of all. I wonder. The ministers and Missus Ministers have been afraid of their chief demon's hunger for them. Perhaps that is what they have been trying to say to me without even hearing themselves. Perhaps the hell they speak of is the hell in which I, Sila van den Kaap, and my children, my friends, and all the people who live and have lived like me—if only it could end with me—have lived in this Cape of Good Hope. Perhaps the hell they speak of is the loss of oneself and the knowledge of this.

I do not even have the language for that loss or that self anymore.

Then. Let me out of hell. Let me be all that I am as I am now for then I begin where I am, Sila.

Big talk.

Fetch me a bag of names. Scatter them all over this island. I want those names to grow and flower so that I may remember them. This place has a way of making names go dull. Their edges go too and lately I have been afraid of knots and tangles. Plant my name there, next to my mother's and my father's. Take special care with my father's. His is the most fragile here. And be sure that it is my mother's real name. They have always wanted to call her Cape of Good Hope but her name is unknown to them. Good. Plant it deep so it can have roots that can take over a world before they realize what has happened.

When it suits them, you are my child. When it suits them, you are born of this Cape of Good Hope. What does it mean? Am I not your mother? Can a place be your mother and your father? Did that place give you milk? Let me tell you that place did not have one second of pain the day you came into the world. Not you, not your sisters, not your brother.

And when it suits them my mother is a Cape of Good Hope too.

At first they said, Sila van Mozbiek. That was the closest they came to truth. Then it was Sila van den Kaap and that is the one they came to believe since that is the one they believed. You see? You see how it goes? They make me sick. And now that sickness has a name. It is forgetting. It is their contagion. They write—the sound of rats in the grain—they want to put down their father's name, their mother's, and their father's father's and mother's mother's. And I know why. I know how their hearts work. They think if they give that sickness to us it will keep them safe, but they are like the min-

337

ister and Missus Minister. They have their god and, worse, they have that book they say is not a book but the voice of their god. Well, that book tells them things they like to hear even as it tells them things that confuse them since that book is filled with their own enemies. And then they are like my deaf ear. But I know how well the deaf can hear and what the nature of those things heard are. Yes.

One day I will ask them a question that has been burning like food swallowed too quickly. What does it mean when they have made a book that says all they want to hear themselves say but dare not, and when they have made people's lives read like a book that says all they want to be heard about these people?

Your mother is a little book. That is what makes me so afraid some days. That is why . . . Well. Why and what are loose things. So, fetch me those names. I spend too much of my time thinking in the language of these devils.

I have a mind to send a message all the way to that king who has sent me—how many years ago now?—a message of his own.

Yela, o! Yela o! Over the edge of the world you go. Find that big chair and take a seat. Yela, o! Yela o! They who are one come complete with buckles and frills. Yela, o! Yela o! Deliver my message, drive it home, make it go deep, deep to the bone. Yela, o! Yela o! Over the edge of the world you go. Find that big chair and take that seat. When you are done, yela o, lalala, I shall be Queen.

Just look at that light on the *fynbos*. And there, on the water, and even over there on that town that grows so quickly. And there on the Blouberge. And there on that Table Mountain. Look at it. In such light I do not mind what the wind is telling me. I can even walk among snakes in such light.

Let me live up to this, what has been demanded of me. It does not matter who has demanded it. All that matters is that I am the one who knows that something has been demanded of her and I am the one who understands that there is no escape in refusing to answer. Let me live up to this and, in doing so, let me dare to follow the line of that demand to its first mouth, to its heart. Let me live up to what will then be demanded and let my right hand be as strong and good where once it was weak and betrayed.

The language of demons is strong and loud. My ears are filled with it. My deaf ear hears the worst things. It is the worst ear, for hearing the worst thing. It has reached the end of all hearing, the end of all deafness. It cannot hear less.

I must be strong.

Baro, stand away, your mother feels the approach of terrible knowledge.

Oh, my boy. My poorpoorpoor boy.

My heart is my enemy. It leads me into darkness. It plagues me with hunger. It confuses me. It speaks to me in the language of these demons and it makes me live out their fullest wishes for all of us, as if I am a book that speaks to them of things they like to hear while I—as if I am the language of this book itself—I must say and do those other things they dare not claim to know or desire.

There. It has been said.

Your mother has been the most guilty of all.

There. There.

I, Sila van den Kaap, I dare to say things that confuse me in a language that has been given me and which strangles all other language, even the language in which my own name lived.

And who I am is loose. My mouth is a mouth of words that are loose teeth. They are the teeth of my childhood and I have been holding on to them for too long. It is time to live up to what has been demanded of me and perhaps I am understanding things none of them can ever understand—with their rats' scratching and their family trees and their letters to the governor and letters to that king's men and their book and their buildings and streets. They think no one can know the truth, how even the cobbles are stones that we pick up and put together to make a passage for their wheels, and how those stones are stones that they make speak of their greatness. And of us, those stones become silent. And that is why who I am loose, as loose as those stones.

I am in need of travel. Let me live up to the demand of its absence.

My heart is my enemy. It leads me into darkness. It plagues me with hunger and I have become a dog howling for its own master in the deepest hour of its stupidity.

And in my deafest ear I hear myself ask, is this all there is?

Baro?

Let me be strong now. Sila, whoever Sila is, wherever she has come from, I am telling you, be strong. This might be all there is, of necessity, but all there is could be less still.

You want to know. What happened to her? Well, some say she left the island, but there is no agreement on how. Some say it was on the center of a piece of paper that she rode like a bier—not a young woman anymore. Indeed, such things are not the domain of young women. Young women might lack the density of shadow one needs to reign such a moment into the right direction. Some say, it was nothing fanciful, all of the women left the island for a house of correction on the mainland. Some say it was nothing so cut and dried, and that a boat came, rowed by men whose faces were wrapped in cloths cut from each dress she had worn when first she landed on that Cape of Good Hope. Some say it was nothing like that, but a long and narrow box, plain and simple. And, to those, some say show us where. And for those long silences or the lines of argument that twist around each other in the air above heads, there is a laughter that might shake an island.

There are wishes: a child of a child came, a guard swallowed astonishment and lost his heart and she hers—hah!—a quiet freedom in the shadow of Signal Hill. Perhaps she would say, wishes are sometimes just stories that have nowhere to go.

Glossary

Arak	A resinous alcoholic drink
Bakkie	Small containers
Boekevat	prayers
Boere	Farmers (also *Boers*)
Bok	Buck; antelope; deer
Branwyn	Brandy
Breidi	Gravy, stew
Bring vir jou ma suur lemoene	Bring lemons for your mother
Broeke	Trousers
Caffer	Black policeman in nineteenth-century Cape Town (related to the localized derogatory meaning given to the Arabic world *Kaffir*)
Dit is what ek sê	This is what I say
Doek	Cloth; also headscarf made of simple cloth
Dom hond	Stupid dog
Dopper	Short jacket worn by farmers
Duiker	A small antelope
Ek is hertseer	I am heartsore
Ek gaan jou klap!	I am going to slap you!

Fynbos	A type of shrub
Gam	Scum, but from the Hamatic myth, i.e., offspring of Ham
Gat	Hole; arsehole (coll.)
Geliefde Spaasie	Dear Spaasie
Genoeg	Enough
Glimlagent	Smiling
Grens	Cliff, edge, border
Hertseer	Anguish; sore of heart (heartsore); distress
Hy sê, meid! meid, is jy wakker	He says, maid, maid, are you awake?
Jirre	Lord! (Or a general exclamation)
Julle stink	You (all) stink
Julle vokking mense maak my vokking siek	You fucking people make me fucking sick
Kaggen	Praying mantis
Kappie	Little cap, hat
Kasteel	Castle (here, the headquarters of the Dutch East India Company)
Kerk klere	Church clothes
Kersfees	Christmas
Kgosi	Ruler, king
Kind	Child
Kindermoord	Infanticide (literally, child murder)
Kleintjie	Little one; child
Knobkerrie	Thick stick with a knobbed head
Koek	Cake
Kom	Come
Konfyt	Preserve, jam

Landdrost	Local magistrate
Lekker soet tee	Delicious (nice) sweet tea
Liefde seun	Darling or beloved son, boy
Mandoor	Overseer
Meid	Maid, girl
Meid, wat . . . wat het jy gedoen	Girl, what . . . what have you done?
Meisie	Girl; little girl
Melktert	Milk tart
Meneer	Sir, Mister, a gentleman
Moeder	Mother
Mooi, mooi meisje	Pretty, pretty girl (*meisje* a Dutch form for Afrikaans, *meisie* or girl)
Mooi seuntje	Pretty little boy
'n Sagte hand vir 'n harde stok	A soft hand for a hard stick
Naai maintje	'Fuck' maid (*naai*, to sow, is a euphemism for sex)
Nè	Is it not so? Fancy! Isn't that so? Yes?
Nee, man	No, man
Nog 'n iets vir jou,	Another little thing for you
Nooi	Woman, girl; also madam
Nooi, nooi die riet kooi nooi, die riet kooi is vir jou gemaak om daar op te slaap	Madam, madam the reed bed, madam, the reed bed has been made for you to sleep on (from slave song)
Nou, ja	Now, yes; very well; OK; right
Nou, ja. Wat maak jy van dit?	Right. What do you make of this?
Nou, waar was ek?	Now, where was I?

Ons is sisters en jou seun
    is onse pa, onse man,
    onse advocaat,
    onse judge, onse god
	We are sisters and your son
	    is our father, our husband,
	    our advocate,
	    our judge, our god

Opstaan	Get up; stand up
Oumiesies	Old madam, old missus
Pik	To pick at; to strike (as in a snake's bite); to harry; *piks*
Poephal	Arsehole
Poes	Female genitalia (rough slang); pl. *poese*
Poff-adder	Puff adder
Pomps en pomps	Pumps and pumps
Prazero	Portuguese landowners, many of who also ran slaves
Riempie	Small strap or thong (from *riem*, strap)
Riet kooi	Reed bed
Rix dollars	Dutch currency
Rooibos	Red bush (a herbal tea)
Rooi wyn	Red wine
Rustig hart	Peace, heart, also peaceful heart
Seun	Son/Boy
Sjambok	A heavy whip made of hide (now plastic)
Slang	Snake
So het God jou gemaak	This is how God made you

Storm wind geduurende de
    nacht, wind
    en regen's morgents.
	Stormy wind during the
	    night, wind
	    and rain this morning.

Zur koud	Very cold

Suikerbos	Sugar bush (used for tea)
Suur	Sour
Tert	Tart
Toe seg ek ook, ja, citrons	Then I also said, yes, lemons
Tronk	Goal, prison
Tuin	Garden
Vark	Pig
Verschrikkelynke storm wind uit het N.W.	Terrifying stormy wind out of the north west
Vet	Fat
Vies	Angry, cross
Viol	Violin, fiddle
Vuilgoed	Filth (literally, filthy things)
Witmens	White people

UNCONFESSED

AUTHOR'S NOTE

In 1825, the newly appointed superintendent of police for the Cape Colony discovered a slave woman languishing in the Cape Town jail. Sentenced to death on April 30, 1823, Sila van den Kaap had not only survived, but also bore two children while in prison. What had she done to deserve death? And what moved the superintendent to petition the English King George IV for a full pardon on her behalf? Inspired by actual nineteenth-century court records, *Unconfessed* moves from the Cape Town jail to Robben Island, where Sila serves a commuted sentence of hard labor. On this low, wind-harried stretch of land, on which Nelson Mandela would later spend more than two decades, Sila breaks stones in the prison quarry, cleans the warden's home, survives in the company of the few other women prisoners, especially Lys, and sings a fierce, sometimes maniacal, sometimes wickedly humorous love song to her dead son. He alone shares with her the deep privacy of what happened that Christmas Eve, and whyfor, in public, when asked to explain her act, Sila uttered nothing but one word: *hertseer*, or "heartsore."

In many ways this novel has emerged out of an accidental, and uncanny encounter—accidental because it was not what I had imagined myself working on, and uncanny because I came to be haunted by a powerful trace of this woman's "voice." Or, perhaps as is *really* the case—that the living long for the dead—I came to haunt her. The "accident" of my encounter with Sila came while reading a memorandum between the Colonial Office in London and the colony's acting governor in 1826. In the midst of bureaucratic demands and explanations, references to new thatch for the prison roof, and bushels of nibs, there she was, a woman who was supposed to have been hanged three years earlier, but who was still alive. Why was she still alive, the Colonial Office demanded? My own questions were straightforward: Who was she? What did it take for someone, a slave, a woman, to survive a death sentence, and for three years?

Trying to answer these questions took years of summers and any other times I could get in the Cape Town archives, the British Library, and the Public Records Office in Kew. What pulled me? It was that trace, the word that all of the official documents seemed unable to resist—that single Dutch word, *hertseer*, which the English translated directly into "heartsore." Not "grieving" or "griefstruck," but this forceful, corporeal, "heartsore." I believed it to be one real word she uttered when the prosecutor outlined and demanded that she confirm her act. She uttered one phrase, "Yes, because I was heartsore." Frustrated, he asks again, "Is it true, that on the night of..." The record shows just that one word as her response. In the prosecutor's silence before her insistence, the court transcript intervenes with a summary of what followed: "the witness was overcome."

Unconfessed is Sila's fierce love song to her son Baro. Like the public record, it is radically fragmented. This is the only form that would resist any narrative longing for a complete, consoling recuperation of the colonial record on my part and, perhaps, a reader's.

—Yvette Christiansë

YVETTE CHRISTIANSË was born in South Africa under apartheid and emigrated with her family via Swaziland to Australia at the age of eighteen. She is the author of the poetry collections *Imprendehora* and *Castaway*. She teaches at Barnard College, where she is the Claire Tow Chair of Africana Studies and English Literature and the director of the Consortium for Critical Interdisciplinary Studies. *Unconfessed*, her first novel, was honored as a 2006 PEN/Hemingway Award finalist.